"You've certainly kept me waiting long enough,"

the deep masculine voice chided softly from the shadows.

"I had to see to my gown," Anne defended without thinking. Something seemed wrong. Nigel wasn't usually so brusque, but perhaps he was nervous about being observed.

"That young fool was certainly determined to make an impression on you, wasn't he?" said the increasingly unfamiliar voice. "Once he's a bit more seasoned, he'll realize a gentleman doesn't pursue a lady, but rather encourages her pursuit of him."

These were definitely not the words of Sir Nigel Conway. "Now see here," Anne began. "I did not follow you out here. I was merely seeking a respite of fresh air."

"Without an evening wrap to cover your lovely shoulders on such a cool night?" the stranger mocked. "I hardly think so, Miss Hargraves. Perhaps you weren't planning on meeting me, but I warrant some fortunate soul awaits your arrival even now under the cover of darkness...."

Dear Reader,

From a haunted ghost town to a widower with five daughters, there is something for everyone in our titles for December.

There is trouble brewing in DeLoras Scott's *Springtown*, and Chance Doyer and Amanda Bradshaw are right in the middle of it. This intriguing tale is sure to delight DeLoras Scott fans who have been patiently waiting for her next book.

British spy Anne Hargraves is on a mission to expose Queen Victoria's would-be assassin, when she finds herself falling for one of her prime suspects in *Dangerous Deceptions* by Erin Yorke.

Promises To Keep from Nina Beaumont is the sequel to *Sapphire Magic*. In this tale of an American woman's journey to unravel the mystery of her birth, the heroine returns to Vienna at a time of political turmoil.

Amity Becker is a mail-order bride in Lynda Trent's *Beloved Wife*, the story of a young woman who is overwhelmed by her handsome new husband and his five unruly daughters.

We hope you enjoy this month's selection, and, from all of us at Harlequin Historicals, we would like to wish you and your family the very best of the season.

Sincerely,

Tracy Farrell
Senior Editor

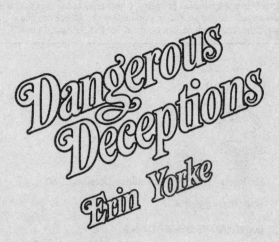

Dangerous Deceptions

Erin Yorke

Harlequin Books

TORONTO • NEW YORK • LONDON
AMSTERDAM • PARIS • SYDNEY • HAMBURG
STOCKHOLM • ATHENS • TOKYO • MILAN
MADRID • WARSAW • BUDAPEST • AUCKLAND

Harlequin Historicals first edition December 1992

ISBN 0-373-28752-6

DANGEROUS DECEPTIONS

Books by Erin Yorke

Harlequin Historicals

An American Beauty #58
Forever Defiant #94
Heaven's Gate #124
Dangerous Deceptions #152

ERIN YORKE

is the pseudonym used by the writing team of Christine Healy and Susan Yansick. One half of the team is single, fancy-free and countrified, and the other is married, the mother of two sons and suburban, but they find that their differing lives and styles enrich their writing with a broader perspective.

For Barbara Bensen, a dear friend
who's always there whatever the need—thank you
and
For my cousin, Rose May McLoughlin,
a delightful lady who admirably combines
strength of spirit with tenderness of heart.

Chapter One

London—May 15, 1887

Ian Kendrick stood alone in the midst of the well-dressed crowd. His stance was casual and his tall, broad-shouldered frame appeared relaxed. Other than his good looks and the meticulous cut of his evening clothes, nothing called attention to the man. Even the wayward lock that usually fell across his forehead had been tamed into place. For all intents and purposes, Ian was merely another member of the aristocracy attending yet another tedious social function. His comely features, carefully drawn into a public display of ennui, attested to it.

However, as Ian laconically sipped his champagne, his half-hooded eyes concealed the intensity with which he was surveying those assembled in the ballroom, just as the soft sigh of boredom that escaped his well-shaped lips hid his avid interest in what was going on around him.

Over the sounds of merriment, the soft chords of the orchestra and the tinkle of crystal, the unsuspected observer strained to catch the undertones of murmured gossip always prevalent at gatherings such as this. Tonight, unfortunately, much of it was merely social and concerned the lovely woman dressed in an expensive and fashionable gown of deep pink, who stood near the piano and was obviously about to sing when the musicians finished the instrumental piece that now engaged them.

When the last echo of the orchestra faded away, an expectant hush descended upon the crowd as everyone awaited the striking woman's unscheduled performance. And as the first notes of her song vibrated throughout the room, the assembled nobility was not disappointed. This was, after all, the renowned songstress Anne Hargraves, and her voice was clear and strong yet inordinately sweet.

With a start, Ian found he had been momentarily distracted from his assignment. Instead of surreptitiously studying the gathering, he had been quite openly focusing on the compelling blonde singing so movingly about love found and lost. Not that his fascination with her would have caused anyone to notice him, he thought with a wry smile. Anne Hargraves had similarly affected every man in the room, and even the women stood listening with rapt attention to her hauntingly wistful voice. Watching her, Ian decided that the singular beauty of her face and the lush womanly curves draped but not quite concealed by the folds of her gown gave credence to the whispers that Anne Hargraves was a woman with a past. She might have the face of an angel, but Ian's experience with women told him that seduction smoldered beneath her ladylike veneer...ignited by a spark from hell's own fire, if the dragons of society were to be believed.

But Ian didn't need their prudish opinions to know that Anne Hargraves was pure temptation. She was a woman fit for a king, or at the very least a prince. Rumors of her liaison with Louis Napoleon still abounded, though he'd been dead nearly seven years now, killed in the Zulu Uprising. But vestiges of scandal had adhered to her, more closely than the gown she wore tonight clung to her curves, and her name had continued to be linked with those of various men. Yet here she was, accepted by polite society, an observation Ian couldn't help but find intriguing.

As Anne graciously acknowledged the accolades at the conclusion of her song, Ian Kendrick found that he wanted to know more about the mysterious and alluring Anne Hargraves. But while his job that evening did not entail ignoring the curvaceous songstress, the dark-haired nobleman reminded himself that she was not his main objective.

After all, he knew who she was and was fairly certain of what she was, and he did have more important things that demanded his attention.

Still, he found his eyes returning to the blonde as she moved gracefully across the room, or when her delightfully melodious laugh traveled above the incessant buzzing of the others to claim his attention. Drawn to the Hargraves woman though he was, Ian hoped that his present curiosity about her arose only from a sense of duty. After all, hadn't he learned to temper his physical appetites long ago? If thoughts of bedding her flitted through his mind with vivid clarity, he found an excuse for his obsession in the realization that most of the men present were probably suffering from the same ailment at the moment.

Running his hand through his hair and struggling to gain control of his primitive urges as Anne once more crossed his field of vision, Ian forced his attention back to his task. The only solace he found in his irrational absorption with the striking singer was that she hadn't seemed to notice him. Had she done so, Ian Kendrick had the sinking suspicion that he would have been completely lost.

This realization vexed him, and he quite illogically aimed his irritation at the siren who was the reason for his discomfort. Shaking his head, Ian sternly reminded himself that the beautiful, blond songstress was not the sort of woman meant for the third son of a mere baronet.

Yet what his mind realized, his body refused to accept. Putting the provocative dilemma aside for later consideration, Ian turned his impassive face to scrutinize those near him, all traces of his inner conflict temporarily concealed. Then, like a soldier going off to war, he turned his back on the ever present image of Anne Hargraves and joined a group of noblemen engaged in a debate about the living conditions of London's poor.

Despite himself, Ian's gaze continued to seek her out again and again, and always she was in the company of one important man or another. Now, when he couldn't find her within the confines of the ballroom, he spent his time wondering where Anne Hargraves was and what she was doing. Was she embroiled in the situation that demanded his own

attention, perhaps tempting some nobleman to spend money
that wasn't his, funds that really belonged to the Imperial
Institute? Or did her absence signify something else entirely?

Excusing himself, Ian Kendrick went in search of her. He
would confront her head-on and satisfy his professional
curiosity and conceivably his personal as well.

With all the attention being lavished upon her, Anne
never noted the handsome nobleman trying so hard to ignore her. During the course of the evening, the songstress
had constantly found herself surrounded by men vying for
her notice. Most of them had been little more than strut-
ting peacocks, yet out of habit she had borne their crowing
admirably. One never knew when something of importance
would be revealed. Men smitten by infatuation or aflame
with lust often divulged things better left unsaid in their attempt to impress a woman. Tonight, however, Anne thought
with a wry smile, little more than her petticoat had come
close to being revealed.

The singer looked carefully at her reflection in the mirror, assessing the damage done by Lord Moreland. Aside
from the quick flash of irritation crossing her delicate features and the slightly disarranged plume of feathers gracing
her upswept hair, she appeared relatively unmarked by the
encounter. Yet she was certain he'd caused some scarring.
Yes, there it was. Fortunately, despite the frightful echo of
tearing fabric still resounding in her ears, the man's elaborate display of swordsmanship had merely caught the flowing train of her gown, slicing across its panel of delicate
embroidery but not destroying any vital part of the garment that stood between her and scandal. To come unclothed at an event attended by the Prince of Wales would
certainly not enhance the ladylike image she was trying to
project.

While her seamstress could undoubtedly effect appropriate repairs, for now, the slender young woman realized, she
had no choice but to remove the surplus fabric and circulate for the remainder of the evening unencumbered by its
weighty length. What a delicious accident, Anne marveled

appreciatively as the door to the ladies' dressing room opened suddenly.

"Oh, Miss Hargraves, I've only just heard about my clumsy brother. I don't know how he can cut such a fine figure on a horse and be a complete ninny standing on his own two feet," despaired Audrey Palmer, so thoroughly embarrassed at the unfortunate mishap that she didn't recognize her own amusing choice of phrase.

"You're rather hard on him, Audrey. I'd say he cut a pretty fine figure on my gown." The petite blonde laughed as she detached the ornamental swathing from the back of her skirt.

"I don't know how you'll ever forgive us," sighed the younger girl, examining the rent in the beautiful rose fabric, her eyes so wide she appeared ready to weep. Here her mother was hostess of a major social event and her brother had not only badgered Anne Hargraves until she had agreed to sing, but then proceeded to shred her gown in an attempt to impress her with his supposed expertise with a blade. "Your poor dress. Is it totally ruined? Of course, we'll replace it for you."

"Nonsense, my dear, a few cuts in the train won't render it useless. My seamstress will see to its repair." Anne smiled, truly less concerned about the garment than the unfortunate notoriety the episode might produce. After all, Conway would most likely have her working soon, and her game was better played in the shadows than the bright lights of unwanted attention. Best to minimize the episode with her gown as much as possible to allow her the freedom to find Nigel. They were supposed to meet at half past ten, and it must be nearly that already. "Audrey, I don't want you worrying about this all evening. Besides, to tell the truth, I prefer my costume to be more simple so I avoid a court train whenever possible."

"You look so devilishly attractive, I warrant you could wear any design and be admired, as long as you steer clear of Daniel," said the young noblewoman, more at ease with her sophisticated guest than she ever would have imagined possible. "I don't suppose it would be acceptable for me to doff my train in order to make you less uncomfortable?"

"I'd approve, but I fear your family might not," said Anne diplomatically, opening the door for the daughter of her hostess. "Shall we rejoin your guests? I really must circulate."

"I'd be more than happy to escort you," a waiting Daniel informed her readily, apparently uncowed by his unfortunate parry. "And I promise to keep my weapon sheathed."

"I appreciate your thoughtfulness, Lord Moreland, but I can find my way. I do wonder though if you could possibly see that this is placed with my evening cloak. I'd hate for it to be misplaced," confided the singer gratefully as she handed the young swordsman the remains of her train. Having dispensed with the cumbersome cloth of her gown, the last thing she wanted now was to be trailed by a lovesick swain.

"Of course, Miss Hargraves; I would go to the ends of the earth for you, let alone the cloakroom," agreed Audrey's brother with a grin. "Perhaps later I could introduce you to some of the other guests; I know everyone is anxious to meet *the* Anne Hargraves."

"Let me get a breath of air first, Daniel, and then I'll join you," agreed the singer, worried that her scheduled rendezvous had been compromised. How long would Nigel wait?

A few minutes later, as she approached the carefully tended east gardens, Anne paused to admire the late spring blossoms raising their brave colors in the silvery moonlight. Even in the midst of man's turmoil, nature managed its change of seasons, she reflected, turning once more to the path and the man who awaited her presence.

"You certainly kept me waiting long enough," a deep masculine voice chided softly from the shadows of a sculpted hedge. "Lovely as you are, my dear, do you think I've infinite patience?"

"I had to see to my gown," defended Anne without thinking, "and assuage Audrey's guilt for the mishap, though of course it was Lord Moreland who was at fault." Something seemed wrong, but she couldn't decide what. Nigel wasn't usually so brusque, but then they didn't ordinarily meet in his friends' gardens; perhaps he was nervous about being observed. After all, should their association draw attention, her usefulness would be lost.

"Yes, that young fool was certainly determined to make an impression on you, wasn't he?" said an increasingly unfamiliar voice. "Once he's a bit more seasoned he'll realize a gentleman doesn't pursue a lady, but rather encourages her pursuit of him…just as I've done this evening, enticing you to follow me to this delightful arbor, private enough for whatever pleasures we choose to enjoy, and no one inside the wiser."

These were definitely not the words of Sir Nigel Conway, Anne's contact with special intelligence for Her Majesty's government.

"Now, see here," Anne began, unwilling to tolerate any more of the stranger's suggestive comments. "Whoever you are, and whatever absurd notions you may have, I certainly did not follow you out here. I was merely seeking a respite of fresh air after the warmth and dancing within."

"Without an evening wrap to cover your lovely shoulders and those delicate arms on such a cool May night? I hardly think so, Miss Hargraves. You were certainly en route to an assignation to warm your blood in a more ancient and enjoyable fashion than conversation. Perhaps you weren't planning on meeting me, but I warrant some fortunate soul awaits your arrival even now under the cover of darkness."

"Well, I never—"

"Now, that is certainly untrue, a woman as striking as yourself," contradicted the tall figure, edging farther away from her even as his steel gray eyes locked hers in challenge. "And may I say that deep rose color does wonders for your eyes, even out here in the silkiness of night. But then, I'll not detain you from your appointment any longer, Miss Hargraves. I have no doubt that we will meet again."

"You think you can just accost me and melt away into the night without so much as an apology?" sputtered the blonde, inexplicably outraged at this stranger's imperial manner. An assignation, indeed! If truth be told, and if she hadn't promised to meet Nigel, perhaps this man's broad shoulders and slim-hipped figure might have attracted her attention, but he had much to learn of proper etiquette if he were to entice her to follow him anywhere. Anne frowned, ready to voice her annoyance. "I haven't finished with you, sir."

"I fear he's finished speaking with you, my dear," offered Nigel, stepping up beside her, his silver hair and mustache clearly distinguishable in the moonlight and his voice a welcome sound. "He's off like a bee after another blossom, seeking after new conquests. If you'll settle for an older man, though, perhaps we can take a walk out toward the duck pond near the rear wall and see if the young have hatched."

"Who is he?" demanded the petite woman as she took Nigel's arm and permitted him to turn her steps toward the far end of the garden. "Do you know him?"

"Not by name, only by type, Anne, so calm yourself. He's just one of many bored noblemen with naught to occupy his time but his own pleasure." Nigel sniffed in disapproval. "Don't worry yourself over him any further."

"Worry? Over him? That's not bloody likely. His sort is not one I'd choose to know, either. Let him gamble away what remains of the family fortune at Ascot for all I care," she declared, settling herself on the bench beside the duck pond and indicating her companion should join her.

"Thank you. At my age, these bones need all the rest they can claim," said the older man, barely fifty and as hale and hearty as men half his age.

"Now, tell me, what is this mysterious assignment we couldn't discuss in our usual fashion?" demanded the young woman, already distancing herself from the peculiar stranger and concentrating on her professional role. "Where is my next special series of concerts to take me? Greece? Africa?"

"No, this time, you'll be working right here at home."

"In England? But everyone knows me here. How can I—"

"They know the singer and the socialite Anne Hargraves, whose presence graces any affair and whose beauty makes men melt while their women glower," acknowledged the man whom she'd trusted with her very life over the past six years, never doubting his instincts or the assignments he'd given her. "What they don't know, and won't learn, is that Anne Hargraves is one of my secret government agents, soliciting information wherever she can to help her country."

"But, Sir Nigel, when I started working for you, we agreed that England was my home and thus not a locale for my work. Here I am just a songstress and nothing more," she protested anxiously, pulling the feathered plume from her hair.

"I remember that quite well," he agreed, taking one of her restless hands and wrapping it in his as a gesture of warmth and reassurance. As Anne's sole contact in the governmental bureaucracy and her superior, Sir Nigel had pulled strings and managed to book some of the most irregular concert arenas ever imagined, but Anne's role of acclaimed entertainer gave her special access to foreign embassies, theaters, high-stakes gambling parlors and ladies' fashionable soirees with no one ever suspecting her purpose. In truth, the information she had provided through her peculiar channels had saved face for Her Majesty's government more times than Sir Nigel would care to contemplate. "This, however, is a far different matter."

"Surely you have plenty of regulars to scour the home territory for whatever details you need, Nigel. People are more aware of me here; my working in London could mean the end of my usefulness abroad if my role were uncovered."

"No one is more aware of that than I, Anne, yet I have no choice but to insist. The situation is that delicate and that dangerous."

Even in the scattered moonlight Anne noticed the lines of tension in Conway's face and the stiff posture in which he held his body, although he continued to pat her hand as if to make everything better. If this bulwark of British stability was so concerned, the trouble was significant; of that there could be no doubt.

"All right, sir, you have my cooperation and my total curiosity, I assure you. What's the source of all this consternation? Don't tell me Bertie has been up to no good again?"

"I only wish it were that simple, dear. No, we've reason to believe Her Majesty will not live to see her Jubilee Day, although it is little more than a month away."

"What? I thought her doctors said she was in fine health for one her age," exclaimed Anne, forgetting to keep her noted tones soft.

"Shh! We can't remain out here too long before some spooning couple seeks the isolation, so just listen to the high points of the situation. The palace has received a few odd letters threatening Victoria's life, and neither they nor I am taking this lightly. I need you to find out as much as you can as quickly as possible."

"But wouldn't the threats be from criminals or foreigners? Certainly no English nobleman or lady is apt to kill the queen because they don't care for her choice of wine."

"Probably not, but she was ill received at the People's Palace yesterday; some of the crowds were quite unpleasant, booing and the like. Unfortunately there seems to be a sense of growing discontentment with her, and not only among the poor and disenfranchised. Even some of the nobility are restless, as well, since the longer Victoria lives, the shorter Prince Albert's reign will be and the less time his cronies will have the influence they seek," hypothesized Conway. "We can't afford to ignore the situation."

"Of course not, but have you considered the political perspective? Maybe the Irish have decided it's time for another violent episode like that in Phoenix Park."

"That, too, is a possibility, but for now, we have others concentrating on them," stated Nigel, his words beginning to penetrate the shock that Anne felt.

"How could anyone contemplate killing the Queen of England? He'd have to be insane," she murmured, not realizing she'd spoken aloud until her companion replied.

"Probably that is the truth. Who else but a madman would proclaim his intentions and boast about them in a series of anonymous letters? We aren't certain, however, that he belongs to Bertie's circle. There is a full complement of suspects in that social reforming crowd in the East End. Some of those characters are complete fanatics, but you'll learn more when I send round the dossiers we have tomorrow. Anne, we really need your help infiltrating these groups. You are the only one who can befriend both people of gentle birth and those with social consciences without arousing suspicion and making them all the more vehement," Sir Nigel stated firmly. "The future of England could well rest on those lovely shoulders your mysterious admirer mentioned earlier, but I for one will feel better knowing you're working from the inside while we take the official precautions."

"I don't suppose there is any chance of curtailing her activities?" asked Anne with little hope.

"After all those years of her remaining in seclusion while the country barely dithered along? I think Ponsonby and Gladstone would draw and quarter anyone who suggested Victoria retire to oblivion again, whatever the reason. And I suspect she anticipates the Jubilee Day adulation of her citizens quite happily."

"Even if someone in those adoring crowds means to kill her?" questioned the startled young singer, rising to her feet.

"Oh, I very much doubt Her Majesty has been informed; you know she doesn't let the petty details of government concern her," said her employer with a rueful grin, turning Anne toward the house. Arm in arm, they presented the image of older uncle and young niece, happily engaged in family gossip.

"I strongly fear the assassination plots are our headaches; hers are Bertie and whoever is the next of her family to be feted with a state wedding."

"Well, I suppose that's one advantage of being the monarch—you can choose your own worries," said Anne, trying to lighten her somber mood. Though deeply perturbed at even the possible threat of a royal assassination, she was professional enough to realize that she could accomplish more as an unflustered investigator than as an emotional subject. "Unfortunately, I have to carry my own worries."

"Nonsense, my dear, I am quite certain any of the anxious swains approaching would be more than happy to ease your mind on any number of subjects,'' said Nigel with a smile as half a dozen young noblemen descended the steps of the terrace to surround Anne, allowing him to slip away unnoticed.

Chapter Two

"Miss Hargraves, you said I might have the next dance," enjoined one gallant hurrying to greet her and executing a deep bow.

"But I haven't even had the opportunity to meet you," protested a soldier in dress uniform. "Surely a man in the service of the queen deserves that much."

"Miss Hargraves agreed that I was to introduce her to Mother's royal guest," protested Daniel with a petulant frown. "The Prince of Wales won't stay all evening, you know."

"Daniel has already caused you enough grief this evening, Miss Hargraves. Let me do the honors," suggested another dapper fellow. "Father hunts with Prince Albert."

As the young men clamored for her attention, Anne couldn't help but notice the solitary figure posed casually at the French doors on the terrace. Unless she was badly mistaken, he was the fellow who had accosted her in the gardens so recently, and he was watching the raging debate for her favor with an inordinate amount of interest. When she realized her eyes were upon him, however, the tall, dark-haired gentleman nodded in her direction and winked, acknowledging her with the outrageously intimate gesture before he turned away as if to deny he felt any attraction for her.

"Lord Moreland," she said sharply, cutting through the continuing chorus of male voices. "Tell me, who is that man on the terrace?" Yet even as she spoke, the object of her query passed through the French doors and was gone from view.

"Whoever he was, he's more the fool for walking away from such an engaging sight as yourself," answered the duke. Taking her gloved hand and placing it firmly on his arm, he smiled victoriously at his rivals. "Shall we go in, Miss Hargraves? I believe refreshments are about to be served, and knowing Bertie's appetite, that's certainly where we'll find our prince."

Nodding agreeably, the delicate blonde smiled apologetically at the others who'd courted her attention and permitted herself to be escorted past the music-filled ballroom toward the dining room. While ordinarily, as Anne Hargraves, private citizen, she would have welcomed the opportunity to dance with such a series of eager partners, on hearing Nigel's words, she'd relinquished her personal interests in the evening's entertainment. She was now concerned only with what she might possibly learn from the other guests, and whom she might meet. She'd been abroad for long periods, and she'd lost touch with many of the nobility. Tonight was a first step toward remedying that... if only she could dispense with Daniel's proprietary attentions long enough to circulate. There were already quite a few young women throwing murderous glances in her direction while they smiled beguilingly at the man at her side. She'd have to do something.

Moving past even the lovely ladies brazen enough to lower their fans in his direction, Lord Moreland led his prize directly to the elegant matron holding court in the center of the main hall. Attired in a deep purple gown of flowing silk and satin panels offset with pearls, she wore a tiara of similar pattern in her dark hair.

"Mother, may I introduce Miss Anne Hargraves? Miss Hargraves, my mother, Aurora Palmer, the Duchess of Moreland."

"Miss Hargraves, it is truly an honor to have you as our guest, let alone to hear you sing so very beautifully." The woman smiled warmly as she took Anne's hand in her own, making her feel quite welcome. "I am only sorry not to have met you earlier, but I'm certain you can imagine the many last-minute details that demanded my attentions. At any rate, I don't know how I can express my appreciation for your sharing our special night, except perhaps to rid you of my son's excessive gallantry—"

"Mother!"

"Daniel, you beleaguered poor Miss Hargraves unmercifully until she sang for our guests, then you made a complete ass of yourself and destroyed her lovely gown, and still you persist in dogging her every step! Have you no consideration for the lady or her feelings?" As any mother chastising her child, the duchess neither minced words nor tolerated debate. "Off with you. Dance with your cousin Hilary if no one else will have you."

"I—" Realizing he was defeated before he could even mount a defense, the young nobleman, blushing furiously, bowed politely over Anne's hand and quickly escaped further embarrassment, all plans to introduce Anne to the Prince of Wales forgotten.

"Really, your ladyship, he did no permanent damage. The gown can be salvaged," said Anne, thankful for her release yet concerned for her former escort's ego.

"Nonsense. At nearly twenty, he should be more responsible for his actions," refuted the matriarch of the Palmer family, sweeping Anne along with her as she crossed the hall toward a group of guests. "Now then, have you met Andrew Brighton? Though he's a bit overzealous at times, he's quite active in the East End, trying to improve living conditions. And this is my cousin, Dame Edith Young, who is trying to convince the queen to fund a nursing school in honor of her jubilee."

"Miss Hargraves, I am pleased to make your acquaintance. You have a delightful voice," approved the noblewoman. "I was just telling Andrew that the sick quite obviously need assistance more urgently than the impoverished. After all, the infirm cannot help themselves but the poor only need find employment to eliminate their distress. Don't you agree?"

"I venture to say, ma'am, that a fair segment of the poor are probably also ill from lack of proper diet. Perhaps your nursing institute might be centered in the East End and help both groups at the same time," suggested Anne diplomatically.

"Where's the good of nursing them back to health if they haven't a decent home or clothes enough to keep them warm? They'll just sicken again," scoffed Brighton loudly, his rather portly body shaking in indignation as his round face grew a brighter red, his mustache a dark splotch in the outraged features. "The government must stop pretending there is no problem and put all its resources into play to salvage its citizens before it is too late for them...and for us."

"Too late for what, Andrew?" demanded Aurora, taking a glass of champagne from a waiter. "You always go on and on about these social issues but you never explain what difference our efforts could possibly make."

Anne waited without comment, wondering if she might be fortunate enough to learn something significant tonight.

"I warrant *Mr.* Brighton wants us to abandon our titles and a major portion of our estates, as he's done to help the less privileged," contributed Dame Edith haughtily. "Personally, I feel if I'm giving them my time and effort, that's sufficient."

"And how much bread will your time buy a starving child?" snapped the angry reformer, now nearly apoplectic. "Just look over there. The Prince of Wales laughs and parties, waiting for his turn at the throne, but as much as we might hope that he'll be different from his mother, there is no absolute assurance our wishes will prevail. Her Majesty, ha! She's spending thousands of pounds sterling for a tribute she doesn't deserve—though ancient as she is, who knows if she will even live to see the day."

"Andrew Brighton! How dare you utter such blasphemy in my house? I must demand that you leave at once. I'll not have such sentiments spoken under my roof. Why, Victoria is my daughter's honorary godmother, you know," announced the Duchess of Moreland.

"As she is of half the children born to nobility each year," replied Dame Edith, "though the woman is too miserly to even send so much as a christening cup."

"Miss Hargraves, you've contributed nothing to this discussion," observed Brighton, the former Earl of Wilton. "What have you to say about our royal monarchy?"

"Nothing of note. But, if you are leaving—"

"He is indeed," affirmed Lady Moreland. "I have sent for his carriage."

"Then may I ask you to see me home, Mr. Brighton? I find I am suddenly quite fatigued," confessed Anne, untruthfully. With the sudden opportunity to get more closely acquainted with Andrew Brighton so unexpectedly available, she couldn't help but proceed in that direction, no matter what laws of etiquette she might be violating. She'd send around a note tomorrow, begging her hostess's understanding. "My apologies, Lady Moreland, and my thanks, of course, for a most interesting evening."

"Think nothing of it, my dear, but why don't I have someone else see you home?" The woman's tone gave clear evidence of her disapproval of Anne's choice of escort. "Certainly a woman as lovely as yourself—"

"Should have better sense than to be seen with someone like me?" finished Andrew Brighton dryly. "Perhaps Miss Hargraves has socialist leanings you never suspected, Aurora, and you're well rid of both of us." Extending his arm to Anne, he looked at her expectantly. "If you don't regret your request, shall we go?"

Within a few moments, Anne had reclaimed her wrap and train, and departed to the noisy speculation of not a few curious guests.

"My gracious, who would have imagined?" breathed Audrey in astonishment. "With Ian Kendrick sending her smoldering glances all night long, she chooses Father's eccentric school chum for an escort. He was only invited because he was best man at my parents' wedding and Mother was feeling sentimental about her first social event without Father. I mean, even Daniel has more sense than to encourage Brighton's attentions."

"Can you imagine?" ran the circuit of the room as men and women alike wondered at the peculiar choice made by the songstress.

Ian Kendrick took particular notice of both Anne's departure and her unlikely companion.

"Well, well, old boy," he muttered to himself as his eyes narrowed in speculation, "perhaps it was some sixth sense rather than lust that drew you to her after all."

Indeed, the only observer not decrying Anne's inappropriate action was Nigel Conway, who took comfort in the speed with which the woman went about her job.

"Well, did you learn anything of significance last night? There's been enough in the press lately about the fiscal irresponsibility of my friends; I certainly need no more unpleasant surprises. But then I trust I shall have none since I saw you deep in conversation with quite a few characters at Aurora's."

Riding horseback in the park, the two men would have little opportunity to exchange confidences before the others joined them, despite the early hour. They had long ago dispensed with the preliminary niceties at these equestrian meetings.

"Yes, but they had nothing of interest to say on the matter at hand. You realize of course, sir, that Brighton left the party unsociably early." The young man was clearly deferential to his royal elder, separated as they were by birth as well as finances.

"Yes, he departed even before I did. Bad form, that, leaving before the Prince of Wales. And why was a certain Miss Hargraves on his arm? I've heard nothing of her social leanings before. It struck me as rather peculiar, and at this point, I think it prudent to investigate anything that appears odd. Is there any special reason for her involvement with Brighton?"

"I'm not certain as yet, but she's more than the golden songbird she appears. I inadvertently upset an assignation she had in the gardens, though, naturally, she denied it. Shortly after, however, she was extremely vocal about the need for social reform, and she did leave with our friend Brighton."

"Was he the one she was meeting?"

"I can't be certain. I would think she'd have been more secretive with the object of a rendezvous," theorized the dark-haired figure as sounds of an approaching group of riders reached his ears. He would have to finish his report quickly.

"If there was anything more to it than a romantic rendezvous in the moonlight. Moreland's gardens are a spectacular sight—"

"Not at this time of year, sir."

"She is quite an attractive woman over whom many men were fawning. She might have simply been looking for some privacy away from the crowd," interjected his employer, the prince, as the first of the riders came into sight.

"Given her looks, why she'd ever choose Brighton is—"

"Something you are going to find out, young man," came the curt instruction, issued in haughty tones the man must have inherited from his regal mother though he seldom used them with Ian, upon whom he so often depended of late.

Surprised at Bertie's officious manner, Ian wondered at its cause, even as the royal continued.

"Oh, and by the way," the Prince of Wales added, his demeanor all too casual given his tone, "take careful note of any disgruntlement you may hear concerning the queen's plans for her jubilee. I don't want her being upset again as she was at the People's Palace." Satisfied his orders would be obeyed, Ian's mentor, ever the wagering sportsman, cantered on ahead, calling out to the other riders, "All right, gentlemen, for a pint, a race to the Serpentine and back to the stables."

As the group disappeared in a flurry of dust, Ian Kendrick smiled at his good fortune. Being ordered to learn more about Anne Hargraves could well be the most pleasant assignment he'd ever received, though Bertie's apparent afterthought about the queen was a cause for puzzlement.

Across town, the object of his musing was in nowhere near as good a frame of mind as she eyed her breakfast. Andrew Brighton had done precisely what Anne had asked

last night and not a single jot more. He had seen her home.
He maintained a proper distance in the coach, stopped the
carriage at her door, declined to come in and had been
driven away without saying another word against Victoria
or the plans for her golden jubilee. Leaving the party early
to be with him had been a totally futile effort and Anne
fumed at the time lost. Despite all the conversational gam-
bits she'd tried, the man had remained steadfastly noncom-
mittal on any topic of special interest to his companion.

Pouring herself another cup of coffee, she wondered
briefly if she could possibly be losing her touch with men.
She was after all twenty-seven and not as young as she used
to be.

"Absurd," she said aloud, placing her cup on the side-
board to study her reflection in the mirror over it. She
turned her head right and left to peruse her profile, tossing
her curls and patting the smooth line of her chin and ever
graceful neck. Not even the hint of a wrinkle, she was glad
to note. "I may be past the age of first loves, but what
woman of sophistication isn't? No, I swear, Andrew Brighton is the one behaving abnormally. Any other man would
have happily seized the opportunity to seduce Anne Hargraves . . . or at least attempt her seduction."

Recalling the many men she'd encountered in her career,
the woman shook her head sadly. Perhaps men craved a
woman to listen to them as much as a woman to hold, but
very, very few had touched her heart or gotten to know the
real Anne Hargraves, and even fewer had succeeded in their
efforts to entice her interest. Yet her reputation as a femme
fatale had preceded her wherever she went.

After all, how many men would voluntarily admit defeat
when it was known that a desirable woman had encouraged
their attentions and invited them to her rooms? It was a ploy
that had served her and the British government well
throughout her foreign assignments. And, for the most part,
she had managed to leave her suitors with a sense of honor
and privilege rather than loss and shame when she escaped
their advances. Anne shivered at the realization that this
time, when failure might mean her sovereign's death, play-

ing at games to secure information seemed somehow awfully risky.

If Brighton wouldn't fall victim to her allure, she'd need
another means of entry into his camp. Recalling the papers
Conway had sent around that morning, Anne carried her
coffee to the table and flipped open the folder on the East
End reformers. Perhaps there was a key there somewhere
that she could use.

Nigel had included a dated article from the *Guardian*
about a failed attempt on Victoria's life, she noted, fingering the clipping curiously.

"Does this tell you anything of our beloved queen's
probable attitude were she to know of the current problem?" he had penned across the top.

" 'It is worth being shot at—to see how much one is
loved,' says Queen Victoria," ran the headline.

"Oh, heaven preserve us," sighed Anne, reading the brief
account of the rifle shots into the sovereign's carriage, the
spectacular capture of the attacker, not by her escort, John
Brown, but by a group of Eton lads, and Victoria's result-
ing sense of destiny.

"If he hadn't missed, I doubt she would feel the same
way," muttered the government agent, understanding Conway's concern. "Well, if she refuses to change her schedule
to accommodate more protection, we'll just have to be twice
as clever. Very well, Andrew Brighton, let's see what your
government knows about you."

Delving into the papers at hand, Anne felt the undeniable excitement she always experienced when beginning a
new assignment. There was a tremendous surge of anticipation, a peculiar sense of power and, at the same time, a
certain anxiety at the responsibility suddenly laid at her feet.
What if, this time, she failed?

Then she shrugged and remembered her Louis; in his
time, no one had even tried to protect him, a dangerous
oversight that caused his death. At the very least, she, Conway and many others would be expending inestimable time
and energy to succeed in safeguarding their sovereign. If
that weren't enough, it was still better than doing nothing,
she consoled herself, opening the file on Brighton again.

Yet, an hour later, the blonde wasn't sure she'd accomplished anything at all. She had read Andrew Brighton's biography, knew the places he frequented, the causes he championed, the arguments he had had with the many branches of governmental bureaucracy and even the members of the church he had offended. Still, she couldn't find a shred of evidence to convince her that caring for the poor as ardently as he did was any reason he'd be an anarchist seeking the queen's demise. As Brighton had implied last night, while Bertie sat on a few royal committees to explore the needs of London's poor, who could be certain he would actually try to improve their lot when he became king? Admiring a man so publicly concerned about social issues, despite the royals' disinterest, Anne reflected on Brighton's background.

As the only son of a profligate devoted to the pleasures of wine and women, Andrew had found himself heir to the title and depleted family fortune at an early age when his philandering father died in a boating accident with another man's wife. Though the woman left behind four young children, they were quickly orphaned when their father took the first chance he had to commit suicide and avoid the shame of the situation. Opening his heart and his wallet, Andrew Brighton had taken his first steps to social reform, pledging to right the world for those devastated youngsters.

That had been almost twenty years ago, and while two of his charges had married and gone on to lead relatively worthwhile lives, one had died a drunken death, frozen in a snowbank, and the other had steadfastly refused his help, preferring to live by providing sexual favors to strangers until one of them had bludgeoned her to death.

Now, Andrew Brighton was rarely found away from the squalor of the East End of London, unless he was agitating for better working conditions or more awareness of the plight of the downtrodden. The only way to reach him, decided Anne, was to support his crusade.

Now, whatever did one wear to a lecture on "Feeding the Body and Soul" in a church in the East End? It was too late to attend today's session, but tomorrow's would suffice.

Having decided the dictates of fashion were certainly un-recognized in London's poorer neighborhoods, Anne dressed comfortably in a soft brown dress and short jacket with delicate braid edging the sleeves and hem. Choosing to minimize its full skirt, she wore only two petticoats rather than the usual five, and was pleased by the simpler, no-nonsense air it gave her. A plain chocolate bonnet with the same braid completed her ensemble, and as she tucked her sun-brushed curls beneath its brim, Anne smiled at her reflection in the mirror.

Certainly not the sophisticated image of the world-renowned songstress the Morelands had welcomed two nights ago, she acknowledged. This somber female might just be the person who could garner Brighton's trust, how-ever. Indeed, if it took assisting in all the almshouses of London to protect Queen Victoria, then Anne would do that. London's slums could hardly be any worse than those she'd witnessed on assignments in Alexandria and Cal-cutta, she reflected as she descended the steps to her wait-ing coach.

"St. George's-in-the-East," she instructed the driver.

"Are you certain you want to go there, ma'am? I could take you to any number of closer and cleaner churches. It would be no trouble," volunteered the newly hired coach-man.

"Thank you for your concern, but St. George's is where I am going and where you will return for me later," Anne said firmly.

"Yes, certainly, Miss Hargraves. St. George's-in-the-East it is," agreed the man quickly. He had warned her; if she wanted to risk her neck, it was out of his hands.

Though it was early afternoon, little sunlight penetrated the grimy windows of the church, leaving it dark and dreary inside, more like a mausoleum than a place of loving wor-ship. For a moment, startled eyes glanced her way as Anne moved to a place on the aisle and seated herself, affording her a strong sense of misgiving.

"Whatcha want here, missy? Bored with yer own fancy digs?" challenged a raspy voice on her right. "We don't need your kind around here snooping."

Turning to look at her accuser, Anne forced herself not to grimace. The poor woman was more skeleton than human, her flesh shrunken on its aged bones, her eyes weary and old before their time, her clothes assorted rags, clean enough but torn and nearly threadbare. Before Anne could answer, however, Andrew Brighton was beside her, gently chiding the woman who had spoken out.

"Now then, Nell, you know I don't turn anyone away from our meetings. I am certain Miss Hargraves has come to help, not mock our poor efforts. I want her welcomed."

"I only meant she shouldn't take food from the mouths of them that need it—"

"She won't," assured Brighton, fingering his mustache. "Now, will you light the candles and distribute the bowls? I'll be along in a minute."

"Aye, sir," answered the gaunt female, scurrying to do his bidding though not without a backward glare at Anne.

"You'll have to forgive my people, Miss Hargraves. They tend to be very jealous of the little I can offer, a slice of bread, some hot soup and a few words of encouragement as they eat."

"When your notice said lecture, I didn't realize," began Anne. "I only—"

"One can hardly advertise free food without offending their pride. There's no need to apologize, though you might be better off sitting toward the back," suggested the reformer. "I must serve their meager fare and get started with my talk. I'll speak with you later."

"Of course," she agreed, embarrassed at taking time away from those who really mattered to Andrew Brighton. "I'm only sorry I troubled you."

"Nonsense, your presence gives me hope that my words may yet make a difference at those interminable house parties, and you give me a vision of loveliness rare in these surroundings. Don't regret coming; you answered a call in your heart," urged Brighton as he moved toward his flock at the front of the church.

By the time Anne had relocated herself in the back of the building, he was busily ladling hot soup into the waiting bowls, sharing a quiet word with each recipient of his bounty. Anne marveled at the gentleness of the big man. When he bent to fill a child's bowl, he seemed a towering giant aiding a dwarf, yet the loving power in his smile made him soften and appear tender. Could such a man really be an assassin? her compassionate nature questioned. But, before she could consider Brighton's true motives further, another visitor sat beside her.

To her immense surprise, the man joining her now was none other than the mysterious stranger in the Moreland gardens, the fellow who had watched her so intently from the balcony and then disappeared into the night. Now, what on earth was he doing here?

"Good afternoon, Miss Hargraves," he began, placing his hat on the chair in front of him. "I realize that we have not been formally introduced, but then how can you distrust someone you meet in a church? The name is Ian Kendrick, and we were both at the Duchess of Moreland's party the other night, so I am not a total stranger."

"You were inexcusably rude to me in the gardens, Mr. Kendrick," said Anne coldly. Shifting over to distance herself from him, she was irate that the rogue was so bold to continue his ill-mannered pursuit in the light of day, and in a house of worship, too. "Quite frankly, I should prefer you to remain a stranger. However kindly your intentions may be this afternoon, I find it difficult to believe you have a charitable nature."

"And yours is apparently quite unforgiving," he retorted quickly, annoyed at her icy brush-off. Just then, Brighton moved away from the cauldron of soup and began to speak.

"My good friends, both those known and those soon to be known, welcome once again to Feeding the Body and Soul. Our bodies are but the temporary shelters of our souls, which need nurturing every bit as fervently as do our bones," began the socialist in a speech apparently not written, but coming purely from his heart.

So deeply was Anne affected by Brighton's eloquence that she forgot the irritating presence of the man beside her and the innate cynicism that ordinarily formed a protective shelter for her own emotions, allowing her to divorce herself from the subject of her assignment. This time, she realized, life would be different; she cared about the outcome of this situation, both personally and professionally, and that could make it very dangerous.

When Brighton finished his talk, the blonde reached obligingly into her reticule and withdrew her purse. Without hesitation, she emptied its contents into the collection cup a small ragged child was circulating. Only as she pulled back her extended hand was it caught in the grip of the man beside her.

"Surely you are sophisticated enough to see through his woeful cry for help?" upbraided Kendrick. "If he is so desperate for funds, let him raise them from his estate or the hierarchy of the church. He needn't milk society women seeking to salve their guilty consciences. Besides, God only knows what the man is doing with the funds he collects here and at Grosvenor Square parties."

"Is that the ugly voice of experience speaking, Mr. Kendrick? Personally I see you as one more likely to steal from women unfortunate enough to trust you," retorted Anne angrily. How dare he cast aspersions on her character? Salve guilty consciences indeed! "Kindly unhand me and let me worry about my well-being. I assure you I am more than capable of looking after myself."

"In this neighborhood? I doubt it, Miss Hargraves. You have already advertised your financial foolishness to a number of witnesses, any of whom might decide to steal whatever you have left. Let me offer you my protection and see that you reach home safely," argued Ian as he urged the woman to her feet and began to lead her to the door. If she was stupid enough to support Brighton financially, he couldn't prevent her from doing so, but he could at least shelter her from the more vile elements of the area and give himself the opportunity to know her better in the bargain.

"No. The only thing I want from you, sir, is your absence from my life. I wish to have a few words with Mr.

Brighton, whom I regard as a much safer guardian than you, Mr. Kendrick. Then my carriage will be outside. I assure you, sir, there is nothing you can do that I would appreciate more than your leaving me alone.'' Turning away from him before her temper got the better of her and she spoke words better left unsaid in a church, Anne made her way up the aisle to where Brighton stood, gathering the empty bowls and plates.

"Mr. Brighton, if you can use another pair of hands to help you clean up, mine are available,'' she offered loudly, her mind still dwelling on the consummate nerve of Ian Kendrick. Who was he to interfere in her life, anyway?

"Thank you, Miss Hargraves. You have been more than generous already, but there's always work for the willing,'' Brighton said, noting her quick glance toward the apparently empty church as the rear door slammed. Neither of them noticed the man in the shadows listening to the peculiar conversation between the social reformer and the woman Ian swore needed to be reformed herself. Only irritation at his own stupidity kept him from leaving without at least trying to hear what they planned, hard as it was in the dark, chilly church. Still, his own comfort meant nothing considering the assignment at hand.

Chapter Three

"Bloody hell, I should have offered to assist Brighton, as well; then I could have heard everything. But no, what did I do? I argued with Anne Hargraves. That's a fine way to get to know more about her. Whenever that woman is in the vicinity, I begin to lose control. What is it about her anyway?" grumbled Ian Kendrick a half hour later as he strode down the street to the small house he rented off Russell Square.

"It isn't as if she's all that special a female. Certainly, the lady is attractive enough and wonderfully vivacious when she performs, but I've had women twice as alluring and a damn sight more receptive," he argued with himself, knowing even as he formed them that such thoughts weren't true. But then, his task had been to explore her relationship with Brighton, and no matter how he looked at it, he had miscalculated the encounter. He had been downright stupid.

Well, there was no way around his problem, the dark-haired young man brooded as he turned into the path to his front door, his ego only slightly more wounded than his professional pride. He had already taken steps to make amends. He hoped she would accept his token of apology. If his efforts didn't succeed, Anne would never permit him to be near her again, let alone allow him to learn about her and Brighton. Scowling once more at the memory of his uncharacteristically impulsive behavior that afternoon, Ian pulled out his house keys and bounded up the steps, almost tripping over the figure huddled on his threshold in the dim afternoon twilight.

"What the devil is this? Has Brighton sent London's poor to camp at my door now? This isn't an almshouse, be gone with you," he exclaimed irritably, even as he automatically distributed the few coins in his pocket.

"Hey, Ian, you can't buy me off that cheaply," protested a youthful voice as its owner rose to his feet and uncovered his head.

"Jack? Why in blazes are you lying on my front stoop? Surely you told Mrs. Land you were family; wouldn't she believe you, you young scalawag, coming without any hint?" asked Ian, unlocking the door and embracing his brother. "Here, here, come inside and let me get a look at you. It's been almost three years."

"I rang, but when there was no answer to the bell, I assumed you gave your staff Thursdays off," Jack replied. Fifteen years Ian's junior, the lad was equipped with a devilishly beguiling grin.

"My staff, is it now? Aye, they've the afternoon off—" Ian chuckled, shedding his coat and moving to light the fire in the front room "—though Mrs. Land and her niece Molly hardly qualify for such an imposing title as that."

"Maybe not, but Mother says with you living in the city, you're apt to be a grand gentleman with all the habits to match."

"And all the equally torrid sins, I suppose?" Ian's last visit home had been spoiled by his mother's vocal distress at his continued preference for the life of a single gentleman over that of a happily settled husband. A granddaughter to a stern fire-and-brimstone minister, Abigail Kendrick envisioned her third son burning amid the flames of hell for his life of excess in the modern Sodom and Gomorrah of London, and nothing he could say would convince her otherwise.

As youngsters, Ian and his older brothers had often speculated on the method of their conception, given their mother's distaste for the physical aspects of life, yet they did exist. And fifteen years after Ian, along had come Jack, now nearly a man himself at seventeen.

"Well, then, have a drink and tell me, what brings you to visit your decadent brother, anyway? Not that you're not more than welcome, of course," said Ian, pouring them each a glass of port.

"I suppose sin is the easiest way to define it," Jack muttered into his glass, his face reddening to the roots of his fair hair as he spoke.

"*Sin?*" sputtered his older brother in disbelief, almost choking on his drink, his voice a raspy croak as he continued. "Don't tell me you've ruined some local girl's reputation?"

At his brother's negative shake of the head, Ian felt less anxious. Still the boy remained silent and Ian felt compelled to get him to speak.

"Could it be Mother sent you to me to teach you the evil ways of the world?" the older brother joked.

"Actually, yes and no. That's why I'm here, but it was Father's idea," confessed the red-faced lad, unwilling to meet his brother's eyes. Quickly swallowing the remainder of his port, he moved to refill his glass.

"Damn it all, Jack. Don't feed me this story in dribs and drabs, spit it out like a man, and fill my drink while you're at it," demanded his brother, already seething at the suspicion growing within his breast. It would be just like his father to make him into a sexual purveyor. Perdition, what was this world coming to that a lad needed to be taught how to enjoy a woman?

"Give me a chance here, Ian. I'm not really comfortable with this myself, you know," defended Jack as he hefted the decanter over their glasses. Handing Ian one, he continued. "Last weekend, I had a bit too much to drink with Tommy Fitzgerald and he dared me... Well, Mother found me in the servant's wing, touching Mrs. Mumm—"

"Mrs. Mumm, the housekeeper? Good heavens, we used to call her Mumm the Mummy years ago—"

"And what other kind of female does Mother permit at Kendrick Lodge anyway? You know all the housemaids are at least sixty and spend all their time in church. Besides, Mrs. Mumm seemed willing, and...well, Tommy says in the dark—"

"I can just imagine what Tommy has to say on the topic," snarled Ian, realizing just how right his suspicions had been. "So I'm elected to protect Mrs. Mumm, the household staff and the virtuous young women of Northumberland by indoctrinating you into the ways of men? Does Mother think that I am the only one equipped to educate you?"

"I don't think so. In fact, she doesn't even know where I am; Father just told her he was sending me away for a few weeks so Mrs. Mumm could recover quietly."

"What about Father or your other brothers? I'm certain they're familiar with male needs and their satisfaction."

"Well, Father says Mother made him forget long ago what was ever pleasurable about sex. Michael is too happily married to consider helping me find satisfaction outside of holy wedlock, and Robert's been assigned a parish in South Anglia and can't risk his reputation on a cause like mine. You're my only hope, Ian," pleaded Jack. "And London is far enough from home that Mother won't even find out about it."

"Heaven help me!" muttered Ian, emptying his glass in one long swallow. Earlier today he'd tried and failed to protect a woman from a questionable do-gooder; now he was being asked to tarnish his brother's innocence. And the worst of it was, he couldn't decide which task he resented most! "All right, Jack, let's find out what Mrs. Land left for dinner and I'll give the matter some thought. We needn't rush into anything tonight."

Following her work in the East End and a quick visit with Conway, a tired Anne finally returned home. The door of her rented town house opened at her approach, and she swept into the large entryway with nary a glance at the rotund little butler with the dour face who had been hired by Conway along with the rest of her staff.

Though the evening was but mildly warm, Anne's face was still burning with anger. Thoughts of her encounter with Ian Kendrick had been foremost in her mind on the journey back to her temporary residence, and her usually lovely lips were drawn into an unaccustomed frown as she heedlessly shrugged out of her cloak and left the garment in the taciturn butler's capable hands.

In her present mood, the simple yet elegant furnishings which had come with the town house melted from her view. Despite the time that had lapsed since they had parted company, no matter where she looked, Anne could see nothing but Kendrick's arrogant face. Her irritation with him was completely overshadowing her mission.

True, he was handsome enough, and his looks might have piqued her interest if she were not on such an imperative assignment, and *he* were not so blasted self-assured and determined in his pursuit.

That was the problem... and the cause of the niggling fascination she felt, as well, Anne admitted to herself ruefully, as she walked into the parlor and settled into a chair much too elaborate to actually be comfortable. Ian Kendrick, with his bold manners and dogged address, was quite unlike the men with whom she usually dealt.

She was Anne Hargraves, internationally acclaimed songstress, and though many men had tried to make her their own, they had approached her in supplication, not really daring to believe that she would smile favorably upon their efforts. There were gifts and expensive dinners, and solicitous notes written in hopeful tones. Never had anyone accosted her and merely assumed that she would acquiesce to his desire, no one, that was, except the insufferable Ian Kendrick.

Damn him to bloody hell, Anne thought angrily as she raised a hand to gingerly soothe the muscles along her throat, which had constricted at the memory of his imperious attitude. From their first words, spoken the other night in the garden, she had known that he was domineering. And the cheek of the man! Why, he had practically announced that he could ultimately have her if he so chose.

This was a new and unnerving experience for Anne, who had always had the upper hand in any relationship she had entered. It was her trademark, and if truth be known, her salvation. She had given her love only once, and the experience had brought her almost unbearable pain. She had vowed then that she would never make herself vulnerable again.

Not that she had any intention of losing her heart to Kendrick, she assured herself haughtily. Even if he were not so uncommonly vexing, she was in the middle of the most important mission of her career. She had no time for any man now, especially one as presumptuous as the tall, dark-haired Kendrick, who had the audacity to follow her about the streets of London in order to corner and confront her, and at Brighton's prayer meeting, of all places!

How could she ever hope to concentrate on doing what she must in order to safeguard the queen if she constantly had to worry about Ian Kendrick's sudden materialization and his stubborn resolve to possess her? Something had to be done about the man, and soon, Anne determined as she rang for the butler, continuing to rub her fingertips gently along the side of her graceful throat.

At Brewster's appearance, she ordered a brandy, hoping that a few sips of the numbing liquid would relax her vocal cords enough so she could practice her scales. Though the short, portly butler nodded at Anne's request and silently retreated, the songstress noted an almost imperceptibly raised eyebrow signifying his disapproval.

Wherever did Conway dig up such a relic, Anne wondered miserably, her ill humor growing. Hadn't Brewster ever seen a woman drink brandy before? No, probably not . . . at least not in the very proper households where he had been employed previously. And certainly never at all in the afternoon. Bother! She had one man chasing her through the thoroughfares of London, and another condemning her actions behind her own doors! There was no sanctuary for her in the entire city! For the first time that she could remember, Anne Hargraves considered men a tiresome lot.

The steel-haired butler's expression was even more severe when he returned a few moments later carrying a small brandy snifter on a silver salver.

Anne pursed her lips in irritation when she observed the absence of the decanter and defiantly reached for the glass. Glaring at her chief servant, she raised the brandy to her lips, tossed back her head and swallowed more in one gulp than she normally would have.

"That will be all for now, Brewster," she said curtly.

"Certainly, miss," the middle-aged butler answered in clipped tones. "Am I to assume, then, that you wish one of the maids to see to the flowers?"

"Flowers?" Anne echoed absently, rejoicing that her skirmish with this crotchety fellow was helping to erase her annoyance with Ian Kendrick, and that the muscles in her throat had begun to relax.

"Flowers, miss," the butler replied, his tone of voice impeccably correct, yet nevertheless laden with reproof.

"Which flowers are those?" Anne inquired, beginning to feel exasperated with the butler's verbal parrying.

"Why, the ones that have just been delivered, miss," the butler replied.

"Who are they from?"

"I'm sure I don't know, miss. I did not open the accompanying card, as it was distinctly marked *personal*," Brewster intoned, the coolness of his reply making Anne feel as though the man was her father chiding her for encouraging some undesirable suitor.

"Very well, have them brought in," Anne ordered. As soon as her instructions were carried out, she waited until the manservant had left once again, before turning her attention to the huge bouquet. It was lovely—hothouse bred to be sure—and very expensive, at that. Admiring the delicate blossoms, Anne smiled, thinking that Brighton's interest in her was not limited to her purse and the contributions she could make to his charitable enterprises after all. And if she allowed the man to suppose it was possible for him to become her suitor, Anne was certain there was nothing about him and his activities that she would not be able to learn. It would seem that despite her earlier misgivings, the day had had its measure of success.

She sipped delicately at the remaining brandy as she reached out for the note affixed to the flowers. At last things were back on course and proceeding as they should, Anne concluded with satisfaction. Of course, something would still have to be done with Brewster, she thought with annoyance. She couldn't begin to imagine the very proper butler's behavior if she brought Brighton home late one evening. Good Lord, hadn't the fellow ever learned that servants were meant to be discreet?

Tearing open the envelope, Anne quickly scanned the page. "Sorry I was not as cordial as I might have been ... Our conversation today does not reflect my feelings for you... I would like to call at your home for conversation of a different nature."

Yes, it had all the signs of a man who was willing to be enticed, Anne decided, quite pleased with the results of her foray that afternoon.

At least Anne *was* pleased until her gaze fell upon the signature. Ian Kendrick! The bounder had the audacity to pursue her within the confines of her own home! Was this supposed to alter her disposition toward him? Well, let him see what sort of change his generosity had wrought. If anything, she was more put out with him than before. Wasn't the word *no* in Kendrick's vocabulary?

The respite from tension induced by the brandy faded almost instantly, and Anne felt her throat begin to tighten once more. Perdition! No man had ever affected her so...for any reason. How dare Ian Kendrick do this to her? Leaving the parlor with a determined tread, Anne went in search of some more brandy, the glint in her eye just daring Brewster to make a comment.

The sedate atmosphere of the drawing room was proper enough to suit even Brewster, Anne concluded miserably the following afternoon. Still, she managed to hide her grimace with a polite smile as she nodded in agreement with the inane comments of her hostess, Mrs. Horace Lipton, Lady Chadwick. Though she had been born and bred in England, practicing her trade as an intelligence agent in the polite society of her homeland was foreign to Anne. She was impatient by nature, and found the restrictions of moving within society's confines exceedingly tedious.

In Northern Africa or the Far East, the simple act of lowering her lashes or the appearance of a dimple would have brought about immediate introductions to the men she

wished to meet. But here in England . . . In England she had
to sit through tiresome teas and gain the acceptance of the
women wedded to the men she was bent on knowing.

This afternoon was a case in point. While Anne's contact
with Brighton might help her gain access into the inner circle of social reformers, it was sitting demurely in the re-
fined morning rooms and parlors of London's most
prestigious town houses that would bring her into the world
of that other group suspected of plotting Victoria's assassination—the men who invested years in fawning upon the
Prince of Wales.

Horace Lipton, Lord Chadwick, was one such individual, and his spouse, the dowdy woman now pontificating so
knowledgeably upon London's latest fashions, was Anne's
entrée into that group. The noblewoman's at home was quite
the dreariest affair Anne had ever endured, but at this moment, despite the fact that she had already suffered through
a multitude of meaningless exchanges with the other women
present, no one looking at the renowned Miss Hargraves
would suspect that there was anyplace else she would rather
be.

Taking advantage of a rare pause in Lady Chadwick's
conversation, Anne smiled gently at Aurora, Duchess of
Moreland, who had arranged for Anne to accompany her to
Gladys Lipton's small social gathering, having evidently
forgiven Anne her social faux pas in leaving her party with
Brighton. For her part, the songstress never ceased to be
amazed at Conway's social contacts. Coming here had been
arranged so easily, and as Aurora answered her smile with
one of her own, Anne wondered if the woman knew how her
standing in society was being utilized by Her Majesty's
government.

But that was neither here nor there, Anne reminded herself as she prettily replaced her teacup in its saucer. The
mission was what counted . . . ultimately it was always what
counted. What difference did it make if she had to consume enough tea to constitute a tributary to the Thames, or
if she learned nothing of value today? The contact had been
made and would grow stronger.

Lady Chadwick had fairly preened at receiving the famous Anne Hargraves this afternoon, and would no doubt desire to take advantage of this social coup by including Anne in her next fashionable event. In fact, if Gladys Lipton was the type Anne suspected her to be, the woman would no doubt plan some gathering or other merely to flaunt her personal acquaintance with Anne Hargraves in front of the rest of London's hostesses.

Conway's agent was entirely ready to signal the Duchess of Moreland that they should be departing when Lady Chadwick sensed a bit of restlessness in her guest and quickly left off discussing fashions, rushing to change the topic to one she felt would suitably impress Miss Hargraves and perhaps persuade her to stay a bit longer.

"But how I do go on, talking of fabrics and patterns," Lady Chadwick simpered. "It's all due to the fact that I am starved for such conversation, as I don't indulge myself with such prattle very often. His Highness wouldn't countenance it, you understand, and usually when my husband and I are out in society, we are in his company. Horace has long been one of the prince's dearest friends."

"How delightful for you," Anne said, picking up her teacup to have it filled once more as she told herself this was a sacrifice for queen and country. "Though I recognized immediately that you are a lady of grace and refinement far above the normal cut, I hadn't realized just how honored I should be to have been received into your drawing room."

"Now, now, my dear. It is my pleasure. We women of quality have no one if not each other," Lady Chadwick drawled, pleased that Anne was properly impressed by Lord Chadwick's relationship with the future king of England. "And after all, you are the one who is favored by fame at present. Horace and I won't take our place in history until after dear Bertie is on the throne."

"Hopefully Her Majesty will reign for many more years," Lady Moreland interjected patriotically, completely ignoring the frown her words had placed upon Lady Chadwick's sharp features.

"Still it is bound to happen sooner or later that the prince will assume control of England," Anne placated in an attempt to further explore this topic. "And until that day, you've plenty of time to enjoy the company of those who, besides Lord Chadwick, will someday advise our king."

"Why, we advise him even now," Lady Chadwick boasted with a haughty glare at Aurora Palmer, Duchess of Moreland.

"But he is not always counseled wisely, is he, Gladys?" the duchess chided.

"Aurora! How can you allude to such a thing in my house?" Lady Chadwick protested, her face aflame with both pique and embarrassment. She was not about to allow Miss Hargraves to sever their blossoming acquaintance due to a misunderstanding. "You know perfectly well that Horace's name was never mentioned in association with the South Kensington Crowd . . . at least not in the newspaper."

"The South Kensington Crowd?" Anne questioned softly.

"Yes, men who used their influence with the Prince of Wales for their own gain. It created quite a scandal," Lady Aurora stated in disapproval, her lips so tightly pursed that Anne wondered how she managed to form words at all.

"But I assure you, Miss Hargraves, that Horace—Lord Chadwick was not among their number," Gladys hastened to interject.

"I'm sure he was not," Anne said smoothly, knowing from the information Conway had given her that the man had indeed been involved but not caught.

"In fact, we were not even on close terms with those who abused Bertie's friendship so shamelessly," Chadwick's wife continued in her husband's defense.

"That may be true enough, Gladys, but I've told you time and again that you would do well to remember that it is Victoria and not her son who sits on the throne of England."

"Forgive me for saying so, when I have only so recently returned home and am therefore terribly ignorant of the politics here, but how much longer can the dear woman hope to reign? It has been almost fifty years already," Anne said, earning a disapproving sigh from the Duchess of Moreland.

"Exactly!" Lady Chadwick crowed with a triumphant smile. "Horace is quite prudent in his support of dear Bertie. After all, men as well received in society as Keating, Bothwell and Warren are doing likewise. And on the fringes of our group, there are others who feel such an association is intelligent. Oh, they are younger men to be sure, but they are beginning to envision the future...Dearborne, Fielding and Kendrick."

"Kendrick?" Anne asked curiously, pretending a struggle to place the name when the man had lately taken over so many of her thoughts. "Should I know that name, Lady Moreland?"

"He was one of my guests at the party you attended, Anne, dear," the duchess replied.

"Then it's a wonder you have to ask who the gentleman is," Gladys tittered, all too ready to sway the topic away from her husband and the Prince of Wales. "I'm surprised that handsome devil didn't attempt to sweep you off your feet. Ian Kendrick has always had an eye for pretty women. He just flits from one to the next without ever coming close to being snared. Why, anyone else with his intense interest in females would be branded a womanizer. But Kendrick is such a charming rogue that he can get away with it, and Lord knows, he has been rumored to have gotten away with quite a bit."

"Is that so?" Anne asked, the indignation and shock imprinted on her face not entirely feigned. So Ian Kendrick, the man who had been so relentlessly pursuing her, was making a name for himself as both a strong supporter of the Prince of Wales and as a rake. There went her decision to ignore him, Anne fumed. This bit of information might mean that Kendrick would bear close watching. Her irritation with the man began to consume her once more, though whether it was his political associations that made her cross or his romantic ones, Anne Hargraves honestly couldn't say.

Chapter Four

A few mornings later, recuperating from a late night spent with some of the prince's friends, Anne sat at her breakfast table and watched Brewster carry in another small pot of coffee. As he placed the intricately adorned container before her, she decided to ignore his sneer of disapproval. It was the best way of coping with his reproof. Though why her preference for thick, sweet Turkish coffee, a taste she had developed during years spent in far-flung corners of the Ottoman Empire, should bother Brewster, Anne wasn't quite certain.

It was apparent, though, that the butler regarded the dark brew as exotic and unseemly, not the sort of thing to grace the breakfast table of a proper Englishwoman. More than once he had tried to persuade his mistress to partake of English tea upon arising, going so far as to pronounce that one was only as socially correct as one's habits.

However, Anne had ignored the man's guidance in that as she had in everything else. And when Brewster served up the coffee brewed so weakly that it might just as well have been tea, as he had this morning, the beautiful Miss Hargraves sent the pot back to the kitchen along with instructions on how to prepare the stuff as it should be served.

Now, as she brought the rich, hot drink to her lips and sipped, she wondered if it was the coffee itself that was so marvelous, or the taste of autonomy it had come to symbolize.

Sighing contentedly that another battle had been waged and won with her pudgy little domineering butler, Anne

reached for the fresh fruit which constituted the remainder
of her morning meal. As she nibbled daintily at the orange
Brewster no doubt considered sinfully extravagant, Anne
vowed that she really did have to talk to Nigel about replac-
ing the man. She had enough to contend with without having surly servants foisted upon her as well.

The thought of her superior provoked a more professional frame of mind, and Anne pushed aside her domestic
concerns to concentrate on more important matters. Going
through the small stack of mail beside her plate, she noted
with satisfaction that the morning post had brought not only
a dinner invitation from Lady Chadwick, but an imperi-
ously worded summons to join a house party in Kent being
given by Lady Bothwell the following month. It would seem
Anne Hargraves had had no difficulty whatsoever in infiltrating the infamous South Kensington Crowd.

Returning to her coffee once again, she wondered idly if
one of these fawning noblemen was actually behind a plot
to put "dear Bertie" on the throne sooner than fate would
have otherwise dictated. Of course if the possibility proved
true, Anne had no doubts as to the complete innocence of
the Prince of Wales himself. Yet she couldn't help but form
the opinion, as had so many others, that perhaps the future
king of England should be more circumspect in his choice
of friends.

As of now, however, she had nothing definite to support
those suspicions. It was only motive that pointed to the
toadies who clustered about the heir to the throne, not evidence. And to be quite frank, the social reformers had their
own reasons for wishing that Victoria's reign would come to
an abrupt end. Still, Brighton didn't strike her as the sort
who would commit regicide in order to implement social
reform, no matter how desperately it was needed. One of his
associates, though, might be more fanatical and a good deal
less scrupulous, as well as more naive about the improvements he could expect a new ruler to make.

Glancing through her appointment book, Anne noted
that today she would be meeting with Brighton for an in-
troduction to his cohorts and a tour of the East End. The
thought of the poverty these men would no doubt relish

pointing out sent shivers down Anne's spine. Still, perversely, she looked forward to the outing. One never knew what would be uncovered there.

That left only one other area that demanded her attention—Ian Kendrick, and the image of his handsome face and dominant manner was not a little disconcerting. Certainly Anne's experience in gathering information for Victoria's government had helped the alluring singer to finally resolve her pique with Kendrick, but not her curiosity. Finishing her coffee, she couldn't help but speculate if the man's interest in her extended beyond the personal and was more than coincidence. But there was no sense in just sitting here thinking about it. No doubt her involvement with the reformers and Prince Albert's circle would soon bring her an answer one way or another... That was, if Nigel didn't provide one first.

Taking another bite of her orange, Anne knew she had to steel herself for the hours ahead. In point of fact, she had seen a lot of poverty and the human misery that accompanied it during her travels abroad. But that had not made her immune to the squalor of London's seamiest streets. For some reason she hadn't expected to find indigence to this extreme at home, and the knowledge that some of her countrymen were forced to exist in such appalling conditions was very disturbing to the wealthy Miss Hargraves. Pity and shame began to well up in Anne's breast, and she hastily fought to keep them at bay. Emotions of any sort, especially ones such as these, were dangerous to agents involved in intelligence missions.

What she needed, Anne thought as she cast about for a distraction, was something to lift her spirits. Within a moment, a devilish light was shining in her deep green eyes. Brewster had, of late, dedicated himself to irritating her; perhaps it was time she repaid the favor.

When the butler answered his employer's summons, he found Anne Hargraves looking quite pleased with herself. Immediately, the portly man suspiciously eyed the room, searching for any clue that might give him an indication as to the woman's uncommonly pleasant mood. He considered her a troublesome female, to be sure, and had no doubt that her enchanting smile portended something of which he would disapprove.

"Yes, miss?" he intoned somberly, as the invitations and open social calendar caught his attention. Though his words were simple and circumspect, Anne knew from his half hidden scowl that the man couldn't care less about seeing her to comfort. "Would you care for some more...coffee?" he asked, his nose wrinkling slightly in distaste.

"No, Brewster, I'd like you to inform the coachman that I'll be needing him this afternoon."

"Indeed, miss?"

"Yes," said, Anne, attempting to sound offhand yet delighting in carefully enunciating each syllable all the same. "I'll be going into the East End."

"The East End?" Brewster echoed, his brow knitting.

"Yes," Anne drawled, amused at how easily her indecorous behavior vexed the man. "And I've no idea how late I'll return, so there's no need to wait up. I *do* have a key."

"Even so, Miss Hargraves, might I again advise you that the East End is no place for a woman of breeding to be found?"

"On the contrary, Brewster, from what I've seen, many of the women there are breeding, and quite rapidly, too, I might add. As to your advising me to keep away from the area...no, I think you may not," the pert blonde stated, her smile broadening as Brewster's shocked face turned a deeper shade of red. What fun it was to bait the proper and stiff butler, Anne discovered. She promised herself to do it more often when things became tedious or Brewster became too overbearing.

"Oh, and by the way, Brewster," Anne added, her softened tones alerting the manservant that this impossible woman was about to announce something else he would find equally unacceptable. "I'm pleased to inform you that you'll be having a few days to yourself next month."

"I beg your pardon, miss?"

"As well you should, but that is neither here nor there and has nothing to do with the matter at hand," said Anne with a laugh. "I shall be visiting the countryside early in June, a house party in Kent given by the Bothwells," she stated quietly.

"The Bothwells?" Brewster repeated, his self-righteous skepticism concerning the advisability of such a visit readily apparent.

"Yes," Anne replied, her smile broadening at her rotund butler's reaction to the news. "So you may either enjoy yourself in London, or go off to visit some friends of your own." That is, if you have any, the songstress thought while she dismissed her unwanted guard dog and watched him leave.

Emerging victorious from the last few moments of conflict had left Anne feeling exceptionally content, and she caught herself humming brightly as she picked up her invitations and calendar and started for the study. This had to have been the most delightful breakfast she had enjoyed since returning to England.

Ian Kendrick put his fork down beside his still heaping plate, his appetite for a hearty morning meal completely gone.

"Did I understand you correctly?" he asked a beaming Jack, who was reaching for yet another helping of ham.

"Probably," the young man replied between mouthfuls, "it's a fairly simple idea and you are an intelligent man."

"Who told you about Madame Duvalier's?" Ian demanded, his normally light gray eyes darkening like ominous thunderclouds.

"How I discovered its existence is of no importance," Jack answered, seeking to protect his sources from his older brother's building wrath. "What matters is that I have quite determined to go there before another day passes."

"And if I tell you I forbid it?" queried Ian, his silky voice so soft and deadly that Jack found it hard to ignore the threat his brother was making.

"But why should you? I'm here for an education of sorts, aren't I?" Jack asked defiantly, feeling so strongly about the matter that he stopped his huge intake of food and met Ian's steady gaze with one of his own.

Anyone seeing the two couldn't help but notice that these were males cut from the same cloth. Both were stubborn, arrogant and given to dominance, and if the older of the two appeared to enjoy a bit more of these qualities than the younger, it was merely a matter of having a few more years under his belt. Though Jack might be a weaker reflection of Ian's character, it was obvious, even now, that he would one day come into his own.

Regarding his brother thoughtfully, Ian couldn't help but be struck by the boy's obstinacy as Jack continued to fearlessly return his glare. It was like peering into some distant mirror and seeing an image of himself as a youth. The idea occurred to him at that moment that perhaps Jack's trip to town had been a form of revenge being vented upon him by their father for Ian's own errant youth. If that were so, it was unpardonable, Ian concluded, though a smile tugged at his heart if not his tightly compressed lips.

"I don't care what you may have heard about the place; Madame Duvalier's is not the sort of establishment you should frequent," he stated emphatically, throwing his napkin on the table as though this volatile discussion was at an end. His actions were stayed, however, by Jack's earnest response.

"Exactly where should I go, then? Would you prefer I further my education with some woman of the streets or do you think I should try to gain experience with some young girl of good family, ruin her and find myself an unwilling husband and still unknowledgeable man at the age of seventeen?"

"No, of course not," Ian was quick to reply, his voice gruff with embarrassment.

"Then what do you want?" Jack asked, mollified enough by the older man's answer to once again resume his meal, his appetite causing Ian to wonder if the boy had ever eaten before coming to London.

"Actually, what I would like is to be left in ignorance of your plans," Ian said, his exasperation with the situation more than evident.

"All right, then," Jack agreed, spooning more eggs onto his plate, "forget I ever mentioned it to you."

"I can't do that, you young idiot! Now I *know,* and my responsibility toward you puts me in a ticklish position."

"Well, from what I understand, you would know plenty about Madame Duvalier's establishment without my ever having mentioned it," Jack said with a laugh.

"And what is that supposed to mean, you scamp?"

"Only that you've found your way there and been seen on the premises on more than one occasion."

Ian's face flamed with anger. It was true. He had been to Madame Duvalier's, but not for any reason he could impart to his infantile brother. In actuality, Ian had only frequented Madame's card room, and had never gone upstairs to the private chambers. He had been there simply to gather information for the prince regent on the comings and goings of some of Albert's followers. The prince had had scandal enough associated with his name and did not wish additional notoriety should his friends' actions in any way reflect upon his own. A whispered suggestion here, a word of advice there, and Albert's friends had soon understood His Highness would frown upon any of his circle who continued an ongoing association with this fashionable, but all too public, brothel.

Drumming his strong, lean fingers on the tabletop, Ian never considered revealing such a delicate matter to Jack. The only decision to be made was whether to be amused or insulted by the fact that the young puppy obviously thought his older brother needed to avail himself of those services of the flesh Madame Duvalier could supply for a gentleman inclined to indulge his carnal appetites. Good Lord! The thought of his having to resort to a brothel, no matter how elaborate, tempted Ian to laugh out loud. But he restrained himself and maintained his stern demeanor as he noticed the smirk Jack was attempting to conceal with yet another biscuit.

"Now, see here, Jack. I could lock you in your room," Ian threatened with a growl.

"I'd only escape, you know," Jack replied, not in the least bit cowed.

"Or make certain that Madame Duvalier's doors are barred to you."

"I'd go someplace more unsavory, the type of place you would disapprove of even more. At least from what I understand, Madame Duvalier's house is somewhat socially acceptable. Would your reputation ever recover if it got around that I was in a house of ill repute never frequented by the gentry? Before you answer, I must remind you, Ian, that I am quite determined to spend some time there today."

"This evening, boy. To go during daylight hours is totally unforgivable."

"Fine, early evening it is then. Just don't wait up for me."

"Don't wait up? Do you think, Jack, that I would send you down there by yourself? No, if you insist on going through with this debacle, I shall take you there myself and make the necessary introductions."

"What!" the adolescent protested loudly. "You'll embarrass me. It's not as if I'm some youngster who needs to be escorted to school."

"That's exactly what you are, and don't forget it," Ian snapped. "Now unless you'd like to be sent back to Father immediately after breakfast, we'll do things my way. Otherwise, you won't do anything at all. Do I make myself clear?"

"Quite," Jack answered, his voice a cross between a sulk and anticipation. "And there's something else I understand, as well."

"And that is?" Ian prompted, swearing that his brother's presence would cure him of any longing, no matter how infrequent, to marry and set up his own nursery.

"In future, to keep my actions and plans to myself."

"Good!" Ian stated with ill-concealed satisfaction as he managed to take a swig of the tepid swill that passed for coffee in his household. "I think that at last we understand each other."

No matter that it was spring. Now that the sun was beginning to set, a distinct chill pervaded the fetid air of the back streets, which spilled one into the other and constituted London's East End. As she pulled her cloak closer, Anne Hargraves shuddered delicately, though whether from cold or from what she had seen this past hour, she was hard pressed to decide.

Keeping pace with her stern-lipped companions, she felt guilt at the additional warmth her light cloak provided, when around her she saw children dressed in rags, running about to keep warm, or shivering in a doorway at an hour when children should be in their homes receiving their supper from their mothers' loving hands. But this afternoon had shown her that there were children living in the capital of the mighty British Empire who ate no supper, possessed no doting mother and indeed had no home. Worse still, those who had families and a place to sleep were little better off than those who did not.

With the descending gloom of impending nightfall, new horrors appeared to claim her attention. No smoke curled from chimneys, as few who lived in this wretched area could afford to buy fuel. The streets themselves, now bathed in mournful shades of gray fast turning black, changed from burrows of despair to sloughs of iniquity, as the creatures of hopelessness who inhabited this awful place began to appear. Under cover of darkness, they seemed ready to give in to the sort of behavior sunlight would never countenance. Desperation and danger permeated the air, making it more foul still, and Anne was glad for the company of Brighton and his fellows.

"Are you certain you are ready for this, my dear?" Brighton asked kindly. "You will see things here tonight that you could never have imagined in your most horrible nightmares."

"It's really not necessary, you know," said Mr. Oliver Digby gruffly. "All we want from people like yourself is your support…and your money, of course. Once you have given us that, you can stay in your fine house, not dirty your costly gown nor unsettle your fragile sensibilities."

Anne regarded the middle-aged Digby and knew, in spite of his protestation that this tour was uncalled for, he was smugly challenging her to go through with it, certain that she would be unable to do so.

"Thank you for your concern, but I feel compelled to see the misery that our government's neglect of the poor has

bred, Mr. Digby," Anne said softly. "I could never expect
to help with the solution if I do not fully understand the
problem."

"Hear, hear," Anne's third companion said with approval. A young man of twenty-eight with large brown eyes,
Alex Morrison had already given evidence of having fallen
under Anne's spell. Her determination to see this day
through to its conclusion only endeared her all the more to
his reformer's heart.

"All right, then, Miss Hargraves, so be it," Digby interjected, stiffly offering her his arm in order to forestall Morrison's inevitable outpouring of admiration for this elegant
woman who was so obviously out of her element yet didn't
have the sense to realize it.

During the next hour, the things Anne witnessed brought
tears to her eyes. There were women no older than she wandering the street with unsteady steps yet worry and despair
caused them to look ancient beyond their years. In their
despondency, they had no jealousy concerning the beautiful, well-dressed woman who stood with a group of gentlemen observing their behavior. In fact, their gin-induced state
made them almost completely oblivious to their surroundings, just as it was intended to do.

This was not the case with the younger girls, little more
than infants really, who stood in doorways and on the
streets. Their faces were heavily painted and their clothing
filthy as well as tawdry. When they noticed Anne and the
others, the girls called to her, their words and manner ob-
scene. Some suggested that she ply her trade in a better part
of town, while others begged her to share the gentlemen she
was with, or asked if she intended taking on all three of them
herself. Then their laughter, hollow and shrill, would spill
along the refuse-strewn streets, sending a chill of revulsion
down Anne's spine.

Though Mr. Digby made no apology for the behavior of
those he was trying to save, Anne heard Brighton cluck his
tongue in disapproval before he muttered support in embarrassed tones, while Alex Morrison reached out to awkwardly pat her arm in consolation, sympathy mirrored in his
eyes.

Despite the presence of the reformers, the taunting of the prostitutes was not the worst thing Anne had to endure. Men tumbling out of pubs or lying in the streets called out lewd remarks as she passed. Though both Brighton and Digby did not deign to dignify the incidents with a response, Anne had to stay young Mr. Morrison from attempting to defend her honor. Bloody ignorant boy, she thought, as she placed her hand on his arm and silently shook her head. Didn't he realize that these people would have no compunction about slashing his throat should he utter even one word of reproach?

"Sorry you came, Miss Hargraves?" Digby asked insolently, as they turned a corner going farther into the decaying labyrinth. "Do you wish to proceed? Now that your experiences with the impoverished have become personal, do you still feel these people are worth saving?"

"More than ever. I am finally beginning to understand the conditions that condemn these poor wretches to behave as they do. Please, let us continue," Anne replied, arching a brow in defiance. She had withstood the worst, hadn't she? Surely she wouldn't be called upon to endure anything more terrible than she had already seen.

"I am proud to say I know you," Andrew Brighton said with hearty approval, while Morrison could do no more than sigh and look at her with adoration imprinted anew upon his face.

Still, as the night continued to descend, Anne found that the situation in the slums could indeed deteriorate further. On one street, she saw a man standing with his offspring, a young boy and girl, on a street corner, mercilessly beating them when they failed to comply docilely. The little ones, their faces filled with despair, were being offered as wares for whatever purpose, to anyone who could pay.

"Oh, please," she pleaded, looking up at an impassive Brighton with tears in her eyes. "You must help them."

"I'm sorry, my dear, there's nothing we can do," the reformer replied, taking her beseeching hands in his own.

"Perhaps we can look for a constable," Anne said, refusing to leave the children to such a fate.

"There aren't many of those in this neighborhood," Digby stated in somber tones. "To interfere would only bring danger to ourselves or more severe physical abuse to the children. It's best we turn our heads and be on our way."

"No, if you won't do something, I will!" Anne retorted, breaking away from the group until she felt the restraining force of Alex Morrison's strong grasp.

"Please, Miss Hargraves, I don't want to see you involved in this."

"Perhaps if we talked to the father," Anne implored, turning the full force of her doleful green eyes on the young man who continued to hold her back.

"I don't think it would do much good," he said by way of apology.

"What kind of reformers are you?" Anne cried, fixing all three men with an accusing stare. "How can you turn your backs on these children? We can pay the man whatever he wants, and send the children home."

"Such an action could be misconstrued by those in authority, Miss Hargraves," Brighton said gently.

"I don't understand," Anne protested in confusion. "How could we possibly be blamed for helping these poor innocents?"

"What Brighton is trying to explain is that if any money changes hands, we ourselves could be charged with buying the children for illicit purposes," Digby answered, his voice ripe with contempt for Anne's lack of comprehension.

"That's how Stead got himself into such trouble, buying that young girl, to prove to decent society how easy it was to do so," Brighton agreed.

"And a heavy price he paid for it, too," Digby intoned in disapproval. "Being incarcerated like a common criminal for making others aware of the sordidness that prevails on these back streets. It is my opinion that he was jailed for making the rest of society, as well as that ignorant woman who sits on the throne, uncomfortable. But be that as it may, we cannot take the risk of being apprehended as he was. Who would continue our work if the three of us were to be arrested?"

"I see," Anne responded, eyeing him coolly. "In that case, the only thing to be done is that I conduct the transaction. Now, Mr. Morrison, if you will kindly unhand me, I will do what I can for these poor children."

"No, Miss Hargraves, I couldn't allow you to converse with such a vile excuse for a man, nor to place yourself in danger," the youngest of her escorts chided gently. "I will see what I can do. Wait here with the others."

A few moments later, money had changed hands, the drunken father was pointed in the direction of a gin house, and the children were sent scurrying off to their home.

"Oh, thank you, Mr. Morrison," Anne said as he joined their small group once more.

"I'd do anything for you," the brown-eyed rescuer assured Anne earnestly. "But please, call me Alex."

"Alex it is, then," Anne replied. "Thank you again."

"Yes, well, not that it will do much good," Digby said sourly. "He will only have them out there again tomorrow night, when he wakes up from his stupor and craves more gin."

"Be that as it may," Brighton intervened, "for tonight, due to Miss Hargraves's kind heart, the children are safe."

"But you can't save everyone who needs saving down here," Digby protested to Conway's special agent. "Do you see that building over there?"

"Are you referring to the only one on the entire street that appears to be in good repair? It's built rather like a palace," Anne replied, struggling to keep her tones from conveying the contempt she had for the man. After all, if she decided that Oliver Digby was the one involved in the assassination plot, she wanted no animosity between them until she could gain proof of his traitorous plans.

"A palace of sin! It is one of those establishments that cater to the carnal appetites as well as to gambling," Digby said meaningfully. "And in a few years the girl you freed tonight could be a resident of such a house."

"Perhaps," Anne conceded. "But then again, it could be that by that time, such a place might have been shut down."

"That's highly unlikely, as it is frequented by gentlemen of the upper class. Do you think they would actually close up one of their amusements?"

"Men of social standing come here?" Anne questioned incredulously. "I find that hard to believe."

"Nevertheless it is true. Come, let us take a closer look at Madame Duvalier's establishment so that you have no doubt about the matter," Digby insisted, steering Anne in that direction before either Andrew Brighton or Alex Morrison could object.

Ian Kendrick couldn't wait to don his coat and leave the premises. Though there were other evenings he had spent in Madame Duvalier's card parlor, departing only in the small hours of the morning, this was not one of those occasions. Never before had his own brother been on his way upstairs. Right now Ian felt damnedly uncomfortable, like a procurer, and it was all his father's fault...and Jack's, too! Good God, what was the world coming to that a seventeen-year-old had to pay for his initiation into sex? Things certainly were different in his day, he recalled, grimacing at the memory of just how scratchy hay could feel against naked flesh. But then, he had been no older than Jack was now, and comfort had not been foremost in his mind. All he had been interested in was getting his first taste of manhood and then hurriedly pulling on his clothes before the squire caught him in his barn.

But Jack, the spoiled youngest child, gets a trip to London for his first experience, Ian thought with irritation. Studying the furnishings of Madame Duvalier's establishment, with its thick carpets, plush settees and velvet hangings, Ian couldn't help but feel envious. He wished his father had been as understanding and generous with him when Ian had been caught fondling the squire's willing and seductive milkmaid. Instead he had received a vicious lecture and been sent out to chop firewood. The blisters had lasted a week!

And now the baronet had the audacity to expect Ian to help Jack learn about women. There was no fathoming parents, Ian decided. Well, he had done what had been asked of him, performing the necessary introductions and

seeing to it that the boy had been placed in good
hands . . . and quite literally, at that. But it was as far as he
would go, Ian fumed, shoving his arms into the sleeves of his
coat. He was not about to wait around for his pampered
brother to perform. The very idea of it was distasteful. No,
he would take his carriage to his club and then send the
driver back to wait for Jack. And God help his brother if he
ever tried to mention this incident again. As far as Ian was
concerned, after tonight, Jack was on his own.

The smile Ian had plastered across his handsome face
when he said goodbye to Madame Duvalier was replaced by
a scowl the moment he stepped through her doors and onto
the street. Shaking his head and muttering at the responsi-
bilities brothers were expected to assume, he paid no attention to where he was going until he bumped into a small
group standing on the pavement halfway between the
building owned by Madame Duvalier and his own carriage.

"Terribly sorry," he began perfunctorily and then
stopped in abashment when he found himself looking into
the upturned, very beautiful and very disapproving face of
Anne Hargraves. Bloody hell! That he should encounter the
seductive blonde while he was leaving this house of ill repute was the final straw! How could he possibly explain that
he wasn't even here for his own pleasure, but for Jack's instead? As the normally composed Ian Kendrick struggled to
find words of greeting, he hoped his brother was enjoying
his experience in one of Madame Duvalier's bedrooms.
With this additional trouble the boy had caused him, Ian
was sorely tempted to extract a revenge that would make it
impossible for Jack to ever enjoy such an interlude again.

"You see, I told you the place was frequented by the upper class," a hawk-faced man was informing Anne while
Andrew Brighton and a younger fellow fixed him with accusatory stares.

"You distinctly said *gentlemen,* Mr. Digby," Anne replied archly, her lovely green eyes becoming cool and distant as they continued to rest on the ignominious Ian
Kendrick. "I haven't seen anyone of that description leave
the premises."

Ian's silver eyes glinted dangerously at the singer's insult. But he remembered himself and restrained his tongue. He had been ordered by the Prince of Wales to get to know this woman, and that would be impossible if she refused to have anything to do with him. As it was, she hadn't acknowledged his flowers, whether from lack of courtesy on her part or lack of interest, he didn't know. Much as it vexed him, he knew that some attempt at excusing his presence here was in order.

"Good evening to you, too, Miss Hargraves, gentlemen," Ian said with as much composure as he could muster.

"Imagine seeing you in this neighborhood, and emerging from that house, too!" Anne interrupted before Kendrick could say another word. She was tired of meeting this man wherever she went, and she was going to let him know it. "One day a church, the next a brothel. I wonder, where will I see you next?"

"But you don't understand. I wasn't here for myself ... my brother, I was searching for my younger brother, but of course he wasn't here," Ian mumbled in spite of himself, coming as close to the truth as his pride would allow.

"Really, I hadn't expected you would have to resort to this," Anne said, her voice echoing surprise and the memory of the child for sale still fresh in her memory. "I would have supposed that there must be some woman somewhere in London who would find you attractive enough to meet your needs of her own free will."

Ian's lean jaw clenched at the affront, and his temper flared. But he would be damned if he would allow this woman to unnerve him more than she already had. It would take every bit of reserve he possessed to keep his tone civil and polite. That was the best that he could do. Let Anne Hargraves make of the words themselves what she would.

"I'm surprised a lady such as yourself would have any thoughts at all ... on such a matter, I mean. Do I dare hope that you have been considering my suit and have been thinking about me, after all, my dear Miss Hargraves? Indeed, do you suppose that you would know any such

woman who would willingly meet my needs? Someone perhaps in close proximity to you? If so, we could meet together tomorrow night for—"

"Now see here, Kendrick," Brighton began angrily, only
to be interrupted by an enraged Morrison.

"I'll not have you speaking to Miss Hargraves in that
manner," the youngest man asserted forcefully, his brown
eyes sparkling when Digby stepped between him and Kendrick. He'd been restrained from confronting the impudent
drunkards they had passed earlier, but he wouldn't permit
this man's remarks to go unchallenged.

"No need to be so upset, gentlemen, I was merely going
to ask Miss Hargraves to dine with me tomorrow evening
and see if I could entice her into revealing the name of any
such female she might know," Ian soothed insincerely even
as he cursed himself for losing his temper and allowing the
blonde to break through his composure yet again. Well, he
could always tell Bertie he had invited the woman to dinner
and that she had refused. He didn't have to acquaint the
prince with the circumstances under which the invitation
had been issued.

Though his sense of professionalism was even now berat-
ing him, Ian tried to console himself with the fact that he
didn't have to be with the seductive songstress to keep her
under surveillance.

But as he reached his carriage, his jealous irritation had
grown quite illogically, and he couldn't help calling over his
shoulder in an offhand manner.

"I anxiously await your presence at my dinner table, my
dear. You'll find that I can provide a delectable repast, I assure you. I shall be at home tomorrow when you send your
note of acceptance."

Before she could issue a retort, Ian Kendrick was in his
carriage and it was underway.

Perdition, but the man was a monumental irritant, Anne
thought. And now, she had to face the others and parry
their responses. Was nothing ever simple?

"I am sorry that Kendrick behaved as he did. Such a poor
end to our evening is regrettable. It was unworthy of any
gentleman," Brighton said.

"When we warned you of the unpleasant things you would face in the East End, I never dreamed it would include such an incident," Alex mumbled. "I cannot tell you how sorry I am for what that man put you through and the insults he rendered."

"Yes. I, too, said you would experience things here tonight that you could never have imagined," Digby drawled. "But then, you have become so quickly dedicated to the reform movement that you could not be dissuaded. However, I might suggest if you are truly interested in correcting society's ills, perhaps you should begin with your own class and start with Kendrick. I've never seen a fellow so much in need of reform."

As a lady Anne would have to agree, but she was surprised to find that as a woman, there was very little about Ian Kendrick that she would change.

Chapter Five

"Madam, a carriage awaits you though the driver refuses to identify his master," announced Brewster indignantly as Anne secured a small hat to her upswept chignon the next afternoon. "I am quite certain I would not go off in a strange coach."

"I realize you might not, but I make my own decisions and you will find I stand by them. Since it is *my* appointment, I intend to keep it, no matter what your opinions," Anne reproved, unwilling to abide the butler's superior manner. Having recovered from her unexpectedly troublesome encounter with Kendrick yesterday and having decided to discuss the man with Conway, she was more than ready to take control of her household staff. "Now then, Brewster, I may or may not return for dinner this evening with a guest. See that Cook prepares a cold supper for two, just in case."

"Yes, Miss Hargraves," replied the servant, begrudgingly draping her wrap over her shoulders and opening the door. "If you insist on leaving with this unfamiliar driver, be assured that I will note his description and contact the proper authorities should you fail to return."

"Very well, but don't be in too much of hurry to do so. I might just be enjoying myself," said Anne in amusement, picturing Nigel Conway as a villainous seducer of young women. For a moment she fell silent, realizing that, in some ways, that was exactly the role he held. Hadn't he approached her when she was lonely and depressed with an offer to work for him? Still, she'd be in no danger from

Conway today. "I assure you my escort this afternoon is eminently trustworthy."

"They all want you to believe that, miss," warned the manservant as she descended the front steps under his watchful glare.

Shortly afterward, as Anne recounted the episode to Nigel Conway, she could barely contain her laughter, soft and feminine as a spring breeze darting across a sunny meadow. Indeed, others enjoying their tea in the open-air pavilion of Regents' Park smiled at the enchanting melody of pleasure.

"I swear I don't know where you found that fellow, Nigel, but he's a relic from the Dark Ages. He makes no secret of the fact that he thoroughly disapproves of my life as an independent woman, not to mention my unladylike career as a singer."

"Granted, my dear, Brewster is perhaps a bit stuffy, but he comes highly recommended. Actually you are quite fortunate I could find someone so qualified; there were a number of others interested in his services. Besides, you did say he is well respected by the rest of the staff and quite efficient in his duties. After all, you don't have the time to start interviewing butlers, nor the inclination, I would think," argued her mentor, not yet ready to confide Brewster's dual function. In truth, the man was a well-trained agent able to provide any necessary assistance and security for Anne while blending in with other butlers in her social strata, lending her authenticity as well as essential protection.

Yet Nigel knew from past experience that the attractive woman across the table from him would never countenance working with anyone, believing herself supremely capable of handling any situation that might arise. For Nigel's own peace of mind, as well as Anne's, it was far better she remain ignorant about the man's primary responsibility a while longer.

"Never mind about him, Anne. I understand that Liam O'Grady is going to contact you about appearing at a small dinner party for the Irish members of Parliament. Can you fit that into your schedule, or are Brighton and Bertie's bunch keeping you too busy?"

"The Irish contingent? I thought your regular people were investigating the Fenians. Why involve me?" she asked in surprise. She already felt somewhat overextended, given her association with Brighton, the South Kensington Crowd and those on its fringes. "I mean, I can accommodate O'Grady if you think it important, but—"

"I have men looking into rumors and questioning their sources, but this wouldn't be undercover on your part. You would merely be a guest at a private reception like any other of your social engagements. It's just that the other guests would all be Irish. You know I've never scorned any opportunity to glean information, no matter how untraditional the source. Look at what you've discovered at embassy parties in the past," reminded her boss. "Besides, the strangest people have a way of confiding their deepest secrets to your sympathetic ears."

"Yes, even when I have no interest in hearing them," admitted Anne, her green eyes flashing as she recalled Kendrick's confused explanation of his presence outside a brothel yesterday. Looking for his brother, indeed! All she had wanted to do was escape his interest, but he'd persisted all the same. "Very well, Nigel, but if I entertain O'Grady's associates, you must do me a favor. I want you to look into that obnoxious fellow from Lady Moreland's party the other night, Ian Kendrick. Wherever I go lately, he seems to appear, however unlikely the locale. It's starting to make me nervous."

"Was Kendrick the one in the garden?"

At Anne's quick nod, Nigel shook his head in disbelief.

"For Heaven's sake, Anne, he's probably just smitten with you like all the other males who were there," he soothed with a chuckle as he lit a cigarette, assuming an avuncular tone. "You know, my dear woman, between that lovely voice of yours and your enchanting beauty, not to mention your personality, a man would have to be three quarters dead not to be captivated by your charms. Don't demean the poor fellow for his good taste."

"Saints preserve us, Nigel! If I can't tell the difference between harmless infatuation and something more sinister, I'd be a damned poor asset to your department," retorted the woman, spots of high color appearing in her cheeks as a sudden coughing spasm closed her throat. "Ian Kendrick—"

"There, there, take a sip of tea," instructed her companion, pleased when the hot liquid eased her distress. "Really, I see no cause for you to be agitated. The man is nothing to fuss over, especially for someone with your experience. You've probably not forgiven him for startling you in the dark gardens."

"Nigel, I tell you, Ian Kendrick is not so innocent as you choose to think, nor I so addle-brained to see specters who aren't there. Twice he's shown up in the East End and interrupted my conversations with Brighton. He was also quite the topic of conversation at Lady Chadwick's social. The Kensington Crowd seems awfully familiar with him. His pursuit of me is much too coincidental for my liking."

"Hmm, the *Financial News* never mentioned his name in their series on that bunch, though."

"That doesn't mean he wasn't involved."

"Possibly. I daresay the whole series of articles was publicity Bertie's friends would prefer to avoid," said Nigel, returning the conversation to its proper track.

"True, but their wives believe the London papers are merely printing lies to discredit the Prince of Wales in order to popularize themselves with Queen Victoria. Everyone knows how she feels about the press," said Anne, momentarily sidetracked from the issue of Ian Kendrick.

"Yes, but given the depth of the improprieties the newspaper cited, I think even Her Majesty's secretary, Ponsonby, will have to bring it to the queen's attention. Otherwise Gladstone will."

"Since she returned from Germany, I imagine Victoria is more than happy to adjust to life at Windsor and anticipate the coming jubilee without looking for problems with Bertie's friends," hedged Anne, not really concerned with the economic scandal or the newspaper's accounts. "About Ian Kendrick, though—"

"We have more serious concerns than your persistent Lothario," snapped Nigel. "Ignore him, or if you don't like his attentions, send him packing. But, for heaven's sake, pull yourself together and concentrate on the threat to Victoria."

"I honestly don't believe his interest in me is just personal."

"What else could it be?" demanded Conway, annoyed at her obstinate return to the topic.

"If I knew that, I wouldn't be asking you for help. His attentions make me distinctly uneasy whenever he's about, almost as though he's watching my every move," admitted the normally poised young woman.

A sudden thought struck Anne, and she fell silent, looking speculatively at her distinguished companion. Was he capable of such treachery as planting Ian Kendrick in her field of investigation? When she continued speaking, her voice was deceptively soft, her anger barely discernible even to Nigel, who knew her well.

"Tell me the truth. Is your lack of concern for my suspicions caused by the fact that Kendrick is working for you? Is that why you are so certain he's harmless?" she demanded icily.

"For me? Without my telling you? Don't be absurd, my dear. You are the only one I have investigating the upper social strata, and the social reformers, for that matter. Besides, you are my very best. Why would I waste my time having someone else follow in your capable footsteps?" asked Nigel earnestly, his eyes open wide in astonishment. What he told her was half true, he assuaged his conscience, more glad than ever he hadn't told her about Brewster. Anyway, she was the only agent covering both areas of suspicion; he wasn't really fibbing.

"If you're sure..." began Anne, a hint of doubt still harbored by her familiarity with Conway's deceptive honesty. Many was the time he had kept details of assignments from her, always with the excuse of protecting her.

"Absolutely. Look, I will investigate Kendrick's background if he bothers you so, but give some thought to the possibility that he is quite innocently fascinated by a lovely lady. Then again, though I doubt it, he might conceivably be somehow involved in this dismal business."

With those words so casually spoken, Anne suddenly perceived Ian no longer as an unwanted suitor, tempting though his physique might be, but as a possible suspect whose capture could safeguard the queen. Perhaps Ian Kendrick deserved more of her time, after all.

"Hmm, it's certainly an idea worth considering," admitted the blonde, suddenly remembering Ian's dinner invitation, which she had discarded so quickly. It could be she would have plans this evening after all. Or would it be more productive to let him stew until tomorrow? There was no need to appear too anxious; Jubilee Day was still four weeks hence.

The paternal smile lingering on Nigel Conway's lips faded the moment he saw Anne Hargraves into her carriage. After watching the conveyance wend its way into the London traffic, he returned to his office to find he had a visitor.

Squaring his shoulders and putting on his best expression of concerned authority, Conway turned the handle and entered the small but comfortable chamber where his caller waited.

"Good day, Matthew! What can I do for you?" he asked, as though it was not unusual for this particular agent to come here during regular hours.

"You can take me off this hellish assignment," came the resolute reply, as the visitor moved his ample bulk forward and stood before his superior, glaring up determinedly at the taller man.

"Now, now, Matthew, what's this all about?" Conway soothed, waving the man into a nearby chair.

"I have told you, sir. I find it quite impossible to continue in my present position."

"And why is that?" Sir Nigel asked, sitting behind the desk and bringing his fingertips together as he leaned toward Matthew Brewster. "You know this mission is of paramount importance."

"I've no quarrel with that," Brewster began, "but my role is entirely superfluous, as well as personally intolerable, and I only wish to be given something else."

"Sorry, old man, it's out of the question," Conway answered quietly but firmly. "We need you where we have placed you."

"I beg to differ, sir," the butler persisted obdurately. "In the entire course of our association together, I have never felt as useless as I do at present. And for that reason, I can no longer tolerate staying in that house in Mayfair."

"Be honest with me now, Matthew. Is it your role in this enterprise you find so unbearable, or is it Miss Hargraves?" Nigel Conway asked.

"It's the futility of acting as a nursemaid to one of your agents!" Brewster answered with a snort. "In all of my years of service with the department, you have never asked me to do anything as demeaning as you do now. Usually I am placed in some household where I can gather needed information. The reputation you have so carefully crafted for me, and not undeservedly, I might add, if modesty can be forgotten for a moment, as the best butler in England, assures my welcome within any home in this nation.

"How many times have I been able to supply you with otherwise unobtainable intelligence about the people you have under surveillance? I tell you what arrives in the post and who comes to call. And because many of the English gentry fail to think of their servants as anything other than household furnishings, and consequently speak in front of us as though we are not present, I often as not relay entire conversations."

"And when the subject fails to speak in front of you, you find other, ingenious ways to listen in on what they have to say, I am sure," Conway interrupted by way of compliment, hoping to pacify the portly little man who had become so valuable during the last few years. "Don't think I underestimate your contributions, Matthew. I am highly cognizant of your talents and your commendable accomplishments."

"Then why didn't you allow me to obtain a position in Brighton's household, or Bradford's, or even, though I shudder to mention it, to enter the employ of one of the Irish MPs?"

"Because I really do need you more where you are, Matthew," Conway replied sternly, fixing the man before him with a hard glare.

"What? As a nanny to Anne Hargraves? I refuse to believe that I couldn't be better utilized somewhere else!" Brewster replied, folding his arms across his barrel of a chest and daring Conway to tell him differently.

"So then it really is your feeling of inconsequence concerning this operation that has brought you here today?" Brewster's superior asked, arching a brow in skepticism.

"Precisely," the butler replied, his voice more than a little adamant.

While he awaited Conway's next words, Brewster's features composed themselves into a rather superior expression, and Nigel inwardly groaned, imagining just how such a supercilious pose would affect Anne Hargraves, a woman temperamental in her own right. Good Lord, that house in Mayfair could become a veritable battleground, unless both Hargraves and Brewster remembered they were professionals and started acting as such. He had enough to worry about in this operation without having to fret over quarrels between his people.

"I am glad to hear that it is not your relationship with Miss Hargraves that prompts you to request reassignment, Matthew. But then I should have known that you are far too seasoned an operative to allow personal prejudice to interfere with as pressing a challenge as the one we face. We are, after all, about the safety of the queen," Sir Nigel reminded him smoothly. Noting with satisfaction Brewster's barely perceptible guilty squirm, the man entrusted with finding Victoria's would-be assassin pressed his advantage. "I do want you to know that I don't suppose working for Anne Hargraves is all that easy."

"That it is not, sir."

"Yes, well, artistes are not like the rest of us. But since it is not Miss Hargraves to whom you object," Nigel continued slyly, "you can return to Mayfair safe in the knowledge that your part in this operation is a vital one."

"How can you say that?" Brewster objected when Conway stood, indicating that the matter was closed. "All I do is run the household and try to advise her as to what is proper behavior in polite society! Tell me how that is helping to safeguard Her Majesty!"

"I had thought you would be more astute. Miss Hargraves is one of my most competent people. Men will tell her things they would never say to anyone else. No, don't look at me in that manner, Matthew, this is a fact that has been proved time and time again. And sometimes, they reveal these things—ahem—under conditions when a butler would not be present, speaking so softly that it would be highly unlikely for anyone to overhear...if you take my meaning. At any rate, Miss Hargraves is an extremely effective agent of the British Crown. The problem is that she has been used to working in areas of the world which are—well, that are not as restrictive as English society. She needs a guiding hand, Matthew."

"Then you should have hired her some gently bred female companion. The woman never listens to a word I have to say regarding her behavior or attire, anyway."

"I grant she is a bit unorthodox, but society has come to expect that of artists. In fact, they almost demand it. Many a door has been opened to Anne Hargraves because of the whispers associated with her name. But that is just it, Matthew, the rumors are merely whispers, speculations if you will. While Anne is ordinarily most discreet, it has been a long while since she has been about in English society for any length of time. I rely upon you to prevent her from making an error that could be all too costly for England. In short, I want you to see to it that no scandal attaches itself to her name. I want you to see to it that she remains acceptable to society."

"I still say a companion could fulfill that role far better than I," Brewster stated, though his determination to dissociate himself from Anne Hargraves appeared to be waning.

"Come now, Matthew. You do yourself a disservice. Who knows the rules of society better than you? And do you think a companion would stay after Miss Hargraves brought home a male guest? No, she wouldn't, and that's another reason I need you in that household. I don't want one of my best agents in the company of someone unsavory, possibly the madman who has been sending those damnable letters, without someone I can trust nearby."

"One of the Crown's best agents?" Brewster repeated haughtily.

"Yes. Do you recall the Arabi uprising in Alexandria? If not for Anne Hargraves, things might not have turned out so well for England," Nigel said.

"She was in Egypt during the uprising?" Brewster asked, impressed in spite of himself.

"And a bloody fine job she helped do," Nigel said with such conviction that the other man couldn't help but begin to view the insufferable Miss Hargraves in an entirely new light. "So you see, maintaining your position in Anne's employ is really a must, Matthew."

"Very good, sir. For the sake of England and Her Majesty, I shall remain," the butler replied stiffly, rising and executing his most formal bow, much to Nigel's relief and amusement.

"I'm glad to hear that, Matthew,"

"You have convinced me that Miss Hargraves is an operative to be respected, and I no longer object to working with her. It's the woman herself I can't stand," Brewster muttered as he exited by a rear door, leaving Nigel Conway to indulge in a soft chuckle.

Later that same evening, as Anne looked over the sheets of writing paper she had already discarded, she grew impatient with herself.

"What is wrong with you?" she muttered in the privacy of her bedroom. "This need only be a few lines, not a great treatise of diplomacy. You've written notes like this a hundred times in the past. A bit of an apology for keeping him waiting for a reply, a touch of flattery at his interest and a hesitant acceptance of his generous invitation to dine. It's not as if the formula isn't second nature to you by now."

Shaking her head at the peculiar difficulty she was experiencing, Anne rose to stretch her stiff muscles and moved to the small table before the fireplace. Picking up the crystal decanter and a small glass, she poured herself some sherry. Since the words she needed would not flow from her pen, perhaps a few minutes of soothing meditation now would permit her to concentrate later.

Deliberately emptying her mind of all conscious thought, Anne closed her eyes, willing herself to focus on the mellowness of the aged liquor, the fruity aroma escaping the small glass, the delicate feel of the dainty crystal, the sharp crackling of the late fire on the hearth. Sometimes, backstage just before a performance, concentrating on the messages of her five senses helped Anne relax in the final tense moments before her entrance on stage. Tonight, however, her sensory distractions failed her as Ian Kendrick appeared behind her closed eyelids.

"No!" she declared aloud. This would not do. Maybe she could employ a different technique.

Seating herself on the divan by the fire, she placed the half full glass of sherry on the table and exhaled. Within moments she had tried each of the rhythmic breathing exercises her various voice coaches had taught her during her career. Yet, even concentrating on the carefully patterned inhalation and exhalation, she couldn't escape the unhappy thought of how long it had been since she'd had cause to gasp for heated breaths at a man's intimate touch. Unbidden, the image of steel gray eyes smiled down on her from under a wayward lock of dark brown hair while a mischievous twinkle appeared and one hypnotic eye slowly closed in a wink as the image widened to show Ian's teasing grin.

Damn, was that the problem? Could she be attracted to the arrogant Kendrick, woman to man, even as Nigel had suggested Kendrick was to her? Startled at the possibility, remote though it must be, Anne lay back on the small divan.

It was as though he was standing before her, attired in the formal wear in which she'd first seen him, his expensively cut dress coat emphasizing the broad reach of his shoulders, the powerful strength in his arms, the provocative narrowing at his waist.

The female within had to admit the man's considerable animal appeal, but the professional agent Anne had become still struggled against the notion, even as she trembled, remembering his purposeful touch in Brighton's church, the anger echoing in his eyes at her donation, and his unreasonable fury at seeing her outside Madame Duvalier's. If he was so easily aroused to anger, how would such a man react to the other passions that might be ignited by their contact, she wondered, unable to ignore this new vision of Ian Kendrick as a desirable male. If he flustered her so in thought, what could he do in reality, and did she really want to find out? For that matter, was it wise to foster this possible relationship, suspicious as she was of the man's intent?

Definitely not, admitted her heart; yet Anne Hargraves had no other choice. She would do her duty as she must or she would not be able to live with the woman she would become. England must come first.

It took a powerful effort of will but, a short while later, she was once again seated at her desk, just sealing the note to the newfound bane of her existence. Its final form was succinct, but she had no doubt that the gray-eyed rogue would fall under its spell as he had apparently woven his own magic about her tonight. Sighing wearily at the world in which she operated, Anne rang for Brewster and a momentary respite from a torn conscience.

"Ah, there you are. See that this is delivered at once," she instructed curtly when he appeared, somewhat disheveled.

"Madam, can't it wait until morning?" protested the butler, having been ready to retire himself. "It is past eleven and you and I are the only ones still up."

"Well, then, you'll have to deliver it," she said with an innocent smile of dismissal, another small battle won, "or awaken someone else to do so. Good night."

"Yes, miss," grumbled the portly fellow, already dreading the damp night air of his journey, but knowing full well that he couldn't send another on this errand that might involve intelligence.

It did Brewster's humor no good to find no one answering the bell at the house in Russell Square, and he momentarily considered awakening Miss Hargraves to return the letter and tell her so.

"But she didn't request an answer," he decided, shoving the letter under the door, his mission done. "I'll not wait."

It was almost sunrise, nearly six the next morning when Ian awoke, late by his standards. He'd have to hurry to make his appointment with Bertie, but he had no choice. "Burning the candle at both ends," his old tutor would have chided him, but damn it, being Jack's nursemaid wasn't his idea. Out till all hours and none of it enjoyable for him, actually much the opposite, he reflected, thinking of the embarrassment Jack had caused him two nights ago outside Madame Duvalier's. He feared a miracle would be needed for Anne Hargraves to voluntarily see him after that debacle.

Well, that problem would have to wait, Ian Kendrick decided, buttoning his vest and drawing on his riding jacket. At least his brother hadn't yet awakened early enough to question these sunrise excursions of his. That was one small thing to be thankful for.

Taking the steps two at a clip, the handsome young man saw an envelope but was in too much of a hurry to read the note written in a decidedly feminine hand and slipped under his door, so he merely placed the waiting letter in his pocket and headed for the park.

The Prince of Wales was waiting on foot, walking his horse a stretch when Ian arrived, an effort he had never seen the royal make before. Indeed the man seemed unusually somber. Had something happened?

"Sir, I apologize for my tardiness, but are you all right?" Ian inquired as he dismounted.

"Oh, yes, just trying to work out a problem. Sometimes if I can't ride like the wind and forget it, pounding the earth beneath my feet with a heavy stride gives me the sense of doing something," confided the man who would one day be king. "Tell me, is there anything new with Somers-Vine since your last report? I can hardly call on him myself after those scandalous pieces in the press, but I had no choice other than request his resignation."

"Nothing, sir. He's handling it well enough though he regrets the fact that you won't take his messages and he hopes you believe him innocent of any deliberate wrongdoing."

"I fear that would be asking too much of even me, Kendrick, but then I've never been known for choosing my friends wisely." The prince frowned, strongly disposed to introspection this morning. "Enough about him, though, we've a greater dilemma at hand. I have a source in the office of the queen's private secretary—"

"Ponsonby."

"Yes, and he's informed me of letters the palace has received threatening that Her Majesty won't live to see her Jubilee Day. Have you heard anything of such rumors?"

"From your friends, sir? No, of course not, and Brighton and his crowd wouldn't be so bold as to say such things. I doubt even the Irish would," considered Ian slowly.

"Hmm, I do agree it's unlikely that my cohorts would be so crass, or so imaginative. Even Bradford is too greedy to want me distracted from my pursuits of pleasure by such a worry as being sovereign is apt to be," mused the prince. "Still, it wouldn't hurt to keep an open ear and watch that East End group especially. The queen's advisers are disputing the reformers' claims about how desperate the conditions of the poor in London are, and since she wasn't well received when she opened the People's Palace, it wouldn't be surprising if Brighton and his crew try to cause further controversy over living conditions down there."

"But, sir, who could seriously wish to harm our queen? It seems too preposterous a notion to take seriously."

"The attack on her a few years ago was real enough."

"But that was one lone madman."

"All the more reason to be concerned in the case of a few fellows acting in concert. They might just succeed," said Bertie quietly.

"And then you'd be king."

"Not that way, Kendrick, never that way!" exclaimed the white-haired royal, nearly fifty and still a prince. "Do what you can to investigate the threats, and don't forget that Hargraves woman, especially if she's still consorting with

Brighton. Previously, she's never returned to England for more than a fortnight at a time, yet now I understand she has no plans to leave.''

"Whatever you say, sir," promised Ian as the nobleman mounted and cantered off, his worries deposited on the shoulders of another, at least temporarily.

"What a foolish notion," Ian muttered as he turned his own horse back to its stable. "Anne Hargraves as an assassin, how absurd. Oh, she could be a killer of men's hearts, certainly, but no more than that. It will be awfully difficult to monitor her activities with her current impression of Ian Kendrick, however. Ah, well, I'll think of something. In the meantime, I'll take breakfast at one of the clubs and listen to what's being said. One never knows..."

It was midmorning when Ian returned to his house off Russell Square, intending to change and return to the East End. Maybe he would accidentally run into the songstress again. Pulling off his jacket, he was surprised at the rustle of paper from within.

"What? Oh, yes, I'd forgotten about this," he said to himself, reaching for the envelope in mystification. The wax seal imprinted with an elegant H did nothing to lessen his curiosity, and rather than go to his study for a letter opener, he furiously tore at the outer covering of the missive, mangling the delicate paper within.

Piecing together the two halves of the sweetly scented note, Ian quickly read it and barely restrained a shout of joy until a thought struck him so forcibly that he found himself muttering out loud.

"Why in heaven's name is she coming to call on me, especially after the other day? Well, no matter. Ian Kendrick has never lost his head over any female, and Anne Hargraves is just another woman, though a good deal more fetching than many. In the course of my investigation, I'll not look askance at a gift as lovely as she," he promised himself. "But neither shall I play the smitten fool. It will be a simple unpretentious evening with no special expectations or preparations on my part."

Yet moments later the normally sedate bachelor was dashing down the back stairs in a state of jubilant elation to confer with Mrs. Land. Dinner with Miss Hargraves must be memorable, perhaps roast baby lamb or stuffed guinea hens, he decided.

"The fly is coming to call on the spider," he thought with a leer, "and a tasty morsel she'll be, indeed."

The ride out from London hadn't taken all that long. But had it done so, the effort would still have been worthwhile because of the peace of the countryside, the man thought. Dressed as a country squire, he trudged across a deserted field, shotgun slung over his shoulder and pistol in hand, reveling in the contentment his surroundings brought him.

Here in the country things were quiet; there were no people for him to contend with, no words to be weighed before being spoken nor emotions to be carefully hidden. Here the air was fresh and there was openness. A man could think what he liked, be what he was and do what he must.

Deep in thought, the solitary figure neared a fence post and rummaged through the sack hanging from his belt, which contained ammunition. After both firearms were loaded, he reached inside and pulled out a flask of whiskey, taking a swig and allowing the liquid to sit in his mouth for a moment before swallowing it with a gulp. Then he sat down near a tree to wait. That was always the hardest part, the waiting. But he knew that if only he was patient, his prey would come to him. The birds who would be his targets today were as unsuspecting as anything he had chosen to hunt thus far. That was what made it so easy, the hunted were usually unaware of their status as targets. But wasn't that always the case? That's why his conscience had demanded he send some words of warning, a warning that would be ignored as his words usually were.

A sudden shift of wind and flap of wings soon brought a flock of starlings to perch on the fence. A smile spreading across his face, the man quietly picked up the pistol he had laid in his lap and took aim at a particularly squat little female sitting with her head tucked beneath her wing.

She made an excellent target, perfect practice, the hunter thought as he began to squeeze the trigger. How very like Victoria the starling looked, all in black, unaware of what was going on in the wide world around her and completely oblivious to being in his sights.

A shot cracked through the air, harshly disturbing the tranquillity of the field. The bird toppled, and the man grinned again at the excellence of his marksmanship. It was going to be just as easy to dispatch the queen at her jubilee celebration, he decided, reaching quickly for the loaded shotgun and bringing down a squirrel that had been startled enough by the blast of the pistol to leave its hiding place in a tall patch of grass.

To the man's satisfaction, the small body flew into the air, fell rapidly, quivered and then was still. Taking another swig of whiskey, he assured himself that it would be no less difficult to dispatch anyone who got in his way or attempted to interfere with his plans.

Chapter Six

"What do you mean you've made other plans for this evening?" Jack demanded irritably as he glanced in the hall mirror late that afternoon and adjusted his cravat. "I thought we were to enjoy a few drinks and dinner at your club and then continue my education in London's seedier neighborhoods. Have you had a better offer?"

"No, no," denied Ian, hoping against hope that his brother wouldn't venture into the kitchen and see the special effort Mrs. Land and her niece were putting into tonight's romantic dinner for two. Unless he could dissuade Jack from remaining here, however, the meal might be shared by three. Rising from his chair in the front room, Ian entered the foyer and laid his arm on Jack's shoulder, but before he could speak, Jack threw it off.

"You're not even dressed to go out," protested the younger Kendrick. "Don't tell me my social expectations are too much of a burden for you."

"Actually, it's just that I fear there's a limit to the amount of pleasure this old body of mine can enjoy. A quiet evening at home is really what appeals to me tonight, Jack," he confided with a sheepish grin, silently praying his brother would not question such an improbable tale.

"You want me to believe you're anxious to sit home in front of the fire with a hot toddy and a lap robe to keep you warm?" hooted Jack, slapping Ian hard on the back. "Now I have heard it all. Give me credit for some common sense. Even Grandfather enjoys more life than that."

"Aye, but then you haven't kept him out every night since you got to the city closing even the late hours clubs," argued the elder sibling, his tone hardening in irritation. On the one hand unwilling to include Jack in his unexpected evening with Anne, Ian was at the same time outraged at the lad's impugning his stamina and was hard-pressed to keep his temper in check. "Look here, I've no need to prove myself to you. I'll have you know I enjoy quite a satisfactory social life and have for a long while. Remember, I'm not the one who needs lessons on debauchery."

"If you've taught me everything you know in four nights, perhaps you do," his younger brother retorted just as angrily.

Then, feeling both his oats and the whiskey he had been imbibing, Jack struck out at his brother in retribution for the imagined slurs cast upon his manhood. Before Ian could jump out of range, he found himself clipped, and without thinking he returned the blow. When his fist encountered Jack's face, the realization of what he had done stunned him, and Ian looked at his hand in horror, wondering what had happened to make him behave in such an extraordinary manner. But before he could call a halt to the uncivilized proceedings, Jack came at him again and Ian was drawn into the fray.

In a moment, the two brothers were locked in furious combat, each trying desperately to make the other pay for his remarks. Their first few lunges left no deep scars as each man took the measure of his opponent and calculated his strategy even as he feinted and parried. Though Jack had struck first, Ian was quick on his feet and fast to answer the perceived threat, but not wishing to harm the brother he still considered a youngster, Ian did not fight as lustily as he was able. Taking advantage of Ian's reluctance, Jack landed his brother a sharp upper cut to his left eye, splitting the skin, even as the elder Kendrick clipped Jack hard on his nose, the impact sending him to the floor as the housekeeper came running.

"What's this commotion then, Mr. Ian? Have you no better sense than to brawl indoors on my clean floors?" cried Mrs. Land in distress at the sight of the two grown men still glaring fiercely at one another, even as one lay prone on her floor, the other standing over him. Seeing both of them were already bleeding, she decided they'd had enough satisfaction and felt no qualms about ending the matter.

"Now both of you, just stop any thoughts of continuing this nonsense right now. Jack, get yourself into a chair and keep your head back to ease the flow of blood while I fetch a cool cloth to wash you up. And you, Ian Kendrick, should be ashamed of yourself, picking on one younger than you are," the woman chided as she hurried off. "You are no better than a street hoodlum, no matter what your education."

For a moment ragged breathing underscored the silence between the men as they obeyed Mrs. Land's dictates and settled themselves in the front room. Ian looked at his brother and cursed the fact that this young rapscallion could have pushed him into so pedestrian a thing as a brawl. After all, Ian Kendrick had learned long ago to handle his passions. Why the hell were they running so close to the surface lately?

Then Ian spoke, an attempt to soothe his conscience and simultaneously keep the upper hand.

"I suppose the woman's right, Jack, I shouldn't have fought you, but you hit me a few pretty good ones, too," he hedged, moving to examine the eye that was rapidly closing as the skin around it swelled. Some evening tonight was going to be, if this was any indication.

"Well, if nothing else, brother, you proved that you are not as old as you claim," said Jack with a halfhearted grin. "I can't tell you the last time anybody's been able to land one on me, let alone knock me down. You did, though, fair and square."

"You're certain you didn't give this *old* man an edge?" Ian chuckled, pleased at his brother's grudging admiration. "You did compare me to Grandfather, as I recall."

"No, he never had that good a right hand."

By the time Mrs. Land and Molly returned to the parlor with two basins of cool water, the brothers were once again fast friends, their argument forgotten in reminiscences over past arguments with their other siblings.

"I've heard about the time you locked Peter in the root cellar with Annie overnight; I'll wager he must have near killed you when he got out," said Jack. "Even Mother tells that story with a sense of awe. She says it took a week till you could open both of your eyes at the same time."

"It was worth it, lad, believe me. He'd been on for weeks about what he would do if he ever got her alone, but I knew he'd never have the nerve to even try, so—"

"Mr. Ian, I'll thank you to stop right there. Molly doesn't need to hear such nonsense," the blushing housekeeper interrupted indignantly.

"Forgive me, Mrs. Land, I apologize to you and Molly for our unruly behavior," said Ian, "and my comments."

"And well you should, supposedly setting a good example for your young brother and then keeping the lad out all hours of the night and engaging him in fisticuffs besides," rebuked the woman, totally mystified when both men burst into raucous laughter. Well, if that was how they chose to behave, she and Molly had things to attend in the kitchen. She sniffed in annoyance, leading her niece from the room.

"Me—keeping you out?" repeated Ian incredibly. "See that, you've even given my housekeeper the wrong idea."

"All right, I see your point. Maybe an evening home wouldn't be so bad after all," conceded Jack when he could stop laughing.

"No, not for you," corrected his brother. "That wouldn't do at all. Bothwell is expecting us at my club for dinner and gambling, Jack. He's been looking forward to meeting you. Just give him this note and you'll be more than welcome to play on my tab," instructed Ian, breathing a sigh of relief at his approaching success, costly though it might be if Jack lost.

"Are you certain you won't reconsider and join me later on?"

"No, I don't think so. Besides, someone had better soothe Mrs. Land's feathers or she'll have us on bread and water tomorrow." Ian chuckled, his gray eyes worried that Jack might insist. "Anyway, how can you ever be a proper gentleman when all you do is tag along with me? You've got to spread your wings a bit and fly on your own."

"Well, if you're sure...."

"Absolutely. This way, you can cultivate your own circle of friends rather than depending on mine. Just watch Bradford, he has a tendency to palm the cards if he's losing."

"Right. Don't wait up then, *old* man," said Jack with a grin, shaking his brother's hand and heading for the door. "And I promise to share my winnings."

"Whether you have any or not, little brother, believe me, I don't intend to. Now to freshen up and prepare for this evening's important diversion," murmured Ian, moving swiftly to the stairs, planning a quick wash, a change of clothes and one of mood, as well.

An hour later, the young nobleman was in the dining room criticizing Molly's final preparation of the table.

"It may be well and proper for us to be seated at opposite ends of the table, but it makes conversation between two people frightfully difficult, my dear girl," Ian objected as he started to rearrange the place settings, even as Molly kept putting the silver back where it had started. "After all, if my brother and I can sit together at one end of the table when there are just the two of us, I don't understand why Miss Hargraves and I cannot do the same."

"She is a woman, sir."

"Yes, Molly, I have indeed observed that fact, I assure you. However, I give you my word of honor, I shan't seduce her on the dining room table," he promised vehemently, raising his right hand, "much as I might like to do so."

"I—I'll fetch my aunt, sir," murmured the maid, unused to this passionate show of behavior from the sensible man she'd served for nearly three years. First fighting in the foyer, now this. Could he be ill? she wondered.

"See here, Mr. Ian," admonished Mrs. Land as she emerged from the kitchen, wiping her hands on a cloth. "I will not permit you to be having your guest think that I cannot set a proper table, no matter what you may say about conversations. Believe me, sir, there are some things that are just not done in polite society."

"Mrs. Land, this is not polite society. This is my home and, more specifically, my private dining room, not open to public scrutiny or comment. Let me assure you, within this house what *I* want done will be done, whether by you or someone else I shall hire," shouted Ian, his patience totally eclipsed first by his dealings with Jack and now by his morally righteous servants.

There was only silence in the dining room, though a hesitant movement at the kitchen door left Ian no doubt that Molly was a curious witness to the scene. He glanced at Mrs. Land and was immediately contrite at his explosion; the poor woman was near to tears, certainly not the effect he'd wished. But then, what about this evening was going as he'd intended?

"By all means, sir, if you wish my resignation—"

"No, Mrs. Land, I do not," he said emphatically. Taking a deep breath, he reclaimed his temper and softened his tone. He'd been behaving in a frightful manner, all caused by his anticipation of having Miss Hargraves as his dinner guest. Good Lord, he'd been acting as distracted and excited as Jack had been on his excursion to Madame Duvalier's. The situation was entirely ridiculous, and he'd put a stop to it right now. After all, his primary purpose in getting to know Anne Hargraves was to investigate her, nothing more.

"You are a very valuable part of my household, Mrs. Land, and I ask your pardon for my angry words, but please try to see my point. You and Molly will be in and out of the dining room constantly, serving and clearing the plates. Nothing untoward will occur, I swear. I merely wish to enjoy the company of a very lovely lady without shouting down the table to be heard. I can't see that that is such a frightfully improper request," Ian said, hoping to make amends.

Mrs. Land studied her employer slowly, her lips pursed in thought. It wasn't as though he'd ever behaved in any way other than as a gentleman, but...

"And you'll tell the lady that you wanted the table set this way?" demanded the housekeeper, still concerned that the impropriety of such a seating arrangement not fall on her head.

"Yes, I will tell Miss Hargraves," agreed Ian, leaving the dining room as the servant set the remaining dishes.

Finally, he thought, finally, the evening will be as I want it. Why, oh why, did such a simple thing as a private dinner for Anne seem so difficult to achieve, he wondered, wincing as he brought his hand up to his face. His left brow had taken the worst of the damage, but glancing in the mirror, he was forced to concede that the swelling did little to enhance his appeal. Well, there was always the possibility of sympathy, he supposed.

Unconventional as it was, Ian had instructed Mrs. Land that he would admit his guest personally, wanting to be the first to welcome her to his home. In many ways he felt like a schoolboy with his first crush, however absurd such a notion might be. And then he heard the knocker and his heart beat in time to its banging rhythm as he moved to answer its call.

"Oh, good heavens, Mr. Kendrick, what happened?" cried Anne the moment he opened the door.

"Really, it's nothing. Don't worry yourself," he answered, unconsciously bringing his hand to his forehead before he escorted her into the foyer and reached out to take her coat.

"I understand there was some trouble in Trafalgar Square this morning. A demonstration by the socialists got out of hand. Was that how you were injured?" she asked solicitously, exploring his cut with a delicate touch. Playing the role of an innocent female came naturally, but Anne was surprised to realize that she did feel a twinge of sympathy for her host. His bruise seemed so raw and ugly, it must be painful.

"No, it was a foolish accident here at home. I do thank you for your concern, Miss Hargraves, but it's not so painful as it looks. I must tell you, though, pleased as I am to have you here, your acceptance of my invitation after our last meeting somewhat surprised me," Ian said offhandedly, probing for some insight as to why Anne had come here tonight. Did she know she was under surveillance?

"It surprised me, too," Anne said, her voice husky and ripe with promise. If she were going to employ her usual tactics, she might as well begin her enticement. "I found," she added in silky tones, "that I couldn't help myself."

Affected by her words as he was, Ian was ever the polite host. He gently removed her wrap, folded it carefully and placed it on a chair before he turned to lead her into the front room. The vision that greeted him when he looked at his guest totally astounded him. For the first time he could recall, the experienced man of the world was at a loss for words.

Anne wore a delicate gown, feminine yet seductive in its cut, a dress without the voluminous skirts that so effectively kept suitors at arm's length and missing the high neck and long sleeves that usually hid a woman's charms. Instead, the cool ivory inset of her bodice was made of elegant lace, wispy and inviting, complemented by the dress's primary fabric, a sea green. The slender skirt that graced her was of the same unusual color, adorned with insets of filmy lace, leaving no doubt as to the exquisite curves clearly suggested by its regal drape.

While pink was Anne's signature color for performances and public appearances, the astute female had discovered long ago that private appointments should be set apart by attitude as well as wardrobe. This particular gown, she'd been told, made her green eyes flash and her golden hair shine with a special, almost ethereal glow, while the simple emerald earrings and necklace sparkled in the gaslight, drawing eyes downward toward her ample décolletage, screened by lace but hinting at secrets about to be revealed. While a garment of absolute modesty by fashion's dictates, it had never failed to produce speechlessness in any man for whom she'd worn it, and she was pleased to note that Ian was no exception.

"Really, sir, if you feel unwell, I would gladly agree to a postponement of our dinner this evening," suggested Anne, reaching for her wrap, when Ian remained silently staring. She couldn't recall anyone so completely taken by her dressmaker's craft, but then the English did seem unfamiliar with innovative fashions. "I did give you rather short notice, I'm afraid. It's probably better that we delay our dinner for another night."

"No, no, please don't even think of leaving," exclaimed Ian, hastily stepping between her and her cloak as he recalled all the trouble tonight had cost him. To lose her now because he was tongue-tied by her lush beauty would be all too cruel. "Besides, if I may be so bold as to say so, Miss Hargraves, your exquisite appearance, indeed your gracious acceptance of my invitation make me feel reborn, a man renewed in health and vigor. That you would grace my table is a rare blessing I would hate to forfeit because of an insignificant wound."

"Well, thank you, sir, but with words as sweet as those, perhaps you'd best call me Anne," invited the blonde, at once annoyed by the transparent ploy of his flattery and intrigued by the man who could deliver such phrases so naturally.

"Very well, Anne, but then I shall be Ian."

"And who else would you be, sir?" sniffed his housekeeper, standing in the door to the front room, holding a tray of biscuits and sherry. "If you'll be wanting a sherry, you should have it now as the roast is nearly done and lamb don't wait well."

"Thank you, Mrs. Land. I'll serve Miss Hargraves," Ian said in dismissal, amazed at the impudence of the woman. She was usually completely circumspect around his guests, but then rarely did he bring women home.

"Anne, please come into my parlor—"

"Said the spider to the fly," finished the beguiling woman, catching Ian unawares with the accuracy of her thoughts, which echoed his very own. Nonetheless, she did follow him into the front room, glancing around approvingly before she chose an armchair at a distance from his.

"Come now, you certainly can't believe I'm dangerous or you wouldn't have agreed to come to dinner, would you?" the dark-haired rogue inquired, more than a little curiously. Pouring their drinks, he looked up suddenly, his deep gray eyes catching hers in a penetrating stare.

"Probably not, or at least not alone," lied the songstress without qualm. Her mission was to learn more about the man, not be totally honest with him. "I would have fetched Aurora or Audrey Palmer along for distraction if not protection."

"Somehow I doubt that," challenged Ian, handing her the sherry and letting his fingers linger over hers, enjoying the feel of her skin. "Having seen you in action in the East End, Miss Hargraves, I suspect that you enjoy courting danger, or at least you disregard its possible impact on you. Not only are you here tonight," he said seductively, "but look at all your foreign engagements. You've spent more time abroad than many military men. Surely a timid woman would not be singing in Paris, let alone Alexandria or Constantinople."

"Hmm." Anne stalled for a moment, extricating her fingers from his and taking a sip of the sweet wine. He seemed to know an awful lot about her activities; just how much of Anne Hargraves's career did the British press cover? Or did he have other sources, she wondered. He would definitely bear further study.

"Actually, Ian, I suspect most people prefer to think of themselves as beyond fear," she said thoughtfully, her heart constricting at the sudden realization that her words might apply to her, even now. "In truth, as an Englishwoman, I have never found Paris or any large city dangerous, once you get past the leering men and greedy carriage drivers."

"But that is just what is so special about you," her host remarked, bending over to brush her hair to one side and plant a quick kiss on the nape of her neck. Rarely had he met a woman so independent and self-assured, ready to take on any challenge, at home or abroad. *Even that of murdering the queen, perhaps?* questioned a stray thought as he raised his lips from her obliging neck, letting the soft blond waves fall into place. The idea caused him to stiffen unconsciously so that his guest immediately became concerned.

"I'm sorry. Is your head bothering you so much?" Anne asked. Suddenly she was standing beside him, her slender fingers reaching up to gently probe his wound, the scent of her making him warm with desire, even as his mind argued the possibility of her treachery. "Shall I ring for the house-keeper? Or perhaps I should fetch a doctor?"

"Nonsense," Ian insisted firmly, catching her hand and drawing it to his lips while bringing his mind under control. "I shouldn't have bent over, but you looked so tempting, I couldn't resist the effort, and I don't regret it though I did feel a bit dizzy. Please don't leave. You are truly the only medicine I need tonight."

For a moment, Anne hesitated; were this someone she really cared about, she would insist on sending for a doctor, yet he did seem well enough now. His forehead had been cool. All right then, her assignment was back on schedule.

"I fear you will turn my head with your eloquent words, sir. You are much too kind to a lonely woman, too often away from home to have many friends," she said, returning to her chair.

"That is the most absurd notion I've heard in a very long time. Anne Hargraves without friends, never," scoffed Ian, seating himself and deciding to let the conversation flow where it might. He'd been about to pursue the issue of her foreign travels, but Bertie could probably get him that information. This avenue of exploration might prove more useful; after all, regardless of the topic, the more the woman talked, the more of herself she revealed, consciously or not. "I warrant you have only to announce an at home and they'd be standing on the street longing for a chance to meet *the* Miss Anne Hargraves, world-renowned performer."

"Probably," agreed the singer, allowing a well-crafted note of self-pity to enter her tone. Never one to tolerate false modesty, she knew she was an excellent musical entertainer, but that was not what this was about. "However, I said *friends,* not acquaintances, those who wish to be or those currying favor. Friends are few and far between, I fear."

"Then may I propose we drink a toast to friendship," Ian suggested. At her nod, he rose and lifted his glass. "To Anne and Ian, who have really met for the first time to-night, away from distractions and society. May their friendship blossom like the glorious roses of June."

And may you not be an assassin out to make those roses into Victoria's funeral flowers, thought Anne as she raised her glass in silent salute. Though it was really too soon to be sure, she had already decided that such a possibility seemed remote.

"Dinner is served. And miss, the seating was his idea," announced Mrs. Land, apparently unwilling to trust her employer to explain. "I told him it wasn't proper, but he insisted. I'll change it back if you prefer."

Following the woman into the dining room, Anne wasn't sure what to expect; in her travels, she'd sat on pillows on the floor, even eaten standing up, separated men from the women and resting on her knees in the dirt. What could be so peculiar to upset the housekeeper? Seeing the table arrangement, Anne could barely contain her amusement. *This* perturbed Mrs. Land?

At the end of the formal salon farthest from the kitchen, one place had been set at the foot of the table while another was laid to its immediate left. A fragrant centerpiece occupied the center of the table while the other end remained barren, clearly a critical breach of etiquette in this provincial woman's eyes, though a clever maneuver on Ian's part if he wanted privacy.

"Thank you for your concern, ma'am, but I see no problem with the table as it is. It will be easier for Mr. Kendrick and I to speak this way," affirmed Ian's guest. "Such place settings are quite common abroad."

The housekeeper sniffed loudly and retreated to the kitchen, her displeasure obvious but her duty done. If the two wanted to play around with propriety, it was none of her affair, but those rules were made for common sense protection, they were. Who knew what troubles would come of their familiarity with each other? It seemed, however, that neither Mr. Ian nor his guest cared a whit for such a possibility—or perhaps they cared too much, Mrs. Land couldn't decide which.

Pulling out the chair to his left, Ian waited for Anne to seat herself and moved the chair forward. Leaning over her, he spoke in a soft whisper, admiring the view as he did so.

"Anne, I must apologize for Mrs. Land. Apparently she fears for your reputation dining in so intimate a space."

"And what about yours?"

"I am certain she believes that I'm totally beyond salvation." Ian laughed, more lighthearted than he'd felt in weeks. Suspect or not, Anne Hargraves was an attractive, attentive female, one whose company he was enjoying more and more as the evening progressed. Perhaps she was innocent and just too naive to see through Andrew Brighton, after all, though common sense warned that wasn't altogether probable.

"Yes, I've heard that whispered around town." Anne laughed as the housekeeper entered with fresh pâté.

"Really? Am I the topic of conversation in your circles? Where? With Andrew Brighton's group of reformers—or maybe the ladies in your social group? Certainly not among musicians of any caliber. Do tell me what they have to say," requested her host, small lines tightening at the corners of his mouth as he awaited her reply while apparently concentrating on his appetizer.

"Brighton, goodness, no, until the other day he didn't even mention your name. You haven't exactly been visible with the social reform movement until quite recently," baited Anne, looking for an excuse for Ian's sudden appearance at St. George's-in-the-East.

"His group has only just come to my attention," evaded Ian, "but tell me then what the women have to say. I trust it's not all unfavorable?" he ventured as Molly served.

"No, not all, though I must admit a good deal of their chatter was not terribly complimentary."

"And, if it were all innocuously bland, would you be here tonight, Anne?" he inquired all too perceptively as Mrs. Land entered with the soup. When his guest didn't reply, but blushed instead, the experienced bachelor decided to answer his earlier question himself. "I've heard it said that I am all too frequently in the company of beautiful, captivating women, but quite honestly, I can't consider that a character flaw, especially when the women and I take such pleasure in each other's company. Tell me, do you disapprove?"

"Not if you don't just use the women for your own enjoyment and then discard them," said the blonde, surprised at her honest reply. After all, what did his womanizing mean to her? And besides, in her time, hadn't she allowed it to be thought that she herself had cultivated many such relationships in the name of God and country?

"Heavens, no, that's not my style at all. Our parting has always been by mutual agreement, with no ill feelings," assured the man with such a roguish reputation. "In truth I suspect those complaints originated with jealous suitors who aren't as fortunate as I."

"Or from the women you don't choose to squire," suggested Anne. "From the way you've treated me here tonight, I would venture to guess that you make your chosen ones very happy women indeed, and there are always those who resent another's joy when they themselves can't partake in a similar manner."

"Many thanks for such high praise." Ian laughed, pushing the ever wayward lock of hair off his forehead. "I'm glad I don't disappoint you."

"I am certain you don't," she said with a smile. He hadn't denied his womanizing reputation; wouldn't he have done so if he had a guilty conscience? Could he be only a renegade playboy after all? He definitely had the appeal for it, Anne acknowledged, feeling herself drawn to the laughing man with such an engaging manner.

Then Ian reached across the table and lifted her hand to his lips, gently kissing its tender palm, trailing his lips across its width and back again, his warm breath and sweet touch sending shivers up and down her spine. Should she allow herself to react, she wondered briefly before she took his hand in turn and repaid his tenderness, unaware of the coughing housekeeper who had entered with their main course.

Shaking her head in blatant disapproval, Mrs. Land plunked the dishes down on the table before them and was gone.

"Good heavens, doesn't she remember what it was like to be young?" muttered Ian, growing increasingly annoyed with his all too present servants. Though his romantic gesture had begun as a ploy to win Anne's affection so that he might gain her confidence, Ian had found it a most pleasurable experience.

"Perhaps she does, and that is the problem," suggested Anne. "She regrets what's lost from her life and resents our enjoyment of it. I'll wager that my butler, on the other hand, has never enjoyed a moment's pleasure, he's so stuffy and provincially disapproving."

"Why keep him if he's so unsatisfactory? Mrs. Land at least cooks like an angel."

"Indeed, the roast is very tender and flavorful, and I've never had such delicious cream of leek soup," raved the singer.

"Oh, is that what it was?" said Ian, his mouth half full as Mrs. Land returned, a scowl marring her normally pleasant visage.

"Is everything satisfactory, sir?"

"Absolutely, Mrs. Land. The cream of leek soup was superb, and this lamb is so sweet it barely needs chewing. You've outdone yourself tonight," praised the master of the house. "Miss Hargraves and I were just saying so."

"Why, thank you, Mr. Ian," replied the woman as she instantly forgave his earlier indiscretions and turned a ruddy hue. "I was hoping you'd be pleased, though I'm surprised you recognized the soup; most people think it's scallion."

"You would never put fennel in that," objected Anne, winning the housekeeper's approval. "Really, it was quite an exceptional meal, better than many I've had on the Continent."

"I hope you've saved room for my dessert," Mrs. Land chided, still blushing. "I've done fresh pastries and cream."

"Well, I don't know, perhaps a small taste," said Anne, thinking sadly of how carefully she'd have to watch her meals for the next week to make up for this feast. If she weren't careful, her gowns wouldn't fit properly.

"Fine, I'll see to it at once and then bring your coffee to the front room," agreed the housekeeper, as she collected the plates and headed for the kitchen. "I'll just have Molly light the fire so it will be nice and cozy."

"I don't believe my ears," muttered Ian. "This is the woman who objected to our sitting together at one end of the table—and now she wants us to be cozy? Miss Hargraves, your knowledge of soups has created a small miracle, yet you claim to have trouble with servants?"

"Not all servants, just my butler."

"If it's a matter of needing a man to discharge him for you, I'd be happy to—"

"It's nothing like that at all. Brewster simply believes he knows more about how my life should be lived than I, and it's very irritating, especially when he's right," confessed Anne as the housekeeper deposited a strawberry tart with fresh cream before her.

"Brewster? I've had occasion to run into him once or twice, and *from* him an equal number of times, I daresay. There was this hunting party where he was serving and... Well, suffice it to say that he can certainly be intimidating," summarized the young man, grimacing slightly at the memory. "Most of London wants to employ him if only so he won't snub them when he's serving them at someone else's house."

"Actually, it's not that he doesn't do his job, but his patronizing attitude infuriates me so that I go out of my way to infuriate him and it becomes a vicious cycle," admitted his lovely guest, wondering if perhaps friendship might be the next tactic to try with the irascible Brewster. It certainly seemed the key to handling Ian Kendrick, she thought, feeling his knee pressing suggestively against hers beneath the table.

"Coffee is ready in the front parlor; Molly and I will just clear up, finish in the kitchen and retire for the night, if that is satisfactory, Mr. Ian," announced the housekeeper with nary a leer.

Her leaving him alone with Anne, Jack out of the house till who knew what hour—damnation, it was not only satisfactory, rejoiced Ian silently, it was ideal!

"Fine, Mrs. Land, and thank you for a lovely meal," he said, rising to assist Anne from her chair. "Shall we adjourn across the hall where we can be more comfortable?" At the blonde's smiling nod, Ian took her arm and led her into his parlor.

Chapter Seven

"I'm sorry, gentlemen, really. I know you think I'm being foolish, but I feel guilty enjoying this run of luck when my brother is sitting home," Jack said, once again trying to cash in his chips.

"From what you told us he was a bit under the weather and wished to remain at home. You, on the other hand, seem well enough. You can't just clean our pockets and then leave," retorted Daniel Palmer, Duke of Moreland, one of Jack's new acquaintances.

"I'd feel better if I check on him," insisted the newcomer to their game. "I'll come back once I know Ian's all right."

"Look, you've been winning every hand for almost three hours, Jack. If he hasn't died yet, I think he'll survive until we have a chance to get some of our own back," protested Bothwell, the man who'd eased Jack's way into the club in the first place.

"Certainly. Can't your conscience wait until I earn back my horse's feed allotment for next month?" pleaded the Duke of Moreland.

"Kendrick, consider the fact that neither you nor your brother might be welcome back here if you leave such an unusually large and ungracious winner," warned the Earl of Bradford. "Why not play another hour?"

"All right, I'll stay another hour, but no more, whether you fellows win or lose," conceded Jack with a scowl, though he obviously had no choice now but to lose a few hands deliberately. "As I told you before, though, you're all welcome to your money back. I've always played for sport rather than coins."

"With your luck, you can afford to be generous," scoffed Bothwell. "The rest of us aren't so fortunate. Just cut the cards and let's hope Lady Luck has left your shoulder for someone else's by now."

At Ian's house, Lady Luck had indeed smiled on the young couple in the front room. The fire was crackling with just the right hint of urgency, they'd enjoyed the brandy and coffee Mrs. Land had set out, and as Ian sat in his chair opposite Anne on the divan, the blonde reflected she'd never before seen a man appear so mellow and relaxed at the same time his eyes so urgently signaled his desire for her. Any minute now, he'd be beside her on the couch, his arm draped around her shoulders, his breath mingling with hers as they kissed, tentatively at first, but soon passionately. What was more, she realized, the chemistry between them was that strong that she wanted it to happen as much as he.

And then he rose in one fluid motion and came to stand before her; she patted the cushion beside her, and he sank down, smiling at her gracious invitation, satisfied with his progress. Indeed, considering the horrible way the day had begun, Ian knew only contentment right now, his arm resting on Anne's lovely shoulders, occasionally allowing a finger to stroke her cheek as they spoke softly of nothing and everything, allowing their enchanted mood to feed their appetites.

Finally he could wait no longer. In spite of himself, his lips so desperately craved her taste that Ian bent forward, willing himself to be gentle as he covered her mouth with his own, savoring the brandy, coffee and woman whose flavor he sampled.

For a few minutes, Anne resisted, desiring to maintain some sense of ladylike decorum before she succumbed to her pleasure and his; this was, after all, England.

Ian, however, had no qualms about pushing past her territorial limits; he'd explored her character and motives over dinner, now the woman herself was on the menu. Besides, with intimacy would come more information, he told himself as an excuse.

Beginning with her mouth, he bestowed tentative touches of his firm lips on hers, feather light and innocent except for the unspoken demand that suggested itself in the slowly increasing pressure. She didn't evade him or fight his advances, he noted. Rather her breath became more labored and her eyes brighter as he deliberately shifted his focus to that vulnerable spot on the nape of her neck just below her ear. Blowing softly, he heated the pulsing skin and kissed it further aflame, sensing her surrender even before she relaxed in his arms and reached to draw his face to hers, claiming access to his mouth.

More than graciously, Anne decided to return the dark-haired rogue's favors, giving pleasure to him as happily as she'd received what he dispensed. After all, she had always believed kissing to be a joint adventure and she wanted to enjoy the experience as greedily as Ian did. Besides, he apparently had no objections, at least none he indicated.

After a languorous period spent enjoying mutual caresses and kisses, Anne felt the need to know Ian's body more intimately and interrupted her loving ministrations long enough to unfasten his shirt studs, drawing the lapels open so she could run her fingers through the soft dark fur that traced its way down his chest. Then she found his nipples and, lowering her head, began to lick them with a slowness that nearly drove him mad even as it seemed to excite him. Were she thinking professionally, were she thinking at all, Anne would have realized this was the time to ask questions about his interest in Brighton, but her mind had been overcome by her own passions. This evening, she'd become Anne Hargraves, a private citizen, behind closed doors, removed from the responsibility of espionage, and she craved nothing more at this moment than to enjoy each glorious sensation of the loving freedom Ian produced in her.

Wondrous as the experience was, Ian was starting to feel a bit peculiar about Anne's taking charge but, encumbered by the jacket that had slipped over his shoulders, he could do little more than relish the physical pleasures she provided. Finally, however, the active male in him demanded satisfaction, and he caught Anne's head, bringing it up to his as he called her magical lips to his own. Even as he drank in the sweet passion she offered, Ian's hands explored the lacy bodice that had so intrigued him when he first saw it. To his amazement, he discovered that it unfastened at his touch and his fingers suddenly delighted in the silky texture of her unblemished flesh.

"Ah, Anne," he murmured, trailing kisses downward until he rested his dark head in the cleft of her bosom, gently suckling her sweetness as she had fed on him, her soft moans signaling her satisfaction even as a door slammed shut somewhere in the distance.

"This is where your charity should begin...at my home," he whispered huskily, "and, believe me, I do appreciate your giving me such joy."

"You're no miser either, sir," the blonde whispered breathlessly, her body so hot from his touch that she thought she'd burst into flames.

"Only because you beg so sweetly—"

"Ian, I say, old man, where are you? Have you honestly gone to bed already? It's barely half past ten," protested Jack as he drew open the sliding door to the front room. "My Lord!"

"Didn't your mother teach you to knock on closed doors?" demanded Anne's host angrily as he drew her bodice together and stood up to shield her from Jack's view. Realizing his own state of undress, the elder Kendrick began to fasten his shirt as he furiously confronted his blushing sibling. "I always believed a man's home was his castle, but you evidently think what is mine is yours."

"Now, Ian," began Anne, "don't you think—"

"What I think is that you and I were having a perfectly lovely evening until my bloody brother had to interrupt," bellowed Ian, venting his mounting frustration in overly loud tones though he really wanted nothing more than to wallop Jack, this time holding nothing back.

"*This* is the way you spend a quiet evening by the fire?" scoffed Jack. "No wonder Mother thinks you beyond salvation."

"I never said I'd be alone," defended the accused man, "not that my affairs are any of your business."

"I wouldn't call this an affair, Ian," said Anne, standing now and trying to decide how she might reconcile the warring males before her, a task she'd performed countless times in the past, though never with brothers. "We were only—"

"Stay out of this, Anne. The impudent rascal needs to be taught a lesson."

"Like the one you tried to teach me this afternoon?" taunted the younger Kendrick. Embarrassed as he was by the intimate scene he'd inadvertently interrupted, he was nonetheless outraged at his brother's deceit, and determined to avenge it. The fact that a beautiful woman would witness his success would only make the victory sweeter.

"I should have done more than bloody your nose, you interfering young pup."

"You want to try it now?" dared Jack. "Fool that I am, I only came home because I was worried about your head, and how you were getting on, and to tell you I won nearly fifty quid before I had to give twelve of it back to get away from the table. Come on, though, *old* man, if you're so all-fired anxious to fight, I'd be glad to take you on."

"You think I care whether you won or lost when I've got my own prize right here?" sneered Ian, so disconcerted by his brother that he overlooked the effect his words might have on Anne. "No matter how much money you had, you couldn't touch a woman like her."

"And with your cavalier attitude, I am quite sorry I let *you* do so," retorted the blonde indignantly. If this was to be the tenor of the evening, she'd learn nothing more here and she was hard put to stomach his arrogance. How dare he use her to taunt the lad? It was best she take her leave— or maybe even entice the boy to accompany her. Perhaps he'd be only too willing to tell her a few unsavory things about his older sibling.

"Mr. Kendrick, for your information, I am no one's *prize*, least of all yours. It is time I left," she announced, entering the foyer to retrieve her cloak.

"No, Anne, I apologize. What I said was uncalled for. I was just angry. Please, let me see you home," Ian pleaded, sending murderous looks in Jack's direction. If he and Anne ended tonight on a bad note, it would be Jack's fault; damn the devil! "It's not proper for a lady to be out alone at this time of night."

"I think it less proper to be in the company of one who considers me something to be won or lost."

"For heaven's sake, I said I was sorry," complained Ian.

"If you like, miss, I'd be happy to escort you," volunteered Jack, straightening his tie and standing tall, thrilled at the prospect of seeing such a glamorous woman home. One never knew what might happen in the carriage.

"No, that's all right," said Anne, with just the right degree of hesitation. "I wouldn't want to take you out of your way."

"Honest, miss, I don't believe it's going to be any too healthy for me around here once you've left," confided Jack with a wry grin. "I think I had best be out of Ian's range for a while."

"Thank you, then, for your gracious offer, and please call me Anne," the woman said softly, handing Jack her wrap as Ian stood watching, his mouth open, his shirt misbuttoned.

"Really, Anne, this isn't how I wanted the night to end," he tried futilely.

"Nor I," she said curtly, "but sometimes, Mr. Kendrick, we get what we deserve rather than what we want."

As the door closed behind the seductive Anne Hargraves and his good-for-nothing brother, Ian was beside himself with rage. How dare Jack come breezing in here like some tempestuous whirlwind and just as quickly blow out, sweeping Anne Hargraves along in his wake?

Good Lord, one visit to Madame Duvalier's and the insolent puppy considered himself a man about town if not a rake of the highest order. And the arrogant stripling had barely seen his seventeenth birthday. If he continued to behave in such a manner, disrupting his older brother's life as he had, the boy would never live to see another one, Ian vowed, his hands clenched into fists and his quicksilver eyes radiating fury.

Did Jack have no common sense at all? A gentleman didn't come barging into a private tête-à-tête spouting accusations, and most important of all, he never offered to take another man's female companion home.

As he stalked back and forth in the hallway of his house, too perturbed to find peace within any of its rooms, Ian knew that he had every right to send his youngest sibling home and let Mrs. Mumm take her chances. It was exactly what Jack deserved for his behavior. Imagine having the cheek to offer himself as an escort to a woman as enticing, sophisticated and famous as Anne Hargraves when he was still wet behind the ears!

Striding with purposeful step into his study and attempting to calm himself with a glass of brandy, Ian knew he had to get himself in check. He never allowed his emotions to run away with him, and yet now they appeared to have free rein. Try as he might, he couldn't get them under control.

An all too solitary silhouette against the fire burning cheerily in the fireplace, Ian ran his fingers through his thick, dark hair, and attempted to exercise some sort of rational thought in connection with the evening's events.

But it was useless, Ian could make no sense out of what had happened here tonight, from his reactions to Anne's proximity to Jack's return home, and finally Anne's departure in the boy's company. What was it about Anne Hargraves that made logical behavior impossible? Perhaps it was her profusion of blond hair, curling around an exquisite face, the perfect setting for her deep green eyes—eyes the color of a lush country hillside come alive in spring. Maybe it was her melodic laughter or her enticing smile, formed by lips that seemed to whisper sweetly of mysterious and unexpected promises. Or could it be her woman's figure, with curves that demanded a man's caress? But beyond all that, hers was a smoldering soul, incapable of being restrained. It presented a danger to any man who saw her, and certainly—Ian cursed beneath his breath—it could be deadly to a green boy like Jack.

Whatever could have possessed the songstress to go along with Jack's suggestion that he escort her home? Though Ian could have sworn otherwise, had his own kisses been so pedestrian that she preferred the company of a mere child to his own?

For God's sake, her behavior here tonight proved her to be a woman of experience. Ian found the idea of just how she had gained that experience enraging, and he wondered what she would want with the likes of Jack. Was she the kind of female who relished seducing young boys? He hardly thought so. She was made for a man. But what else could it be?

Of course there was always the possibility that the captivating Miss Hargraves had gone off with Jack merely to irritate her dinner companion, though Ian, his brow knitted in consternation at the idea and his head starting to ache anew, couldn't see the sense in that. Overall, during the course of the evening, she had seemed more bent on pleasing than teasing him. Unless maybe he had tempted her beyond her limits and she used Jack as a means to protect herself?

Slamming a fist down into his open palm, Ian decided he wasn't going to stay here and fret about it any longer. He felt like a caged tiger, and that did not bode well for a restful remainder of the evening. If he left the house for a while, he might forget about the effect Anne Hargraves had on him. Perdition, the effect that mere *thoughts* of the woman had on him!

What he needed was to expel her image, to blot it out completely. But there wasn't a woman he knew who would be able to make him forget the bewitching Anne. No, he didn't need another woman. To bloody hell with all women, with their fluttering eyelashes and flirtatious manners, that only set a man on edge and ultimately rendered him a complete idiot. No, what he needed at the moment was to be with his own kind. To find peace in the comfort of male company, in logical, masculine conversation...and in a few stiff drinks. What he needed was to go to his club, an orderly, tranquil world of males, a place where the huntresses of this world couldn't course after him and bring him, anxious and bewildered, to bay.

Full of determination, Ian stormed into the hallway, took his coat from its peg and left for the sanctuary of his club. Climbing into his carriage a few moments later, he told himself how much he anticipated the next few hours and the opportunity to enjoy sensible yet stimulating conversation. Let Anne Hargraves try to find him there, he gloated, until he realized that the lovely Miss Hargraves wasn't looking for him anywhere at the moment, and the knowledge prompted a string of oaths that only would have made Anne laugh had she heard them.

Settled in a comfortable leather chair across the room from a table of card players, Ian raised his hand and signaled for yet another whiskey. He was totally bored and well on the way to being completely drunk, as well. In fact, he was nothing short of miserable.

He stared morosely into the fire and wondered how such a short acquaintance with such a tiny bit of a woman as Anne Hargraves could have driven him to his present state. He, who had always been so proud and self-possessed, he thought, with a trace of morbid amusement. But being taken with the exotic singer was only half his problem, he reminded himself reluctantly. There was his duty to the Crown to contend with, too. And what would he do if Anne Hargraves was actually involved with a plot to assassinate Queen Victoria? Anne's games, and Jack aside, that was the greater part of his problem at the moment.

Good Lord, he had chosen the world's unlikeliest woman with whom to fall in love, he berated himself silently, and then almost spilled the contents of the glass being handed to him by the waiter when he realized where his musings had led him.

In love . . . with Anne Hargraves? It was preposterous, he assured himself, and most likely nothing more than his wounded pride and the whiskey talking. It was simply that he wasn't used to a woman deserting him after he had taken the time to urge her on to greater things with his caresses and kisses. But even as he tried to convince himself of that fact, his lips remembered the sweet softness of Anne's mouth pressed against his, and the breathless, raspy little moans she had made when they had been entwined in each other's embrace.

Damnation! He refused to consider that he had fallen in love with the renowned Miss Hargraves. It made him no better than countless other men worldwide. In order to refute such a possibility, he vowed not to spend another moment thinking about his dinner companion.

Believing his mind to be more befuddled by the alcohol he had consumed than by Anne herself, Ian shook his head in an attempt to clear it. Then he rose and wandered over to stand behind the card players, hoping that either their game or their conversation would put an end to the nonsensical thoughts that had so recently been plaguing him.

"Ah, Kendrick," Charles Crosby, Earl of Wallingcroft, greeted him, "your brother made a killing earlier on this evening. He's one lucky lad!"

"He certainly is," Ian replied through clenched teeth. Good God, he didn't want to spend his time discussing dear brother Jack and his good fortune, either at the gaming tables or with Anne.

"How long will Jack be up?" Wallingcroft asked. "I hope it will at least be time enough for me to have a go at winning back what he took from me tonight."

"I don't know how much longer my brother can afford to stay," Ian said dryly, his public face now very much in place, though his bruised eye still showed the effects of Jack's visit.

"Well, you certainly can't send the chap home before the jubilee, now can you?" Bothwell commented as he picked up the hand he had been dealt. "Destiny doesn't decree an event such as that very often, does it?"

"Who would have imagined the old lady would have lasted so long?" Tyler Fielding, Earl of Bradford, asked, looking at his cards and discarding his hand. The voice of the man who had fawned upon Bertie for so many years held a clear note of disgust, but whether it concerned the cards he had been dealt or Victoria's many years on the throne, Ian couldn't tell. Whatever had prompted the comment, it erased all thoughts of both Anne and Jack from Ian's mind, and caused him to focus on the group seated at the card table: Bothwell, Wallingcroft and Bradford. Could any of these men be so desperate for power that they would plot against the reigning monarch in order to see her son ascend to the throne?

"Who is to say that she will even see the jubilee?" asked Bothwell. "She is, after all, sixty-eight years of age, and fate is sometimes ironic."

"Well, that's a merry notion," Bradford said with a sly wink as he won the current hand. "If the queen were to go to her final reward before the big event, it would plunge a nation expecting a celebration into yet another period of mourning. How jolly! But then there is a bright side, isn't there? Our man would be king."

"And high time, too," Bothwell stated to the murmured agreement of the others.

Ian remained silent, though the topic of conversation had sobered him quickly enough. It was surprise that tied his tongue now, that and the embarrassment he suffered for ever having considered these to be fellows of a decent sort. Though it was no secret that every one of them wished to see the prince become monarch, they had never expressed themselves so openly before—at least not in Ian's company. Their remarks both offended him and caused him to wonder if they alluded to anything more than a desire to see Bertie crowned king. It would seem the prince had been correct; they would bear watching.

"Do you want to sit in?" Wallingcroft asked, breaking the serious mood that had followed when the sentiments the card players had all harbored in their hearts had been spoken.

"No, I'm on my way home, actually," Ian said, his tall, muscular frame casting a huge shadow on the wall behind him.

"Don't tell me that you are priggish enough to have found our recent drollery in poor taste, Kendrick. Surely you know we were speaking only in jest," Bothwell protested, all the while studying Ian's reaction.

"Of course, my dear fellow," Ian lied easily. "After all, which one of us has not wondered when the prince will actually take over the reins of the empire? No, no, Bothwell, I fear I must be off in search of that rogue, my brother. The boy is quite taken with London and its attractions, and it would be bothersome should he wind up in some scrape so that I had to attend his wedding before ever we saw the jubilee."

The men laughed, remembering their own errant youths, all of them happy they had not had to answer to an older sibling of Kendrick's ilk when they were Jack's age.

"That's too bad. I had thought to wager my new mount against that fancy carriage of yours," Bothwell pressed.

Ian looked at the men, knowing full well that he was being tested, that Bothwell was wondering if their fellowship had been tainted by the offhand comments of those at the card table.

While it was more important now than ever that he be thought one of them, Ian's disgust was so great that he couldn't force himself to sit down in their company. A compromise, however, would be in order.

"I'm sorry to say, Bothwell, that I really must be off," Ian replied, his tone as casual as ever. "However, I'm intrigued by your proposition. I would not be adverse to a cut of the deck to determine the outcome of such a wager."

"Hear, hear!" Bradford cheered by way of approval, and proceeded to shuffle the cards, glad of a new diversion to combat his chronic ennui.

Ian cut first and then Bothwell. Laughingly congratulating the other man, a gracious Ian made arrangements to deliver his coach the morning. Then with his most charming smile, he bade the others adieu.

It would seem, he thought, as he trod angrily down the steps of his club, that all his luck this evening was destined to be bad. Now, on top of everything else, he had lost his expensive carriage, as well. Ironically, Bothwell had drawn a queen, and he, well, he had wound up with nothing more than a jack!

Chapter Eight

Ian decided to return to his home on foot. There was no sense in subjecting his coachman to his ill humor, and he wasn't yet ready to explain that the carriage was no longer his. Besides, there was always the chance that strolling through the almost deserted streets of London would do him some good.

With angry footsteps he set off, muttering to himself his assessment of just how dearly the evening had cost him. There was his argument with his brother, the deprivation of the company of an enticing and willing woman and now the loss of his expensive coach. Most important of all, however, was the forfeiture of his own composure.

What had become of him to behave as he had? He, who had always prided himself on his ability to remain unruffled under the most trying of circumstances? Within his entire recollection, he had never acted like this before—before Anne Hargraves had come into his life! Since first meeting her, he had not been himself at all. Was the blond beauty some sort of enchantress, he mused, feeling almost as if a spell had been cast over him. The cause for his recent emotional behavior had to be external. After all, Ian reassured himself, it was most definitely not in his character to be irritable, rude and intractable. He was not that sort of man.

Trudging onward, he vowed to regain control of himself and learn to ignore his illogical impulses where Anne Hargraves was concerned. Yet nevertheless, Ian looked up to suddenly find himself passing in front of Anne's town house, though coming into this neighborhood had taken him out of his way.

Cursing himself for his weakness, he scanned the imposing edifice anxiously for some sign of its occupant's presence. The house loomed dark and silent before him, except for the soft glow of gaslight in one of the upstairs windows, in all likelihood Anne's bedroom.

How ironic, he told himself as a small smile of relief played about his lips, that such a weak light should be so comforting. It appeared that Anne was indeed home. Quite unexpectedly, Ian conjured up images of the scene behind that window. In his mind's eye, Ian could see Anne's provocative gown draped over a chair, to be gathered by servants the following morning, along with her petticoats and other feminine garments. And to complete his idyllic musings, he visualized Anne herself sweetly reposing in the middle of a gracefully carved bed.

But was she in that bed alone? a small, taunting voice suddenly asked. Thunderstruck by the idea that she might not be, the anxious and jealous male turned on his heel and hastened his steps toward home, swearing that Jack had better be there before him.

Deftly twisting his key in the lock, Ian let himself in and stormed down the hallway, checking kitchen, dining room, study and parlor. There was no sign that his bothersome brother had returned.

Infuriated, Ian took the stairs two at a time, bounding past the landing and down the upper corridor until he stopped, breathless, just outside Jack's room. Somewhere in the depths of his soul, he managed to find a vestige of the self-control that had once been both his pride and his trademark in society.

He would be tranquil about this, he told himself, as he rapped sharply on Jack's door.

"Go away, I'm trying to sleep," came a mumbled reply.

So his brother was there. How fortunate for the boy, Ian thought, his breath coming more slowly and evenly. Still, this confrontation was not one to be put off until the morning. Ian knew that he was capable of being somewhat civil at the moment. The Lord only knew how a night of festering curiosity would affect his demeanor. No, now was the time to talk to this ingrate of a lad, and to tell him calmly but firmly just what behavior was expected of him if he hoped to remain in London.

"Jack, it's Ian. I want to talk with you."

"And I want to sleep. It would seem one of us is bound to be disappointed," Jack called out irritably. "Now leave me in peace. Surely, this can wait until morning."

"No, it can't," Ian replied, making his way into the room and throwing off Jack's covers in order to claim his attention. Take hold, the older man commanded himself when he felt a scowl forming on his face. In an effort to expunge the tarnish marring his former image of imperturbability, Ian casually seated himself in a chair rather than continue to loom ominously over his brother's bed, though it cost him dearly to do so.

"This is about Anne, isn't it?" Jack grumbled, sitting up and looking about for his blankets.

"Anne?" Ian asked, his face darkening as one eyebrow rose in disapproval, even as he reminded himself to remain tranquil. "Shouldn't that be *Miss Hargraves?*"

"You heard her when she said I was to call her Anne," Jack replied with a self-satisfied smile.

"It probably meant no more to her than it does to any soft-hearted woman who invites a child to call her by her given name," Ian pronounced, pretending that this proffered intimacy had no impact on him in the least. "However, you will find that women do not extend that privilege to *men* they have but so recently met."

"Anne is not like most other women," Jack protested sullenly, his ego more than a little wounded by his brother's insult and the fact that Anne Hargraves had done very little in the time they had been together other than ask questions about the insufferable Ian.

"That might be the case, but I am here to tell you, boy, that Anne Hargraves is not for you," Ian stated quietly, pleased that he had enough control over his voice to make it sound so frostily polite, when in reality he was fighting the urge to trounce the young rogue as he deserved.

"I'd think that was a decision for the lady to make, wouldn't you?" Jack asked defiantly, unaware of how close to danger his words placed him.

With restraint, Ian managed to stay where he was, though his hands, resting on the arms of the chair, craved nothing more than to curl themselves into fists. Instead, he shook his dark, handsome head in disdain.

"Surely," he began in a superior voice, deep and rich in tone, "you are not such a boy that you don't know the behavior you exhibited tonight is totally unacceptable. Gentlemen do not attempt to steal the feminine companions of their fellows."

"Nor do gentlemen lie to each other," Jack shot back crossly. "You led me to believe that you were to pass a solitary evening at home. Perhaps if you had taken me into your confidence and told me that you would be entertaining a woman tonight, none of this would have occurred."

"Are you trying to say that if I had informed you the lovely Miss Hargraves was to be my dinner companion, you would have gone off and left us in peace?"

"No," Jack conceded. "Anne Hargraves is the sort of woman most men only dream of encountering. I couldn't have passed up the opportunity to meet her. But don't look so smug. That doesn't mean you're right about everything you've said here tonight. As for my behavior, certainly even you must admit that among men of the world, all's fair in love and war."

There, he'd said it, Jack thought with satisfaction. He had set up a competition with his brother over the lovely Anne Hargraves. And though he had no chance of winning such a beauty, his enjoyment of the situation stemmed from the irritation it would cause his very vexing older brother. For that reason, he refused to be cowed under Ian's fierce stare.

The insolent confidence of the boy shook Ian to his very center, as did the message he imparted. But then what male who knew her couldn't imagine himself in love with Anne Hargraves?

"How can you talk of love when you have only just met the woman?" Ian asked, a dark lock fallen onto his forehead making him appear less authoritarian and sage than he would have wished. "I fail to believe that Anne did anything to encourage such a notion."

Jack didn't respond to his brother's comment. In fact, his stubborn silence did nothing to assuage the rising anxiety now evident in Ian's furrowed brow, when he could not read the younger man's enigmatic expression. Was Jack refusing to admit that Anne had not demonstrated any interest in him, or was he wisely holding his tongue for other reasons?

"*Did* she?" the elder Kendrick pressed at last, his soft but deadly voice finally breaking the stillness of the bedchamber.

Studying his brother, Jack found himself enjoying the situation immensely. Ian hadn't always been so confident, so coolly detached from life's goings on. He had become so only after he had fancied himself a grown man and moved to London. It wouldn't hurt this inordinately unbearable gentleman to be brought down a peg or two. Besides, nowhere in English law did it read that it was only the youngest Kendrick who could learn something during his sojourn in London.

"A gentleman wouldn't say," Jack began with a grin, quite pleased with himself for sorting everything out.

"You had better say," the man sitting in the chair fairly growled. Though his voice told of his unsettlement, he managed to keep his anger from implanting itself upon his face.

"But Ian, don't you remember?" Jack protested, a wicked gleam alight in his eyes. "I'm to do whatever I want as long as I don't make you aware of it. Those were your instructions, given me only two days ago. Did you think I forgot? And in keeping with them, I choose to maintain my silence concerning how I spent my time with Anne. There, don't tell me that doesn't make you happier than actually knowing what went on, and what my plans are for seeing her again. In fact, it gives you nothing at all to think about and brood over. Now if you don't mind, I'm going to get some sleep."

While Jack retrieved his covers and made himself comfortable, Ian was forced to clamp his lips together tightly in order to keep from giving way to the indignant outrage that threatened to erupt.

His brother had formed a tendresse for Anne Hargraves, had he? Didn't the boy realize that the woman had to be at least ten years his senior. But then, Anne had an ageless beauty, Ian admitted. A sigh escaped him as images of the blonde came all too readily to mind. She was provocative, witty, sophisticated. Surely a woman such as she would have little use for a boy like Jack.

At the moment that was his one hope, he realized, as he rose from his chair, too tired now to harass his brother further. To continue to clash with the boy would serve to make him more stubborn and determined to prove his manhood, and God only knew where that would lead.

Damn Jack! How could he impose himself in this way? The idea that his older brother might be attracted to Anne Hargraves obviously meant little to him, Ian thought as he entered his room and began to undress for bed. And it was unthinkable to reveal to Jack that he was investigating Anne by command of the Prince of Wales.

It had been difficult enough to gain even a small degree of her confidence and attention without Jack vying for the woman's favor. How could Ian carry out his orders with his young rascal of a brother getting in the way?

There was only one manner in which to deal with this situation, he concluded, pulling back the sheets and sliding his unclad body between them. If Jack had decided to ignore his brother's decree concerning Anne, Ian would have to deal directly with the enticing songstress.

He'd go to her and explain about Jack's boyish infatuation, suggesting that she sever all contact with the lad in order to spare him further unnecessary hurt. For good measure, Ian determined, he would do what he could to distract her from all thoughts of Jack, indeed all thoughts of other men. It would not be an unpleasant task. Ian was adamant, however, that the word *love,* which had so surprised him when he had nearly been in his cups at his club, had nothing to do with his plan. He was merely being practical...and exceedingly patriotic, but then he'd always loved England.

Pleased with his cleverness, and afire with anticipation, he fell asleep, a smile decorating his ruggedly handsome face.

The next morning, Jack's solitary breakfast was rudely interrupted by the loud and cheerful tune that heralded his impeccably tailored brother's arrival in the dining room.

"Have some mercy and cease that racket," Jack, still attired in a dressing robe, said plaintively.

"Not in a good mood, are we?" Ian asked, a grin lighting his countenance.

"Once you woke me, I had trouble getting back to sleep," the younger man all but moaned.

"How dreadful for you. I slept very well indeed," Ian stated before he took up his cheery whistling once more as he heaped his plate with eggs, fish and hot, thick bread.

He set the plate before him and looked at the mound of food. A hearty breakfast was important, he silently told himself. A man never knew when he would need all of his stamina. His secret pleasure made him grin once more, which only served to increase Jack's irritation. This in itself was cause for a good mood. If Jack wasn't happy here, the young whelp might well go home. Yes, this was bound to be a very good day, Ian thought, as he stopped whistling and attacked his eggs.

Talented cook though Mrs. Land was, Ian was surprised that he hardly tasted any of the things he had piled on his plate. But then, he supposed, he had other things on his mind...things most gentlemen in society didn't think about before breakfast. Well, bloody hell, perhaps they should, he decided. Most people could stand to start their day a bit more pleasantly.

Even Jack's continuing scowl had little effect on Ian as he dutifully consumed his breakfast. The sun was shining, and outside his window the birds were twittering melodically. Their song reminded him of his own little songbird, the beautiful woman he intended to visit this morning. Ah, but he would teach her a sweeter song than ever she had sung before. Taking a final sip of coffee, he pushed himself away from the table, bade his brooding sibling good day and left the house, the sun all the more glorious as he started toward his destination.

Anne replaced her cup in its saucer and sighed. Though the coffee had been near perfection this morning, Brewster had been at his worst. Why, the man had all but demanded to know who had escorted her home last night, and Anne was finding his meddling increasingly difficult to deal with.

Why was it that men felt women could not see to their own affairs, in every sense of the word? Tired, she allowed herself the luxury of leaning her head back and closing her eyes. She had slept little last night, trying to piece together the few shards of information the Kendrick boy had given her concerning his older brother with what she already knew about Ian Kendrick.

No, that was a lie, she berated herself with a shake of the head. There was another reason she had failed to sleep, and a much more disturbing one, at that.

Try as she might to avoid them, Anne couldn't help but think about the events of the previous evening. The warm memories painted her finely sculpted cheeks a becoming shade of pink. By all that was holy, she had never meant to respond to Ian as she had. She, who had always been in control of every situation, had found herself on the verge of being dominated, of submitting without questions or reservations to the urgings of that dark-haired rogue.

She could only thank Providence that the boy had barged in and interrupted them. Otherwise Anne had no delusions as to what would have occurred between herself and Ian Kendrick....

But Jack's sudden presence had not saved her entirely. This morning, the emotional residue of her intimacy with Ian refused to be washed away, and Anne was wise enough to know that her present discontent and edginess was due to the fact that she craved the touch of a man.

With the admission came a small, self-deprecating laugh. Imagine society's shock if its members ever guessed that the notorious Miss Hargraves found herself in need of a lover. After all, everyone surmised that she had paramours by the score. But in truth, that had not been the case.

While countless men had been attracted to her, that attraction had not been returned. Her relationships with men had been more talked about than existent. Yet, because she had been seen on the arms of so many powerful males, because she had laughed and flirted and listened to them with rapt attention, her scandalous reputation had persisted. Aided, of course, by the fact that those men who had been her escorts would rather have perished than have told the world that they alone had failed to sleep with Anne Hargraves.

It was really quite amusing, Anne told herself, that with all the time she had spent in the company of the opposite sex, her life these past few years had been a solitary and lonely one.

She didn't want to be alone anymore. Despite her present longings, however, not just any man would do. It was Ian she wanted, though it was Ian whom current circumstances forbade her from having.

Not since Louis had any male affected her as the tall, rugged Englishman did. He filled her with yearnings and desires that she had thought destroyed long ago. In fact, until last evening, she had assumed most of her emotions had died along with Louis in Africa seven years before.

Anne had all but considered herself a cold, unfeeling woman since then. She had carefully fashioned a wall of stone around her heart to spare herself the searing despair and pain she had felt when she had so suddenly and tragically lost her first love. Of course, she had experienced some emotions in the intervening years, though not many. There had been sorrow, anger and occasionally compassion. But love, happiness and even fear had become foreign to her. And now, inexplicably, after Ian's preliminary lovemaking, Anne knew all three with an intensity that startled her.

Lord, why did this Englishman, with his sophisticated good looks, affect her so? Was it because beneath his prepossessing exterior there raged passions which beckoned to her own, restrained though they had been? Was it his smile, his strength, his stubborn male pride that spoke to her buried emotions, awakening them from their long slumber with his expert kiss, like the prince in the fairy tale?

But Ian wasn't a prince, Anne reminded herself sharply. That had been Louis Napoleon, son of the emperor of France and ruler of her girlish heart. The golden-haired singer sighed. That part of her life had been a long time ago, and the past was a province where one could not live.

Still, Anne could not resist squeezing her large green eyes shut and willing images of Louis to come to her, floating across the years to the present moment. It had been eons since she had allowed herself to dwell upon him, though in reality thoughts of her one great love were never really far from her mind.

Yet now, when she sought to indulge herself in the bitter-sweet memories that were all she had left of Louis, she found she could not do so. Instead of his tender, loving face, she saw Ian Kendrick's striking features. And rather than hear Louis's voice so charmingly accented in French, she heard Ian's husky and compelling timbre.

It saddened Anne that Ian was able to intrude even here, in the most secret core of her soul. But it didn't astonish her. She was all too aware that Ian Kendrick was the sort who would want to totally possess any woman he claimed as his own. Such a woman would have to give herself to him completely. There would be no secrets, no privacy, and that was what made him so dangerous, especially for someone involved in the deadly game of espionage.

Finding herself frowning, Anne determined she had had enough of such introspection. Dwelling upon the past solved nothing and only created more problems. As for thinking about Ian, that was a futile endeavor. There was a place, however, where Anne knew she could hide from the phantoms that shrouded her morning. She would turn to her music, to the sweet strains of melody that had been her salvation many times in the past. So deciding, she rose and made her way to the piano in the music room.

Though it was a difficult task for Matthew Brewster to look down his nose at a man so much taller than he, the butler managed it admirably. He recognized Ian Kendrick immediately and hoped that the presence of this scoundrel who ran on the fringes of the South Kensington Crowd portended only business and was connected with Anne's work for Nigel Conway.

It was not an easy thing to determine, however, as the bounder had the audacity to stand upon Miss Hargraves's doorstep, his arms full of posies, at the undignified hour of ten o'clock in the morning. Whatever would the neighbors think? But then, the manner in which Anne Hargraves conducted herself left her continuously open to gossip. As always, Brewster determined that he had to be on guard.

When the butler's imperious stare failed to quell the man into depositing his floral offering and departing, Brewster hastened Kendrick inside before too many passersby noted his appearance.

"Good day, here is my card. I should like to see Miss Hargraves if she is available," Ian said. Though his voice was all that was proper, Brewster noticed and deplored the amused gleam in Kendrick's eyes.

"I believe the term is good morning, sir," Brewster replied haughtily, the simple words conveying his disapproval of a gentleman who would presume to call unexpectedly upon a lady's household at such an hour. "I will see if Miss Hargraves has arisen and is receiving."

"If she rises much higher, I'm afraid she'll crack all the crystal," Ian said with a laugh as Anne's voice drifted into the entryway. "Just tell her I'm here, will you, old boy?"

"The name is Brewster, sir. And I'm afraid that's quite impossible. Miss Hargraves does not like to be disturbed when she is attending to her music."

"Ah, I see," Ian responded gravely. "I shall wait, then, until she is finished. Put these in water, will you?" Ian directed as he casually thrust the huge bouquet at the squat man guarding Anne's residence so fiercely.

The butler's only response was to stare disdainfully in the direction of the flowers and then to shuffle off below stairs with the intention of handing Kendrick's tribute over to one of the maids. Upon his return, Brewster planned to inform his employer immediately concerning the present invasion.

The moment the ominous little butler was out of sight, Ian sauntered down the hallway, following the sound of Anne's lovely voice to the music room. There, he stood upon the threshold and was quite content for a moment to observe Anne at her work. She was all that was feminine and lovely in delightful dishabille, dressed in a pale pink ensemble of satin, lace and ruffles. Her sun-kissed hair was swept up off her neck and formed unruly curls around her enticing face, and her woman's body swayed gracefully to the notes produced upon the piano.

Even from the doorway, Ian could see that she was quite immersed in the melody that claimed her attention. Unaware she was being observed, Anne gave herself over to the music completely, and thus afforded Ian a glimpse into her very soul. He liked what he saw. As much as she had shared last night, there was a softness and vulnerability to Anne Hargraves that she had never fully revealed to him. In spite of his purpose in being there this morning, Ian's instinctive reaction was to enfold her in his arms and protect her from all of life's cares.

It was at that moment Anne chose to look up. There, about to enter the room, was the very man her song was supposed to exorcise from her thoughts. He was handsomely dressed this morning, and upon his lips hung one of the tenderest smiles Anne had ever seen. It caused her heart to skip rapidly, and in a panic, she felt the traitorous muscles of her throat begin to squeeze and cramp. Before her voice became nothing more than a series of ugly squeaks, Anne closed her mouth abruptly, her song ending in midrefrain.

Boldly, and against all better judgment, she returned Ian's stare, allowing herself to be captured by his piercing gaze. And when his eyes continued to hold hers, Anne was surprised to find that she didn't feel constrained. Rather, she was quite content to remain as she was.

The magic of the moment was broken, however, by Brewster's ill-timed appearance. Sallying forth with Ian's card on a silver salver, a little maid carrying the bouquet scurrying in his wake, Matthew Brewster entered the room like a knight protecting a damsel in distress. He went directly to Anne, but not without sending Ian a contemptuous glare, which all but told Anne's visitor that he would

endure eternal damnation for his social transgression in not
waiting to be announced.

"A Mr. Ian Kendrick to see you, madam," the butler intoned solemnly. Then he turned to take the vase from his
underling and slam it quite forcefully on the top of the piano, telling all concerned just what he thought of Ian Kendrick.

"Thank you, Brewster. That will be all," Anne stated
quietly, her usually clear voice evincing a whispery quality
that Ian found utterly seductive.

With a stiff bow in Anne's direction and a cynically raised
eyebrow addressed to Ian, the belligerent servant left the
room, making certain the door was properly ajar.

"So that is how Brewster behaves when he's miffed," Ian
said, his silver eyes brimming with laughter. "It's no wonder half of London society is terrified of the old codger. I'm
certain that if I hadn't needed to see you as urgently as I do,
I would have left before ever I set foot inside your house. It's
quite apparent he doesn't want me here."

"Is that so?" Anne asked in that low, raspy voice, the tilt
of her head making it obvious she had yet to decide whether
or not to welcome his visit.

"Quite," Ian confirmed, moving to stand beside her piano bench as though he expected an invitation to sit down.
"I assure you, I would have been quite cowed."

"I can't imagine you being frightened of anything," Anne
replied softly and hesitantly.

"Oh, but I am," Ian hastened to assure her, his husky,
tender cadence one of the most beautiful sounds Anne had
ever heard. "For instance, I'm afraid of you, right now. I've
come to apologize for what happened last night," he continued with a nod at the flowers awkwardly gracing the piano.

Anne cleared her throat before she could respond. "Oh,
I see," she said. "You are sorry for the advances you made
last night."

"No, not for that," Ian said, lifting her hand from the
keyboard and bringing it to his lips before he sat down beside her, his thigh brushing hers. "I'll never be sorry for
that."

"For the interruption, then?" Anne questioned so quietly that Ian had to bend his head close to hers in order to hear her. "Is that the reason you're apologizing?"

"Unfortunately, I couldn't have foreseen that," Ian growled, his words hardly more than guttural until he turned her face toward his so that there was no more than a breath between them. "No, I'm sorry for the things I said, the way I spoke to Jack in front of you, the manner in which I acted when you chose to leave in his company. In short, I am contrite about anything I've done to cause you upset. Say you forgive me."

"I forgive you, Ian," Anne replied, barely able to mouth the words.

And then his lips descended upon hers, urging, demanding, pleading and commanding so that the harsh light of reality was all but eclipsed by the brighter flame of their aroused desires. Each became totally lost in the kiss they shared, forgetting all the reasons they had for keeping the other at a distance.

Anne felt her self-control vanish completely until Louis's visage suddenly appeared, unsummoned, behind her lowered lashes. No matter how tightly she shut her eyes, she couldn't banish his image. Instead it continued to haunt her until the memory of what she had felt for him and the recollection of her suspicions concerning Ian Kendrick compelled her to turn away and end the kiss.

"I'm not sorry for that, either," she heard Ian vow.

"Yes, well, there's no need to be," she croaked, rising from the piano bench and striding to the other side of the room. Clearing her throat, she continued brightly. "It was something we both wanted, both enjoyed, and now we have experienced it. There's no more to it than that."

"There's a lot more to it," Ian insisted fiercely, daring Anne to contradict him.

"Not really," Anne said with a laugh, slipping into her public persona in order to hide behind it. Though she studied the enigmatic expression in Ian's quicksilver eyes, she could not decide if it was really she he wanted, or if it was the world-acclaimed songstress of reputation he wished to conquer. In either case, she knew she couldn't grant his request.

"I refuse to believe you've responded to any other man's kiss as you just now reacted to mine," Ian pressed, illogical pangs of jealousy besieging him.

"Countless times," Anne lied with a bored sigh.

"Prove it," Ian challenged, his lips pressed tightly together in determination.

"What?"

"Come kiss me again and tell me it isn't something special."

"Oh, Ian, I'll do no such thing," Anne stated, dismissing his suggestion as if it was of no significance.

"You're afraid of me," he uttered in amazement.

"That's entirely untrue," Anne sputtered, barely finding enough breath to deny his accusation.

"But it is true," he insisted softly, taking a step toward her. "It's there in your eyes, no matter what you say. Anne, you have no reason to fear me. And I swear you never will."

"Ian, no. I…" she began as he continued to draw closer, his arms held out from his sides, an invitation for her to come into his embrace.

"No matter what you think, this is where you belong, Anne," Ian said with gentle authority, taking yet another step in her direction.

All that Lady Bothwell had told her was true, Anne decided, as Ian continued to advance, his overwhelming magnetism banishing her hesitancy. With his dark good looks and consummate charm, it was no wonder he had earned such a reputation as a womanizer. Under her own present circumstances, Anne doubted very much there existed a female who could spurn his overtures. Yet that knowledge alone couldn't strengthen her resolve to resist him, as Anne discovered to her consternation that she was no more immune to Ian Kendrick than any other woman would be.

He was standing in front of her now, looking down at the pink-clad artiste anxiously, willing this provocative woman to come into his arms.

"Ian," she began to protest hoarsely, even as she moved toward him.

"You rang, miss?" came the peevish voice of Matthew Brewster, whose unexpected presence put an effective end to the fiery spell Ian Kendrick had cast over her. Good God! The man must have been listening to everything, Anne realized self-consciously. She, after all, had not summoned him, had not even thought to seek his assistance. Now, she didn't know whether she should fire him instantly or raise his salary.

"Yes, Brewster," Anne said with some effort, trying to maintain a degree of dignity though she could have sworn her voice betrayed her, raspy with desire as it still was. Quickly she turned from the spot where she had stood rooted to the floor and walked to the center of the room. "I should like some more coffee, and I think Mr. Kendrick would enjoy some, as well. Would you please bring us a pot?"

"It will take but a *moment*, miss," Brewster told her, though his message seemed somehow intended for Ian Kendrick.

"I won't press you further," Ian promised when the butler had departed and Anne appeared at a loss as to what to do next, "at least not today. Why don't we seat ourselves over there?" he suggested, indicating two chairs facing the hearth with a table thrust between them.

"Will it be safe, do you think?" Anne asked, the absurdity of the situation threatening to cause her to burst out laughing. She was in her own home, after all, with a watchdog for a servant! Besides that, she was Anne Hargraves, experienced espionage agent, not some empty-headed school miss. Now that she had regained control of herself, there was nothing she needed to fear.

"All too safe," Ian rejoined mournfully, laughter crinkling the marvelous gray eyes that never ceased to intrigue her. "Tell me, have you ever considered pensioning that fellow off?"

"Brewster? He's rather useful, really," Anne said, a cool smile catching the corners of her luscious mouth.

"So I see."

"Truce?" Anne suggested, pretending it was she who had the upper hand.

''For the moment,'' Ian conceded, though his eyes narrowed speculatively as he wondered what it would be like to make Anne Hargraves his own.

''Fine. Do you think we can find something to talk about, then? Something other than . . .''

''Our mutual attraction?'' Ian finished for her gently. ''Yes, I do. As a matter of fact, I'd like to speak to you about Jack.''

''A sweet boy,'' Anne murmured automatically.

''Sweet is hardly a description of my wayward younger brother,'' Ian corrected dryly. ''Since his arrival in London, the boy has been nothing but an irritant.''

''Did your presence at Madame Duvalier's really have anything to do with Jack?'' Anne asked, feeling somewhat more comfortable with Ian now, but still wanting to have her curiosity satisfied.

''It had *only* to do with Jack,'' the handsome Englishman assured her, glad to rectify his lovely companion's misconceptions concerning that matter. ''And now I find he has placed me in another embarrassing situation. In fact, that was part of the reason, a very small part, I promise you, for my visit here today.''

''What is it?'' Anne asked, wondering what any of this had to do with her.

''I fear the boy fancies himself in love with you.''

''In love!'' Anne exclaimed.

''I told him he was being ridiculous. You are, after all, a good deal older and more sophisticated than he. . . .''

''A bit older will do, Ian,'' Anne said drolly.

''Oh, you know what I mean,'' Ian protested, embarrassed by his faux pas. He would never have uttered such a statement to another female. What was it about Anne that made him say whatever popped into his head, to share with her the workings of his mind, and why didn't she appreciate it?

''It's all right, I'm not offended. Nor am I disconcerted by Jack's adoration,'' Anne said with a titter.

''Well, I am. And I fail to see what is so amusing about a young man wanting to give you his heart.''

"It's not his heart he wants to give me, Ian," Anne said, actual laughter now bubbling from her lips.

"I beg your pardon?"

"I get the impression that Jack is your brother in every sense of the word," Anne said. "But, then, I have become accustomed to dealing gently with boys who are blinded more by my reputation than they are by me. Don't worry, I will be firm but kind when I see him next."

"But you misunderstand me entirely. I don't think you should see him again," Ian protested.

"Don't you feel such a move will cause him unnecessary hurt?" Anne asked.

"I think he'll experience even more hurt, which I personally intend to deliver to him, if he tries to secure your company in the future."

Before Anne could reply Brewster had returned with a steaming pot of coffee, a mound of tiny cakes and a platter of fresh fruit. He placed all of these on the table between Anne and her guest as if he was erecting a barricade.

"Shall I stay to pour, miss?" he asked meaningfully with a slight nod in Ian's direction.

"No, thank you, Brewster, I think I am capable of handling everything by myself at the moment," Anne answered, trying to reassure this normally difficult servant that he no longer had to worry about her.

"Very good, miss. But do have a care with the coffee. It is scalding, and if it were spilled upon someone it would cause considerable pain."

"Thank you, Brewster," said Ian's hostess, hard put to conceal her merriment as she picked up the weapon her butler had thoughtfully called to her attention. "I shall remember that. But for now, I believe that will be all."

"Bloody hell, the man's a menace," Ian muttered as soon as the butler was out of hearing.

"He's only trying to protect me," Anne assured him.

"He doesn't like me much," Ian continued, taking the lethal cup of coffee Anne handed him.

"Usually it's me he dislikes," the pretty blonde confessed. "I must say, having you here is a refreshing change of pace. Perhaps I should ask you to call more often."

"I was hoping you'd suggest that," Ian said with his most devilish smile.

"I'm afraid that's impossible," Anne said, practicing with Ian the technique she intended to employ with Jack.

"Why?" asked Ian as he leaned forward and gazed into Anne's blushing face. "Because I was correct before when I suggested that I frighten you?"

"You don't scare me in the least, Ian Kendrick," Anne lied with a stubborn tilt of her chin. "It's simply that as a single female, it would do me irreparable harm to have you calling here constantly."

"Then why don't we meet in public?" Ian suggested, prompted partly by his duties to the Prince of Wales and partly because he knew he had to see Anne Hargraves again. "You know that under the watchful eye of society, I can do nothing untoward. Although I must say that in all probability, Brewster is a much more effective guardian than the dowager dragons of society."

"I am certain we shall meet at one party or another," Anne said.

"Yes, but then I shall have to share you with everyone else. It's not the same thing as being your escort."

"And are you so intent upon being my escort?"

"Without a doubt," he replied, his eyes caressing her delicate face in a manner that quite blatantly told her what he wanted and left her breathless. "Then, when you become better acquainted with me, and are ready to admit the fondness you feel, we can think about meeting more privately. Of course, I only mention this because you tell me you are not afraid."

Anne found herself highly amused by the persistent male who was Ian Kendrick. He was nothing short of incorrigible in his pursuit, yet utterly appealing at the same time. Besides, his proposal did have some merit. Nigel Conway wanted the man watched, and if she went about with Ian in society, she could comply without having to worry about disgracing herself by giving way to the longings that raged within her. Yes, seeing him in public might solve her problem very nicely.

"I've told you I'm not the sort of woman to be easily frightened, Ian, by you or any man. Would you find it agreeable to accompany me to a small dinner party being given by the Irish MPs tomorrow night?" Anne queried seductively.

"I shall be delighted," he said. "And now, I think I should take my leave before your butler feels he should come charging in again, and perhaps this time douse me with scalding coffee himself, since thankfully you have failed to do the job."

"I had no reason to do so," Anne stated with sincerity, letting Ian know that for all her femininity, Anne Hargraves could be a formidable adversary.

"I'll bear that in mind tomorrow night," he said with a chuckle, and left the room to the sound of Anne's delightful laughter.

As she watched his broad-shouldered form retreat from sight, Anne sighed softly. For the first time she could recall, she wished she had never become involved in espionage work at all.

Chapter Nine

Anne glanced at the pink satin gown embroidered with darker cashmere roses and sighed, almost dreading the long evening ahead. Clearly it was her duty to explore every possible avenue that might help them protect Victoria, but, just as certainly, her impulsive invitation to Ian Kendrick to be her escort this evening added an emotional burden she didn't relish.

At the time she had thought she could monitor his behavior and that of the Irish simultaneously. He did eventually turn up wherever she happened to be anyway. Now, however, she was having second thoughts about the situation. Was she uneasy at the possibility, remote though it was, that she would learn something to place the Irish members of Parliament under suspicion? Or was her dismay more that she would uncover further discrepancies about the man who would be squiring her?

This morning Nigel had reported that Kendrick, as the third son of a respected though minor baronet, had been educated in philosophy at university, but apparently had no career, few political convictions and evidently even fewer obligations, since he was frequently present at social events involving the Prince of Wales or his associates. Also intriguing was the fact that other than a small amount settled on him by his father, Ian seemed to possess no visible income to sustain his elite social position. But most damning of all was that so many of Bertie's friends were anxious for Victoria's demise.

There was no doubt that Ian was a charmer, a man who could easily ingratiate himself into the affairs of those who interested him, playing on their needs while revealing nothing of himself. Was that what he had done to her, Anne wondered with a start, reddening at the memory of her surprising loss of control in the face of his romantic advances yesterday morning. True, their encounter had been enjoyable, but had he been as affected as she... or had he only played the game for some ulterior motive of his own?

Tonight, she would have to be on guard against his overtures, despite the fact that her traitorous body craved his touch the way it had no man since Louis. Rarely had Anne suffered misgivings about an assignment, though she'd handled many more complicated ones in the past. However, dividing her attentions between the interests of the Irish and the growing enigma who was Ian would be a balancing act requiring supreme concentration.

Examining her reflection in the mirror, she found some consolation in her appearance. Her green eyes, with the aid of petroleum on the lashes, appeared to sparkle with excitement; a touch of rouge enlivened her cheeks and heightened her normally red lips. If the evening went as so many had in the past, men would forget the cautions of their governments in an attempt to impress her, and she would learn all she and Nigel needed to know. That happy thought filled her with self-confidence as she directed her attention to her hair.

How should she wear it for the best effect? Uncertain of her mood, the blonde dawdled before the mirror trying one style then another as the moments passed. Having traveled so often in areas where accomplished ladies' maids were unheard of, she had come to prefer dressing her own long curls, knowing she would be satisfied with her work.

Finally she chose the traditional style she preferred for public performances, and the job was quickly accomplished. Her golden hair was swept upward and piled high atop her head with a few pearls entwined for romantic effect while the back was arranged in a plait, looped with a velvet ribbon that matched her gown. Around her neck she placed a similar band displaying her most precious gift from

Louis, a delicately etched cameo of ivory and ebony, presented just prior to his fateful mission to Africa. Now it was her lucky charm, an exceptionally fine piece of jewelry that graced her every official performance but, more importantly, it was her reassurance that Louis was still a part of her life. This night, something told her she would need the comfort of his memory.

Finished with her toilette, Anne rang for her maid. She had long ago shunned the unnecessary discomfort of corsets and horsehair bustles, but the elaborate draping of her gown required an extra pair of hands to adjust it. Bess had the perfect touch.

To the singer's immense surprise however, it was Matthew Brewster who answered her summons.

"You rang, Miss Hargraves?"

"Not for you, Brewster, unless you have a mind to help me dress. What is keeping Bess?"

"Don't you recall, miss? At luncheon you told the entire staff they might have the rest of the day off since you were going out for the evening and wouldn't require anyone's services. I thought such a gesture inappropriate since tomorrow is their half day, but you insisted." The disapproving servant sniffed.

"Then why are you here?" asked Anne, annoyed at her unusual forgetfulness in her anxiety to clear the house of unnecessary eyes and ears should Ian return with her.

"I had no special plans and thought to enjoy a quiet evening with a good book," the servant explained uncomfortably, quite unable to reveal the truth—that Conway had forbidden him to leave Anne unprotected any time she was home.

"Oh," the blonde replied, trying to decide what to do now. Brewster would likely be absolutely horrified, but despite his sartorial shortcomings, he had to be better than no one. Didn't butlers often double as valets? "Well, then, what do you know about dressing women?"

"I very much fear my knowledge is limited to undressing them, miss," the portly butler confessed with the barest suggestion of a smile. "I am, however, a quick study."

"Hmm." She considered, startled by the manservant's nearly humorous reply. While the idea of his studying her unclothed body made her faintly uneasy, if she was to be ready when Ian arrived, she had no other choice. Abandoning her silken robe, Anne stood boldly before the butler in chemisette, bloomers and stockings and issued curt instructions.

"All right. Take the silk underskirt, the deep rose colored one. Slip it over my head, draw the ties in the back and fasten the small buttons at the bottom of the bodice to the underskirt."

"You don't wear a corset, Miss Hargraves?" inquired Brewster, red-faced now but gamely complying with her orders.

"My waist measures only eighteen inches in its natural state, sir. I see no logical reason to suffer unspeakable torture to reduce it by two more, do you?" Anne demanded, annoyed at his impertinence yet amused at the man's attempts to avert his eyes and avoid touching her as he attached the bodice and skirt. For such an ungainly man, he had gentle hands.

"No, miss, I just—ah, what comes next?" Deciding even Nigel wouldn't expect him to answer so dangerous a query, Brewster wanted nothing more than to be finished with the Hargraves assignment, especially this aspect of it. Surely such a task as playing lady's maid was beyond the call of duty, particularly since he couldn't allow himself to enjoy the experience.

"The gown itself. Slip your hands down through the neck opening, raise the gown over your arms and lower it gently over my head, but be careful not to muss my hair," directed the blonde. Realizing she'd have to accommodate the butler's short stature, she leaned forward, allowing the garment to fall from his arms onto her slender form. "Good. Now look toward the bottom of the skirt on the left and right below my hips. There are two cashmere roses, which have small loops of material in them. Gather the loops to the back and secure them to the hooks at the waist. Then arrange the draping of the skirt carefully. It should fall symmetrically in neat gathers all the way around."

Standing patiently as the man tut-tutted and circled her, repeatedly adjusting the skirt an inch in one direction, then a half inch in the other, and again a smidgen back, Anne awaited his approval. When his words came, however, they weren't exactly encouraging.

"Well, I suppose if that's the effect you want, miss, then we have it," he muttered as the door knocker sounded loudly below. "I'd best answer that."

In an instant, the butler had escaped, leaving Anne to twist and turn before her mirror in a futile attempt to discover what was lacking in her appearance.

"Damn that man! There is nothing, absolutely nothing wrong with this gown or the way I look," she fumed in exasperation as she put on her shoes, gathered her handbag and gloves and descended the stairs. "I will not permit that oafish butler to make me doubt myself."

Once Anne saw Ian Kendrick's face, however, she had no further qualms about the effect of her costume. Indeed, it appeared that for the third time in their brief acquaintance, she had rendered the poor man speechless, though this time it was thankfully for reasons other than fury. His mouth opened and closed twice; he cleared his throat and coughed, but still words failed Ian.

"Thank you for being so prompt, Mr. Kendrick," Anne said at last, feeling charitable toward the poor fellow. It was, after all, the first time he had seen her in full performance regalia, and it wasn't his fault that he was unaccustomed to such dramatic apparel.

"I only regret that I wasn't earlier, Miss Hargraves. It would have allowed me that much more time to drink in your intoxicating beauty. You do look ravishing in that gown," he answered at last, bowing regally from the waist.

"Thank you, sir, though I must say that you look quite fashionable yourself," replied Anne, noticing not for the first time how splendid a figure Ian Kendrick made in dress finery. "It is nice to know that a *gentleman* appreciates a lady's efforts," she added, directing a pointed stare at Brewster, who was waiting by the door. The butler, however, remained professionally impassive, ignoring her implied criticism.

"If you will just help me with my cloak, Mr. Kendrick, we can leave. Brewster, you needn't wait up; I did promise you the evening off."

"Yes, miss, though since you did have need of my services earlier, I warrant you might again later."

"I doubt that, Brewster," she answered, uncomfortable at the memory of his comments about undressing women. *That* was surely a chore she would not want him to undertake.

"I will be more than happy to see to the lady's needs," added Ian.

If you're up to it, thought the manservant, though his verbal message was far more deferential.

"Very good, sir, miss. Good night." As he closed the door on the departing couple, his thoughts dwelled on their eventual return. "I shall, nonetheless, be available."

Outside, as Ian handed Anne into the private carriage he had hired for the evening, he was quite pleased that he had specified an enclosed vehicle. Anne was so remarkably lovely this evening, he would never be able to control his desire for her until the end of the night. The fact that she had dismissed the butler was a good sign but, in the meanwhile, they could at least share a few unobserved embraces en route to their destination.

Entering the coach and seating himself beside the singer as though such was common practice, he pretended not to notice her look of surprise, even as he cautioned himself not to take too much for granted. She had, after all, limited their physical enjoyment of one another yesterday; perhaps she was not as available as he had assumed.

However, Bertie's recently voiced suspicions of Anne echoed in Ian's brain even as his body reacted only to her womanly charms. Realizing that this evening was an unexpected opportunity to observe her in her professional mode, Ian determined not to forgo his own professional impartiality. The life of his sovereign could conceivably depend on his investigations; he must not let her down. First, though, he reasoned, perhaps the man in him could enjoy the woman in Anne before the performers took to the stage.

"As overblown as my compliments may have seemed, Anne, you do look splendid this evening. Every man present will envy me with you gracing my arm," he assured, resting his hand lightly over hers.

"Who said I would be on your arm? I'm not like Victoria yet, infirm enough to need a man or a cane to support me," she bristled, rejecting her desire to encourage Ian's advances. As debonair as Louis had always appeared in evening finery, she had always believed that no other man could compare; yet Ian did.

"But you asked me to be your escort. I thought—"

"That Anne Hargraves needed an escort, the protection of a man, sir? That is hardly true." The woman laughed, relenting as she saw his crestfallen look. "I invited you because I enjoy your company and I thought the evening would amuse you, not because I am a helpless woman in need of support."

"I never pictured you that way," affirmed the broad-shouldered male, taking her gloved hand in his and slowly slipping away the kidskin so he could caress her silken fingers. When she didn't protest, he lifted her hand to his lips and kissed each fingertip in turn, murmuring between kisses. "I find you beautiful...gracious...intelligent... sophisticated and...extremely seductive, especially tonight, but certainly never helpless."

"Good, because right now I have every intention of reclaiming those five kisses you just stole from me," Anne informed him, firmly banishing Louis from her mind. Leaning toward Ian, she placed her hands, one gloved, one bare, on his cheeks, and held his head still while she slowly, excruciatingly teased his lips with her own.

The light, almost ethereal sensations made Ian want more, but he knew better than to press her now. This escalation from hand to mouth had been of her choosing; he mustn't interfere. Finally she finished.

"There, sir, payment in full."

"Maybe you would consider starting again," he suggested tentatively. "Though kissing is more fun if we work at it together, you know."

"I'll not argue," Anne murmured, allowing herself permission to enjoy this small intimacy with Ian. Yet moments later, as the carriage turned a corner, she came back to reality, sensing herself surrendering too completely to Ian's practiced touch. She panicked, pushing him away and gasping for breath.

How could I do this now? How can I possibly behave so irresponsibly, so impervious to the danger facing Victoria? The accusations echoed in her skull as her throat constricted, further disconcerting the woman juggling two roles. What was it about Ian Kendrick that unnerved her, Anne Hargraves, who had conquered three continents, she wondered helplessly, struggling still for air.

"Anne, what's wrong?" Ian cried in concern. "Are you all right? Did I—"

"No, no." She stalled, relieved that her voice, though a husky whisper, was still functioning. After all, shortly she would be on stage, a command performer before an adoring if limited audience…at least Nigel presumed they would be adoring. "No, Ian, it isn't you. Sometimes, as silly as it seems, I still become a bit nervous before public appearances and suddenly I couldn't breathe and—"

"I'm sorry. The last thing on earth I would want to do is to get you excited, my dear—no, I fear that's not quite the truth." Ian chuckled self-consciously when Anne laughed. "Now is not the time for that type of excitement, though."

"Nor the place," agreed the blonde, feeling more at ease that he hadn't misunderstood and considered her a tease. She found, to her surprise, she did care for him, perhaps more than she should, and that continued to be upsetting. "Later, Ian, when I've finished working, maybe we could continue—"

"If you like," he interrupted, attempting to reassure her by bringing her ungloved hand to his mouth and gently kissing its palm, "we can do anything or nothing."

"With an offer like that, Mr. Kendrick, don't be surprised by my demands," she said as the carriage halted.

"I will be counting the minutes," he assured her, opening the door and hopping out, ready to take on the world, knowing the woman he escorted was indeed interested in furthering their relationship.

Two hours later, however, the man was not quite so overjoyed. Small though the gathering was, a dinner party for twenty, including Anne and himself, it seemed every man present, and there were fourteen of them, had a greater claim on Anne's time than he did. As soon as the two of them had arrived, she had been swept from his side and surrounded by two, three or four men at every instant, each intent on edging a bit closer to her, clamoring for her full concentration. Once or twice he had managed to catch her eye and smile encouragement, but he was unable to actually get near the lovely blonde he was theoretically escorting. Deciding to devote some time to the job at hand, he attempted to circulate among the men and discuss politics, home rule and Victoria's jubilee, but the only topic the Irish were concerned with tonight was Anne Hargraves.

Even at dinner, he and Anne had been separated, he on the right of the hostess at one end of the long table and she on the right of the host at the other. For his part, Ian was forced to converse politely with Mrs. O'Grady on the problems of keeping a proper Irish garden flourishing on English soil, while Mrs. Feeney held forth on the peculiar lack of good Irish stout in English public houses. Once the meal had concluded, he'd been captured by Miss Amanda Feeney, whose brother was a missionary, and her friend, Margaret Ryan. They had a great deal to say on the dearth of suitable entertainment for respectable young women in London, and actually asked him to recommend some places. For a moment the devil in him almost mentioned Madame Duvalier's, but he couldn't bring himself to embarrass Anne that way, and he mouthed the typical attractions instead, the museums and gardens, even as his mind raced along different paths.

In actuality, of course, the only thing all the women had really wanted were the details of his relationship with Anne Hargraves. Where had they met? Had he known her long? What were their future plans?

What could he tell them? Ian didn't know the truth himself. Was it possible that Anne was only a suspect who required investigation? Or, no matter how often he denied the idea, had the woman already stolen his heart?

In any case, the dark-haired Englishman was not about to discuss the matter with females he barely knew. Hell, he couldn't afford to discuss it with anyone, even Bertie, his only real confidant. What could he say to the prince? Sorry, old man, I can't continue to suspect Miss Hargraves in the possible assassination plot—I love her, so she must be innocent. The prince would think him mad... and perhaps, for the first time in his life, Ian acknowledged, he was, mad with love rather than just desire.

Straightening his tie and excusing himself from the ladies, he made his way to Anne's side and handed her a glass of champagne, taking the liberty of allowing his hand to linger over hers. She smiled briefly and sent a nod in his direction before including him in the conversation, apparently a political one.

"I was just saying that I cannot believe Mr. Parnell actually wrote that letter the *Times* published," she explained. "As much as he wants Irish home rule, he is too honorable to condone murder, especially a member of Gladstone's own family."

"Gladstone's family?" echoed Meg Ryan, who had followed Ian across the room.

"Lord Cavendish, whom the Fenians killed in that ambush, was married to Gladstone's niece," Anne said. "Anyway, Charles Parnell would never support violence as a means to political change—let alone advocate it in print."

"No man in his right mind, Irish or not, considers violence a legitimate means of resolving disputes, be they personal or political," agreed Ian, suffering only a small twinge of conscience as he remembered his brawl with Jack.

"So we've all been saying in letters to the *Times*, and even to the queen herself," commented O'Grady.

"And all the years the Irish starved while the English landowners got fat should just be forgotten?" demanded Flaherty indignantly. "No one who's not one of us knows the price the Irish have already paid. It's time the English learned.''

''Then tell them, man, don't kill them,'' urged Ian, wondering if this was the break he'd been looking for. ''One or two dead Englishmen, no matter to whom they're related, won't change governmental policy.''

''Maybe not, but a deceased monarch might, that is if she doesn't outlive us all,'' said Anne with a small laugh, trying to encourage criticism of Victoria. Ian looked at her oddly, but the others nodded. ''After all, sooner or later, Bertie has to take the throne.''

''Aye, but will he be any different? Given his sporting ways, gaming and hunting, he's barely interested in his own heritage, let alone ours,'' argued Feeney.

''Kendrick, I've seen you at the races with the prince. How do you think he views home rule?'' asked O'Grady.

''I'm really not a confidant of his,'' denied Ian, ''but the few times we've spoken, Ireland was not a topic of conversation. To my knowledge, he's most concerned with the plans for Victoria's jubilee next month, presuming she lives that long,'' he added with a nod to Anne.

Was he merely echoing her words or was he making her a promise, the startled agent wondered. She remained silent, deciding to allow this interesting conversation to set its own course.

''Well, if she does, not everyone will be cheering,'' grumbled Flaherty. ''If home rule hasn't passed by then, the Irish members will boycott the festivities altogether.''

''Liam, you didn't tell me that,'' complained Mrs. O'Grady. ''I especially ordered a new bonnet and gown for the occasion.''

''Miss Hargraves, perhaps now is the time for you to share your wondrous gift with us,'' proposed O'Grady suddenly to avoid listening to any more of his wife's carping. ''Surely your beautiful voice will lift all our spirits.''

Nodding agreeably as the others took seats around the drawing room, Anne finished her champagne, handed her glass to O'Grady and moved toward the piano. Ian came to stand beside her, unexpectedly squeezed her hand and whispered in her ear.

"I am certain your audience will love you as much as I do, Anne. My heart already knows how wonderful you are. Show them."

Startled by his words, the golden-haired beauty opened her mouth to reply but only a tiny squeak escaped. Oh, Lord, what she had feared most had happened: her personal interests had impeded her professional talents. Now what?

Seeking to give herself time to recover, Anne tried to clear her throat, but succeeded only in coughing uncontrollably. Oh, why had she ever let him into her heart? But suddenly Ian was beside her again with a glass of lemon and water and a kind word.

"A bit of an unhappy audience at the moment, Annie, my girl, but you have the charm and talent to make them smile as though they'd found the pot of gold at the end of the rainbow. Take deep breaths, that's better. Sip the lemonade, don't gulp it, and you'll be fine," he assured her, totally unaware that he or, rather, her unexpected feelings for him, were the source of her problem. "In my opinion, sweetheart, you couldn't sing a sour note if you tried, but don't try just in case these folk aren't quite as in love with you as I am. I know you'll bring them around."

Swallowing deeply and blinking back the tears, Anne forced her instincts to take over. Softly, slowly, she emptied her mind of all but the need to perform. Then she opened her mouth and sang, her voice as sweet and clear as a crystal bell, its tone pure enchantment even as her thoughts began to tumble one upon the other again, distancing her from her own performance.

In love? Ian Kendrick said he was *in love* with me? She marveled, her throat starting to tighten until she concentrated on separating her frightening thoughts from the words she was singing. Damn him, just when I'm under such pressure to find Victoria's possible assassin, he casually tosses out those words I've longed to hear ever since Louis died. But, at the moment, there is so much happening, I can't afford to believe him. It couldn't be . . . or could it?

There is no real evidence connecting Ian to the rumors of an assassination plot. All Nigel has are my own suspicions, reminded her heart. Should those foolish thoughts deny me happiness? she argued silently, even as she began one of her most popular love songs. Wasn't I the one who insisted Nigel investigate poor Ian, all for no real reason except my own discomfort around him? Now it seems that uneasiness might have been a shield I was using to protect my heart, and if I'm satisfied with his innocence...

All of a sudden, Ian felt a charge of energy as Anne's brilliant green eyes sparkled at him, as electric as lightning itself, holding him tightly in their gaze as the songstress seemed to be singing to him alone. There would be no more pretense, no avoiding the inevitable, he realized from her manner; she had made up her mind to acknowledge her needs and permit him to fulfill them. Anne was as ready as he to take their passion that final step to the ultimate pinnacle of existence.

Nothing could interfere with their pleasure tonight, Ian reflected, if only they could escape this infernal reception that threatened to last forever, especially if Anne kept singing so beautifully. Looking pointedly at his pocket watch, the gray-eyed rogue signaled her to close her performance, but when she tried, her audience wouldn't permit it. Two encores were demanded, then a third before, finally, they accepted her pleas of exhaustion, an excuse Ian fervently hoped was untrue. Still, elaborate words of praise, expressions of gratitude and amazement at her talent continued to echo over them as he retrieved her cloak and hurried her to the waiting carriage.

Then they were alone again, but given the emotions running rampant between them and the inescapable climax ahead, their first words were a few minutes in coming. Ian sat across from Anne, and the silence, though easy, was unexpected until she took the initiative.

"Thank you. I thought I'd never be allowed to leave," she said, patting the seat beside her in invitation. At his raised eyebrow, she laughed delicately. "Well, Mr. Kendrick, you did say we could do anything we chose this evening."

"Or nothing whatsoever," he teased, moving across the swaying coach to draw her into his arms, his actions clearly indicating his choice for the night ahead.

"Whatever you like," Anne murmured softly against his chest after they'd exchanged kisses long enough for each to feel confident about the road they'd chosen. Comfortable now with what was to come, they delighted in holding hands, sharing sweet kisses and tender embraces as the coach carried them homeward. The flames of passion would yet find them.

Had Ian any doubts as to Anne's intent, they evaporated when he assisted her from the carriage.

"Why don't you send the driver home for a few hours?" she suggested softly. "That is, if you would care to come in."

"By all means, I would love to," he said, quickly sharing a word with the coachman as coins exchanged hands and the vehicle pulled away.

Seeing Anne standing patiently in the circle of hazy light from the street's gas lamps, the Englishman was again taken by her near-ethereal beauty. Her flaxen curls shone while the small pearls in her coiffure seemed to wink in amusement as she waited for him to join her at the foot of the steps. Instead, spurred by a mad impulse, Ian charged forward, lifted her into his arms and carried her up the stairs to the front door while she giggled uncontrollably.

"You are not quite a knight in shining armor, but I'll admit you swept me off my feet," she said when her voice returned, a tender echo of vibrant emotion.

"Good evening, Miss Hargraves, sir," intoned Brewster suddenly, standing at the open door and guarding the entryway though Anne had neither knocked nor used her key. His sudden appearance as well as his next words would have banished all of the enchantment Ian and Anne had been experiencing if Ian were not carrying his lady close to his heart. "Are you all right, miss? Is there something wrong with your feet?"

Ian frowned as he brushed past the overly conscientious servant and entered Anne's home. It would appear the butler had been awaiting their return despite Anne's orders, not a good sign unless he could outmaneuver the man to allow

them some privacy. Though servants weren't supposed to
carry tales, Ian, for one, didn't want even a silent observer
to tonight's events.

"I know you are concerned for your mistress, Brewster,
but I assure you nothing is wrong with her," he explained,
"and she is in very capable hands."

"Of course, sir, but perhaps you should put her down,"
suggested the manservant with a disapproving glance at the
hall clock. "It is rather late."

"Which is exactly why I told you not to wait up," rebuked Anne with a carefree tone, once more on her feet
though still slightly flushed from Ian's attentions. "As it is,
we decided to return earlier than we'd planned, but I've no
need of your services."

"Since I am here, miss, I'll take your wrap and wish your
caller a good night so you can retire," stated the butler,
pointedly holding the front door ajar.

"There is no need for that. Mr. Kendrick is not leaving."

"Not leaving?" repeated Brewster in shocked tones.

"Not at the moment, no. So you may take his coat as well
as mine, and shut the door," instructed Anne, her words
polite but her tone becoming icy. This was one time she
would not tolerate the servant's interference, and she'd be
certain he knew it.

"His coat? But he's not wearing one," protested the butler, obediently shutting the door even as he hoped against
hope the woman wasn't suggesting what he thought. How
would he ever explain this to Nigel?

"Of course he is, a formal dress coat, which, attractive as
it may be, isn't necessary for an informal evening in my
music room," said the woman, helping Ian off with the
garment in question. "Now, hang this up and bring us some
brandy. Then you are dismissed for the night, and Brewster, I do not wish to see you wandering about. I will see Mr.
Kendrick out when he is ready to leave."

"If he ever is," muttered the butler beneath his breath.

"What was that?" challenged Anne, not really caring
what the man had said; it was his manner that continued to
irk her. She would not permit him to display such disre-
spect. "I would remind you, Brewster, that this is *my* home.

The manner in which I choose to entertain my guests is absolutely none of your affair.''

"Anne, perhaps that was not the wisest choice of words," cautioned Ian, gentleman enough to worry about the servants' gossip.

"Or precisely the correct one," she replied. "In either case, it is nothing Brewster will worry himself about, is it?"

"No, miss, but which brandy did you want?" asked Nigel's man, burning at her rebuke and the fact that he had to accept it.

"The best, of course. Mr. Kendrick is a dear friend," stated the blonde without hesitation. As the butler turned to the back of the house, she caught Ian's hand in hers, leading the way to the music room. She confided softly, "And soon, I hope, to be much dearer, though Brewster needn't know that."

"I imagine the man suspects as much," Ian said with a smile. "He isn't exactly doltish, you know."

"No, but this might be easier if he were. As foolish as it is, I feel almost as though he were my disapproving father," she confessed, amazed at her own sense of embarrassment that the butler knew her intentions for the evening.

"Well, imagine how I feel. I half expect the fellow to return with a loaded shotgun along with the brandy." Ian chuckled, pulling a pliant Anne into his arms. "But I am more than willing to risk his wrath for one of your delicious kisses."

"Ah, you give me such courage," she said with a smile, happily obliging Ian's suggestion.

So enraptured with one another were they that Brewster entered, noisily deposited the tray with its brandy snifters and departed without disturbing them. It was only when he emphatically slammed the door on his way out that his absence was noted and appreciated.

Moments later, finding herself suddenly overwhelmed by the ever increasing sensations Ian's kisses were evoking in her body, Anne gently eased herself from his embrace and led him toward the center of the room. She was almost afraid to stop touching him for fear he'd misunderstand, but she had no choice; she needed a respite. As much as her

racing pulse, ragged breathing and overheated being wanted
to hurry their joining, the artist in her relished each subtle
change and wanted to enjoy every nuance of their loving . . . or, asked her heart, were thoughts of Louis interfering? Brushing aside the question, she looked at Ian with a
smile.

"If you will light a fire while I lock the door and fetch our
brandies, we can be certain of our privacy," she suggested,
needing to offer an explanation for her withdrawal. Besides, knowing Brewster, the man could well be camped
right outside the music room door, ready to barge in at the
least excuse.

"Good idea. I've seen all I want of your butler for a
while," Ian agreed, brushing his errant forelock off his face
as he accepted the brandy and downed it in one gulp, giving
her a rakish grin. "To tell the truth, I had hoped I was
warming you sufficiently that we'd not need a fire."

"You are, my love," said Anne, sipping at her brandy and
setting it down, "but then, I'm still dressed. We can rem-
edy that situation, though, if you'll do me the favor of un-
fastening the loops at the back of my gown, under the
waist," she added with a teasing grin.

Turning her back to him, she was momentarily startled
when his firm hands encircled her waist, hugging her to him
before he did as she asked. Even as his hands were occupied, his roving mouth descended on her nearly bare shoulder and left a trail of kisses, leading to that vulnerable spot
behind her ear. Tenderly, his lips delivered pleasure, ex-
ploiting her weakness there, allowing his mouth to heat her
flesh so thoroughly she thought she would ignite more
readily than the kindling in the fireplace. Then, nudging
aside her braid, Ian began to pay loving homage to her neck,
making her shiver with anticipation, even as his long slender fingers started to unplait her hair, trailing golden flames
down her back.

"Oh, do fix the fire, Ian, please," she asked suddenly, her
voice tremulous as her shaking fingers grasped the ribbon
displaying her cameo and unfastened it. As much as she had

loved Louis, this was a new time, a new man and a new love, one that ought not be spoiled by the past; wondrous as it had once been.

"Of course," Ian said agreeably, ready to comply with so easy a request. Indeed, the way he felt about Anne now, he could refuse her nothing—even, he thought desperately, if she should ask that he leave. Yet in his heart he knew they'd become so much a part of one another already, that was one thing she'd not demand of him. So confident was he of that fact that after he'd started the flames dancing over the logs, he removed his waistcoat and opened his shirt before turning to face her. For a moment he was startled not to find her near the door where he'd left her. Where had she gone? But then, his anxious eyes discovered her and were well pleased with the object of their scrutiny.

Having abandoned her silken and cashmere gown, shoes, stockings and, unbeknownst to Ian, her bloomers, Anne was still nearly covered by the filmy V-shaped chemisette and her rose-colored underskirt. Without the least hesitation, she moved toward him, almost dancing into his arms while strains of music from an invisible piano suddenly echoed in the air.

"What is that?" Ian asked as he embraced her slender form, holding her close to him, massaging her spine, sensing her growing need. Trailing his fingers down her back, he began to unbutton her bodice from the skirt while nibbling gently at her already swollen lips. He had always imagined hearing music when he kissed her, but this time it was different. There *was* music in the room with them, imperfect though it was when compared to Anne's voice.

"One of Mr. Edison's phonographs," she explained, running her hands over his chest, her fingers curling the fine hairs and teasing them in her grasp. All at once her mood was impatient, her need more desperate; could it be because she'd finally discarded Louis? "I use it sometimes to rehearse and I thought the music in my heart should be shared by the man who is causing it to play."

Opening his shirt further, she kissed his nipples and suddenly could wait no longer for the satisfaction after which she hungered. As he released the underskirt from around her waist and it dropped to the floor, revealing her unshielded womanhood to his startled glance, she unbuttoned his trousers.

Though she still longed to feel his lips upon hers and his caress upon her breasts, those desires were nothing compared to the cravings that took control of her body. After so many empty years, she fairly shook with the need to feel a man within her. But it could not be just any man. No, only Ian Kendrick would do.

"Anne, are you sure?" he questioned hoarsely, unprepared for her abrupt escalation of their loving.

"Absolutely. I want you, Ian, now," she declared, sinking to the floor and positioning herself to admit this welcome invader. Then he was part of the moment, helping her. Catching her buttocks in his anxious hands, he lifted her as she raised her legs to encircle his waist.

Moving against him as he held her, Anne felt the beginnings of pleasure as waves of excitement began to build, the tide of passion driving her forward. Faster and faster, harder and harder, she urged him onward as though she was trying to obliterate years of loneliness with this one glorious interlude. Then came the ultimate reward, the sudden shudder as Ian found his release and triggered her own, sending sparks of electricity cascading over her as he called her name.

"Annie, my love." His words echoed in the air.

Otherwise there was only the crackle of the fire in the room. Mr. Edison's magic machine had played its limited tune, but in their hearts, the symphony's crescendo sounded yet as their breathing slowed and life returned to itself.

"Annie, I've never felt—what I mean is," Ian began as they lay before the fire a while later. "Usually..."

"I wanted our first time to be primitive and fierce," murmured the sated woman in his arms, feeling a twinge of fear as she realized her forward behavior might have offended him. "Did you mind?"

"Of course not, but are you ready to try it again, my way this time?" he asked, wanting to pleasure her even as she had so excited him.

"Whatever you like." Anne giggled, repeating their phrase of earlier in the evening.

Rolling her to one side, Ian slowly undid her chemisette, freeing her breasts to accept his attention, and drew her to face him.

"Oh, I know I'll like this just as much," she sighed, already feeling shivers of excitement as he licked at one nipple while his fingers caressed the other. Stretched out beside him before the fire, Anne luxuriated in Ian's concentration to detail as he left no part of her unattended. From her toes to the crown of her head, she experienced his loving worship, her body rippling with building tension as his touch fulfilled needs she'd never before been aware of, until finally she had to beg for release.

"Ian, now, please—"

"Whatever you like," he answered huskily, his own desire so intense that he now craved satisfaction as urgently as did Anne. Entering her swiftly, he thrust to meet her motion, and again the earth exploded for him, unleashing passions he hadn't known existed. Together, they rode the aftershocks of an epiphany that surpassed all others, relishing the closeness they felt as their breathing slowed and the world resumed its normal pace.

Words couldn't express what they had lived through, so Anne remained silent, perfectly content to be in Ian's embrace, watching the flickering flames that embodied her heart's racing.

"Annie, I loved you before tonight, but now I think I adore you," he murmured in her ear as he watched the fire, knowing full well their own consumption had been even more spectacular.

"Those are difficult words for me to say," she whispered tentatively, "but I think I've shown you how I feel, Ian.

Don't ask any more than that right now.'' She did, after all, have an assassin to catch; much as her heart wanted to abandon the effort, her sense of duty wouldn't permit it.

''All right,'' he agreed, surprised and somewhat relieved that for now at least Anne didn't want total commitment. Though he would have liked to forget everything but this moment and time, he did have a job that had to be done. For tonight, however, he was a man first and an employee of the Crown second, and for that small blessing, he fervently thanked God.

Chapter Ten

Hours later, in the pale sunlight of early morning, the delicious memories of Ian's persistent lovemaking caressed Anne's body with a pleasurable tingling sensation. Unconsciously, she squirmed into her pillows, and a contented sigh escaped her lips as she recalled the smoldering manner in which last night had drawn to a close.

They had stood in the central hallway, Ian's coat draped casually over one arm as the other had reached for her.

"How can you tell me to leave you now? After what we have just discovered in each other's arms? I want to spend the night with you, to hold you close and hear your heartbeats echo mine," Ian had murmured, pulling Anne closer, dipping his head and kissing the sensitive hollow at the base of her throat, the muscles of which had become remarkably relaxed, she recalled now in amusement.

"You know you can't." She had fairly giggled. "If Brewster should find you here in the morning, I would never be able to deal with him."

"What do you care? Sack the blighter," Ian had insisted between kisses, his words muffled against her skin as his lips moved along her collarbone and then down over the swell of her breast. "You know you find the man unbearable anyway."

"So I do," Anne had absently replied, her breath becoming faster and shallower at the persuasion Ian was employing. "But no, Ian, not tonight," she murmured, struggling to retain some degree of control, denying him her bed even as she made her body so readily available.

Blinded by passion, Ian had continued to employ every gentle inducement he knew in an attempt to change her mind. But in the end, he had reluctantly though gracefully acceded to her request and gone home.

Now, much later, Anne ran her slender fingers over the cool sheets and wondered what it would be like if Ian was lying beside her. Though her dark-haired Englishman had not shared her bed, Anne found it quite easy, after the intensity of the lovemaking that had been theirs, to picture him there, to feel his presence lighting the dimness of her room.

Oh, how sorely tempted she had been to pass the dark hours before dawn enfolded in Ian's muscular arms. Yet how could she have told him that while she had accepted the passionate homage he had paid her, she couldn't permit herself to give him more than that?

In reality, if she had had any sense at all, she would have kept him at arm's length, though somehow she doubted so lusty a man as Ian would have stood for that. But last night, her desire had won, overpowering any logic she might possess so that she had surrendered quite willingly to Ian's bold demands. Ian Kendrick wielded mastery over her body and could ignite her desires whenever he wished with a mere whispered word, a gentle touch or a smoldering look.

Tracing the lips Ian had made his own with the tip of her finger, Anne found the idea both disturbing and exciting. But she excused her reactions to him with the thought that she had not yet surrendered her heart. Nor would she do so until Victoria had safely celebrated her jubilee and Anne knew for sure that Ian had no connection to any plot to harm the queen.

Though she was fast coming to believe that Ian was no traitor to England, she was not so overwhelmed by him that she was willing to wager the queen's life on her own feelings. And despite her professional instincts crying out their warning that she be careful, in the aftermath of Ian's loving, awash with the lingering sensations of his expert ardor, Anne was content with the position she had taken. At least, she was content for the moment. She wanted no searching examinations of her soul to diminish the joy she was still experiencing hours after her lover had left.

It was almost mid-morning before Anne appeared in her dining room. For some reason she had found herself ravenously hungry, and did not bother to dress before she descended the stairs, clad in a soft peach nightdress and wrapper, both festooned with yards of delicate lace and velvet ribbons.

Brewster took one disapproving look at her attire and with a scowl set an extra place at the table.

"I trust you slept well, miss," he intoned in the manner of a vicar delivering a sermon.

"Yes, when I finally closed my eyes, I fell into a deep sleep indeed, Brewster. Thank you for inquiring," Anne said with a delicate yawn designed to both aggravate the old fossil and hide her amusement at the same time.

"How fortunate for us all, miss," he rejoined with blatant insincerity as he moved to pour steaming liquid into a cup and then proceeded to place it before Anne.

"Ah, tea! How delightful," Anne said, raising an eyebrow in surprise but refusing to be piqued. "I believe in a change of pace every once in a while. How astute of you to realize that, Brewster."

"I realize more than you know," Brewster muttered, placing additional flatware beside the second plate.

"Do you?" Anne asked archly. "Then perhaps you can tell me who is to be my breakfast companion, since I myself have no knowledge of having invited anyone to share my table this morning. If I had been made aware there was to be a guest, I would have donned something more becoming," she continued, indicating her semisheer ensemble.

"Your pardon, miss. My mistake," Brewster replied implacably, a slight reddening of his cheeks the only sign that he was disconcerted. Deftly, he removed the extra service and then with great dignity began to serve Anne her breakfast.

As he removed a platter to the kitchen, however, Anne could have sworn she heard him muttering, "Harrumph!

From the look of him I would have thought he'd have been worth feeding afterward."

With a joyful laugh, Anne drank her cup of proper English tea. This morning she would keep doubts and problems and irritable servants at bay. What a wonderful change Ian Kendrick had wrought in her world!

A few moments later brought a pleasant surprise, when, as though he was relieved to finally be able to announce a guest of quality, Brewster came into the dining room to inform Anne that the Duchess of Moreland and her daughter Audrey were calling.

"Show them in here, please," Anne directed, unable to keep herself from adding a small barb. "I suppose we'll be having guests for breakfast, after all. How you manage to anticipate such things, Brewster, is no doubt one of the many reasons you have earned such a remarkable reputation as a butler. How lucky I am to have you in my employ."

Ignoring Anne's remarks and unusually good humor, the cause of which he suspected only too strongly, Brewster was back in a moment, ushering in the two women.

"Oh, my dear, how sorry I am to have caught you still at breakfast," Aurora Palmer gushed. "But then you must have been quite naughty and stayed out until all hours to still be at table with your morning meal when so shortly it will be time for luncheon. It is good of you to receive us, considering the circumstances, but then, I hope that we have become well enough acquainted that we do not have to stand on ceremony."

"Indeed, we do not. Won't you both please join me?" Anne asked with enough graciousness to satisfy even Brewster, as she indicated that the ladies should take seats on either side of her.

"Now, my dear, since we have found you just stirring you simply must tell me where you were engaged last evening, and who was there," Lady Moreland commanded, settling in for a session of gossip.

"Tea, milady? Or coffee?" Brewster interrupted, holding both pots before him, the mention of her favorite morning drink causing Anne to regard him through narrowed eyes.

"Coffee for me, and of course my daughter will have tea," the duchess directed to an approving Brewster, who for once poured without comment.

"The man is a veritable treasure, you don't know how fortunate you are to have him," Aurora said when she thought Brewster out of earshot.

"No. I can assure you I don't," Anne replied dryly.

"But you still haven't told us what it was that kept you so busy last night," the noblewoman pressed.

"It was a dinner engagement and musicale, quite intimate and inordinately lovely, I might add," Anne replied, watching in delight as Brewster's back stiffened.

"I hadn't heard of any musical reception being give in town yesterday evening," Aurora noted with a sniff, ready to condemn any affair to which she and Audrey had not been invited.

"It was a small dinner for the Irish MPs," Anne commented, unsure from his reaction whether or not Brewster objected to her socializing with the Irish even more than he did Ian.

"That explains it," the noblewoman said, her satisfaction at not being slighted evident. "I do not normally concern myself with their goings-on."

"Was Mr. Parnell there?" Audrey asked, a girlish romanticism creeping into her voice.

"Now, now, Audrey. You shouldn't be the least bit interested in such a rogue, no matter how handsome he is," her mother remonstrated. "You'd do far better to concern yourself with young men acceptable to society. That nice fellow Daniel brought around yesterday is a case in point."

"And who is that?" Anne asked in teasing tones when the young woman turned pink at her mother's words. "Has someone captured your attention at last?"

"No," Audrey protested. "It's nothing like that at all. He is simply another of Daniel's friends, though he is more handsome than most and much nicer, as well."

"Hmm. Sounds serious, your ladyship. You'd best be on guard. Who is this young man, anyway?" asked Anne as she spooned sliced fruit onto her plate.

"His name is Jack, and he has the most charming way
• about him," Audrey gushed, not giving her mother a chance to speak until the matron's glare silenced her quite effectively.

"He is a young man of good family, though his older brother is considered a bit of a rake," Aurora pronounced. "He is Jack Kendrick, of the Northumberland Kendricks, and Ian's brother."

"Ian's brother?" Anne asked softly, surprised at hearing her lover's name on the lips of others so shortly after he had left her side.

"The very same. And Audrey does speak true. The boy is every bit as charming as his older sibling but gives evidence of being much more manageable," the duchess stated with authority before turning her attention toward her daughter. "You'd best take care, miss, lest you find yourself irrevocably smitten before you have given yourself the opportunity to be courted by others. The Kendrick men are known for being irresistible."

"So it would appear," Anne muttered, only to be cut off by Aurora Palmer.

"But then, Anne, dear, you really are but newly arrived home after spending so much time abroad, and not aware of who is considered a good catch and who is not. Quite frankly, I've heard whispered inquiries as to why a lady of your standing should be so involved with Brighton and his charitable enterprises. And the responses have been ones that do not please me at all."

"Really?" the blonde replied.

"Yes, forgive me for saying so, but there are those who feel that because of his enormous wealth, you have set your cap for Brighton. I assure you that I did not believe such faddle for a moment. He's much too old for you, and the only thing he has to recommend him is his soft heart as concerns the underprivileged. You understand, I hope, that should he ever choose to marry, his wife would never see a sixpence of his fortune. The only thing on which he spends his money is in caring for the poor."

"There's no need to worry, your ladyship," Anne said, hard pressed not to laugh out loud at society's speculation that she was pursuing Andrew Brighton. "It is the needy who have captured my attention and a piece of my heart, not the gentleman who tends to them."

"That is exactly what Mother has said," Audrey interjected.

"Audrey, you've been listening to gossip. It is a trait most unbecoming in a young girl," her mother reproved before resuming her conversation with her hostess. "And as for you, Anne, surely you do not mean to spend the rest of your life traveling the globe and then ministering to others during your infrequent visits home. Perhaps it *is* time you looked about for a husband. Now with your permission, I can arrange for introductions to some of the most—"

"No, thank you," Anne said, holding up her hands and laughing.

"I suppose you're right. A woman as attractive as yourself.... But then, I really must admit that I have not observed you looking in the right places. Think of how you've been managing your time. Mingling with reformers, socializing with the Irish and accepting Lady Bothwell's invitation for a weekend at her country house. Really dear, I do think—"

"How did you know I've been invited to the house party?" Anne asked curiously.

"Why, Violet Norris, Lady Bothwell, has spent the last few days bragging to everyone who will listen that you have accepted. And when I learned that, I accepted for Audrey and myself, as well, something I wouldn't have ordinarily done."

"Why not?"

"Because Bothwell's crowd is not the one with which I normally socialize. Of course there are some of them who are acceptable, Bothwell himself and Kendrick, to name two. But some of the others are a despicable lot, and I prefer to avoid their company."

"Then why are we attending, Mama?" Audrey asked, her curiosity overcoming her sense of good manners.

"Yes, why?" echoed Anne suspiciously. This couldn't be another of Nigel's operatives, could it? The idea that this noblewoman was working for the Crown was absurd, but then one never knew where one would find Nigel's people at work, and the idea that he may have planted someone to watch over her was a blow to her pride.

"Well, the truth of the matter is that Violet and I attended school together, and I could not hurt her by refusing an invitation to what will surely be her greatest social triumph. And then there is another matter entirely. And that one, my dear, concerns you."

"Me? How?" Anne asked, her qualms and conjectures about her companion growing.

"It goes back to what we were talking about before. You need someone to guide you in your search for a husband, as you have given no indication that you know who is considered acceptable and who is not. I would hate to see you make a mistake."

"Thank you for your intended kindness, but I am not looking for a husband," Anne protested.

"Then you should be," the older woman pronounced. "And my matchmaking skills have never been called into question. After all, who more than a widow knows how much a woman truly needs a man? Deny it all you like, but I refuse to believe you."

"You don't understand. I have my career. My music means everything to me."

"Then I suggest that you are far too easily satisfied. Music may be sweet, but a husband's symphony is sweeter still. Though you may doubt the truth of what I say, I know that you would be happier by far sitting before your own hearth in the company of a good man than you could ever be standing on a stage receiving the accolades of strangers."

"But..." Anne began, only to be interrupted by Brewster's flower-laden entrance into the dining room.

"These have just arrived for you, miss," he said more decorously than usual, presenting Anne with an enormous bouquet. Though there wasn't a trace of rancor in his voice,

Anne was quite aware that his deference was no more than a show for Lady Moreland and her daughter. And even that could not keep him from adding a comment of his own.

"I would be quite careful if I were you, miss. I'm certain *these* are rife with thorns."

"I beg your pardon?" Anne asked icily, forgetting her guests at the impertinence behind her butler's words. It was wonderfully romantic of Ian to send so lovely a token of his devotion. How dare this little man seek to dampen the warm glow the flowers had evoked as he cast aspersions on the rapture she and Ian had found in each others arms?

"Roses, miss. No matter how marvelous they look, they always have thorns. I wouldn't want to see you forget that in your excitement," Brewster continued with a false benevolence that made Anne want to empty the contents of the teapot over his head.

"How solicitous!" the duchess murmured. "Your butler is without compare."

"Quite," Anne managed to reply through the smile that she hoped hid her clenched teeth. "I'm certain there's no one else like him. Anywhere!"

"How true," the noblewoman echoed speculatively as the servant departed. "But now on to more important things. Look at those lovely roses! There are dozens of them there. I know they are far too costly to have come from Brighton. Do you have any idea who sent them?"

"I think so," the pretty blonde said, feeling suddenly shy at admitting a relationship with Ian Kendrick. A hint to Aurora Palmer was tantamount to placing a notice in the *Times*. The intimacy she shared with Ian was still so new that she rather fancied the idea of keeping it to herself for the moment and relishing it like some delicious secret. However, Lady Moreland was not to be deterred.

"There appears to be a note nestled among the blooms. Don't keep us in suspense, my dear. Open it."

"Really, there's no need to attend to it right now. It can wait until later," Anne demurred, bending her face into the scarlet blossoms and inhaling their seductive scent.

"Your face is as red as those roses, Miss Hargraves, and it's quite obvious that you want to be alone when you read your letter. This looks much more serious than my noticing Jack Kendrick," Audrey exclaimed innocently.

"I should say so," the girl's mother concurred. "But really, Audrey, you mustn't think of prying. Anne deserves her privacy. Of course, she should wait to read her love letter after we have gone. Though I must say, it would make leaving much easier if our curiosity wasn't there to delay us."

"You're quite convincing, your ladyship," Anne conceded with a laugh. "If you must know, this is simply a tribute from someone who admires my music."

"And that admirer is?" the older woman prompted.

"Ian Kendrick," the object of Aurora's inquisition finally admitted, knowing she would have no peace until she did so.

"Ian? Jack's brother?" Audrey almost squealed.

"Why, you sly puss!" Lady Aurora said with a smile. "No wonder you refused my matchmaking efforts. You've already set your sights on that intriguing Kendrick man."

"You misunderstand. It's my music he admires."

"Ian Kendrick wouldn't care if you couldn't sing a note, child. Don't allow him to make you believe otherwise. I know the man, and it's not just your voice he finds alluring. I must say, I can't fault your taste, though I don't know how serious that handsome rogue is about marriage."

"I'm not interested in wedding anyone," Anne protested.

"Yes, dear, so you've said. Still, I'm sure that with gentle prodding and the right encouragement we can bring him around. Perhaps I should give a small dinner party next Thursday. You're not engaged that evening, are you?"

"No, but..."

"Fine. Audrey, we must be leaving," Lady Aurora commanded, rising to her feet and signaling her daughter to do the same. "We've kept Anne from her schedule far too long. Besides, we have invitations to write."

"Oh! Can we include Mr. Kendrick's brother Jack?" Audrey asked, her eyes taking on a dreamy, speculative look.

"And a menu to plan," the duchess continued, paying no heed to Audrey's request. "Come along, dear. Don't dawdle."

Anne watched the ladies leave, a bemused smile on her face. It would not surprise her to learn that Aurora Palmer considered going directly to the nearest church in order to inquire about wedding arrangements, hoping she could finalize them after Thursday's dinner party.

Oh, dear! Thursday! She would have to warn Ian about that so they could both beg off. For some men, there was nothing like the mention of marriage to extinguish their passion. Though last night had hinted that Ian Kendrick was a man whose ardor was limitless, right now Anne didn't want to put him to the test. After all, she thought as a soft smile played about her mouth, at the moment things were quite lovely as they were.

She and Ian had made no plans to meet that day, yet Anne was not surprised to look up from her correspondence that afternoon to find Brewster announcing her lover's arrival.

Elation flooded her heart as the handsome man who had so expertly rekindled her passions followed the butler into the room rather than wait in the vestibule.

For Anne, the sight of him was enough to eclipse Brewster's disgruntlement at the situation. And certainly being in her company once more was all that Ian needed to forget the butler's presence as he walked purposefully toward his lovely lady to plant a gentle kiss at the nape of her neck.

"Hello," he murmured huskily against her delicate skin, enjoying the way the tendrils that had escaped her upswept hair teased his lips. "Are you glad to see me?"

"What do you think?" Anne asked, her normally clear green eyes turning the same smoky hue and her voice exhibiting that raspy quality that had driven him almost mad with desire the night before. Though they were but slight physical changes, they spoke to Ian of welcome more loudly than any words Anne could have uttered. The realization of the effect he had upon her provoked a tender smile, transforming Ian's rugged face into an expression of adoration so overwhelming that it left Anne almost breathless and practically unable to speak.

In the charged silence of the room, Anne returned Ian's look with an enticing smile of her own, noticing how he unconsciously licked at a corner of his lips in a most predatory way. It was a dangerous game they played, Anne reflected, especially when she was all too willing to place herself within his grasp. But then, Ian was not an ordinary man. He was magnificently wild and savage, thrilling in his dominance, the epitome of all that was wonderfully male.

Still, she had a task to perform before she could give herself up completely, Anne recalled dutifully as she gestured for Ian to take a seat opposite, rather than on the settee beside her.

With a questioning raise of his eyebrow, he nevertheless complied with her wish.

"You shooed me out so efficiently last night that I didn't think to ask when I might see you again. That was bad form on my part. And as rude as it was to arrive unannounced just now, I couldn't take the risk of being rejected. You see, I discovered that I simply had to be with you," Ian said earnestly.

Anne looked at him in uncertain silence. Though she had become an expert in gently discouraging all sorts of men, Ian was not like any of them. Neither was the situation in which she now found herself similar to any she had encountered before. Anne was bewildered. She was not certain of what she should do, what Ian expected.

"Have I come at a bad time?" he asked gently, an amused smile lighting his handsome face. Good Lord! He didn't care what sort of reputation this exquisite woman had. Her actions told him that she was a good deal greener than many a society miss.

"Not really," Anne responded in that small, breathy voice that emerged only when she was in his company.

"Good," Ian pronounced, his eyes holding Anne's and his tone soft yet determined.

Anne shifted uncomfortably in her seat. Could she really trust herself not to fall headlong into this man's powerful arms, forgetting anything else of importance that mattered? This morning it had been comforting to think so, but now, with Ian here, she wondered if it was not an impossible expectation.

Her hungry eyes traveled over the lean, hard lines of his body, from broad shoulders to expansive chest, along his taut abdomen, slim hips and muscular legs, before rising to caress his lean jaw and near perfect features. Now that she knew exactly the sort of strength his clothing concealed, she discovered that her passions were far from being spent. Instead they gnawed at her like some beast demanding to be fed.

What sort of man was Ian Kendrick, that he could have wrought such changes in her? What had happened to the woman she had been, cool and evasive, keeping men at a distance with no difficulty at all? Dear God, she felt like some poor creature in a harem, waiting and hoping for her master's signal that he wanted her. That tonight she was to be his. Well, she would have none of it! She refused to remain in this room with Ian Kendrick any longer, and if he didn't understand, that was just too bloody bad!

She was just about to send the dark-haired seducer on his way when an understanding Ian rose from his seat and joined her on the settee. Casually draping his arm along the top of the furniture behind his golden-haired beauty, he allowed his hand to rest on her shoulder, the fire of his touch silencing Anne rather effectively.

"What do you say," he whispered suggestively in her ear, "to going for a ride in the park?"

"A carriage ride?" Anne echoed in confusion. Had she misread his intentions so completely?

"Yes," he said with a rueful laugh. "If we continue to stay here confined and alone, I'm afraid I won't be able to resist you much longer. But I am not such a rake that I come here only to enjoy your favors and then leave again. I want to get to know you better, to converse, to savor your company."

"How clever of you to suggest such a delightful outing. It *would* give us the opportunity to talk, and you do realize, I suspect, that I'd be utterly fascinated to find out more about you," Anne said, playing the part of the coquette even as the agent in her recognized the opportunity she was being given and seized control. Perhaps she would be able to handle the danger that was Ian Kendrick after all.

"Then let us go," Ian said, kissing the top of Anne's delicate ear, "before I lose my composure."

"If you do, I shall help you find it again," Anne said tartly, happy to once more feel confident in her abilities to resist temptation when need be.

"I'm sure you would, wench," Ian commented with a laugh as he helped Anne to her feet and they left the seductive atmosphere of the small room behind them.

"I just thought you should know, sir," Matthew Brewster said sullenly.

Nigel Conway studied the man before him. The agent's face was bright red, though whether from embarrassment or from anger, Nigel couldn't determine.

"Thank you, Matthew," the head of the intelligence operation said, exasperation creeping into his voice. "But I thought I had made myself clear. You are not there to report on Anne Hargraves. She is one of my finest agents, and I trust her explicitly. You are there simply to protect her should something go awry."

"And should I protect her from this Kendrick fellow?"

"Anne knows what she's doing. Besides, the chap didn't stay the night, did he?"

"No, sir," the stout little man muttered. "He didn't have to."

"See here, I simply want you to leave Anne and Kendrick alone. He's one of those Anne is investigating," Conway said, his patience at an end.

"And a very thorough job she did, too," the butler remarked.

"Good God, Matthew, you are not the girl's father! Now let it rest."

"And if I notice one of our people becoming personally involved in an assignment, am I supposed to let that rest, as well? I can't believe you would want me to do that, sir," the butler observed, a smug expression settling over his rather pudgy face.

"I've told you, Anne Hargraves is one of our best. She knows what she is doing."

"I hope you're correct, Sir Nigel. But I want it understood that I am not reporting this irregularity because of any animosity or resentment I might have toward Miss Hargraves. If truth be known, I have come to rather enjoy our verbal sparring. It is the only excitement we have had in that morgue of a household. And as long as I am in the mood to confess, I will tell you that I almost admire the young woman. She is quite spirited, if misguided, and not at all easily quelled. That can be said of very few people of my acquaintance. The reason I am mentioning Kendrick, and what went on last night, is that it might have something to do with an attempted forced entry at the town house."

"What's that you say?" asked Conway in alarm.

"I suppose I should describe it as a possible attempt," the butler said, his tone serious. "I thought I heard a noise at the back door late last night. When I went to investigate, I found nothing. I must have frightened off whoever it was. This morning, I saw scratches in the metal plate surrounding the keyhole, as though someone had been trying to force the lock. Perhaps it is nothing. The scratches might have been there before, though they do look new to me. I just thought I should mention it, sir."

"And you think this has something to do with Kendrick?"

"I'm not certain, sir. I don't even know if the man was still there when this occurred, as Kendrick seems to have departed rather stealthily sometime before morning... Miss Hargraves's magnanimous concession to propriety, I'm sure. What I am saying is that some unknown person wanted to get in that house last night."

"Do you think Anne has been targeted? That some party might wish to do her harm?"

"It could be. And the possibility exists that Kendrick was supposed to serve as a distraction while an accomplice made his way into the house. I am not positive about any of it, Sir Nigel, except for the fact that in my opinion, Miss Hargraves is not able to trust her own judgment where Ian Kendrick is concerned. And given the gravity of the situation, I thought you should be informed."

"All right, Matthew, all right. You might be on to something. Or the entire episode could be as simple as a lover who had left something behind trying to regain entrance to the town house without disturbing the staff and making them aware of his presence at such an odd hour."

"It could be, sir. But maybe it was that same lover, surreptitiously returning to do what he had left undone."

"Until we make some sense of this, the only thing we can do is double our vigilance as far as Anne Hargraves is concerned. With all of the contacts she has made since being assigned to this case, she might have stirred up some viper's nest somewhere. It's your job to know exactly when Kendrick enters and leaves that house. Anne needs your protection now more than ever. In fact, she has a house party scheduled for next weekend. I want you to accompany her to Bothwell's estate."

"I beg your pardon, sir," the very proper butler protested, "but I hardly see how I can do that."

"Well, you certainly can't go in the guise of a ladies' maid." Conway chuckled, surprised at the red flush creeping up Brewster's jowls and stealing across his cheeks. "But I depend upon you to be clever enough to think of something."

"But, sir . . ."

"Not another word, Matthew. It's time you were on your way home. I want you there before Anne returns from her carriage ride."

"Yes, sir," the rotund servant grumbled. "But if this wasn't for the safety of the queen . . ."

"Goodbye, Matthew. Enjoy the countryside," Nigel said, dismissing the man and then busying himself with paperwork.

After closing the door behind him, Matthew Brewster was more than unhappy. The very hallways of Whitehall vibrated with his muttered indignation as he made his way to the street, and those who chanced to cross his path very quickly removed themselves, wanting no contact at all with such an odd, scowling little man so preoccupied with talking to himself.

"I don't mind doing my part for my country, but really this is too much. The roles I've been forced to play—nanny, ladies' maid, chaperon and now traveling companion. Next Nigel will want to dress me up in skirts and pass me off as somebody's mother."

By the time Anne and Ian returned to her home, it seemed natural to have him by her side, to feel his hand upon hers, his thumb gently stroking her own.

"Would you like to come in for a short while?" she asked with downcast eyes as Ian handed her down from the hired carriage. No longer afraid of his power over her, Anne had uncovered very little she hadn't already known about Ian that afternoon. Additional time together would give her further opportunity in that quarter. But more than that, she found herself reluctant to have these magical moments spent in his company come to an end.

"I would find it delightful," Ian replied softly, very much touched by Anne's sudden shyness. What an enigma she was, a puzzle that obsessed him far more than was good for either of them, he thought. Yet even with this conclusion firmly in mind, he discovered himself powerless to reject her impulsive invitation.

"Just a bit of dinner perhaps," Anne suggested, pleased with herself for taking precaution enough to set limitations before they entered the town house.

"Just for dinner," Ian echoed in agreement as he took Anne's arm and led her to her door.

Chapter Eleven

Anne stretched lazily beneath the sheets, enjoying the solid masculine presence beside her, daydreaming of the future, a time when Ian would always be there, when her name might be the same as his. It *was* a dream, she acknowledged silently. A veteran of too many foreign intrigues, she knew full well how tenuous any future plans were and had long ago accepted the need to be content with the present. Today she would enjoy the man here with her.

Trailing her fingers lightly across his aristocratic jaw, she let them wander upward till they captured that errant piece of hair that plagued him so. Indeed, to hear him complain, it was the only thing in life he couldn't properly control.

Oh, how his life would change if I were to remain a part of it, Anne thought with amusement, remembering their past skirmishes over Brighton and Jack, among other things. She toyed with the dark thatch, curling it gently about her fingers as he waved her hand away, even in sleep aware of the source of his disturbance.

Sitting up, the petite blonde allowed the sheet to slide down as she leaned over the man beside her, intent only on kissing the unmanageable lock into place. All of a sudden, however, Ian's eyes flashed open and he smiled at her, pulling her into his arms with practiced ease.

"What a glorious sight to wake up to," he murmured, kissing her tenderly, "you hovering above me, sunlight enriching your golden hair, your body firm and ready—sunlight! Oh, Lord, what time is it?" he exclaimed anxiously.

If the sun was already this bright, it had to be well past sunrise.

In what seemed like an instant, Anne found herself alone in the bed while Ian rooted through his discarded clothes, searching apparently for his pocket watch.

"Well, I certainly don't know," she answered petulantly as a knock sounded on the bedroom door. "It can't be too late or Brewster would have called me already."

Again came the knock, this time more of a pounding rhythm, accompanied by the butler's disapproving tones.

"Miss Hargraves, are you awake? Your maid says you didn't respond to her call, and you did order breakfast for eight o'clock. It is now nearly nine and it is unlike you to be so inconsiderate," conceded the servant. "Are you unwell?"

"Unwell? No, we—I just overslept," she called through the door, watching in dismay as Ian rapidly dressed, apparently intent on leaving at once. "I will be down shortly."

"Very good, miss," answered Brewster. "And will Mr. Kendrick be joining you for breakfast this morning?"

"No, he won't," announced Ian as he stood and finished tucking his shirt into his trousers. Worried now about how to contact the prince since he'd failed to make their sunrise rendezvous, he was oblivious to Anne's look of displeasure.

"Did you have to let him know you were still here?" she cried in dismay, more upset that Ian was preparing to go than at his lack of etiquette, but unable to confess such a weakness.

"Darling, I am frightfully sorry, but I suspect Brewster knew already. I did leave my coat downstairs last night, you know. I had intended to leave before the sun or your overly nosy butler arose," said Ian apologetically. "Now, I've embarrassed you and I've missed a rather urgent early appointment so I must hurry off. Can I make it up to you with tea at the Claremont, say around four?"

What could be so important in his life this morning after what they'd shared last night, Anne wondered, even as she suddenly recalled her own date to meet Nigel at nine o'clock. Well, it couldn't be helped; she'd get there as soon as she

could, and if he asked the cause of her tardiness, she'd tell
him she was occupied with the investigation and pray he
didn't ask just what she was investigating.

"All right," she agreed, "but you do have time for a kiss
goodbye, don't you?"

"Certainly," her suitor replied, embracing her as he momentarily put aside his professional failure this morning and
relished his personal successes of the night before. Anne was
no assassin, of that he was certain, unless she was regarded
as the sort of woman who could kill a man's yearning for
unencumbered freedom, he reflected, as thoughts of marriage entered his head for the first time in his life. Casting
them aside even as he kissed her deeply, Ian drew strength
from the passion they had shared. It would be a difficult
day, he knew, but this was a pleasant way to start it.

Then he was gone in such a hurry that he left the bedroom door partly ajar, allowing Anne to overhear Brewster
greeting him on the stairs.

"Ah, good morning, sir. I trust you slept well."

Though Ian didn't reply, she could just imagine his furious scowl at the butler's impertinence as the front door
slammed behind him. Donning her chemise and ringing for
her maid, she wondered idly which of the two arrogant
males had slammed it, deciding it was perhaps better she
didn't know.

The clock chimed nine as Nigel looked up in surprise from
the reports he was reviewing. It was highly irregular for
Anne to be late for an appointment, but then it was also
unusual that he had her come to his office. Undoubtedly
she'd be along shortly, and in the meantime, perhaps he
could fathom some plan for their further investigation of
this assassination plot. The latest threatening letter Ponsonby had sent round this morning added a new element of
ominousness to the matter, but did nothing to spur his own
insight.

Rather it seemed their investigation was heading everywhere and nowhere at the same time, an ungainly hydra with
too many possible avenues of attack, he mused, many too
many if they couldn't convince the queen to take some pre-

cautions. Bloody hell, Jubilee Day was over two weeks away, but there was no guarantee this fellow would wait till then. Any day now, the would-be killer might fire a lucky shot and the woman would cease to exist. Fortunately, Ponsonby had taken his advice and encouraged Victoria to go up to Balmoral for a bit. It had made her happy to escape London and would give him more time to find her enemy.

As it was, what else could he do, hands tied by governmental regulations as they were?

"Don't involve the press. Don't reveal more than you have to to anyone. Even your best agent might not be truly loyal to the queen. We can't afford mistakes. Find him now!"

Following directions like those would have seen him long dead. Nigel frowned, remembering his own experiences in the field. But now he had other problems to resolve. His two best agents seemed to be impeding one another's progress, what with Brewster's constant carping about Anne's methods and she about his impertinent service in the household. Maybe it was time he told her the truth, he considered. No, not yet, he decided, there were too many other issues to deal with today.

Honestly, he couldn't begrudge the fieldwork of either agent. Brewster's association with the butlers of noblemen from among Bertie's associates who supposedly disdained the queen had eliminated a few of the South Kensington Crowd who apparently spoke one way in public and another in the confines of their own homes. And Anne had penetrated Brighton's group, going so far as to discount the reformer himself from involvement, though a few of the others in his group seemed overzealous, in her opinion, and capable of supporting any activity that would promote their reforms. Her dealings with Bertie's fawning crowd, though, had yet to yield much information.

Well, his people were looking into it—and Flaherty, the loud-spoken Irishman the other night, as well, but the immediate question bothering Nigel Conway was Ian Kendrick. Did Anne still suspect him of being involved? Nothing Nigel had uncovered seemed to either acquit or

convict the fellow, but the very coincidence of his being so
regularly in Anne's field of investigation was disconcerting. Why would he place himself in proximity to Brighton
one day and the Prince of Wales the next, and then be willing to accompany Anne to the Irish reception, if he didn't
have an ulterior motive? Unless... Had his foremost agent
abandoned her governmental concerns for a personal liaison?

In the six years he had known Anne Hargraves, it would
be the first time her needs as a woman had ever disrupted
her work. What she did on her own time was her business,
of course, Nigel acknowledged, but when the queen could
conceivably suffer, embarrassment be damned, he'd say
what he must.

Where the hell was she, anyway? He fussed, pouring yet
another cup of tea as his resentment of the upcoming topic
built. It was half past nine already.

Where would the prince try to reach him, pondered Ian,
hurrying down Anne's front steps. Perhaps he should check
at home first; it was a good twenty-minute walk from here,
but Bertie certainly wouldn't be in the park any longer, and
to reach the prince at the palace was neither an easy task nor
one that would be appreciated. He hoped the royal would
have sent a message setting up a later appointment, though
Ian could just imagine what the future king would have to
say about his agent's dereliction of duty—and the thoughts
were not pretty.

"And where have you been, big brother?" challenged
Jack as Ian entered the small house off Russell Square.
"Your bed wasn't slept in last night and you are still wear-
ing your evening clothes."

"Tell me something I am not aware of," snapped Ian, in
no mood for his brother's games.

"Well, you probably don't know that Prince Albert was
looking for you," announced Jack in a condescending tone,
"but I had to tell his messenger that I didn't know where
you were."

"You still don't—and you won't, either," retorted the older Kendrick, his temper at a flash point. "What was the message?"

"Something about joining him at the racetrack before noon if you could manage it," replied Jack, admiration shining in his eyes though his voice remained casual. His brother, hobnobbing with the Prince of Wales, who would believe it? "Mind if I tag along?"

"Sorry, but I do. It's business, not pleasure, definitely not an outing for children," explained Ian, hurrying up the stairs to change into clothes more suitable for the stables where Albert's horses trained.

Jack scowled, but had no rejoinder. Anne Hargraves hadn't considered him a child, he thought with resentment.

"Mr. Conway, a Miss Hargraves is here," announced his overly efficient secretary.

"Send her in, but no need to note it in the log," he instructed, rising as Anne entered the office, immediately brightening its governmental gloom. "Thank God you're all right. I couldn't imagine what kept you."

"I'm sorry to have worried you, Nigel, and good morning," she said, hoping to avoid an outright deception as she circled his desk to kiss him on the cheek. "Time simply got away from me this morning and before I knew it, I was late."

"Anne, you are one of the most organized people I know," he challenged. "You have never missed a rendezvous, even in the field. You know better; too much can depend on it."

"Everyone has an off day once in a while," the attractive blonde replied with a bright smile, still hoping to avoid stating the reason for her tardiness. "I suppose mine just happens to be today. Now, tell me what you've learned."

"After you tell me what's wrong with you," Nigel demanded in annoyance. She had never evaded issues before this; could Brewster be right after all? Was Ian Kendrick the culprit behind her change in behavior? "I have always relied on your sense of responsibility and discretion. Surely you can trust mine, as well, and share whatever is bothering you. And don't tell me that it's nothing, I know you too well," he chided.

"Really, Nigel, I'm fine, maybe just a little edgy because things aren't coming together on this assignment, that's all," she lied, feeling her heart pounding away with the tension that gripped her body. "I haven't had much success at all in routing out our villain, but believe me, I'm working on it."

"Evidently quite actively for you to miss a strategy meeting," he said dryly. Lighting a cigar, he watched Anne closely; she was nervous and hiding something. Well, he might as well bring it out into the open. "Tell me, is Ian Kendrick still hounding you?"

"Kendrick...hounding me? No, not that I've noticed," she replied uneasily. Just how much did Nigel know? "I mean, I think he's attracted to me, but I don't believe he's of any political threat where the queen is concerned."

"And to you? Could he pose a threat there?"

"To me?"

"I think it's time you looked at your relationship from a purely rational level, Anne. You may well be drawn to the man—"

"I never said that."

"No, tell me the possibility doesn't exist," her employer challenged, reddening slightly at the thought of just how much Brewster had told him. "Anne, I don't want to see you throw your career away for a man who may be using you for his own purposes."

"That's not what's happening."

"Perhaps not," Nigel conceded. "But we haven't fully cleared Ian Kendrick's background or his financial status. There are still too many unknowns. I care too much about you to see you hurt this way—and maybe allow others to be hurt at the same time. Just how well have you come to know this man?"

"Well enough," Anne admitted, her cheeks tinged with pink.

"Good, then you will not have to spend much more of your time with him," commented Nigel, making no secret of the fact that this was an order, not a suggestion. "Just because you think of him as a lover doesn't mean you should stop considering him as a possible assassin.''

For a moment Anne was silent, weighing her choices, considering what she knew to be true and what she only felt was true. While part of her recognized Ian's conceivable culpability, a doubt she had never been fully able to dismiss, her heart and soul demanded she cry out his innocence and call for Nigel to retract his harsh words. But then, as she had been trained by Her Majesty's government, she made the only decision possible despite its high personal cost.

"All right, Nigel. Until this is over and we know that Ian Kendrick is indisputably a respectable Englishman, I will see him only when necessary in the course of my investigation,'' she promised sadly. Looking out the window at the clouds gathering in the sky, she wondered how she would explain her sudden change of heart to the man who'd held her so tenderly just that morning. However, that was her concern, not Nigel's.

"Good, now about this latest letter Ponsonby received. He's sent it over for us to examine,'' began Nigel, his counseling accomplished and his mind back on the business at hand.

Ian left the track as unobtrusively as he'd arrived, head down, avoiding contact with any of the trainers or riders about, still somewhat stunned by Albert's controlled fury. Never before had he been witness to such deadly anger expressed so vehemently yet quietly that no one in the adjoining boxes noted anything unusual in the prince's manner. All the same, Ian felt his wounds so acutely, he was rather surprised to find that he wasn't bleeding.

It had been nearly twenty years since he'd received a dressing down like the one he had just suffered, and then his father had punctuated his remarks with strokes from a cane. For Albert, however, a cane would have been superfluous; his words alone had cut deep enough, flaying Ian's self-respect more effectively than any weapon could have bruised him. The disgrace was all the worse, Ian realized, because he fully deserved every painful phrase of the prince's sharp rebuke.

For the first time in his career, Ian Kendrick had been irresponsibly arrogant, presuming his own enjoyment took precedence over the assignment he had accepted. He had violated his own sense of honor in permitting self-interest to blind him to the problems of Victoria's safety. It was true, Prince Albert had admitted, that the queen had retired to Balmoral for a time, but that was all the more reason this matter had to be resolved before she returned to the arena where danger lurked.

"If Miss Hargraves is really a suspect in your investigation, rather than a sexual diversion to satisfy your own untimely needs," charged the royal, "then treat her as such. If not, put a stop to it, now!"

"Yes, sir," he'd answered solemnly, one of the few times in the interview he'd been permitted to speak. It had torn at his heart to verbalize his agreement. Yet Ian knew he had no choice but to agree.

Now the problem was dealing with Anne. Knowing full well that he'd become overly devoted to her in too short a time was one thing; convincing his heart of that and explaining it to her was a punishment even he didn't deserve.

It was after one when Anne returned to the house, having spent some time walking in the park, attempting unsuccessfully to rid herself of the nervous energy she felt after her session with Nigel. She had always recognized her job and done it willingly, to the exclusion of all else . . . till now. Morally and professionally, her duty was clear. But whether her rebellious heart would obey was still undetermined, despite the ongoing arguments playing over and over in her mind. Her mood therefore was not the best when Brewster greeted her.

"Good afternoon, Miss Hargraves. Cook was uncertain if you'd return for luncheon, but she's prepared a lovely meat pie. Shall I have her serve it?"

"What may be lovely in your eyes is not even remotely appetizing in mine, Brewster," the blonde refuted, removing her hat and gloves and handing them to the servant. At this moment, her stomach would not tolerate food; of that, she was certain. "I will be upstairs, but I am not home to callers."

"Even to Mr. Kendrick?" questioned the butler, eyebrows raised. He could understand her wishing to avoid others, but the man who'd shared her bed this morning?

"To anyone," Anne emphasized, starting up the stairs. She needed time to think, time to decide how to explain the situation to Ian without really telling him anything. She did not need the petty disruptions of visitors or meddling servants.

"But, Miss Hargraves, you—"

"What is it, Brewster?" she demanded, irritated at the man's continued intrusion when she wanted to be alone.

"You haven't said what you wished for luncheon."

"Absolutely nothing, nothing at all. You eat the meat pie if it's so lovely," she snapped. "I have no appetite." Damn it, if the butler was as intuitive as everyone claimed, he should have known that.

Unfortunately, her bedroom did not prove to be the peaceful sanctuary she had hoped. Despite the maid's having tidied up, Anne could yet see Ian in her bed, remember the sweet words he'd whispered only last night, feel his masterful touch on her overheated flesh and taste the passion they'd shared with such abandon. Now, so very shortly, she would have to tell him that it couldn't happen again.

Still, she had no other choice, she told herself, unbuttoning a shoe, kicking it off and watching it fly across the room. Nigel was right, damn him! Ian Kendrick, suspect or not, would be too great a distraction to her work if she allowed him to linger in her life, much as she might want to do so. If she could just find an excuse that would occupy her time for the next few weeks, one that would seem logical and urgent enough for Ian not to doubt its veracity, maybe after Jubilee Day...

She pondered her dilemma, pacing back and forth over the soft carpeting. What would Ian Kendrick believe so important to her that she would willingly sacrifice their time together, the joy they'd shared? Of course, her music, a concert, or better, a concert tour that she had to prepare for.

That was it! He had seen firsthand how her voice reacted to him; he couldn't question her need to avoid the passion they generated when they were together. Her career, no, both of her careers, would depend on their remaining apart.

Suddenly finding herself ravenous now that her problem was beginning to resolve itself, Anne rang for the butler. It was nearly two hours until she'd meet Ian for tea; there was no reason she should go hungry. Besides, a lady did not eat heavily in public anyway; she could dine now and nibble fashionably at tea with no one the wiser as to her real appetites.

"Brewster, fetch me a luncheon tray," she instructed. "Tell Cook nothing elaborate, a small salad and cold meat, perhaps."

"But you said you didn't want anything," he protested. "Cook has taken the kitchen maid and gone to the shops."

"Then you'd best see what you can prepare. Surely a cold platter isn't beyond your many talents," Anne said dryly, totally unsympathetic to the man's complaints.

"No, miss," sighed Brewster, unhappy but resigned to his fate—butler, lady's maid, now cook's helper. Damn it, he had warned Conway. She was eccentric enough before her involvement with Kendrick; now heaven only knew what the woman would demand of him next.

Examining her reflection in the mirror after the portly manservant departed, muttering as usual, Anne frowned. She had dressed rather hurriedly for her meeting with Nigel this morning, wearing a functional but simple outfit, a high-waisted dark gray skirt and a white chiffon blouse with gray piping. It was attractive enough, she supposed, but certainly not what she would want Ian to remember her in. If this was truly to be their last private meeting, she wanted to look special for the man.

By the time Brewster returned with her tray, it appeared two-thirds of the woman's wardrobe was cluttering her bed, the chaise, the chairs and the floor, haphazardly scattered over the whole area as she had considered and discarded dress after dress. The apparent favorite of the moment was hanging over the wardrobe door, a forest green gown with a short matching jacket, but the singer was still rooting about among her other options, continuing to scatter accessories about the floor.

"My Lord, miss, are you cleaning out or has a whirlwind struck without warning?" he exclaimed in distress. Though his mistress had never been known for neatness, this went far beyond the norm. "Never mind. I'll set your tray here. Why don't I send Bess to straighten up while you dine? I am certain she can find whatever it is you were looking for so unsuccessfully."

"I doubt she will, Brewster, but very well."

Seating herself at the place he'd quickly arranged before departing, Anne frowned, thinking of his words. *What I'm looking for is a suit of armor*, she reflected, *an outfit to protect my heart from pain even as I wound the only man I've allowed myself to love in years.*

In an instant, her napkin was tossed aside and the luncheon tray abandoned. Then she was up again, her anxious movements echoing the frenzy within as her mind and heart continued their ongoing battle.

He is a possible assassin. There's no evidence of that; he'd never kill anyone. *He has expensive friends and tastes and no purse to provide for them.* That doesn't mean he is a criminal. *Then how is it he knows your movements almost before you've made them?* Maybe because we're so close he can sense my actions, or perhaps it's just coincidence. *And is it coincidence he managed to get himself into your bed in two short weeks?* No, that is love, exclaimed her heart. *On your part, perhaps, but what about his? How can you be certain he's not just using you?*

"Miss?" The maid's voice broke in on the angry debate within Anne's head. "Brewster said you needed me."

"Yes, please put my clothes away and then help me out of this and into the green," instructed the singer, seating herself at her dressing table as the maid complied. Even her hair was inappropriate for this afternoon's tea, Anne decided; it was much too severe a look. Quickly she began to extract the pins securing her chignon, and started to brush her long blond curls, enjoying the feel of the bristles against her scalp.

"When you've finished that, I'd like you to do my hair, Bess. I've very little patience for it today."

"Certainly, Miss Hargraves," agreed the maid, surprised at the unusual request but more than happy to oblige. Her mistress had lovely, soft tresses that were a pleasure to work with.

Shortly after three, Anne descended the stairs, looking feminine and totally bewitching, in her maid's opinion. The green ensemble set off her sparkling eyes, her blond hair was arranged in wavy tendrils about her face, and a small green hat, more feathers and veil than fabric, secured her upswept locks, leaving her slender neck vulnerable to admiration. It was that particular effect that startled the songstress as she passed the hall mirror on her way to speak with Brewster.

"Yes, Miss Hargraves?" inquired the butler coldly, annoyed that she had returned his luncheon tray to the kitchen without even sampling what he'd prepared.

"Send for my carriage, please. I'm having tea at the Claremont at four."

"Very well, if you think they set a better table than I." The butler sniffed.

But Anne didn't even hear his answer, transfixed as she was by the sight of her barren neck. Void of the cameo Louis had given her, her naked neck emphasized the sacrifices she was making. She had given up the security of loving Louis, pushing aside the past to welcome Ian into her present life, and now she was on her way to send him off, as well, she reflected sadly. No! There was no way she could look this soft at her meeting with Ian today or she'd crumple into his arms at his first objection. She was about to do her duty, not enjoy herself, and she had better look the part, if only to give her strength of purpose.

When Brewster entered to announce the arrival of her carriage, his mistress had gone back upstairs, a fact that didn't perturb him unduly. It was only when she returned again in what she'd worn that morning, even her hair redone, that he admitted his concern. Was the woman all right? Refusing luncheon one minute, demanding it the next but not eating it, changing her ensemble and her hair, then suddenly altering her appearance again to look *less* attractive? These were not the actions of the efficient, analytical agent Anne Hargraves was reputed to be, worried Matthew Brewster. Yet what could he do about it, other than remain on guard? He had already warned Conway.

"Have a good afternoon, miss," he offered.

His voice seemed a bit less gruff than usual, Anne thought briefly as she descended the front steps, but then it was probably her imagination.

Crossing the lobby of the popular hotel, Anne glanced at the historic clock and reflected how peculiar it was to be early for an engagement. Over the years, she had found that five to ten minutes of anxious anticipation sparked a man's interest and lowered his self-confidence, two conditions very helpful in her line of work. More than ten minutes of waiting, however, turned interest into irritation and anticipation into impatience in most cases, so she had carefully mastered her arrivals to take advantage of men's natural responses.

Ian Kendrick, however, had already proven he was not like most men, and today especially she wanted every advantage she could possibly garner at this meeting of supposed lovers. She had decided that arriving ahead of Ian would put him off guard and give her an edge, so it was ten minutes to four as she approached the head waiter. Unfortunately, she realized as the man led her to Ian's table, Ian had been more anxious to see her than she had anticipated.

"You're early, my sweet," he exclaimed, rising to his feet and kissing her hand as she was seated. "How lucky I am to find a woman who believes a timepiece is more than ornamental jewelry. It gives me all the longer to enjoy your gracious beauty."

"Ian," she began nervously, withdrawing her hand from his grasp to play with the teacup before her. "I'm not one of your idle South Kensington socialites, always seeking a compliment. You really needn't—"

His fingers gently brushed her lips to silence her.

"Anne, I'm not one to say what I don't mean," he said emphatically as he stroked her cheek with a gentle touch.

"You should realize by now that I value every moment we share."

"So do I, but I—"

"All the more so because, much as I regret it, I won't be—"

"Won't be able to continue seeing you," Anne finished, amazed that the words seemed to be leaving his mouth even as they did hers.

"What?" Ian asked, not quite certain he'd heard her properly, speaking as he had while she was talking. Here he'd gathered the nerve to tell her he wouldn't have time for her and she was putting him off? How was that possible—unless Bertie was right and her goal was the assassination?

"I just found out this morning that a new concert tour is being arranged for me on the Continent. What with helping to coordinate the itinerary, learning new songs, rehearsing the music, enduring dress fittings and trying to continue charity work with Brighton, I'm going to be frightfully busy," offered Anne, ashamed at how lame her excuses sounded. Surely if she had time for the reformer, she should have time for her lover.

"How soon do you leave?" he asked quietly.

"The date hasn't been set yet, but probably in about two weeks," she hedged. "That's why there's so much to do."

Right after Jubilee Day, after you kill Victoria perhaps? Ian frowned. The ugliness of the conjecture mirrored itself briefly on his face as he stopped his hand from touching her, but Anne read it as disappointment at her rejection.

"Maybe we could see each other once or twice a week, in public," she offered. "I'm afraid I really can't commit to more than that for a while. You know how you affect my voice." Even now, she reflected, it was trembling as she spoke her lies to the impassive man across the table.

Ian sat silently for a minute, weighing the anger and pain he experienced against the relief he should be feeling. Though the words she'd spoken had placed her high on his list of suspects, at least he didn't have to worry about breaking it off; she had done so. Should he tell her his side, false though it was, or let her assume the blame for their parting? he debated. No, that wasn't fair. His story was prepared; he might as well use it. If she wasn't the killer, he might one day be free to love her.

"Actually, Anne, I was starting to tell you the same thing, though for different reasons, of course. No one wants to hear me sing," he said with a forced laugh. "I'm really concerned about Jack; you know how naive he is. Well, more and more often he's been haunting the worst dives in the East End. In fact, last night, while you and I were enjoying ourselves so marvelously, he lost a bloody fortune of my money gambling. I fear I must supervise the lad more thoroughly, despite the heavy price it will cost me in not being with you."

"Maybe once my tour is finalized, and he leaves," suggested Anne, admiring how convenient an excuse Ian's errant brother had become. Yes, he had visited her house in Mayfair once or twice, but he'd left pleasantly enough without ill feelings when she explained her situation, but then that made it all the more probable that Ian was only using the boy as an excuse. She frowned. "Do you have any idea when that will be?"

"I'm sure he wants to be here for the jubilee," he replied, watching her green eyes harden and her gentle mouth grow firm, "but I'll try to hurry him home, I swear."

So you'll be free once Victoria is dead, she thought, a chill pervading her heart as Nigel's suspicions of Ian haunted her very soul.

"That's not so far off," she said aloud.

"No, perhaps we'll have a few days before you leave on tour," speculated Ian, "or maybe I could join you for a bit when we're free to enjoy ourselves without worrying about all these other obligations."

"Wouldn't that be wonderful?" sighed the blonde, picking up her menu though she had never felt less inclined to eat. All she truly wanted was to leave and begin her investigation anew, but that, too, would have to wait. "Shall we order?"

"Yes, they have excellent cream cakes," Ian advised, signaling the waiter as if nothing was amiss, though his heart was heavier than he'd ever thought possible.

Chapter Twelve

A short while later, Anne breezed through the door of her town house, her expression distraught and her manner distracted. Absently depositing her coat in Brewster's waiting hands, she all but flew to the music room, abruptly and emphatically slamming the door long before the curious butler could make sense of her continuing strange behavior.

All he was left with was the observation that whatever had disconcerted Anne Hargraves before she had left the town house earlier that afternoon was far from being resolved. The young woman was evidently more at odds than ever. But whether her upset stemmed from her assignment or problems with her lover, the butler was unable to determine as he winced at the discordant notes being pounded out upon the piano.

As Anne sat at the keys, she struggled to recover her composure, seeking to find an outlet for her churning emotions. But for the first time she could remember, her heart had no desire, no room for melody. The solace she sought from music was elusive, a pale imitation of the very different release she had experienced in this very room.

"Dear God, what has come over me?" she whispered, her slender fingers continuing to wander stiffly over the keys in no particular order. After all, she was no green girl. She was a special agent for Her Majesty's government.

She was a woman who had learned long ago to disregard her own feelings in the service of her country. And because she had repressed her emotions, treating them as if they did not exist, she had always been able to accomplish the objective set for her, even if she had not been particularly proud of her actions in doing so. But now those powerful, long-pent-up feelings had been unleashed by one Ian Kendrick, and like a pack of wolves, they beset her, tearing at her reserve, ripping it apart and hungrily devouring it, leaving her inner self raw, bleeding and vulnerable.

Chiding herself for her weakness, Anne leaped up from the piano bench and like some restless demon began to pace the room. When had she started to lose control? Was it the first time Ian had kissed her, his sensuous mouth possessing hers so completely that she had forgotten who she was and what she was supposed to be doing? Or had it begun at Aurora's party, when she had encountered a man so self-assured and commanding, so unlike any other she had ever known, that she had been intrigued in spite of herself?

Ian! Anne's soul cried out his name even as her mind told her that she had to forget her feelings for him. But Ian Kendrick was not the sort to be forgotten easily. As Anne tried to gain mastery of her thoughts, to concentrate on the task Nigel Conway had set for her, haunting visions of Ian arose before her. No matter that she closed her eyes, he was there.

She remembered his lean, determined jaw and visualized his silver eyes when they sparkled with laughter as well as when they turned that smoky hue which bespoke his desire for her. And then there was that endearingly rebellious lock of hair which persisted in tumbling over his forehead, as though inviting her hand to attempt to push it back into place.

Good God, Anne thought in despair, her head was so filled with thoughts of Ian that she couldn't concentrate, couldn't conceive of what she should do next to try to safeguard the queen from her would-be assailant. But perhaps it was this room, and the bittersweet memories it contained, that made it impossible to dwell on anything other than the rapture she had shared here with the Englishman who had captured her heart.

That had to be the reason. After all, this room had been the site of her downfall, though she had initially thought it to be her resurrection. It was the place she had finally capitulated to the cravings she had felt, the yearnings Ian could evoke so effortlessly, with no more than a nod of his head, a seductive smile or a light caress. That first night she had burned with passion more hotly than the blaze in the hearth. No wonder she could not focus on anything else as long as she remained here, where an atmosphere of desire still pervaded every inch of carpet, every nook and cranny. She had to escape this place and quickly, Anne concluded as she started for the door and the impersonal coolness of the hallway.

She *would* attend to her work, steeping herself in it for personal reasons as well as those of state. The basis for her dedication didn't matter, she told herself. The thought cheered her immediately. This is exactly what her attitude would have been before Ian Kendrick had captured her in his seductive snare. The realization eliminated any lingering traces of guilt that loving him might have left lurking in the background. Perhaps the changes he had wrought in her were not so irreversible after all.

Heartened further, Anne had to decide what to do next. Surely there was somewhere she could go tonight, someone she could contact in order to continue her investigation. Entering her study and consulting her engagement calendar, she noted that she had jotted down Oliver Digby's address and information concerning a meeting of reformers, which she had overheard Brighton mention a few days earlier. Though at the time she had registered it carefully, fully intent upon being present, she had not thought of the gathering once in the past two days. Horrified by her negligence, Anne was immediately all the more resolved to reclaim her professional concentration. Only then, once she had been successful in finding the man who threatened Victoria, could she deal with Ian Kendrick, assuming, of course, that he was not at all connected to this dirty business. And Anne perceived with growing unhappiness that this was no longer so certain a premise.

In spite of her distress, she smiled slightly. She was becoming more her old self with every passing moment. The fact that she could consider Ian's implication in the assassination attempt without immediately dismissing such an idea as absurd proved as much. Yet even as she called for Brewster, instructing him to order her carriage, Anne experienced no elation at her newfound impartiality. Instead, she was left with a bittersweet sensation, and as she departed her home for Digby's residence, she feared that her heart had been emptied rather than merely hardened.

Such thoughts were swept away instantly when Anne arrived at the reformer's home. Though not palatial, the decor nonetheless whispered of wealth. The house's rich but understated furnishings and trappings indicated something else, as well. Digby had none of the personal reasons that Brighton had to be involved in the reformers' movement, other than that he deemed it important enough to demand his attention. A man with a cause was always dangerous, Anne concluded, as the butler took her cloak. And she would do well to realize it.

As she waited for the servant to dispose of her garment, she could hear masculine voices coming from a parlor off the main hallway. From the sound of it, there were more than a handful of men gathered, and attempting to discern what they were saying, Anne was surprised at the mention of her own name.

"I don't understand why a woman of Miss Hargraves's standing would want to associate herself with us so closely. Ladies of society never become personally involved, they merely send round money or cartons of clothing their sewing circles have produced. I don't mind telling you that I find that singer's presence to be a hindrance."

"Now, now," Brighton's voice sounded, gentle and soothing, "I've made it a practice never to turn away anyone who wants to lend a hand."

"But a woman!" came unfamiliar tones in obvious disapproval.

"Much as I both like and admire Miss Hargraves," Alex Morrison's voice came echoing softly through the open doorway, "I must admit that she presents a problem. It is, at times, difficult to shield her delicate woman's sensibilities and still do what has to be done."

"Hear, hear," interjected angry tones Anne recognized as Digby's. "She's a nuisance, an obstacle standing in the way of our accomplishments. And I don't trust her! The staunch monarchists as well as those supporters of the prince who believe quite strongly in their own superior nobility are constantly observing us, trying to trip us up or catch us breaking a law. They would like to see us all in prison, or at least disbanded so that the status quo can continue."

"What has this to do with Miss Hargraves?" Brighton asked.

"I'll tell you," replied Digby. "She socializes all too frequently with those who would like to see our movement lose impetus. Haven't you noted how easily she flits from one set to the next, from loyal defenders of the queen such as the Duchess of Moreland to that dishonorable lot with whom the Prince of Wales has surrounded himself? Don't you think the possibility exists that her true sympathies could lie with one of them? That she has joined us merely to monitor our actions and report to those who are our enemies? And don't forget, Morrison, how she enticed you into paying that father for his children. You could have been arrested for that. In fact, you could still find yourself being visited by the constables and at the mercy of an unjust law."

"Do you really think so? I could never believe such a thing of Miss Hargraves," said Alex Morrison.

"You're too idealistic, boy, to see the world as it really is," Digby responded rudely, just as the butler returned to the vestibule and Anne. "Mark my words, we have to protect ourselves. How can we go ahead with our plans to change the plight of London's poor if we have Miss Hargraves constantly looking over our shoulders? I don't mind telling you, what with the importance of our next undertaking, I don't want her around. There's too much at stake."

"Digby, I want change as much as you do. As for Miss Hargraves—" Brighton began.

His words were drowned out, however, as the butler asked politely, "Whom shall I say is calling, miss?"

"Anne Hargraves," the shapely woman replied, watching the servant's face turn bright red as he hastily went to the meeting room to announce her and effectively put an end to the conversation of the moment.

Soon Anne was being ushered into a conspicuously hushed room. Of the dozen or so men present, a few appeared flustered and embarrassed, others curious, but only Digby had the effrontery to scowl.

"It would seem that I have arrived late, gentlemen. Do accept my apologies," the consummate performer said, her lashes dipping downward coquettishly. "In future I promise to be on time and never again allow tardiness, that unfortunate female trait, to materialize. I hope you will understand and find it possible to forgive me."

Amid a few mumbled assurances that there was no need for so charming a creature to ask for pardon, Anne took a chair at the head of the assembly vacated by one of those who felt guilty enough to stand until another seat could be procured. The vantage point this provided was an excellent one, and Anne proceeded to make eye contact with all present, smiling shyly at some and invitingly at others depending upon her assessment of each individual. Even Digby was extended an overture of friendship, though it only made his face appear much more grim in contrast. With the exception of her one main detractor, Anne was pleased to see that she had swayed this group of previously hostile men into accepting her, at least for the moment.

"Please don't allow me to interrupt this meeting more than I already have. I thought I heard someone talking about a new project. Go on with your discussion. I'm most anxious to know what this newest endeavor involves."

An uncomfortable, chagrined silence hung heavily in the air until Brighton cleared his throat and addressed the elegant intruder.

"Yes, well, you see, Miss Hargraves, we had just been discussing...that is, we were referring to a tenement we have but recently purchased."

"A tenement?" Anne queried, the soft cadence of her voice inconspicuously urging more details.

"Yes, we want to provide a home for children who have no one to take care of them, those who are now living in the streets of one of our poorest areas."

"An orphanage or perhaps a school?" the lovely blonde prompted.

"Neither," Digby responded gruffly. "What decent couple would want to adopt children of the lowest class? And what would those ill-bred infants do with an education? No. We mean to be much more practical. What we intend to do is make them productive members of society who will be able to support themselves in those professions for which they were meant."

"And how will you accomplish this?" Anne asked, conscious of Digby's peculiar lack of sympathy.

"We will scrub these children clean, get them jobs in the factories and furnish them with a safe place to sleep at night. Their salaries, of course, will go toward the running of the home."

"Of course," Anne replied, frowning in spite of herself.

"It really is a worthy goal," Morrison said, "a charitable and practical solution to the dilemma."

"I quite agree," Anne lied, forcing her exquisite features into an expression of approval. "And surely you realize that I would like to be involved. I know I could be of some use. Where is this building? I would very much like to see it."

"It's in the East End on Cornwall Street," Morrison blurted before Digby could stop him.

"Splendid. I shall go there the day after tomorrow, and hope that a few of you gentlemen will be able to meet me there in the afternoon.

"Why?" Digby asked pointedly.

"I would like to get some idea of how much money will be needed to refurbish the place."

"And are you volunteering to foot the bill for this yourself, Miss Hargraves?" Digby asked smugly.

"I will make a substantial contribution. But I believe I can do better than that," Anne replied, a plan beginning to form. "What would you gentlemen say to the idea of my giving a concert, with all of the proceeds going toward the renovation and furnishing of this house of yours?"

Anne's suggestion met with an enthusiastic reception, and there were those who were now only too happy to take her on a tour of the near-crumbling building the society had acquired.

Soon Anne found herself embroiled in planning the logistics of her concert, not the least of which was when and where it should take place. It was many hours later, therefore, before Brighton escorted her home.

Though she invited him to stay for coffee or a brandy, the reformer characteristically ventured no farther than Anne's vestibule, where he stayed for but a moment before he left under Brewster's approving stare.

By now exhaustion began to settle over Anne like a mantle of snow over a forgotten garden. It had been an emotionally wrenching day, as well as a long one. Yet as she mounted the stairs to her bedroom, she knew that she would find sleep an elusive thing that night.

How differently the day was ending from the way it had begun. This morning she had awakened within Ian's strong, comforting arms, and this evening she was going to bed alone, the dark-haired Englishman no longer a part of her personal life. Reaching the landing, Anne sighed and told herself that she had accepted the situation.

Acquiescence, however, did little to ease her pain as she undressed and climbed into her lonely bed. Running her palm along the spot where Ian had lain beside her, Anne wondered if perhaps the Duchess of Moreland had not been right. What was public acclaim compared to private devotion?

Seeking to banish this depressing idea, Anne turned to thoughts of more immediate matters. Tomorrow was the dinner party being given by Lord and Lady Chadwick, and there she would continue with the course of action she had set in motion at this evening's meeting.

First, there were preparations for her concert, which, if things could be arranged to her satisfaction, could promote some degree of safety for Victoria upon the sovereign's return to London. Second, if what she had overheard at tonight's gathering of socialists was any indication, it would be easy enough to provoke the assassin, no matter to which group he belonged, into believing that she was a hindrance, an enemy who could put an end to his plans and therefore had to be removed.

With any luck, the madman would attempt to take Anne's life before the queen's jubilee and thus be apprehended. And, if he could not be prompted into acting beforehand, the concert at the People's Palace would put her on center stage, in full view of the killer. Anne hoped, as a last resort, it would be a temptation he would not be able to ignore.

It hardly mattered, she thought, if these operations proved a bit dangerous. She had lived under the shadow of greater hazards in the past. But it wasn't mere loyalty to her country that made Anne reckless and lacking in concern for her own safety. Rather, at the moment, she felt that she had very little left to lose.

The next morning, Anne was surprised to find Brewster almost solicitous. Her coffee was made exactly as she liked it, her fruit chilled and her toast warm when she came to the table. But in addition to that, the meal was served without muttered comments or caustic admonitions.

Watching Brewster suspiciously as he glided silently in and out of the room, speaking only to ask after her comfort, Anne had the vague but improbable notion that he sensed she was distressed and he was seeking to make things better. But she immediately discarded the conjecture as ridiculous. If Brewster was quiet and acting as a butler ought, it was most likely because he was having an off day.

"I don't know about this, Anne," Nigel Conway found himself saying a short while later. "Some of it sounds rather too perilous, and I don't want to find myself without my best agent."

"Oh, Nigel," an amused Anne protested, her laugh rich and vibrant. "The danger is really minimal. If you knew half the things I've done while working for you, this wouldn't cause you to fret one bit."

"Somehow, that's not an altogether comforting thought. However, the point is that I *do* know about these plans, and I can't say as I agree with all of them."

"You certainly can't object to my giving a concert on the day the queen returns from Balmoral. The reformers will have to attend, and I can see to it that the prince's crowd feels it is a social event not to be missed. And since I've already sung at *their* dinner party, we might be able to press the Irish contingent, as well. Anyone we suspect of doing the queen harm will be in the concert hall. That should make Her Majesty's return to Windsor a bit safer.''

''And if the person we seek is not present, or leaves early?''

''He will be conspicuous by his absence, and we will know with whom we are most likely dealing. That will make our job a bloody sight easier.''

''I have no quarrel with that part of your scheme,'' Nigel pointed out, sighing softly in exasperation. ''It's the other that bothers me, and well you know it. I don't want you drawing out the madman by calling his attention to you.''

''But we have to do something, Nigel. Time is passing all too quickly, and we haven't been able to single out anyone...''

''Anyone but Ian Kendrick,'' muttered Nigel.

''Anyone,'' emphasized Anne, ''as the individual who poses a threat to Victoria. Surely, if I made that person, whoever he is, suspect that I stand in his way or that I have an inkling as to what he is plotting, he would have to do something about it.''

''My point exactly,'' Conway said, his expression one of concern. ''He *will* do something, and I'm not prepared to have you pay the consequences.''

''Should it be the queen who pays for your reluctance in this matter?'' Anne argued. ''Really, Nigel, you speak as if I am a novice. I can take care of myself. I've been doing it quite well these past six years.''

''So you have, my dear, but—''

''No buts. Neither one of us has any choice in the matter. We must simply do what we have set out to do, protect our monarch.''

''I suppose you're right. And it is only for that reason that I give my unwilling blessing to this undertaking of yours. But what bothers me most is the excitement dancing in your eyes at the prospect of stalking this would-be killer. I don't want you putting yourself in any unnecessary danger. Is that clear?"

"Perfectly," Anne said, her green eyes a bit too wide and guileless to suit her superior.

"I mean it, Miss Hargraves," Sir Nigel called out after Anne, who smiled at him sweetly before turning her back and exiting his office.

That evening, readying herself for the Chadwicks' dinner party, Anne was more meticulous than usual concerning her toilette. The dark pink material of her lavish evening gown fell seductively off her shoulders, exposing a daring amount of décolleté, which was emphasized all the more by the ruby and diamond necklace that ran across her delicate collarbone to sparkle and dangle just above her cleavage.

As Anne fussed with the curls that framed her face, she told herself that wanting to look her best was part of her job, and her attentions to appearance had nothing whatsoever to do with the fact that Ian Kendrick might be present. In fact, Anne thought, a crease marring her brow, it would be better for both of them if he played the gentleman and refrained from attending.

But if he should be there... well, she would deal with the situation as best she could. There was no sense in making herself anxious beforehand concerning a predicament that might not arise.

When Anne entered the ballroom of Lord and Lady Chadwick later that evening, she immediately became the center of attention. What had originated as a small, private dinner party had quickly escalated to a gathering of a good size when members of society had learned that Anne Hargraves was to be one of Lady Chadwick's guests.

Though she had met a few of them briefly around town, Anne looked out over a crowd of at least sixty and recognized no one she knew well until she gratefully spied the Duchess of Moreland in a far corner of the room. Making her way slowly in that direction, Anne breathed a small sigh of relief after her gaze swept the crowd. Ian Kendrick was nowhere to be seen.

Again and again, as she tried to cross the floor to converse with Aurora, Anne was stopped by men and women intent upon making her acquaintance. During each encounter, she was gracious, feigning interest in everyone she met. She was the master spy at her best, evidencing such sympathy and understanding concerning all that was said to her that people found it easy to talk with her, and to confide in her, as well.

She had already heard from their mother about the Randolph twins' bout with the measles, an illness that had left a pockmark on the shoulder of the livelier of the two girls. Then there had been Mrs. Wilson's concern that her daughter was interested in a man who was socially inferior, as well as the fact that Lord Davin had lost heavily on the races that very afternoon.

None of this information had been spoken as gossip, but rather given to Anne by those involved. As usual, she had dutifully commiserated or advised as each occasion had demanded. Her ability to invite confidences was a natural talent, one that made her valuable to both Nigel Conway and the British Crown.

Extricating herself from a group of middle-aged men discussing the advantages of their country estates, Anne turned to find Aurora, oddly enough without her daughter in tow.

"Not that I am less than overjoyed to see you, your ladyship," Anne began amicably, "but I could have sworn you told me that you do not travel in these circles."

"And so I don't, my dear, which is why I have so prudently left Audrey at home. There's no sense in exposing her to anyone who may be undesirable."

"And will you feel this way when Albert finally ascends the throne, and these people assume positions of power?" Anne asked with a glint lighting her eyes.

"My darling girl, for one so experienced, you're such an innocent. With a handful of possible exceptions, when His Highness finally becomes His Majesty, he won't need persons of this sort toadying to him. He'll have an entirely new circle of friends. I'm certain of it."

"I see. Then what is it that has tempted you to join the gathering this evening?" the guest of honor inquired.

"Why, to see for myself exactly what is going on between you and Kendrick, of course! Especially when both of you sent your regrets for the dinner party I had planned to hold," the older woman exclaimed as though Anne were extraordinarily dim-witted. "My curiosity is the only reason I am here tonight. I must admit, though, to being bitterly disappointed."

"Because Mr. Kendrick isn't here?"

"Why, no, my dear," Lady Moreland said, choosing her words quite carefully as she reached out to place a consoling hand on Anne's arm. "It's because Mr. Kendrick appears to be so utterly engrossed with Lady Chadwick's goddaughter."

Anne's usually supple body stiffened and her smile all but froze into place as she slowly turned toward the direction in which Aurora had subtly nodded. It was true; he was here. And he was more attractive than Anne had ever seen him. His broad shoulders filled his evening jacket admirably, while his trousers had been tapered to closely hug his slim hips. As Ian bent to hear what Lady Chadwick's breathless goddaughter was saying, that appealing lock of unruly hair fell across his forehead, a visual intimation of his engagingly roguish character. But it was his smile that tugged at Anne's heart; that captivating, lazy grin she had found so alluring was now being bestowed on another woman.

Holding her emotions in check, Anne turned to her companion, the graceful sway of her body concealing the tension she felt.

"I told you there was nothing between us, your ladyship," Anne admonished gently. "But you would have none of it. Now perhaps you'll believe me."

"Well, I still say there should be something there," the noblewoman insisted. "The two of you are so well suited."

"I think not," Anne declared lightly, all too conscious of Ian bending ever closer to that abominable young woman and whispering something in her ear that made the minx blush, flutter her lashes and smile all at the same time.

Straining to pay attention to the constant chatter of the duchess, Anne nevertheless found it difficult to do so. Instead, her imagination was running loose, suggesting a veritable plethora of wicked things Ian might have drawled to the female gazing at him so adoringly. Wasn't he supposed to be busy chaperoning Jack rather than pursuing young socialites himself? Anne thought irritably.

Why hadn't the man had the good grace to stay away from this dinner party? After all that had passed between them, how could Ian Kendrick have expected her to ignore him, to stay on her side of the room instead of flying to his side?

Could it be because their interlude had meant so little to him? The idea produced a small frown until Anne caught herself and turned her attention to Aurora Palmer once more.

"But, my dear," the woman was saying as if talking to her own daughter, "if you have no interest in Mr. Kendrick, I can't see why you should grimace at my suggestion that I introduce you to Wallingcroft before we are all summoned to dinner. After all, the man possesses a title and is fairly attractive, even if he does travel with Bertie's crowd. Besides, who knows who that ninny, Gladys, has placed beside you at the dinner table? And what with all these predatory males circling, many of whom are married, mind you, I would feel much better if I delivered you to the hands of someone I deem worthy of such a privilege."

Before she could demur, Anne found herself standing beside Charles Crosby, the Earl of Wallingcroft, and none too subtly deserted by the indomitable Duchess of Moreland. From the first, it was obvious that the man was quite taken with Lady Chadwick's chief guest, so taken, in fact, that he failed most miserably at all attempts to converse. It was with a sense of relief that Anne looked over her shoulder to see another guest in the process of joining them.

This, she learned from Wallingcroft, was Tyler Fielding, Earl of Bradford, a man as different from Charles Crosby as spring from winter. While Wallingcroft held himself stiffly, Bradford was smooth, charming and more than a little flirtatious. In fact, unbeknownst to the puzzled lady upon whom Ian had been lavishing such regard, it was Bradford's attention to Anne that caused Mr. Kendrick's words to suddenly turn frosty and his sparkling gray eyes to transform into shards of ice.

But Anne, unlike Ian, was very much unaware of what was transpiring across the room. Instead, she was concentrating desperately on the conversation at hand, her sole defense from the grieving heart this evening seemed to promise.

It was only when the topic turned to Prince Albert that Wallingcroft suddenly became animated and quite comfortable with seeking to dominate the conversation, a fact Anne noted with interest. Here was a subject obviously quite dear to the earl's heart, and he waxed eloquent concerning Bertie's more favorable attributes, giving particular emphasis to what it would mean for the nation once the prince ascended the throne.

Not to be outdone, Bradford more than held his own, each man vying to demonstrate that he was the more knowledgeable about the Prince of Wales. But when the men had exhausted their sentiments and were in the course of expressing them a second time, Anne interrupted and introduced a topic of her own, designed to mark her as a reformer and a danger to the future of the high-living South Kensington Crowd.

Sweetly yet zealously, she fairly pontificated about the plight of the London poor, voicing a reformer's social conscience. She talked of plans to influence the prince so that he might see things from her viewpoint, a goal the two gentlemen standing beside her had no doubts she would be able to accomplish, as beautiful and seductive as she was. But when Anne went on to speak about a better society molded by the future king, wherein there was no place for noblemen interested only in their own wealth and power, both earls were appalled.

Telling her shocked companions that she realized things must begin on a small scale, she mentioned the tenement on Cornwall Street, which she would be visiting the following afternoon. Finally, she concluded by briefly outlining her plans for a charity concert at the People's Palace and her intention of inspecting the premises two evenings hence in preparation for that event.

When Anne had finished, both men looked at her askance. Wallingcroft hurriedly excused himself and stalked away. For his part, Bradford stood his ground, deciding that a pretty little thing like Anne Hargraves could never be capable of forming an original thought and was merely parroting what the reformers had been preaching to her. He found the thought a soothing one and considered it his duty, as a superior intellect, to help shape this impressionable young woman's mind. After enough conversations with him, he'd soon have her on the right track... and perhaps in his bed, as well.

His thoughts were interrupted, however, by the announcement that dinner was being served. Reluctantly, he relinquished Anne's company to their host, Lord Chadwick, who had come to escort the renowned singer to the dining room.

Here, rather than the formal table she had been expecting, Anne saw an elaborate supper buffet laid out, and a score of small, damask-clothed tables where guests could enjoy their repast quietly and intimately while still being able to observe the actions of almost all those around them.

For Anne, such a design dissolved the stigma of being put on display in a place of honor beside her host and allowed her to continue mingling with those assembled, as all were free to go from one table to another whenever they so chose. It was a delightful concept, and Anne smiled sincerely as Lady Chadwick joined her husband and the three of them found a table with just enough chairs to suit their party.

Complimenting the hostess on the success of her evening and the superior quality of the food, Anne nevertheless managed to mention in passing both her concert and her scheduled visits to the tumbledown house on Cornwall Street and the People's Palace.

Though the information drove Lady Chadwick to glance at her husband, who responded with a questioning lift of his brow, neither the earl nor his lady gave voice to disapproving comments concerning Anne's proposals. Despite her present standing in society, Anne Hargraves was an artiste, and therefore could be counted upon to be somewhat un-orthodox in her behavior and ideas. Both host and hostess appeared to feel that this explained, if not excused, the woman's odd interest in the reform movement.

After a bit more conversation, the Chadwicks left the ta-ble, ostensibly to see to the comfort of their other guests, but in all likelihood, Anne thought wryly, to increase their own importance by circulating the gossip about her eccentric plans. Busy with her plate, Anne was not surprised when she sensed someone immediately slipping into one of the va-cant chairs. There were, she knew, at least a score of men present who wanted to be seen having a private word with Anne Hargraves, the seductive songstress of controversial reputation.

She was not prepared, however, for the shock of looking up to see that it was Ian who had put himself at her table. The nearness of him, and his powerful, utterly masculine presence, all but took her breath away, so that at first, Anne was quite incapable of speech.

"Good evening, Anne," he began. Though his voice was deep and rich, Anne wondered if she didn't detect a trace of awkwardness underscoring his simple greeting. Strong and sophisticated as ever, Ian nevertheless gave subtle evidence of wistful discomfort at being in his former lover's com-pany.

Such a boyish attitude in so virile and commanding a fig-ure practically demanded Anne's sympathy, but she waged a valiant and silent struggle against the emotions he so ef-fortlessly called forth.

"Ian," she replied curtly, her traitorous throat beginning to close as tension raced through her body. "How's Jack?"

"Look here, Anne," Ian insisted, dropping his voice to a whisper and bending closer in imitation of the gesture a bristling Anne had seen him employ with Lady Chadwick's goddaughter. "Though we've suspended our relationship for the moment, there is no reason to ignore each other when we meet in public."

"I assure you, Ian, my purpose wasn't to ignore you," Anne protested hoarsely, a wistful trace of a smile playing about her lips when he captured her small hand within his large, proprietary fingers. "I've simply been kept fright-fully busy by the attentions of others."

"Yes," Ian murmured, a frown flitting across his aristo-cratic features so swiftly that Anne questioned whether she had seen it at all. "As long as you're not trying to avoid me, dearest girl. Because there is no need for that."

There is plenty of need, Anne wanted to scream. How can I think of anything else when you are near? How can I keep myself from running to your side and pleading with you to take me to your bed? And worst of all, how can I imagine you would ever be involved in an attempt to assassinate the queen when I am half mad with wanting you whenever I glance in your direction?

But Anne, a master of deception, hinted at none of these feelings churning within her breast. Instead, she gently ex-tricated her hand from the warmth of Ian's grasp and pre-sented him with her most dazzling smile.

"I know that, Ian," she said, her raspy voice ringing with a sincerity that no one would suspect of being false. "In fact, I'm glad we have a few moments alone to chat as friends should. I have planned a concert, you know, since last I've seen you."

"Yes, I've just heard buzzings to that effect," Ian re-marked coldly. "I had thought plans for your upcoming tour and your charity work would be taking up all your time. It surprised me you were able to attend this evening."

Oh, and is that why you were obliged to seek the affec-tions of another, Anne wanted to cry, because you sup-posed I wouldn't be here? Instead she smiled coyly and patted his hand.

"You know how it is, Ian. One can't work all the time. Even I have to relax periodically, just as you slipped the role of Jack's guardian tonight. At any rate, this new concert is to be given for charity, raising money for Brighton's cause."

"How magnanimous of you," Ian replied, his gray eyes narrowing as he studied the exquisite face before him with sudden intensity.

"Oh, bother," Anne decried. "In reality it's little more than a dress rehearsal for my tour. But I was wondering if I couldn't count upon you for some assistance."

"In what way?" he inquired, refusing to release her from his dominating gaze.

"The evening after next, I'll be inspecting the People's Palace, the site proposed for this hastily planned performance. Because it's so new, I've no idea of the lighting or acoustics. If you're free, I thought you might go with me and help decide if it is, indeed, a suitable place."

"I don't know anything about lighting and such," Ian proclaimed, while suspicions quickly surfaced concerning Anne's purpose in inviting him to escort her.

"No, I don't suppose you do," Anne said in that throaty voice that had always preceded their lovemaking, the voice that even now ignited a fire in Ian's loins. "The lighting I can judge for myself. But I need someone I can trust to sit in the balconies and listen, to tell me if I can be easily heard."

"I'd like to accommodate you, but I'm afraid it's impossible. I'm engaged for the evening," Ian lied, deciding prudently that he could not trust himself to be alone with this enticing woman.

"Oh, I see," Anne murmured, her expression of disappointment making it clear that she assumed his engagement included another woman. "Well, never mind. I wouldn't want you to think of changing your plans."

"But they're not my plans; they're Jack's," Ian hastened to add in an effort to correct any conclusion Anne might have erroneously drawn.

"Not another trip to Madame Duvalier's, I hope," Anne teased, her pouting lips glistening so alluringly that Ian was finding it difficult to focus on their discourse.

He wanted nothing so much as he wanted to ravish her, here and now, without thought or care as to who was present. To love her so intensely that she, too, would forget where she was and who else was there. Good Lord, if he felt that way at the moment, he certainly didn't need to be alone with this enchanting creature in an empty hall. No, that was one place he couldn't accompany Anne Hargraves, Ian decided. It would be nothing less than direct disobedience to the orders he had received from the prince, and he congratulated himself on being able to deny her request even as he

sought to create some elaboration for his excuse in not doing so.

"Thank God, no," Ian responded with a laugh that hid,
for a moment, the husky tones of desire creeping into his
voice. "No, actually I'm keeping Jack close at hand. I've
suggested he do some entertaining, though only on a small
scale, that evening. And I fear I should be present. Though
the boy is seventeen, there are times I question his maturity. Actually, most of the time. If I were to go out that evening, I suspect I would come home to a veritable bac-
chanalia, complete with wine, women and song."

"Oh, dear, I wonder wherever he learned such hedonis-
tic behavior?" Anne commented dryly.

"Surely you're not suggesting from me," Ian objected in
a fierce whisper. "Come now, Anne, certainly you don't
think I am forever seeking to indulge myself in the sort of
thing we shared. That's not a fair assumption to make."

"I suppose not," the blonde replied with a tender yet enigmatic expression.

"Look, if there's anything else I could do to help you,"
Ian began.

"Of course, I'd turn to you. But as of now, I can't think
of anything. Tomorrow I'll be going to Cornwall Street to
have a look at the building Brighton and his associates have
purchased."

"The East End! Really, Anne, you should stay out of that
neighborhood. It's not safe for you."

It's much less hazardous than sitting here with you, Anne
wanted to say. Instead, she replied with other words, ones
that meant much less to her.

"Be reasonable, Ian! I've walked through the back alley-
ways of Cairo and Alexandria, wandered along the narrow,
twisting streets of Calcutta, explored the medina in Constantinople..."

"That's all very well, but that was before I could stop you
from such foolish behavior," Ian argued in hushed tones.

"Stop me?" Anne questioned in amazement.

"Yes, stop you," came Ian's angry reply. How could this
woman possibly think he would allow her to put herself in
danger, he wondered peevishly.

"You have nothing to say in the matter," Anne stated simply.

"I have plenty to say."

"What I mean is that you have no right," Anne insisted with quiet dignity.

"I don't care what you think my rights are, Anne. Your upcoming concert is more than enough involvement in the reform movement. I won't have you going into the East End again, as well. I simply will not allow it."

Before the words were out of his mouth, Ian knew he had made a mistake. He had simply wanted to keep this stubborn woman from possible harm. However, the need, deep within him, to safeguard Anne was an urge so fierce, so acute that it had completely taken control, and he had managed only to brand himself a boor. Yet even this knowledge could not help the dark-haired Englishman master his protective instinct, and it drove him to continue his diatribe in the face of Anne's sudden, angry silence.

"I mean what I said, Anne. You are not to go to Cornwall Street tomorrow. In fact, I expressly forbid it. Do you understand what I've said?"

"Quite," came the frosty reply as Anne rose gracefully from the table and walked away. Finding her host and hostess, she bade them goodbye and never once looked over her enticingly bared shoulder to see the impact her departure had upon Ian.

Ian heaved a long, drawn-out sigh as he watched Anne go. What had happened to his sophistication, his élan, his bloody civilized conduct? What was it about Anne Hargraves that made him want to respond to her on such a primitive level? Confound it, but civilization was something he had always admired. It fostered impeccably polite speech and socially correct behavior, building a wall behind which a man could hide his primal instincts. But no matter how desperately he tried to reinforce that wall, Anne had no difficulty whatsoever in dismantling it brick by bloody brick.

Right now, Ian was so furious with Anne that he wanted to throttle her, yell at her, shake her and then, inexplicably, to tenderly swoop her up in his arms, carry her off and show her how much he wanted her. Bloody hell, how would he ever deal with it if he discovered that she was truly involved with a plot to kill Victoria?

Chapter Thirteen

A solitary figure walked along the London streets in the dissipating gloom of early morning. At every corner along the proposed parade route, he slowed, his trained marksman's eye assessing the opportunities afforded by such a vantage point.

Would it be a pistol round from the street or a rifle shot from one of the buildings fronting the road along which Victoria would travel for her jubilee procession? He'd have to make up his mind soon. Of a certainty, his aim with a pistol was much more deadly, but the use of a rifle promised him a chance to escape. If he stood alone in the shadows of a curtained window, who would be able to identify him once he had completed his task and joined the throng on the streets?

Of course he would like to remain at large, to participate in the changes that would take place once the old woman was gone. But he couldn't be selfish, he berated himself, a glaze descending over his eyes as he became lost in visions of his homeland without Victoria. No. His own feelings didn't count. After all, heroes never allowed their own emotions to shape their actions. They were drawn on by something much grander, much nobler. It was immaterial whether or not he ever enjoyed the bright days to come. What was important was that he would be the person who would give England her future.

He was immersed in reverie, and a beatific smile lighted the dreamer's face as he continued his march along Victoria's planned route. His sense of importance was as great as that belonging to any monarch when he pictured the homage history would pay him. Was it too pompous to imagine being called the savior of the British Empire? He couldn't quite make up his mind.

Surely he would earn that title only if he employed the pistol and stood among the crowd, allowing them to witness his great deed. If that meant instantaneous death for himself, it would be a martyr's glorious leave-taking. But if he was apprehended and executed after a trial, that was acceptable, too. In the years to come, his country would discover just how much of a patriot he had been. Then his bravery would be extolled and his name added to the ranks of acknowledged English heroes. It would be more than an adequate compensation for death.

With such thoughts dominating his mind, the inconspicuous madman almost stumbled over a crate of kale outside a greengrocer's establishment. As he worked hard to keep himself upright, his euphoria vanished as though it had never existed, and an uncalled-for wrath took its place. The man's face darkened and his smile twisted into an expression of anger so intense that the greengrocer's boy hid behind the door, too afraid to come out and ask if the gentleman had been injured.

Obstacles! There were always obstacles to watch out for. The man cursed silently, hurrying now to reach Westminster, as though some force was trying to keep him away. Nothing was going to stand in his path, he vowed, a demonic look glimmering in his downcast eyes. Not crates of kale, nor passersby, not the army, nor the government, not society or even the Prince of Wales. He would allow no one to stop him from changing the course of English history.

This especially included the intrusive Miss Anne Hargraves! Didn't she think anyone would notice how easily she moved back and forth between the diverse social circles of the reformers and those attending the Prince of Wales? Or did she think her beauty would blind them all? One night she was at a reformers' meeting and the next she was sparkling at a society party!

But he was too smart for her. He knew that she had to be working in some capacity for the other group, carrying

whispers and rumors to their ears. Perhaps she even suspected what he planned to do. But it didn't matter. What
more was she than another obstacle that had to be overcome, better still, removed? he thought, giving way to the
violence the crate of kale had unleashed. What was one
more human life when weighed against the fate of the empire?

Once the decision had been made, he felt the peace that
had eluded him ever since he had made the singer's acquaintance. His steps slowed from their frantic pace, and his
facial features relaxed. The little wren may have flown to
Balmoral, but she was expected to return soon. And in the
interim, there was the warbling songbird to dispatch. One
plain little wren and one magnificently plumaged songbird... What contrasting targets he had to claim his attention. He could hardly wait to get home in order to write
about them.

"I must repeat that I don't find this at all appropriate,
miss," Matthew Brewster said in a clear and strident voice
rather than resorting to his usual muttering.

"And I repeat that I don't care whether you consider my
behavior bloody appropriate or not," Anne stated calmly as
she pulled on her gloves.

"But really, miss, the East End again?"

"Yes, Brewster, the East End. Now why don't you run
along and polish the silver, or whatever it is you do, until I
return?" the diminutive woman suggested as the portly servant followed her out onto the front steps. "I promise you
that I shall be in no real danger on Cornwall Street."

"But your reputation will be," the stocky little man persisted gruffly, searching for something to conceal his concern for this young agent's well-being. "What happens if
you are seen?"

"Ah, I should have guessed what was at the crux of this
matter—my reputation, and I suppose yours, since you do
work for me. Well, I hate to disillusion you, Brewster, but
my good name vanished quite some time ago, and I must
enlighten you to the fact that life has been jolly more fun
without it. You should try it for yourself."

With that, the determined blonde walked to her waiting carriage, and after accepting the driver's assistance, gave him instructions to be off immediately. She was not about to give Matthew Brewster further opportunity to dissuade her from this afternoon's business.

Men! There was not one of them who realized she could fend for herself, had been doing just that for years, and anticipated doing so in the future.

As the carriage jolted forward and then pulled quickly away, Matthew Brewster found himself quite put out. There was just no reasoning with that obdurate woman.

Turning to go inside the building, which he considered his own purgatory on earth, a small bundle of drab cloth at the corner of the step caught his attention. Clucking his tongue in displeasure at such a shabby sight, he bent to retrieve it and was surprised to feel something wrapped within the confines of the nondescript rags.

He unrolled it curiously and almost gasped when the contents fell into his pudgy hand. It was a finch, a little songbird, and its neck had been quite deliberately broken.

Staring at the tiny, grotesque figure sprawled in his palm, Brewster couldn't help but connect this threatening affront with those strange noises at the rear door a few nights previously. Whoever was behind this was likely to act here, at the house, the butler decided, recalling the odd scratches at the back door.

While Miss Hargraves was most probably safe for the moment, the situation certainly called for increased vigilance as well as a visit to Nigel to inform him of the repulsive warning that had been delivered.

That resolved, Brewster gently enshrouded the small, still form of the finch once more, straightened his shoulders and entered the house.

Ian found it difficult to write the report he had promised the prince. What with Jack knocking on his door over an inconsequential matter, and Mrs. Land barging in with a luncheon tray, ready to converse before she returned to her duties, there was just no getting down to work.

"No," he muttered, being honest with himself as he threw his pen down with a half-strangled curse. "It's not that at all, is it?"

Ian Kendrick knew that his inability to complete the afternoon's task had very little to do with the routine goings-on of his household. It was something much more serious that was distracting him. It was his constant thinking about Anne Hargraves. She haunted him incessantly, giving him no peace. And whose fault was it but his own? He had allowed himself to succumb to her enchantment, he who had never thought to lose his soul to the demons of love. And they were demons, he was convinced, because they did nothing but torment him mercilessly.

For their weapon they had chosen a female who constantly perplexed and bewildered him, he, Ian Kendrick, a man who had always understood women so easily! But Anne...Anne was unlike any other woman he had ever known.

The talented beauty was a creature of contrasts. She was worldly yet vulnerable, fragile but strong, loving though distant, all at the same time. Good God! Was it any wonder she was driving him mad, Ian asked himself disgustedly as he pushed his chair away from his desk.

Though all temptation was by its very nature attractive, had any man ever known the degree of enticement she delivered, this lovely and unique woman who was a part of society yet stood apart from its rules? And it was Anne's flouting of society's dictates that made Ian so apprehensive. Could she care so little for accepted morality that she saw nothing wrong with committing a heinous crime in order to institute what she considered to be a greater good? Ian would have wagered his life that this was not the case, but it was the life of the queen that concerned him, and not his own.

Tapping splayed fingers on the highly polished surface of his desk, Ian once more considered the enigma that was Anne Hargraves. No matter what Bertie's suspicions were concerning the beautiful songstress, Ian wanted nothing other than to protect her. That damnable and illogical sentiment was what had caused him to enrage her last night.

But, he consoled himself, feeling very much a martyr, it had been for her own good, if not for his. At least her going to the East End this afternoon was one less worry with which he had to contend, he rationalized, pulling himself closer to his desk in an attempt to get down to work once more. After his orders last night, she wouldn't dare stir in that direction. Or would she?

Suddenly Ian was none too certain of Anne's behavior, and the words of his report blurred before him as he picked up his pen. Damn it! She wouldn't completely ignore his wishes, would she, especially when he had stressed that his prohibition had been issued for good reason? Despite the fact that his ego balked at entertaining such a possibility, doubts nibbled away at Ian's conviction that Anne would obey him in this matter until he realized he was not able to do anything other than brood.

What he needed was a respite from his labors, perhaps a breath of fresh air. Yes, that was what he would do. He would go for a walk, quite possibly along Cornwall Street, and then, when he was assured that Anne had indeed heeded his instructions, he could return refreshed, ready to tackle this bleeding report. Within an instant he was on his feet, coat flung over his shoulders, then out the door, leaving Jack to wonder just what was bothering his moody brother now.

As her carriage approached Cornwall Street, Anne was still struggling with her anger at both Ian Kendrick and Brewster. Imagine them thinking her incapable of looking out for herself in the East End! To Anne's way of thinking, a shoddy area and some poor but desperate people presented very little in the way of real peril.

And if such an excursion angered them, she shuddered to think how they would react should they ever have any inkling as to why she was really here. Brewster would be positively apoplectic if he knew she was attempting to entrap a would-be assassin. And Ian, well, Ian would be enraged as no one had ever seen him. The thought of his passionate fury, originating in his concern for her well-being, caused a thrill to journey down Anne's spine and center in her most

secret being until she was jolted by another idea. Ian's rage
might very well stem from the fact that he was the man she
was trying to bring to justice.

Brushing such frightening thoughts away as the carriage
came to a stop before a dilapidated edifice, Anne carefully
arranged her facial features to hide her emotions. By the
time she stood at the doorway of her conveyance, she wore
a sweet, unconcerned smile, which completely belied the
turbulence of her heart.

Standing on the walkway were Andrew Brighton, Oliver
Digby, Alex Morrison and two others. Anne ignored Digby's scowl as she granted permission for Alex to help her
down from the carriage. Greeting the rest, she allowed herself to be ushered into the deteriorating building that cried
out so plaintively for repairs. Even the door handle appeared to stick before it could be properly turned.

The interior was dank, a foul odor permeating the air, so
much so that Anne wondered if cleaning and paint alone
would rid the place of its smell of despair. It was difficult to
immediately assess the condition of the room in which she
stood, as most of its windows, like those in the rest of the
house, had been boarded up to keep out intruders.

But as Anne's eyes adjusted to the dim light while one of
the men started a fire in the grate, she could see that the attempt had been unsuccessful. Piles of rags gave evidence
that some desperate souls had been sleeping here until very
recently. So recently, in fact, that mice and rats had yet to
eat the stale bread and moldy cheese left behind on a rickety table, or to devour the bit of gruel congealed in a pot.

"Well, my dear Miss Hargraves, perhaps it is best that
you see this place at its worst so that you will be all the more
enthralled by its appearance once we have renovated it and
put it to good use," Brighton said enthusiastically, warmed
by his vision of just what would be accomplished in the near
future in this very building.

"I for one apologize that you should be exposed to such
squalor," Alex said with a soft smile.

"Not to worry," Anne reassured him as she continued to
look about the depressing room. "Dreams can sweep away
cobwebs in an instant."

"Besides, she wanted to come, didn't she?" Oliver Digby asked gruffly. "And didn't we get here an hour beforehand to chase away the squatters so that she wouldn't be offended by their presence?"

"Poor blighters, I wonder where they will spend tonight?" Alex asked, his brown eyes awash with sympathy, as though he actually felt their hurt.

"Probably back in here if we don't board up the remaining windows," Digby replied. "I suggest we attend to it before we leave."

"Much as I hate to displace people, I fear I must agree," Brighton said. "We can't afford to have any further damage done here. There's always the off chance those poor devils would accidentally burn the place to the ground in an attempt to keep warm or cook whatever food they can scavenge."

"If you don't mind, I would like to tour the house in its entirety," Anne requested, hoping to forestall a debate. "It would give me more of a feel as to what needs to be done, how much material has to be purchased and so forth, before the place is habitable."

"Would you like us to fetch you a bucket and scrub brush as well, so you can clean the place, too, before we depart?" an irritated Digby asked, his supercilious manner most unkind.

"Here, here, there's no need for that," Brighton reprimanded, his tone stern. "Miss Hargraves is in no way overstepping her bounds in wanting to inspect this building and to help decide just what is needed to repair it. She is, after all, making much of this possible with the concert she has planned for the People's Palace."

"So everyone has told me, but it's not an actuality yet, is it?" Digby asked.

"No, but it will be shortly. In fact, I am going to the hall tomorrow night to ascertain its appropriateness as the site of the concert. If it meets my expectations, we can publicize the date of the event as early as the next day," Anne said soothingly.

"There, you see, we'll pull this off yet," Morrison said, his eyes glowing softly at the prospect.

"I have no doubts that we shall," Brighton said. "But until that time we'd best get busy here. Why don't a few of you escort Miss Hargraves upstairs so that she can have a look? Morrison and Digby, perhaps you can give me a hand with boarding up those windows."

"Certainly, I'll help. But I'd like to go back upstairs and search for my silver matchbox. I had it when we first came in to dispossess the squatters, but I seem to have dropped it. The thing was given to me by Stead, and I would hate to lose it," Alex mumbled, as he walked around poking about the floor of the room.

"Right. We'll meet you outside, then," Brighton said, he and Digby moving toward the doorway.

Anne walked to the broken-down stairway. While the other two men preceded her up its rotting skeleton, she allowed Alex the privilege of keeping a hand at her waist in order to assist her up the treacherous steps. Intending to examine the upper floors first, she thought she would finish her investigation of the downstairs level afterward, once the fire in the hearth had warmed the main room and quite possibly removed a bit of the dampness.

Anne discovered that the upper rooms were little better than those below. They, too, were filled with refuse, the pitiful, decaying remnants of broken dreams. While Alex went from one tiny cubical to the next searching for his matchbox and making certain, he assured her, that no trespasser had managed to sneak onto the premises, Anne toured the upper levels in a more leisurely fashion in the company of the other two gentlemen.

Soon, however, she tired of their silent company at her elbow as she tried to visualize what potential each room held. Besides, how could she offer herself as a victim should the queen's possible killer be one of the reformers if she was forever being guarded by these two?

Sending them outside to help Brighton and Digby, Anne heard Alex calling to her from below, informing her that he would be outside should she need him when she descended the stairway. It didn't bother her to be left alone in the house, where, she assumed, her only companions were the shattered hopes of another, happier era and, if fortune smiled upon her, the man who proposed to do Victoria harm.

Noting that all the windows on this floor were boarded, Anne nonetheless had enough light from chinks in the wood to make out the physical condition of each chamber. The dimness, and the silence, broken only by the occasional scuttle of tiny rodent feet, reminded Anne of other slums she had seen during her years of working for Nigel Conway. Without meaning to do so, she began to remember those other places and other intrigues, so that she was not as vigilant as she should have been.

She had to have been alone for ten or fifteen minutes before she noticed the first signs of the fire. Initially there was a crackling noise she couldn't quite place, and then the fearful smell of smoke coming up the decaying staircase.

Anne's first instinct was to rush to one of the windows and push out some of the wooden planks covering the paneless frames, in order to alert the men outside. But the slats were thick, and she was small and not as strong as she had supposed. She called out anyway, but not even the power of her well-trained voice could penetrate the thick walls of the house with sufficient volume to be heard over the noise of the streets with their screaming children, squabbling adults, passing carts, barking dogs and the clanging of the hammer and anvil coming from the smithy next door.

Going to the top of the stairway, Anne's heart began to thump wildly in her chest as the smoke became more dense, and she could feel heat rising from below. There was no escape from the second floor other than this. Her only way out was to go down the rickety stairs and face the flames situated who knew where.

Pulling her shawl over her head and holding its fringed edge over her nose, Anne groped in the billowing gray clouds for the wall that would lead her down the steps. Then, feeling about gingerly with her foot, she distinguished the first tread and began her descent, hoping that she could recall which sections she should avoid. Praying she could hold her breath long enough to avert the possibility of being overcome by the thick, acrid puffs of gray smoke, she made her way downward.

Halfway through her suffocating journey, one of the planks beneath her foot sagged so severely that Anne thought it was about to give way. Struggling against instinct, she hastily jumped to the next level of the staircase, hoping she would find something solid beneath her when she landed. Finally, after a few more torturous moments, Anne found herself on the main floor of the house. Safety, however, was still far away.

It was difficult to orient herself in a setting that was so new to her, and the task became almost impossible due to the ever blackening smoke. Throwing herself down on the filthy floor, she found breathing only minimally easier. Lying still for a moment, she listened for the shouts of the men who were outside the house. Why weren't they trying to rescue her? Was it because, boarded up as the house was, the heavy dark clouds of smoke had still to find a means of escape, and therefore hadn't informed the men of the danger she faced? Or did they know exactly what was happening, and were only waiting for her to die before they returned to their homes?

Her throat was burning as Anne slithered along the floor in what she hoped was the direction of the door. Miraculously as she hunted along the wall, her probing fingers discerned the door frame. All that was left to do was stand, open the bloody thing and leave this inferno behind. But after all the effort of dragging her gasping body to its feet, Anne tried the doorknob only to feel it stick. She pounded on the thick oak, but to no avail. Was it the faulty handle that held her prisoner, or had she been deliberately locked within the burning tenement?

Though the wall running perpendicular to the one at which she stood appeared to be radiating more heat, Anne remembered that a few of the wooden slats covering the window situated there had come undone. Since the path to the rear of the house was blocked by hungrily licking tongues of flame, she hoped that perhaps at the wall she could force a means of escape.

She dropped to her stomach once more and made her agonizing way forward. Finally she reached the spot where the window should be situated. Reaching above her with great exertion and hindered by constant choking, she felt the sill directly overhead. But when Anne pulled herself up and tried to poke about for the openings she remembered seeing, her fingers only met with newly installed lumber nailed tightly into place.

A terrified sob escaped her lips as she fell to the floor once more. She hadn't thought her lungs contained enough air to make such a sound, just as they now denied the screech she attempted to emit, turning it into a frightening silent scream instead.

The crackling of burning wood was growing louder and more persistent, so that Anne thought she was breathing her last. But suddenly there was a shattering splinter of planks. Gratefully, she realized the sound wasn't caused by the fire, but by someone ripping the newly installed boards from the window above her.

Watching dazedly as smoke found a release from the confines of the house and poured out the window, it took Anne a moment to realize that this was her escape route, as well. Gathering what was left of her quickly vanishing strength, she made a monumental effort to stand and threw herself headlong through the opening, only to be caught in Andrew Brighton's waiting arms.

Cradled by Brighton and gasping for air as she lay amid her singed skirts on the pavement, Anne thought that she had never seen a bluer sky. The sight was all the more beautiful, she realized, because she had never thought to see the sky again.

After a moment, Anne's chest stopped heaving, and her breaths came easier. Slowly, the great pounding in her ears subsided, and she became conscious of the others inquiring as to her well-being and asking her what had occurred.

Slowly she surveyed the anxious men surrounding her, and to her surprise noted Tyler Fielding, the Earl of Bradford, among them. Her curiosity as to his presence had to wait to be satisfied, however, as Brighton took charge. In a commanding voice he began to direct an effort aimed at saving the burning tenement, the activity of the men leaving Anne in the care of her coachman.

It was obvious, by this time, that entry into the front room, whether by window or pried door, was out of the question. Though access through the rear entrance was possible, the reformers and Bradford soon learned that any endeavors to beat out the blaze without help was beyond them. All they could do was await the fire brigade as they watched their dreams turn to ashes.

"How could this have happened?" Brighton asked mournfully when the men collected around Anne Hargraves once more.

"Do you mean how could *she* have allowed this to occur?" Digby asked, his lips tightly drawn together as he launched a look of condemnation at the woman now struggling to her feet with the aid of Alex Morrison.

"I allowed it to happen?" Anne asked, swaying in exhausted outrage, too tired to slap this noxious man as he deserved. "The fire started downstairs while I was still on the upper floor."

"So you say," Digby intoned, quite blatantly dismissing her explanation without considering it seriously. "But how do we know it wasn't you who began this fire in the first place?"

"And why would I do such a thing, trapping myself inside a burning building?" Anne asked, her words edged with condescension.

"Really, Digby, she's been through enough. Leave her alone," Alex Morrison ordered, his voice sharper than Anne had ever heard it.

"Yes, she has," Brighton agreed sympathetically, "but still I must ask you, Miss Hargraves, can you give us any insight as to how this catastrophe took place?"

"I assumed I was alone in the house, upstairs as I've said. Suddenly I heard that horrible snapping sound a fire makes when it devours everything with which it comes in contact, and I smelled smoke coming from below. My guess is that the blaze started in one of those heaps of rags in the front room."

"But how, my dear, if you were alone?" Brighton pressed, gently offering his support when it appeared that a still wobbling Anne might sink down to the pavement. "Did you hear anyone?"

"No. But then there was a lot of hammering going on. How is it, though, that no one else noticed the smoke?" Anne demanded, fixing her companions with a hard stare as she fought to regain her equilibrium.

"You were the one boarding up things in the front of the house, Digby. Surely you must have smelled something," Morrison stated, his words rife with insinuation.

"I was situated downwind of the smithy's fire, you young fool. Smoke was all around me standing where I was. Since I didn't expect the tenement to be set aflame, I didn't notice whether the odor was coming from inside or outside the bloody building."

"I'm certain the entire thing was an accident," Brighton interjected before things could get out of hand. "After all, we had lit a fire in the hearth. In all probability, an ember escaped and landed on the refuse inside."

"Or one of the squatters returned and torched the place, disgruntled that he had been evicted," Morrison offered as he patted Anne's hand solicitously. "It could also explain why I was unable to locate my matchbox. The blighter must have taken it with him!"

"But all this supposes that the man was able to enter by the rear door, go into the front room and exit as he had come, all without being seen," one of the gentlemen who had escorted Anne upstairs objected.

"Though he could have dropped a lit match onto the rags through one of the spaces in the window boards," the other man suggested. "Damp as that cloth was, it might have smoldered a bit before catching flame."

"But all of this is conjecture," Andrew Brighton said, shaking his head wearily, listening attentively for the sound of the fire brigade in the distance. "Did anyone actually see anything?"

As Anne had supposed, all of the men except for Bradford claimed to have been too busy with their own tasks to have detected anything out of the ordinary. And to make matters worse, no one had been in any one spot for the entire length of time that she had been in the house.

"When did you first become aware of my predicament?" Anne asked the group, trying to wipe sooty smudges off her face with a dainty handkerchief and only succeeding in spreading the dark dust that stained her cheeks.

"Why, when I heard pounding on the other side of the front door," Digby asserted. "But when I tried to open it, the damnable thing wouldn't budge."

"So I noticed," Anne commented dryly, not voicing her suspicion that the man had either held the door shut or else jammed it closed.

"Other than Miss Hargraves, who of us was the last one out of the building?" Brighton asked.

"I suppose I was," Morrison admitted. "But I assure you, I saw nothing amiss."

"What about you, sir?" Brighton asked, turning his attention to the stranger in their midst. "Did you see anything?"

"Me? I had only just arrived as Miss Hargraves was being dragged from the building," the Earl of Bradford protested.

"But what are you doing here at all?" Anne questioned sharply, her eyes hardening and making a vivid contrast to the vulnerable picture she otherwise presented.

"Doing here? My dear Miss Hargraves, surely you don't mean to tell me that you have forgotten inviting me while we conversed at Chadwick's gathering? You did, after all, make a pointed reference as to when you would be here." Bradford snorted indignantly, acting for all the world as though no woman had ever tendered him such an insult before he remembered himself and finally relented. "But then, I suppose your recent ordeal has unsettled you past all rational thought. Have no fear, my dear. Under the circumstances I take no offense."

Was the man really so arrogant as to assume that when she had mentioned she would be at this address this afternoon she was issuing an invitation to a rendezvous? Or, Anne wondered, as she leaned against her coach, had he been here for more ominous reasons?

Before she could decide, her thoughts were interrupted by the clangor heralding the long-awaited arrival of the fire brigade. With their appearance came chaos as everyone began to talk at once, and Brighton issued booming orders to direct the newcomers to the back door where they might enter the building and possibly salvage some of it.

In their haste to accompany the fire fighters, Anne was forgotten once again, and left to stand alone at the front of the tenement house. Even the crowd of locals who had gathered retreated to the other side of the building, hoping to be entertained.

Breathing a sigh of relief at her narrow escape, Anne pushed aside her own considerations and began to analyze the afternoon's events, recalling every small detail in her endeavor to uncover the identity of the arsonist. That it had been arson she was quite certain. It only remained to puzzle out who and why. If she was lucky, she would find some connection between the fire and the threats made against the queen.

The young Englishwoman was so deep in thought that she was unaware of the figure who had separated himself from the crowd in back of the house, managing to slip away without calling any attention to his absence. He stood staring at her, pistol in hand, his eyes glazed over as he contemplated putting an end to her interference now. She mouthed pretty words, but her presence caused dissension no matter where she appeared. It would be an easy enough shot to bring down this noisome songbird, but did he dare do it? Would the confusion and din of the fire mask both the sound of the shots and his movements?

A rational man would have dismissed the situation straightaway, but the gunman gave it serious consideration. Before he could make up his mind, however, an unwelcome figure appeared, making his decision for him. Reluctantly, the madman pocketed his pistol and traced his steps to join the others, consoling himself with the thought that there would be other opportunities to rid the world of Miss Anne Hargraves.

Dangerous Deceptions

Wrestling with possible theories, Anne had been unaware of being watched, just as she was ignorant of Ian's presence until she heard his fearsome roar.

"What in God's name has gone on here?" he demanded, as he spun Anne around and grasped her slight shoulders in his large, inescapable hands. His intense gaze swept over her anxiously from head to toe, taking in every departure from her usually fastidious appearance.

Her face and hair were covered with soot, an area over one well arched brow was unnaturally pink, and several areas of her dress were most definitely singed. Ian's fury was irrepressible. Not only had the little ninny come down here, she had obviously almost been killed. By God, when he realized that he might have lost her today, he felt like killing her himself. How dare she disobey him and put herself in such danger?

After her frightening ordeal, the sight of Ian made Anne want nothing more than to throw herself into his arms and feel the safety and comfort she had discovered within his embrace. But before she could do so, she chanced to look into his face, and the hardened glint she saw reflected in his silver eyes stopped her before she began.

Standing there like some impassive marble statue, Ian waited for Anne to speak. Needing no words, his august silence commanded her to do so.

"There was a slight fire," she offered in a small voice, wincing as she felt his fingers dig into her upper arms.

"A slight fire! A slight fire!" Ian growled, shaking her so violently that she thought her neck would snap. "Why did you come down here?"

"I had to come," Anne cried out in defense. "Brighton needed me."

"What?" Ian replied in amazement. How could she say that to him? Though the baronet's son had ceased to rock Anne back and forth, his hands unconsciously remained where they were, cutting off her circulation like iron bands.

"I suspect that you came for no other reason than to prove to me that what I say means very little to you," he continued. "Well, now you've proved it, and almost managed to get yourself killed in doing so. But from now on, Anne, you'll do as I say. Do you understand?''

"How dare you!" Anne exclaimed, ineffectually trying to disentangle herself from Ian's powerful and punishing fingers.

"I said you will do as I say. Damn it, woman! Don't you know that I am only trying to keep you from harm?''

"If that's the case, then why are you hurting me now?'' Anne asked in a frosty whisper, looking pointedly at the hands still clasping her too tightly.

Good God! Ian thought, meeting Anne's gaze with horror, he had been doing just that. Immediately, his grip relaxed. Yet unwilling to let her go, he refused to release her. It was as if he needed to touch her, to feel her beneath his hands, to reassure himself that she was indeed still alive.

"I'm sorry, sweetest Annie," he mumbled, more contrite than he had ever been in his entire life. "There was no excuse for that. But surely you understand how much I care for you.''

"I only understand this, Mr. Kendrick. My actions are none of your concern. And it's time you understood it, as well. With that in mind, I will speak quite simply and clearly. You have no right to say anything about where I go or what I do.''

"No right! Woman, this gives me the right," Ian growled fiercely, pulling Anne against his chest, bending his dark head to her pale one and capturing her lips with his own. His kiss was hungry and full of passion as he attempted to tell her without words just what she had come to mean to him, how deeply he longed to protect her and how overjoyed he was that she was unharmed.

Though her lips responded of their own accord and she uttered a soft moan, Anne knew she couldn't permit this man to control her now. The future of England might very well be at stake, and for that reason she fought to keep Ian Kendrick from claiming her soul.

Raising his head from hers and allowing his hands to rest lightly at her waist, Ian looked at Anne with loving expectation, certain that now she knew what was in his heart.

But Anne was all too aware what he expected of her at the moment. For her part, she had never known a temptation such as the one she faced. With that unruly lock of hair hanging on his forehead, his face smudged with soot transferred from her own, Ian Kendrick had never appeared so appealing. It would be so easy to yield to him, to forget about the world around them and to spend the rest of her existence at his side. But it was something she could not do.

She fought back the urge to laugh. How ironic it was! Despite her lapse from morality, and society's opinions to the contrary, Anne Hargraves had a very strong sense of honor. And it was that stubborn honorable streak that prompted her to gather every ounce of determination she possessed and give Ian Kendrick a response he wasn't expecting.

Leaning back in the Englishman's arms, Anne raised her hand and quickly, before she could think about it, soundly slapped his handsome face.

"You'll take only what I give you, Mr. Kendrick," she said coldly, even as she fought the desire to apologize and comfort him when she saw the hurt and confusion displayed in his gray eyes.

Ian stood looking at the diminutive female before him, his expression quickly transforming itself from warm tenderness to restrained fury. Bloody hell, he told himself as he grabbed her wrist to stop her from delivering another such insult, he had kissed her, declaring his love, in an attempt to reassure her after what must have been a most frightening brush with death. He had acted in direct contradiction to orders received from the Prince of Wales, and it had meant nothing to her! It had meant nothing at all! Damnation, but she was an unfeeling female. Why had he ever had the impression that she was warm and passionate?

If she had deliberately set out to tear apart his heart, she couldn't have been more successful. Quite a trick, Ian decided angrily, when it came to a man who had always been immune to love's arrows.

Rage swelled impulsively deep within his breast. Despite Ian's resolve to do otherwise, he sought, like a wounded tiger, to hurt Anne Hargraves as she had hurt him.

"I see," he said quietly, letting her go and stepping back. "I won't trouble you by asking for anything ever again."

With that, Ian turned away, wanting only to reach the sanctuary of his home, just as the injured beast seeks its lair. He wanted quiet and time to heal before he had to face a cruel and unpredictable world once more.

As she watched him go, tears appeared at the corners of Anne's emerald eyes. She longed to call him back, to explain everything and beg his forgiveness. But that was a luxury England could not afford, and so she remained silent, ignoring the others who had returned to the street and joined her again.

"I say, isn't that the chap you met up with in the East End?" Morrison asked. "What was his name?"

"Ian...Ian Kendrick," Anne replied softly, wiping away her tears and leaving streaks running through the sooty patches on her face.

"He hasn't been rude to you again, has he?" Brighton asked gruffly, surprised at his instinct to shield this plucky little woman from unpleasantness.

"No, not at all," Anne lied. "I fear I am merely reacting to the excitement of the day and the despair I feel at the tenement's destruction."

"As long as you are quite certain that disreputable fellow didn't insult you," Morrison stated, casting an angry glare in the direction in which Ian had disappeared. "Say the word and I will find the bounder and thrash him for you."

"There is no need," Anne insisted.

"Then it's really not so bad, Miss Hargraves," Brighton said, patting her hand awkwardly. "Though there was extensive damage done in the front room of the house, the building can most definitely be salvaged. We'll have our home for children after all."

"I'm glad to hear that," Anne murmured, sincere in what she said in spite of her own heartbreak.

"Yes, but it will cost many more pounds than it would have had there been no fire," Digby complained. "I would still like to know how it began."

"We'll never find an answer, I fear," Morrison spoke up. "After all, this is not the best of neighborhoods. Not only are there the poor and the squatters to suspect, but gentlemen of Kendrick's ilk swarm through the place as well, it would seem. Of course, I'm not referring to you, Bradford,'' he amended.

Anne looked at Alex in alarm. Surely he didn't think Ian could have set the fire that had almost killed her.

As if he could read her mind, Morrison instantly tried to allay her fears. "My dear Miss Hargraves, please don't be so upset. Just because Kendrick was in the neighborhood so shortly after the blaze broke out, that is no real reason for us to suspect him, no matter how disreputable he may be.''

Anne nodded in tired agreement, thankful for Morrison's attempted comfort. But a seed of doubt had been planted nevertheless. Dear God, she prayed in desperate silence as cold fear washed over her, don't let Ian have had anything to do with this. Don't make him the man I am seeking. And though Anne had prayed many times in her life, she had never before been so frantic that heaven should listen.

Chapter Fourteen

Enjoying the sunny morning in the garden of her town house, Anne ran her slender fingers through her long unbound hair and sniffed at them suspiciously, but she could find no lingering smell of soot. She knew full well her hair was perfectly clean. Bess had seen to her bath last night, carefully warming and scenting the water, and then the maid had washed Anne's long blond hair twice before applying a scented cream.

Still, the acrid smell of the fire, indeed the very taste of the smoke, lingered in her memory till she expected the odor everywhere. Looking around at the well-ordered shrubs and the immaculate beds of bright color, the seasoned agent shuddered, wondering if she'd ever forget the initial jolt of terror when she'd realized her predicament, the momentary understanding that she could actually meet her death in a squalid tenement only a few miles from home. For all the close calls she'd experienced in exotic locales, this seemed somehow more personal, more vindictive, perhaps because it happened in London, where she expected civilized behavior rather than violence.

Yet for all the horror of the fire, Anne reasoned, some helpful conclusions could be drawn from its occurrence. Just as she had hoped, her tactics had frightened someone enough to make him react, and if she'd flushed the villain from cover once, she could surely to do it again before he went after Victoria.

Bending over to sniff a particularly appealing white rose, the blonde inhaled its heady sweetness and finally succeeded in expunging the noxious odor that had haunted her sleep. Quickly she used the rose shears and laid the chosen bloom in her basket atop the flowers she had already gathered as an excuse to escape Brewster's anxious hovering this morning.

Often when an investigation stymied her, the veteran agent found inspiration amid the simple lessons of nature. Even the roses growing in her temporary garden gave evidence of shifting loyalties in Nature's creations. Lovingly planted years before by a family now retired to the Cotswolds, the bushes continued to thrive, deriving sustenance and nourishment from the soil, completely indifferent to their nominal owner.

"Aren't most humans the same, living their lives with an impressive disregard for the world around them as long as nothing disturbs their pleasure?" reflected Anne as she clipped another blossom. "Now that I've disturbed my quarry, rooting around in the soil of his existence, he's angry enough to come after me. Oh," she cried as a hidden thorn pierced the soft flesh on her thumb, causing a drop of blood to stain the white petals in her basket even as she brought the wounded finger to her mouth.

"Take better care, or more of your blood than that will be spilled," warned a stern voice from behind her.

Anne turned with a start, reaching for her basket of flowers, then relaxed as she recognized her visitor.

"Nigel, what are you doing here?" she began in surprise. Ordinarily her superior took great effort to avoid being seen in her company. What had happened to bring him to her town house?

"I slipped in through the rear gate. I had to be certain you were truly all right," he explained. "I heard about the tenement fire and have a list of all those who were in the vicinity—"

"You were worried about me," concluded the blonde, her eyes reflecting her appreciation that this tough, experienced man, responsible for scores of personnel, still had the heart to be personally concerned for her. "Thank you for caring, Nigel, but you should show a little more faith in my abilities. I'm fine, really. My clothes and my dignity suffered the only damage. I'm accustomed to much more peril than this assignment has yet offered."

"Well, don't you get any ideas about increasing the stakes to draw him out again, do you hear? I'm even reconsidering this whole notion about your giving a concert to distract the man."

"Nigel, we agreed that would be best."

"That was before our would-be assassin sent another message, changing the rules."

"So soon? Didn't the palace just intercept one last week?"

"Yes, but it appears our man is furious that Victoria has gone off to Balmoral before the jubilee. He sees her trip as a deliberate ploy to keep him from reaching her."

"Well, it is, isn't it? You said yourself you had urged her secretary to pack the queen off to safety."

"Victoria usually flees London during the summer anyway. We merely encouraged her to go up to Scotland before the big day and then again after Jubilee Day, rather than limit her stay to July and August," defended the government's man. "It makes perfect sense, but never mind about that. Our real problem is that apparently this madman has decided *you* should take Victoria's place while she's away. He says practicing on you will make him more accurate when it comes to kill her," Nigel said quietly, watching the effect his words had on his lovely companion.

Predictably enough, Anne shrugged her shoulders as if throwing off the possible danger and offered a positive interpretation of the threat.

"For heaven's sake, Nigel, then why are you looking so glum? Clearly I've done what we wanted. I've rattled him enough to make him change his plans," the blonde explained. "You know it's much more likely he'll make a mistake now that he's flustered. The situation couldn't be better."

"Perhaps," conceded her superior, "but I won't have his mistake costing us your life."

"Am I irreplaceable then? Is that the message, that you've no more singing agents?" Anne laughed, her teasing bringing a begrudging smile to Nigel's face.

"You know you're that and more, but I'm serious here. I want your word there will be no more independent little escapades that could put you in danger."

"Fine, I'll simply discontinue my snooping and sit back and wait for the man to strike at me and then Victoria," she snapped irritably. Why couldn't Nigel Conway trust her experience and let her function as she chose?

"You know that's not what I want."

"And it's not what I want, either. You agreed to let me run the investigation my way, to trust my instincts."

"I don't want you hurt, Anne."

"I promise I won't be. See, I'm prepared," confided the delicate-looking female. Reaching under the flowers in her basket, she extracted a small pistol. "Had you been a stranger, I assure you, you would never have gotten this close to me."

"I should hope not," sighed the intelligence officer. Too many things about this case were irregular for him to be comfortable, from watching Anne function so close at hand to her personal involvement with Kendrick, but he knew he had no choice other than to trust her. "All right then, but one more thing before I'm off. The whole Irish contingent, even Flaherty, was present in Parliament yesterday afternoon for another session on home rule. I think we can safely eliminate them all from suspicion."

"See, I told you. There's another positive outcome from that little fire," said Anne. "Our field is narrowing."

"You just see that you take care of yourself at that house party given by Bothwell this weekend. Should you need help, I'll have someone nearby."

"Whoever—" she began, only to be distracted by Brewster's appearance in the upper level of the garden near the house.

"Miss Hargraves," called the butler. "You've visitors, Lady Moreland and her daughter, Miss Audrey. Shall I bring them out or will you come in?"

"I'll come in," she answered quickly, moving toward the house as Nigel disappeared into the shrubbery near the back wall. "Though it's only mid-morning, the sun is already becoming rather warm for sitting outdoors."

"My heavens, Anne, are you truly all right?" gushed the noblewoman, pushing past Brewster to greet Anne outside. "When we heard what had happened from Bradford, we just had to come and be certain for ourselves that you were truly unharmed. I did warn you, however, of what might happen associating with those reformers the way you do."

"I doubt they would burn down a tenement they wanted to refurbish," disputed Anne as she reached the veranda and handed the basket of flowers to her butler. "Please see to these, Brewster."

"Yes, miss, and will you want coffee and tea for your guests?" inquired the servant.

Anne shook her head in bewilderment as she led Aurora and Audrey indoors. If the man wasn't being insufferably condescending to her, he was unbearably considerate; was there no middle ground to his behavior?

"Yes, thank you, that would be quite lovely. Ladies, shall we go into the drawing room?"

"I still say, Anne, even if your reformers didn't light the fire personally, you are putting yourself in danger by just being with them. Who knows whom they may have offended with their socialist nonsense?" began Aurora, warming to her theme.

It would be a long morning, reflected Anne, but then she had nothing to do until her visit to the People's Palace tonight anyway.

By three that afternoon, Ian was dirty and discouraged. He had started the morning with his usual early conference in the park, but Bertie had refused to accept the tenement fire as evidence of Anne's innocence.

"More likely she'd been working with the assassin and had let him down or he decided he didn't want any witnesses," argued the royal. "This could well be a scheme to convince us of her innocence while she's up to her neck in the whole plot—especially with the devil's mentioning her name in his latest letter."

"He mentioned her name?" Ian had repeated in amazement. Why hadn't the prince told him that first?

"Mmm, supposedly he's going to practice on Anne Hargraves before he kills Victoria Regina, or at least that is what he wants us to believe. Maybe I will, if he actually does, but otherwise she's still a suspect in my book."

Had the royal's involvement with Lillie Langtry so colored his judgment of all performers that he'd trust none of them? It was something Ian couldn't help but wonder about, but he was prudent enough not to voice his thoughts aloud. That might explain the nobleman's attitude, yet all the grandiose speculation in the world wouldn't do as much as a few solid facts to change the man's mind, Ian decided.

"I tell you, Kendrick, watch that woman carefully, but don't let her fool you. I'm certain she's a clever plant to keep us off guard," the future king had insisted before cantering off to rejoin his party. "Stay with it."

If this man is to rule our country upon his mother's death, Ian had thought, frowning, he had best learn more about people first. Determined to find the would-be assassin and prove Anne innocent, Ian set out for the site of the tenement fire.

Yet, after scouring the neighborhood, paying numerous children and bedraggled adults for their memories of the previous day, he still had nothing to show for his efforts. Many of the East End folk had seen Anne and the reformers tour the property, but the unexpected sight of such a fine lady in their part of town had pushed aside all interest in anything but the songstress herself, how she moved, what she wore and what she said. As to whom she had said it to— no one could recall, and of course they hadn't been in the tenement itself.

There had been plenty of strangers around, everyone agreed, but as to which of them might have acted suspiciously, his informers could reach no consensus.

Knowing he could expect no help from Brighton, Morrison or Digby, Ian called upon one of the other reformers present during yesterday's near fatality. Awkward as the interview was, it had given him no insight. The reformer was reluctant to cooperate with this man whom Anne Hargraves had seemed to dislike. Still, he had finally told Ian the bare facts of the moments leading up to the fire. Yet even this knowledge offered Ian no clue as to what had actually happened.

Frustrated, he went to the tenement and crawled around the charred floors, trying to decide what had started the fire, but again, he had no luck. There had to be something he'd missed, worried Ian, his gray eyes steely as he concentrated on what he'd seen when he had arrived. Yet nothing new came to mind.

He hoped the woman was at least safely home today. He frowned, heading for his own residence, sorely in need of a bath and change of clothes. Just to be certain she stayed out of trouble, he might venture over to the People's Palace tonight, he decided, unwilling to test Anne's welcome at her home. For now, however, soap and water called.

Summer days in England are lengthy, and it was barely dusk when Anne ordered her carriage brought around. Dressed in a simple navy gown with a short cloak and hood to cover her pale blond hair, the singer intended to reach the People's Palace long before she expected anyone might join her, Brighton, Digby, Morrison, Bradford, Wallingcroft or maybe even Bothwell. Who knew? While Ian had declined her invitation, there was still the dismal possibility that he would be the one to appear, wishing to do her harm.

When she'd set this trap, she had mentioned her visit would take place about nine, well into the twilight hours, ostensibly to allow her to see Queen's Hall as it would be when she performed. In truth, the agent had hoped her quarry would feel more secure tracking her under the cover of darkness. Despite Nigel's fears, she theorized that if she could only draw the man out this once more, she'd have him.

Dismissing the carriage a half mile from her destination in order to avoid notice, Anne walked hurriedly through the crowded streets, her head down, her costume chosen specifically not to attract attention, her very demeanor so servile that none of her acquaintances would have recognized her. Indeed, those who did notice her at all saw only another weary woman, perhaps a touch more well dressed than others, but hurrying nonetheless.

"One institute, no matter how grand, won't be enough to change this area," she thought to herself, inhaling the pungent odor of hops as she passed the breweries of Mile End Road on the approach to the People's Palace. Queen's Hall, the only finished part of what was planned as a complex of buildings offering training in technical skills and handicrafts as well as popular entertainment, had been located plumb in the center of an area better designed for destruction than construction, mused Anne wryly. Maybe someday it would spur further efforts at improvement, but now it stood, a suspiciously displaced anomaly, sadly emphasizing the squalor surrounding it.

Nonetheless, this was her destination, acknowledged Anne, knocking at the small shack that housed the watchman.

"I don't know if I can do that, miss. No one said nothing about visitors to the palace tonight," disputed the sentry when she requested him to unlock the building.

"I'm sorry for the confusion," said Anne, slipping some gold coins into his hand, "but Mr. Brighton was supposed to be in touch with you. He said the home secretary had approved."

"Ah, Brighton, maybe, yes, I suppose I'm just a wee bit forgetful these nights," said the old man, readily pocketing the money. "Most likely, by tomorrow, I won't even be remembering you and your Mr. Brighton were here at all. Will you be wanting the lights turned up in the hall?"

"Maybe in the orchestra and stage area," the singer agreed hesitantly, not bothering to correct the old man's assumption that this was an assignation. She didn't want the room too bright or the assassin wouldn't feel safe, but there had to be some illumination.

"Right then. Just knock on my box when you leave, so I can lock up again," instructed the guard, hurrying ahead of Anne to do her bidding. Tonight was proving to be quite a profitable evening.

When Anne entered Queen's Hall, she found herself immediately exploring it from two perspectives: that of a possible target seeking hiding places, and that of a performer anticipating an audience's reaction. For either scenario, the setting was absolutely magnificent; truly, it deserved to be part of a palace, no matter how dingy the outside of the building might seem.

Queen's Hall was at least one hundred and twenty feet long and seventy or eighty feet wide, but it was the glass ceiling, more than fifty feet overhead, that enchanted her. Some panes appeared tinted, others clear, but the overall effect was that someone had forgotten to draw the drapes, permitting the rapidly darkening sky and its eventual array of glittering stars to be part of the room's decor. On a moonlit evening, it would be a truly spectacular arena. Huge marble columns stood along the edge of the main floor, supporting the roof in elegant style. In between the white columns stood pedestals supporting famous queens of history, twenty-two, Anne counted, unaware of the eyes that watched her. Victoria didn't appear to be included in the display, marveled the singer, but then she would undoubtedly be added later, or demand to know why.

Continuing her tour of the elliptical room, Anne counted the gilded balconies adorning the side and rear walls, twelve in all. Potted palms appeared at regular intervals around the room, interspersed among the chairs. The only drawback she foresaw to a concert was that the seats were grouped as though in a huge drawing room, in sets of four or six, not all facing the stage as they would be in a theater.

"Performing here could present quite a challenge," said Anne as she moved toward the orchestra area, satisfied now that no one lurked in the shadows prepared to kill her. "With a glass ceiling, I wonder how well the sound will carry."

From his vantage point behind the second statue to the left of the stage, Ian fumed at her stubbornness; he had half a mind to pull her across his knee right here and now and teach her the meaning of obedience. While it had been easy enough to pick a lock to get in here, Ian wasn't certain he would be happy with what he would see tonight. If Bertie was right, Anne could be meeting her nefarious partner here, be it Brighton or someone else entirely. In truth, he didn't know what to expect; it could all be perfectly innocent, as the songstress had told him, an exploration of the theater, no more.

Annoyed at the necessity of his forced inactivity, Ian trained his eyes on Anne, determined to be ready should she need his protection but to stay out of sight if all was well.

Intent on her musical concerns, Anne proceeded to the stage. Off in the distance, she heard a door slam somewhere out front, but assumed it to be the watchman leaving, now that the lights had been lighted.

Ian, however, uncertain whether he awaited an assassin or an accomplice, tensed as he worried over Anne's lack of stealth. But, asked his heart, why would an innocent woman want to hide her presence in a theater she was considering for a performance? Damn it, how could his mind vacillate so between her guilt and innocence? It was all Bertie's fault for loving and losing Lillie Langtry, he was sure of it.

On stage waiting for her trap to be sprung, the blonde couldn't resist the temptation to run the scales, inordinately pleased at the sound she created, soft and mellow in the huge room. There was a slight echo, to be sure, but the hall seemed to welcome her voice, embracing it and sending it skyward where it seemed to hover near the stars before melting away. Indeed, the notes of the scale had sounded so natural, Anne was unable to deny the call of her music.

Breathing deeply, inhaling and exhaling slowly to relax her nerves, the songstress opened the piano and fingered the ivory keys. Then, closing her eyes, she opened her mouth and sang her signature melody, a love song with a haunting refrain and a particularly intricate final chord that even she occasionally missed. Tonight, however, her performance was magical, her rhythm and pacing clearly attuned, her breathing unlabored, the overall effect a perfect melding of talent and effort.

Indeed, when she'd finished singing and the last note faded away as she closed the lid of the piano, the sound of applause greeted her. At once, Anne was alert as, from backstage, two lone hands clapped, slowly, deliberately, almost mockingly. Turning to look about her, she could see no one, yet the eerie tattoo continued. Ian heard the sound, but couldn't decide where it was originating or what it portended. Still, he moved closer to the stage, hugging the shadows, trying to be invisible.

"Who's there?" called Anne as the applause echoed its peculiar beat. "Ian, is that you? The hall isn't open to the public," she announced, perhaps sensing his presence even as he froze in the darkness. "Who's there? Come out where I can see you, for heaven's sake," she urged as the flickering gaslight backstage faded, leaving the entire hall gray and shadowed. "Ian, is that you?"

"No!"

It was only one muffled word, reflected Anne, and maybe it was a lie, but the simple staccato syllable gave her chills, though at least the clapping had stopped. This was her quarry then, the would-be assassin; she had no doubt of it. Anyone else would have come forward to greet her. His applause meant nothing other than that he had found her and wanted her to know it. Deciding to play innocent as long as she could, Anne reached into the pocket of her cloak, grasped her pistol and spoke again.

"Andrew, then? What did you think of the sound?" asked the small blond figure on the stage, seeking to draw the man out as she circled to the opposite side of the platform and went down into the orchestra.

"I don't think you'll be doing the concert, my dear, so it hardly matters how you sound," came the hoarse reply, only feet from where she had been standing a few moments earlier.

Was that a threat? Ian couldn't decide for certain; maybe Brighton, if that were he, had simply reconsidered the proposal and decided against it. Still, the fact that the lights had gone out was worrisome and prevented identification of the shadowy figure on the stage. Inching forward, Ian remained in the darkness, needing to hear more of their exchange before he could take action.

"What a strange thing to say," Anne baited, moving to her right as a floorboard squeaked behind her. Was there someone else here now, as well?

"See, you've left the stage behind you already," mocked her quarry. He jumped down from the platform, a black-garbed figure, his eyes busily searching the shadows for her tellingly blond tresses as he awaited her next words. All he needed was one clear shot and she'd be gone.

This time, however, Anne remained silent. Having covered her hair with the hood of her cloak, she became the hunter, stalking her quarry soundlessly as he moved away from the stage.

"Where have you gone, my little songbird?" demanded the intruder, growing anxious now at the continued silence in the cavernous hall. The huge room seemed a kaleidoscope of blacks and grays, some small light entering through the ceiling, distorting shapes and distances as he sought his prey. Could his effort tonight be futile? No, he couldn't fail . . . he *wouldn't* fail. "Anne . . . Anne?"

"Here," she whispered softly, pulling her gun from her pocket even as she raised it to be ready if he threatened her.

As a sudden flash of light reflected off the metal in front of her, the man grew desperate and fired into the darkness from which she spoke. Barely aware of the sound of his shot, Anne automatically took aim and pulled the trigger, blocking her mind to who the man in her sights might actually be. Even as her bullet found its human target, she crouched to avoid the chance of another shot from the marksman.

A sudden cry echoed through the hall and then all she heard was movement; her quarry must be heading toward the door. Yet as Anne prepared to follow, a sudden shove knocked her to the floor and a second shadowy figure took off after the first.

"Could there be two madmen involved in the plot or did Nigel send someone to help me?" she wondered, recalling her superior's words about assistance being available if she needed it. But that was to be at the house party, or so she'd thought. Whoever the two figures were, they were long gone by the time Anne rose from the floor and regained her breath. Hopefully she had hit the man wielding the pistol so he would be easier to find even if his friend wasn't. At the moment there was little more she could do other than report what had happened here to Nigel and hope that her gunshot had wrought some real damage.

* * *

Outside an anxious Brewster had just found the night watchman trussed and gagged in his box when he heard a noise that sounded suspiciously like gunfire. Damn, he knew she'd get herself killed, and Nigel would blame him for it, too!

As quickly as he could, the portly butler reached into the guard's pocket just as the man began to come to. Glad the fellow was not dead, Brewster grabbed a ring of keys and headed for the entrance to Queen's Hall. Better to have the keys with him in case the place was locked than have to run back, he decided. Unused to heavy physical exertion, however, he was panting so hard he had to stop to catch his breath at the top of the steps. It would do Miss Hargraves no good at all if he entered loudly gasping for air and alerted the villains to his presence before he could determine what to do.

Examining the keys in his hand, Brewster never expected the door before him to be thrust outward so suddenly. Consequently, the force of the movement propelled him backward down the steps. He landed so forcibly that his head slammed into the pavement. Momentarily dazed, he fought off unconsciousness, struggling to overcome the pain and nausea sweeping over him from the fall. When he opened his eyes a bit later, he was surprised to see the dastardly fiend just leaving the front gates, running like the devil was after him.

And, a moment later, he was. Huffing and puffing, Matthew Brewster hurried down the street as quickly as his short legs and elaborate girth would permit, intent on at least getting a glimpse of the villain's face, well aware he could never hope to apprehend him. Finally, just when he thought he could go no farther, a properly functioning gaslight obliged, and the butler halted his pursuit, relieved and at the same time distressed at the features he thought it had illuminated. Still, he frowned. The distance was great and his eyesight not so sharp.

"Well," he considered as he turned to the People's Palace, "if she's dead, at least she'll never have to know what I might have seen."

But she wasn't, Brewster was surprisingly relieved to learn as he returned to the gates outside the hall. Anne Hargraves was there, in the yard, tending gently to the building's guard, stanching the wound on his forehead as she murmured words of consolation amid her probing questions as to what he had seen before he was attacked. That being the case, the butler decided, he'd best hurry to report to Nigel and be back to her house by the time she returned. What he would tell her, he didn't know, but Nigel might.

"You've no idea then who did this?" Anne asked the old man.

"Not unless it was your friend Brighton. Wasn't that what you called him?"

"Oh, I doubt he would hit you," the blonde demurred, not really knowing if Brighton had been there but allowing the guard to use his name for lack of another. "Are you certain there wasn't anyone else around here tonight?"

"I told you—just that young fellow I saw running out of the place—dark-haired, tall, unruly hair. Brighton, you said?"

"No, that's not Brighton," whispered Anne, her heart constricting at the guard's description of a man who might be Ian. Was it he who had called to her in the hall after all? "Where did that man go?"

"I didn't really see, miss."

"All right, thank you. And that's for your troubles." Placing another gold piece in the watchman's palm, Anne made up her mind. She had to go see Ian—to prove to herself his innocence and feel his strong arms around her, comforting her, reassuring her that no one, nothing could keep them apart, that tonight's nightmare was only that. It didn't matter what Jack might think; she needed his brother!

If Ian had no wounds, he couldn't be the assassin—though of course she'd have to undress him to be absolutely positive. Concentrating on that pleasant prospect to forestall an attack of conscience that awaited her for disregarding Nigel's instructions, Anne straightened her cloak and headed to her carriage, giving the driver Ian's address.

He had said he would be there tonight, and he would, she told herself, unharmed, healthy and very happy to see her.

Damn that bitch, cursed Anne's real quarry, already gone to ground. Safe in his own quarters, he wrapped the gauze about his wound, muttering all the while against Anne Hargraves.

Why the hell did she have a gun in the first place? Women didn't carry weapons, especially pretty ones like her. And why did she shoot? Did she recognize me, even in the shadows of the hall? What if she tells someone? Now she can't live; I'll have to be more careful the next time. He planned, already conceiving his next attempt. While he didn't relish changing his agenda yet again, that squawking crow couldn't be allowed to destroy his hopes for Victoria. Once she was gone, there would be a new world, and he would be its founder, of that he was certain.

In the back alleys off Mile End Road, Ian strode angrily, kicking at the shadows, shaking drunken tramps and sleeping citizens, trying his best to be certain the assassin hadn't escaped through such a simple subterfuge as pretending to be one of them. But that didn't appear to be the case, he concluded sadly. Wounded or not, the devil must have gotten to safety somehow. And now, with the unexpected shooting at Anne, the whole thing began to unravel. Could Bertie have been right? Was tonight the falling out of two accomplices? Ian debated. He hadn't really heard anything that would prove that, but nothing that would disprove it, either.

Was she a victim or a villainess? His heart told him one thing and his head another, and despite his training, he had to believe his heart. Someone had tried to kill Anne Hargraves twice in the last two days, each time coming all too close to success, and he had to find out who and why. The Bothwells' house party could wait; tomorrow morning he would examine the hall and the tenement and see what he could learn before he went down to Kent. With that comforting thought in mind, he headed homeward, tired and disgusted with his lack of progress, but at least pleased that he had a plan of action.

"Oh, Mrs. Land, good evening," Anne said in surprise when the housekeeper finally answered her persistent knocking. Though lights were on in the house, for a while Anne wondered if anyone was home. The place had appeared very quiet for one that was supposed to be the site of an evening's entertainment. Perhaps it was canceled or Jack and his friends had decided to go out. That didn't mean Ian wouldn't be here. "I came to see Mr. Kendrick."

"And which one would that be, miss?" The older woman sniffed, remembering full well the problem this female had caused between the two brothers. "It is rather untimely a visit."

"Mr. Ian."

"Well, then you've wasted your time. He's not here," Mrs. Land announced with no small degree of pleasure.

"Oh." For a moment Anne's knees trembled and she reached out a hand to steady herself against the newel post. *He wasn't home... He could have been at the People's Palace... He could have been the man trying to kill me.* Her head swam at such unpleasant notions and she closed her eyes to reorient herself, only to find herself sitting in the parlor with the housekeeper pressing a glass of sherry in her hand and belittling a sheepish Jack at the same time.

"Now, you see here, I don't care what you were doing. She's your brother's friend. You've got to do something for her," insisted Mrs. Land as she left the room.

"I—" Jack was inordinately nervous, it seemed to Anne. His shirt was open and not tucked into his trousers, his hair was mussed and he wasn't even wearing shoes; it appeared Mrs. Land had awakened him to tend to her.

"Jack, I'm frightfully sorry to disturb you so late—"

"What? Oh, you didn't interrupt us, ah, disturb me. No, not at all," he blustered, turning beet red as he prattled on. "I, ah, I was alone in my room, reading, just a quiet evening alone, you know."

"I thought you'd be entertaining here tonight," Anne said.

"Enter—entertaining," Jack stammered. "No, I had no plans to entertain anyone here tonight."

"I see. Then have you any idea where Ian might be?" she pressed, still hopeful that he might have had some legitimate appointment, though it obviously hadn't included his brother.

"Ian? Oh, no, I haven't seen him since dinner at all, but then I've been *alone* upstairs," the young man repeated, unwilling to meet Anne's eyes.

Upstairs perhaps, thought Anne sadly, but definitely not alone. The only question in my mind is whether you were busy nursing your brother's wounds or pleasuring some not-so-innocent female. Somehow I don't think you'll tell me the truth in either case.

"All right, Jack, thank you."

"You are well enough to leave?" he asked with a show of concern, though his eyes strayed toward the stairs. "You gave Mrs. Land a scare."

"I'm sorry. My carriage is right outside, and Jack, don't tell Ian I called tonight. I wouldn't want him to think I didn't trust him."

"No, of course not," Jack agreed, blushing again as the songstress left.

Chapter Fifteen

Anne stood in the middle of her room overseeing the packing of the clothes she would need for the Bothwells' house party. There was no sense in staying in London when she had announced to all concerned that she would be spending the weekend in the country. If the man who had tried to kill her was still mobile after having been wounded, he would only be the more desperate and would certainly find his way to Bothwell Manor. But whether he would appear as a stalking interloper or an invited guest, Anne still didn't know.

However, she admitted to herself while mechanically depositing necklaces and rings into her jewelry case, more than ever it looked as though that person would be Ian Kendrick. Dropping the case bulging with gold and precious gems into a small valise, Anne once again listed her reasons for finding him so highly suspect. He had been inordinately interested in her ever since she had begun this assignment, had been on Cornwall Street when she emerged from the blazing tenement and had not been at home last night as he had stated he would be. And then, of course, as a member of the prince's circle, this impoverished nobleman would benefit when Victoria's son became king.

The agent in Anne argued that she had more evidence implicating the handsome man who had become her lover than she had pertaining to anyone else. Still, this morning she hadn't gone to Conway to press him into having Ian taken into custody. Was it her professional instinct that made her hesitate, or was it something else entirely? Was the heart Ian had awakened within her so enslaved by him that it refused to see things as they really were?

Calmly hiding her painful ambivalence, Anne directed her maid as to which evening clothes she would be taking with her, quickly going through her wardrobe dismissing one garment after another. But narrowing her selection of clothing was a far easier task than weeding out suspects, Anne thought as she fingered the exquisite lace decorating one of her gowns.

If Ian didn't appear at the house party as he was supposed to do, she would send word to Nigel Conway, telling him to ascertain if one Mr. Ian Kendrick had sustained a bullet wound the night before. And if the handsome nobleman was at Bothwell Manor, she could judge for herself if he was in any discomfort. It would be an easy enough thing to do, despite the halt they had put to their relationship and their angry words in front of the tenement.

Astute as she was, even when smitten by love, Anne realized that should she find Ian to be in the best of health, it was no proof of his innocence. He could have been the other man who had appeared at the People's Palace last night. And right now, Anne had yet to decide whether that second party had been accomplice or savior.

Of course the possibility did exist, however dim, that Ian had nothing at all to do with the attempt to be made on the queen's life, Anne reminded herself as she supervised the closing of her trunks. Yet rather than find comforting joy in such a thought, she reacted to it instinctively. There was no room for sentiments of any sort in this assignment, and it was certainly not the time for dreams. Without hesitation, Anne immediately brushed aside her confused emotions. By the time she descended the staircase to the main floor of the town house, she had been successful enough to banish everything from her mind except the job she had been assigned to do.

When Anne entered the dining room for breakfast, Brewster couldn't help but be impressed by her cool and levelheaded demeanor. Her behavior was certainly not that of a woman who had so recently twice faced death, and in all likelihood was about to confront it this weekend, as well.

Watching her from the corner of his eye, the butler had to admit that it had been no lie when Nigel Conway had told him Anne was one of Britain's finest agents.

Pouring coffee into Anne's cup, Brewster only hoped that she would remember her professionalism should she ever discover his part in her mission. He had no doubts that a woman as icy as the one at the breakfast table would have few qualms about extracting some sort of humiliating revenge if she felt her abilities had been questioned. An involuntary shudder swept over him at the thought.

Coming into the vestibule to see to the loading of her luggage, Anne observed a small, unfamiliar trunk being toted out behind her maid's satchel.

"I see you are going to heed my suggestion and enjoy a small holiday while I'm away," the songstress said, addressing Brewster absently while she pulled on her gloves.

"You did say I might have the time, miss," the butler said defensively, but unable, for once, to look his employer in the eye.

Brewster's odd manner drew Anne's attention at once. Her supercilious servant had rarely been flustered before and never given to evasiveness. She questioned what could have made him so. Suddenly it occurred to her that the pudgy little devil might be off to an assignation. Perhaps, Anne thought, a wry smile playing about her lips as she recalled Brewster's own words, this was how he gained his experience in helping females to undress.

During dangerous or difficult moments, Anne had learned, along with most of those in her trade, to take humor where she could find it. And here was Brewster, presenting her with an opportunity that was much too good to ignore. Ribbing the normally stuffy butler would surely give her a respite from the tensions besieging her.

"Where are you off to, then, Brewster?" she asked, an impish glint in her eyes. "Somehow I have the feeling that all this involves a lady."

"No, there's no lady at all, I assure you, miss," he stated, plunging bravely ahead. "I'm going with *you*."

"What! With me! How dare you speak in that insolent manner!" Anne railed, her powerful voice echoing through the house. "And what makes you think that you can inform me at the last moment that you are going to accompany me to Kent?"

"Because I knew, miss, that if I had broached the topic beforehand, you would have forbidden it," the butler pronounced with his usual exasperated superiority.

"You're bloody right I would have forbidden it! In fact I am going to do just that right now. You can stay here, or go to bloody hell if you prefer, but you are not going to Kent with me," Anne concluded emphatically.

"Really, miss! I was not aware that I was not free to travel about England as I see fit on my holiday."

"Not on any holiday I give you," Anne interjected.

"It is simply that I had thought to visit with some friends in the Bothwell household where I was once employed. But perhaps you are right to ask that I refrain from doing so. Should I go with you, Lord Bothwell would only spend the entire time trying to lure me back into his service. And I should admit, miss, that at the moment, with your attitude, I would be sorely tempted to accept. It is no wonder that you seek to keep me here. And who, after all, could blame you?"

"You pompous little man! Do you think I care if you leave my employ? Believe me, there is nothing I would like better than to take you along so that I could leave you behind with the unfortunate Bothwells. The only thing that stops me is that I find I cannot deprive myself of the few days I had been joyously anticipating away from your pretentious company."

"Of a certainty, miss," Brewster replied evenly, sounding as if Anne could never convince him of such.

This continually haughty manner of his set Anne on edge. Her emotions were already strained. Now she was angry with herself for giving way to her irritation, and at Brewster for causing her to feel it in the first place. How wonderful it would be to pawn him off on the unsuspecting Bothwells. That way, if the house party did not accomplish all that she hoped it would, at least she would be able to return to London and continue her efforts to save the queen without further hindrance from this officious butler.

But no, she couldn't do it, no matter how enticing the idea, Anne decided. It was no time to be selfish. This weekend was of paramount importance, and there was enough for her to do without giving Brewster the opportunity to get in her way.

"Believe what you choose," Anne said coolly, her success in composing herself most admirable. "But you will not be coming with me to the estate in Kent."

For the first time in his dealings with Anne Hargraves, Brewster allowed his dour mask to drop, and his face evinced signs of concern and amazement. No matter how well he thought he knew her, he had failed to read her correctly. His gibe had been constructed to induce her into allowing him to make the journey with her, even if her sole purpose in doing so was to demonstrate that she didn't care whether or not he deserted her household. But it appeared he had underestimated this woman's power to control her emotions when it became important to do so. Oh, blooming hell! Hadn't Conway informed him that Hargraves was that good?

Brewster realized he had no options left. With things as dangerous as they had been these last few days, he could not permit Anne to travel to Kent alone, even if he intended to meet her there. No, unfortunately, as he watched the young woman smooth her cloak and make ready to depart, there was only one course open. He was that desperate.

Coughing softly to engage Anne's attention, Matthew Brewster clasped his hands behind his back, and began to rock on the soles of his feet.

"I am sorry, Miss Hargraves, but you cannot go to Kent without me."

"And why not?" Anne asked with a mocking smile. "Lord Bothwell's own carriage is waiting outside even now to whisk me down to the country."

"Because," the man began, lowering his tones so that only Anne could hear, though the house was all but clear of the other servants, "your *uncle* wouldn't like it."

"My uncle?"

"Yes. Your uncle *Nigel,*" Brewster said as he stared at the floor, remembering Conway's fury at his failure to capture or at least clearly identify Anne's attacker the night before. "He specifically ordered me to go with you."

"What?" Anne asked, her fierce whisper hot with rage as she realized what it was Brewster was saying to her. "Do you mean to tell me that you've been plaguing my life these last few weeks at the request of *Uncle Nigel?*"

"I do indeed, miss," Brewster said, lifting his chins in defiance.

"Then you and Uncle Nigel can go straight to bloody blazes," the vocalist asserted, turning to leave. "For the love of God, if Conway was so determined to put an agent here, it should have been someone who could have helped me, not made things more difficult than they already are."

"I can understand how you feel, miss. But orders are orders, for you as well as me. You are not to go to Bothwell Manor unless I go with you."

"I will take great personal satisfaction in strangling that lying bastard when next I see him," Anne muttered, all but forgetting Brewster's presence.

"He thought it might upset you to know, which is why we have hidden the fact for so long. I would have continued to do so, but you left me no choice."

"Might upset me? Why, heavens, no! I've enjoyed your bullying, your insults, your interfering and your caustic comments. What makes you think I would be upset by you or by them?" Anne asked with such deadly sweetness that an uneasy Brewster suddenly felt perspiration beading across his forehead.

"Is that all, miss?" he asked, fervently hoping that this remarkable woman had enough self-control in reserve to forestall a full-scale eruption of what she was feeling at the moment. "There's no reason to call the servants' attention to our squabbling any more than need be."

"Just one more thing, Brewster. If you must come to Kent, I want to make one thing clear. You *will* stay out of my way. I don't want to see your face. Do you understand?"

"Very good, miss," the rotund agent said, as he retreated to the cloakroom. "I'll just fetch my coat and meet you in the carriage."

"Yes, I'll meet you at the carriage," Anne muttered, adjusting her hat and walking to the front door, angry at everyone including herself for being so easily duped by Nigel, a man to whom she had often entrusted her very life. Brewster—Nigel—Ian. Good God, wasn't there anyone in this world she could trust?

In spite of her barely controlled temper, the ride down to Kent was a comfortable if silent one for Anne. Lost in her thoughts, and trying to sort things out, she hardly spoke at all. But Bess didn't seem to mind. As for Brewster, he deserved to be treated horridly, Anne decided, sinking back into the plush seat of the coach, which was luxurious beyond words. It certainly made the carriages she had shared with Ian appear shabby by comparison. She would have imagined one such as this would have suited him infinitely better.

Finding her thoughts settling on Ian Kendrick yet again, Anne bestirred herself, shifting against the plump cushions of the seat as she sought to set her mind to something else. There were plenty of other people in this world besides Ian Kendrick, Anne rebuked herself, surely she should be able to concentrate on one of them!

Though scores of men had told her that her face was angelic, it was a devilish smile that lit Anne's face as she wondered wickedly if Brewster was finding the ride a comfortable one as well, perched where he was beside the coachman. But then it served him right to be banished to the top of the carriage, wearing only a thin coat in air unusually brisk for June. Nigel might have dictated that her troublesome watchdog accompany her to Bothwell Manor, but nothing had been said about the man actually riding within the compartment of the carriage which had been placed at her disposal. That was a privilege the bounder did not deserve.

At the end of her journey, Anne emerged from the coach and glanced up, satisfied to see that a sickly looking Brewster was not only shivering, but having trouble disentangling his tightly clenched fingers from the edge of the seat, an indication, surely, that he was afraid of heights. How careless that no one had so informed her, Anne thought wryly.

Turning to find her hostess, Anne was warmly greeted by Violet Norris, Lady Bothwell, who after she had finished her words of greeting began to gently scold her latest arrival.

"We always treated Brewster like a prince when he was part of our household, and still he left us. Don't tell me that you made him ride all the way out from London atop the coach! Aren't you afraid of losing him?"

"Not in the least," the petite singer responded airily, while managing to deliver a baleful glare to the object of their conversation, who was even now awkwardly trying to scramble down from the driver's perch.

"But, my dear, most of London wants him!" Violet assured her.

"Then permit me to share the secret of my success with him. It is a hint you or one of your friends can utilize when I leave on my next concert tour and Brewster becomes available once more," Anne replied, lowering her voice as she relished the sweet taste of revenge. "If you allow the old boy to act in a superior manner, he will think he is superior. Then there is no controlling him. But if you treat him callously, he will thrive on it, as he longs to be employed by those who are better than he and act accordingly. Those are the only sort he deems worthy of him, you understand."

"Indeed?" asked Violet glancing at England's supreme butler skeptically.

"Oh, yes," Anne replied, "you have my word on it."

Lady Bothwell was reputed to be the sort of woman unable to keep a secret. Telling her would ensure that all of society would soon be so informed. And Brewster, well, Brewster might have to endure condescending arrogance no matter which household Conway next placed him in.

Glancing at the carriage only to ascertain that someone was attending to Bess, Anne followed her hostess into the manor house, her bright green eyes routinely sweeping the area to discern where danger might lurk.

After being shown to her room and refreshing herself from the journey, Anne changed from her traveling dress, then was on her way to meet with the Bothwells and their guests before a late luncheon.

As she came into the drawing room, Anne saw that though most of the others were here, all had yet to assemble. Those who were present were conversing in quiet groups of two or three about the room, but an anxious Anne was disheartened to see that Ian Kendrick was not among them.

Violet was there along with her husband, who, Anne was surprised to see, was confined to the settee, a bandaged foot propped on a stool before him. Could this have been the man she shot last night, Anne asked herself, even as she moved forward, a sympathetic smile gracing her face.

"Your lordship, how kind of you and Lady Bothwell to have me here," she said, "especially when it would seem that you have met with a mishap of sorts."

"We are delighted you are with us," the earl responded, reaching out to take Anne's hands in his. "And as for this," he continued with a rueful glance at his foot, "it is but a bit of gout which became bothersome late last night. However, it seemed to us there was no sense in allowing this inconvenience to spoil everyone's fun. You are not to worry your pretty little head about it."

"Indeed. I am glad it is nothing serious," Anne replied, wondering what it was the bandages actually concealed.

"Nothing at all," Lady Bothwell joined in with a trilling laugh. "But come, my dear, let us mingle with the others, most of whom you already know."

Accompanying her hostess, Anne saw Tyler Fielding, Lord Bradford, who nodded pleasantly at her in the midst of enthralling two young ladies of the gentry with tales of his recent brave exploits during a London fire.

Wallingcroft, Chadwick and Dearborne were talking as usual about the prince, while some of the ladies, who had been busy chattering before Violet's approach with Anne, suddenly fell silent, an indication that the scandalous Miss Hargraves had been the topic of their conversation.

Deciding to allow the women to resume their idle amusement, Anne found a place with Chadwick and his fellows. Her reception was a warm one, with only Lord Wallingcroft regarding her warily. Ever alert to subtle nuances of human behavior, Anne considered that the nobleman's reaction could just as easily have been caused by a recent encounter in the People's Palace as it could have been by the socialist lecture she had delivered at the Chadwicks' dinner party.

The lovely spy was ready to start investigating which one it was when she was interrupted by the arrival of more guests, all traveling together in one party.

With a bearing regal enough to compete with any monarch, in marched Aurora, Duchess of Moreland, followed by her son, daughter and young Jack Kendrick. Anne peered past them, her heart beginning to beat rapidly as she waited for Ian to appear. To her horror, he did not.

"Is everyone here, then?" Chadwick called to his hostess, hoping that luncheon would finally be served.

"No, Jack's brother, that naughty devil, has yet to arrive," Lady Bothwell informed her guests, who were now congregating around her in the center of the room.

"Ah, but Kendrick might show yet." Bothwell chuckled. "Knowing that rogue, he was up to something entirely wicked though infinitely pleasurable last night, and was paying the price this morning."

While the men guffawed and the ladies tittered, the Duchess of Moreland shrugged her shoulders in a gesture of helplessness directed at Anne, who pretended to ignore it. As for Jack Kendrick, he could do little more than smile at the others weakly. He had little idea of Ian's movements last night, and even less knowledge of his older brother's plans for the day. He certainly didn't know what to tell these people concerning Ian. The young man silently cursed his brother for placing him in such an uncomfortable position, especially where Anne Hargraves was concerned. Besides the fact that Jack resented being his brother's keeper, the young man had problems enough dealing with his own devil at the moment, the residue of last night's excesses. Who would have thought that learning to be a rake could be so taxing?

After a luncheon during which Anne's spirits had continued to sink with each minute that slipped by and Ian did not appear, the men decided upon a riding party as the afternoon's diversion.

Though she briefly considered begging off, Anne decided to ride with the others in an attempt to discourage both Jack's and Daniel's reviving attentions, when she heard the two youngest men state their intentions of remaining behind in the house.

Soon the beautiful Miss Hargraves was gathered with the others near the stables. Her elegantly tailored riding ensemble of deepest black made her the center of attention, just as she had intended it to do. Not only was it a departure from the pastels she usually favored, but the inky hue emphasized the flawlessness of her pale complexion and the singular shade of her golden curls.

The majority of the men surrounded her immediately, but it was the arrogant Bradford, the man who had been on Cornwall Street, whom Anne asked for assistance when it came time to mount.

"Do you ride well?" he inquired, his hands caressing Anne's trim waistline as he lifted her to her saddle.

"Passably," Anne said with a smoldering smile. "But then you must realize that I have traveled by everything from camel to elephant to braying ass. Horses present little problem, I assure you. Why do you ask?"

"Just indulging in friendly conversation. It's my way of letting you know that I bear you no ill will for slipping away from me on the afternoon of the tenement fire," the nobleman said, his hand lingering at Anne's ankle after her foot had found the stirrup.

Before Anne could reply, the party was ready to set out, and she found herself off with the rest, traveling at a quick trot.

Crossing the meadows, so green and alive, Anne wondered if she could manage to pull away from the chattering group. If one of these men, specifically Bradford, was the assassin, he wouldn't dare act while in the company of the others. She would have to present him with the opportunity to find her alone.

* * *

Ian Kendrick had been riding for some time at breakneck speed when he pulled up before the stables of Bothwell Manor. The morning's investigation had yielded nothing. Among the reformers, Brighton had been involved with some activity at St. George's-in-the-East, and therefore unavailable, Digby had refused to receive him, and Morrison had not been at home.

A return to the People's Palace had uncovered nothing more than a few bloodstains on the floor of Queen's Hall. While this told him that Anne's shot had been true, he knew the wound it had inflicted was not all that serious. Hadn't the man who had tried to kill her last night been able to run off and escape pursuit?

Overcome by the frustration of his fruitless search for information, Ian had returned home only to find Jack had departed with the Morelands for Bothwell Manor. Surprised to see how late it was, Ian had decided to follow immediately.

Unable, after so much effort, to connect any of the reformers with Anne's most recent brush with death, Ian had to consider that perhaps it *was* one of the prince's friends who was behind everything, after all. The thought had so unnerved him that in spite of the icy reception he had felt he would receive, he had called at Anne's residence to offer his escort to the Bothwell estate. When he had found her already gone, he had cursed himself for a fool and had galloped off, riding harder than he had ever ridden in his life.

Now, leaving his mount, its sides heaving and flecked with foam, in the care of a stable hand, Ian raced up the path toward the main house. Before he arrived, however, the nobleman spied his brother Jack and Miss Audrey Palmer enjoying a stroll in the garden under the Duchess of Moreland's watchful eye.

"Good day, your ladyship, Miss Palmer," Ian called, nodding at his brother when he came abreast of the tiny group. "Has Miss Hargraves arrived yet from London?"

"She was here before we were," the duchess replied, pleased that the man was inquiring about Anne's whereabouts at first opportunity.

"She's in the house, then?" Ian asked, ready to excuse himself and head in that direction.

"No, actually, she went riding with some of the others," Jack said casually. Good Lord, why didn't his brother and Miss Hargraves get their signals straight? She had come looking for Ian last night when he was not at home, now Ian was searching for her and she was not about. The two of them must waste more time than they ever enjoyed, Jack decided, with all the presumption of the newly sophisticated.

"Riding?" Ian echoed, knowing full well that his own horse was in no condition to travel anywhere at the moment. "Where did they go and when did they leave?"

My, this did sound promising, Aurora thought, even as Audrey spoke up to answer the questions Jack's brother had asked.

"They began in that meadow to the east with the intention of riding the perimeters of the estate. Of course that was some time ago. In all probability, you would be able to catch up with them in the woods over to the west."

"Thank you," Ian called and then he hurried off in that direction on foot, causing the duchess to smile.

It gets better and better, she thought. The poor man is so anxious to see her that he entirely forgot to take a horse.

Anne had easily managed to separate herself from the other riders. Now, in the solitude of the small forest, she could not help but appreciate the lush greenery of the trees and the sweet, damp smell of the woodland floor. With leafy branches meeting overhead, allowing only intermittent shafts of light to shine through, and the peaceful silence, the place reminded Anne of a cathedral, hardly the setting in which one would expect a murder to be attempted. And yet if she was lucky, that is exactly what her presence would entice someone to try.

Slackening her reins and allowing her horse to nibble at the growth alongside a shallow stream, Anne thought she heard a rustling of leaves nearby. It might have been the wind, except that the churchlike forest suddenly produced a choir of excited birds, their voices reaching a crescendo of warning.

Before she knew what was happening, there was movement in the underbrush to her left, its suddenness frightening her horse so that it reared up onto its hind legs, and she had to struggle to control it.

The noise sounded again, much louder now, only to be answered in kind by a violent crashing through the brush on the other side of her. The proximity of these new eruptions caused Anne's high-spirited mount to become frenzied at the danger it sensed. Once more it reared up, thrashing its great head and becoming almost impossible to handle.

Suddenly, in the dimness, through the horse's wildly tossing mane Anne saw Ian emerge from the shadows close to her steed's flailing hooves. Then, before she could see anything else, there was a gunshot.

The horse bolted, unseating Anne, who tumbled to the ground, her lungs compressed so badly by the fall that there was no air left within them. Her body stunned, Anne's frantic mind urged her to draw a deep breath before she was forever incapable of doing so again.

Oh, dearest God, it *was* Ian who was trying to kill her after all, her desolate heart cried, even as she clutched at the ground in an effort to drag herself away before he could effectively put an end to her life. Why else would he have startled her mount?

More crashing of branches sounding in her ears, Anne was finally able to force searing air into her lungs and pull herself up onto her knees. She looked over her shoulder, expecting to see Ian Kendrick coming toward her, but was surprised to see him running off through the underbrush instead.

Still gasping for breath, a confused Anne was trying to understand what had just occurred when she heard the thunder of approaching hoofbeats. Was it this noise which had saved her life, prompting Ian to flee?

Within moments Anne found herself surrounded by solicitous men and women. Unwilling to explain what had happened for fear that one of these people might be in league with Ian, she despondently mumbled something about surprising a poacher and losing control of her horse. When Bradford looked at her skeptically, Anne could only hope that it was a result of the bragging she had done concerning her horsemanship, and not because he was Ian's accomplice.

Too sore and weary to worry about that possibility at the moment, Anne made no resistance when the Earl of Wallingcroft placed her on his horse and led her to the house. Here Lady Bothwell took command and swiftly put her chief guest to bed, brushing aside a worried Brewster and banishing him, heedless of his objections, to the servants' hall along with Bess so that their mistress could get some rest.

Chapter Sixteen

Most of the guests were clustered in a small sitting area at the end of the broad upper hallway where Anne's room was situated when their whispered speculations were interrupted by a slamming door and a booming voice.

"Where is she?" came a bellow followed by frantic footsteps ascending to the second floor.

The startled houseguests and their hosts turned to see a disheveled and breathless Ian Kendrick pushing his way determinedly through their group.

He appeared now as no one there had ever seen him. His dark, normally well groomed hair had been tossed by the wind, and his usually meticulous clothing was in disarray, shirt open down to the center of his powerful chest, jacket torn. But it was his air of untamed savagery coupled with the anguish of his handsome features that held the assembly in awe.

"Where is she?" he demanded of Bothwell in a lupine growl.

"Kendrick, how fortunate that you could join us," the lord of the manor said, hobbling forward on his cane and depending upon the polite strictures of society to circumvent a nasty scene.

"Perhaps you didn't understand me," Ian said, his voice dangerously soft as he fixed Bothwell with a brutal glare, bringing his face so close to that of the nervous host that the man almost tumbled over backward. "I want to know the whereabouts of Miss Hargraves."

"Calm yourself, Kendrick," commanded Lady Moreland, putting a staying hand on his arm. "The girl is, for the most part, unharmed."

Ian swung his head sharply to regard this pillar of society, who was currently exhibiting more bravery than any of the men present.

"That's right, Ian," Jack ventured hesitantly, quite overwhelmed by this unsuspected feral aspect of his brother's character. "Anne is fine, she's in that last room over there on the right. Alone," he added nervously.

"Perhaps I can see if she is up to receiving," Lady Bothwell said, hoping to put an end to this highly irregular incident.

But her words were ignored as Ian had already broken away from those congregating in the hallway and was moving toward Anne's door.

"I say, Kendrick," Bothwell protested weakly, "you can't go in there."

"Try to stop me," Ian muttered as he softly opened the door and stepped inside, locking it behind him.

Certain that her mother would swoon at the shock of such impropriety, Audrey Palmer was surprised to see her parent bring clasped hands to her bosom in a show of romantic compassion, a victorious smile lighting her face.

But when she happened to glance at her impressionable daughter, the Duchess of Moreland caught herself. Straightening her already rigid posture, she allowed a condemning frown to slip into place before she firmly marched Audrey and the others away, placating Lady Bothwell with the promise that her house party would be the talk of London society for months to come.

With the curtains drawn the room was dim, and Ian approached Anne's bed stealthily. So great had been his fear of losing her that he dared not believe his beautiful Anne was uninjured until he saw her and judged as much for himself.

Alone in the large room, Anne lay in the center of her bed, sleeping fitfully. Paler than usual, she looked so vulnerable that the sight of her wrenched Ian's heart. At the moment he didn't care what she had done or what she was involved in. Unable to help himself, he bent low to place a feather of a kiss on her brow.

Instantly, Anne came awake and alert, her years in espionage having trained her to sleep lightly. But when she perceived who it was standing over her bed, Ian was taken completely aback by the fear he saw registered in her eyes.

"It's all right, Anne, it's Ian," he said, misunderstanding the reason for her apprehension as he sat on the bed and enfolded her rigid form in a gentle embrace.

Then, before she could remind herself of what had happened in the forest, her arms, with a life of their own, entwined themselves around Ian's neck. Yet even as her mind fought to persuade her that this man meant her harm, Anne's heart, reveling in the tenderness of Ian's loving hug, insisted that such a notion was untrue.

After showering the contours of Anne's lovely face with a multitude of soft, warm kisses, Ian's lips finally sought hers. The effect was so potent that both Anne and Ian could do nothing else but lose themselves in the taste of each other. Helpless, they allowed all doubts, all suspicions, all sense of duty to recede, subdued by the force of their undeniable attraction.

But when Anne permitted herself the pleasure of sweeping her hands across Ian's chest and around to his broad back, he involuntarily winced and withdrew from her touch before claiming her lips with his own once more.

His actions and the grimace he had worn immediately summoned Anne's reluctant memories of the bullet wound she had inflicted on someone the previous night. Dear God in heaven, why was he playing with her in this manner? It was all too evident that Ian Kendrick *was* the man she had wounded *and* the man who had tried to shoot her this afternoon.

This unwelcome realization aroused Anne's slumbering sense of obligation to her assignment as well as her will to survive. Recognizing that she had no choice, Anne continued to answer the demands of Ian's passionate mouth while she reached beneath her pillow and brought forth the pistol hidden there.

Ian was bent forward and in the midst of untying the ribbons holding Anne's chemise closed when he felt the cold, unmistakable touch of a gun barrel at his temple.

Even as his eyes widened in surprise, he swiftly brought his head up, catching Anne beneath the chin to send her falling back into the bed's soft surface. Immediately his huge hand wrapped, ironlike, around her wrist, and within seconds he had managed to relieve her of the small, ivory-handled weapon.

Pinning her to the mattress, he looked at the volatile beauty, his eyes narrowing in cool speculation.

"You could have just said no," he joked grimly.

"Let me go, you bastard," the blonde commanded in a fierce whisper, her heaving chest and dishabille making her appear so alluring and vulnerable that Ian almost forgot the threat she had posed but a moment before.

"We have to talk," Ian said at last with a heavy sigh, pulling Anne to a sitting position and capturing both her wrists in one strong hand. "What do you know about plans to assassinate the queen?"

Anne returned his hard stare, her own eyes unfathomable. She wondered if this man meant to brag of his evil intentions before he killed her. How he hoped to get away with it, she didn't know, unless he thought to smother her and blame her demise on the fall from her horse. But she'd not make it easy for him.

"I asked what you know about the threats against Victoria," an impatient Ian stated, his free hand coming up to grasp Anne's stubborn chin, directing her face to his. Though his voice was imperious, he was conscious of his touch, not wanting to hurt her no matter how guilty the moment made her seem.

"Not as much as I would like to know," Anne said defiantly.

"Oh, bloody hell," he groaned in despair. "Out with it, Anne. Tell me how deeply you're involved in this damnable plot. Even at this stage there might be something that can be done."

"To silence me?" she asked quietly, as though her life were nothing but a trifle.

"Silence you! I don't want to do that, woman. I want you to talk," Ian erupted angrily.

"Well, I'm not going to do so," Anne pronounced, her eyes challenging his. It would not be from her lips that this potential assassin learned just how much, or rather how little, British intelligence knew of his activities.

Ian's face reflected more misery than he had ever felt before in his life. Had this woman ever cared for him, or was her pretended affection part of the intrigue in which she was embroiled? Angered by the question that haunted him, Ian addressed Anne harshly. "At least tell me one thing. Why do you want to see the queen dead?"

"Me? Don't try to take me for a fool," Anne snapped, "when it is you who have been working to kill Her Majesty."

"If you believe that then you are a fool," Ian muttered, studying Anne's face for some clue as to the meaning of what this was all about.

"I may have been once, when I let you into my bed, but I'm not any longer," Anne declared. "You were enraged when I left your house in the company of your brother, and a carriage almost ran me down. You were on Cornwall Street when the fire broke out, and I suspect you were in the People's Palace last night, as well."

"Anne, I..."

"Can you deny it?"

"No, but you don't understand. I was—"

"And that's not all, Ian. It was you I saw in the woods this afternoon, just before the shot rang out," Anne concluded with an accusatory stare.

"I was there, yes, just as I was at the tenement and the music hall, but my intent was to protect you. Look at me, Anne. No matter what you have done, do you honestly think I would ever set out to hurt you?"

Wavering momentarily under the intensity of the spell cast by his silver eyes, Anne had to fight the urge to fall into his arms and believe that everything was going to be fine.

"I've known innumerable men to do what no one would suspect of them," Anne hedged. "There are too many coincidences for you to deny that you're involved in this despicable enterprise,'' she objected, looking away in order to break the enchantment between them.

"And what is your connection to this dirty business that you should come to such a conclusion?" he asked, growing tired of her damning view of his actions. His quiet tones were rife with barely contained fury, his anger burgeoning not as a result of her accusations, but because her treachery threatened to put her forever beyond his reach. How could he help her if she wouldn't confide in him?

"It's none of your affair," she said in a deadly voice.

"Yes, it is, you little idiot," he argued savagely. "Don't you understand? It's no longer just the task I must accomplish. In spite of it all, God help me, I still love you."

"Is that why you shot at me this afternoon, and last night, as well?"

"Damn it, Anne! I never did," he avowed in frustration.

"Don't lie to me, Ian. I wounded my assailant last night. Just a few moments ago you winced when I touched your ribs. And as much as I didn't want it to be so, that reaction confirmed my suspicions."

"I *have* no bullet wounds," the dark-haired Englishman cried, tearing open the rest of his shirt with one hand and drawing her attention to his side. "Look, Anne. It's a bruise, nothing more. I was clipped by your horse's hooves as it reared in the forest. See for yourself."

As dim as the room was, Anne was able to discern the truth of what Ian had just told her. He released his hold on her, and gingerly Anne ran her fingers over his muscular torso. There was no bullet hole. His injury was nothing more than a purple discoloration. Still, Anne hesitated to embrace relief until she learned more. In almost every instance, when someone had tried to kill her, Ian had been there.

"This only proves that you are not the man who shot at me last night. But you might be his accomplice."

"I told you, I have nothing to do with him. But why does he want to harm you, Anne? And why are you so afraid? Have you double-crossed him?"

"If what you're telling me is true," Anne said, ignoring his question, "why did you run away last night as well as today?"

"I was trying to capture him, damn it! If I was making a run for it would I have come back?"

"Perhaps if you wanted to finish the job you and your partner have continued to bungle," she retorted, hoping to push him into revealing something, anything.

"Look, how many times do I have to tell you that I have nothing to do with him? But it doesn't make any difference what you think of me right now," Ian pronounced wearily, his patience beginning to weaken under the assault of the puzzling game she was playing. "I don't know how or why you're involved in this, but I do know I have to send for the authorities."

"The authorities?" the petite blonde asked sharply, caught very much by surprise.

"I'm sorry," Ian said, gently tracing her chin with his forefinger, a visible sign of his regret. "But there's nothing else I can do. No matter how much I have come to love you, Annie, the Prince of Wales has entrusted me with uncovering the source of the threats being made against Her Majesty. And you're caught up in it somehow."

"You're working for the Prince of Wales?" Anne asked incredulously. Ian's affirmation flooded her with joy, giving credence to the assertions her heart had insisted on harboring concerning his innocence. While her innate skepticism had saved her life many times in the past, Anne knew that now it was time to listen to what her heart had tried to tell her. In this instance, it was speaking true.

Tears glistened in her luminous eyes, and a sad little smile settled upon her mouth. She reached out to caress Ian's cheek. "What dangerous deceptions we've been playing at, my love," she said, thinking of the gun she had placed at his head.

"What do you mean?" he asked gruffly, his manner an attempt to hide the anguish that was tearing at his very soul.

"I'm with British intelligence," she replied simply.

"What!" he exclaimed. "The famous Anne Hargraves is a British agent?"

"For six years now."

"But why?" he demanded, clasping her shoulders lightly and locking her eyes to his, wildly hoping that what she told him was true, even as he began to piece together all the evidence that supported her claim.

Before she knew what she was doing, Anne found herself explaining about Louis Napoleon, and how he had been slain in Africa because England had had no inkling of the danger he had been in. As Ian watched her intently, Conway's most beautiful agent went on to tell him about how she had been approached by Sir Nigel and how she had agreed to work for her country so that the tragedy that had taken Louis from her would never again be repeated.

"You must have loved him very much," Ian said, his voice husky with gentle sympathy.

"I did," Anne confirmed, meeting his searching gaze. "So much so that I spent many lonely years before I found a man I loved even more."

"And who might that have been?" he asked, his breath catching so that he felt his chest would burst while he anxiously waited for her answer.

"The man who escorted me to the Irish reception, of course. The man who—"

Before Anne could utter another word, Ian caught her to him and held her tightly against his chest while his grateful lips rained gentle kisses upon her head.

"Dearest Annie," he murmured, resting his cheek atop her soft, blond curls, "you don't know how much I love you, how relieved I am to learn that you aren't guilty of trying to harm the queen."

"But I know exactly how you feel," Anne corrected him, caressing his lean jawline with the back of her hand.

"I suppose you do," he agreed, that devilish lock of unruly hair falling dangerously and enticingly across his forehead. "But tell me, are we so in concert that you share everything I feel at this moment?"

"I think so," she replied, her voice raspy as she swirled her fingertips lightly around his navel.

Ian lowered his lips to hers, his masterful kisses alternately coaxing and demanding, and his eyes burning so hotly with desire that Anne thought his touch would turn her to cinders. His strong hands, sweeping over her body in tender possessiveness, stood in marked contrast to the primitive urgency of his obviously searing needs. Easing his palm across the sensitive tips of her now exposed breasts, Ian was just bending forward to cover one taut peak with his mouth when there was a tremendous banging upon the bedroom door.

Hearing only a muttered curse coming from within, Brewster pounded more insistently.

"Miss Hargraves, are you all right?" he asked before thumping on the door once more.

"You'd better see to him," Ian groaned, while Anne left the bed and put on a wrapper. Unlocking the door, she opened it slightly.

"Oh, miss, you're unharmed then! How fortunate. Conway would have had me flayed alive otherwise. I was down in the servants' quarters and heard some rumors of Mr. Kendrick storming into the house and then into this very room," the butler began.

"It needn't concern you, Brewster," Anne said firmly, though her tone was hoarse, indicating to the portly servant that Kendrick was indeed lurking somewhere close.

"Is he here?" the butler demanded, becoming agitated as he noted not only Anne's breathy voice, but her swollen lips.

"Yes, if you must know," Anne hissed, attempting to shut the door. "Now leave us alone."

"But, miss, you don't understand. I think I saw him leaving the People's Palace last night."

Brewster had been at the Queen's Hall, too? It was beginning to seem that almost everyone she knew had been there.

"Yes, Brewster, I know. Not to worry," she said soothingly.

"He's a dangerous man!"

"In some ways," Anne murmured, thinking of the barechested masculine figure waiting in her bed. "Though if you don't leave, you'll find I can be more dangerous still."

"But, miss, you can't be too careful."

"That is all, Brewster," came Anne's threatening voice through the keyhole as she locked the door.

"But..."

"Keep this up and I'll see to it that you spend the next few years working in the household of an Irish MP. I assure you, I have everything under control."

"That's not a lie," said Ian, coming to stand behind Anne and holding her in his arms, the sound of the muttering butler stalking down the hallway bringing a smile to both their faces. "You control me well enough, you enticing witch. However, there's one thing I must insist upon."

"And what's that?" she asked, bending her head back to look up into the eyes of the man she loved.

"I won't have the woman I marry working as a spy. It's much too dangerous," he stated, spinning her around and tilting her face to his. "Say you will marry me, Anne. Say it now."

"Oh, Ian, yes! Nothing would make me happier," Anne exclaimed, completely forgetting her protestations to Lady Moreland as she stood on tiptoe and pulled his head down to meet her kiss.

"When?" he murmured, his lips pressed against hers.

"As soon as we catch the man we're looking for," she responded almost incoherently, thoughts of all else save this glorious male receding from conscious.

"Right," Ian said, breaking their embrace and taking Anne's hand to lead her to the bed. "The sooner we find this bloke, the sooner I can make you my wife. I say we pool our knowledge. Besides, we don't want our wedding bells to follow Victoria's death knell, do we?"

Readily agreeing, Anne heard all that Ian had to say, any questions she had now answered. Satisfied, she then explained her plans and insights to him.

"This concert is to gather the suspects and allow the queen the opportunity to return to Windsor safely while they're distracted?" he asked.

When Anne nodded, Ian heaved a deep sigh and placed an arm around her shoulders. "It's a decent strategy, but still, we are not any closer to knowing who this madman is. Last night he gave me the slip under cover of darkness, and today I lost him in the woods without ever seeing who he was. He could be anyone staying here, or not Bothwell's guest at all. Damn, but I feel it's all my fault we've gained nothing concrete!"

"Don't blame yourself," Anne said, her voice a symphony of consolation. "Yesterday evening it was dark and everything happened so quickly. Today, you were in no condition to chase anyone with your ribs bruised as they are."

"I chased you and managed to catch you, didn't I?" Ian asked with a devilish smile, placing a light peck on the tip of her nose. "But you're very kind to make excuses for me. I think I am going to enjoy having such a supportive wife."

"But it is true," Anne protested. "And besides, I allowed him to get away, too."

"Which brings me to a very important matter," Ian said, his mood becoming more serious. "Until this man is caught, I don't want you returning to Mayfair. It's not safe. I'll just have to find some secure and well-protected spot for you to stay."

"Do you have somewhere in mind?" Anne inquired seductively.

"Well . . . I do know this little place off Russell Square," he replied with a smile. "While the decor is not up to your usual standards, the food is decent and I can promise you, you'll find the host most attentive."

"It sounds quite cozy, though you do realize that means taking Brewster, as well."

"Good Lord, I hadn't thought of that!" Ian joked in mock horror. "Do I suppose correctly that you will make such a sacrifice worth my while?"

"I can try," Anne replied.

"Good," he drawled with lazy satisfaction. "Now as for this concert of yours, I've some suggestions. First of all, I think you've been making yourself too accessible to this killer. If you were to stay at my place, we could put about the story that going into seclusion is how you always prepare for a major singing engagement. I think not being able to find you will make the man nervous, and nervous men make mistakes."

"And what am I supposed to do with all my free time until the night of the performance?" Anne asked.

"I'm certain I can think of something," Ian said meaningfully.

"That sounds extremely promising," Anne replied with a giggle. She couldn't help but be astounded that Ian Kendrick had it in his power to make her feel like a girl again, even under such dire circumstances.

"Stop that squirming, woman," Ian complained halfheartedly as Anne snuggled closer to the man who had uncovered the secrets of her heart. "You're apt to make me forget any thoughts I have."

"Actually, I was intending to give you new ones," Anne commented suggestively.

Undoing the sash of her wrapper, Anne lay back upon the bed. Her outstretched, welcoming arms spread the colorful material of her dressing gown, causing it to flare out on either side of her so that she looked like some erotic Psyche, awaiting the arrival of Eros.

The image she presented was temptation in its purest form. With a groan of surrender, Ian fell into her arms, his head resting on her naked torso.

"Show me how much you love me, Ian," Anne pleaded, the touch of his skin upon hers inspiring her wanton behavior.

"As if I could do anything else," he fairly growled, his virile instincts set afire by her simply stated request.

Though his needs were great, Ian's touch was teasingly light as he removed his lover's clothing and then his own. Zephyrlike, his hands drifted over Anne's body, barely skimming the surface of her form, taxing her patience and evoking whimpers of anticipation as she began to writhe provocatively atop the sheets.

"Hesitantly...that's how I loved you the first time I saw you, wanting you yet unwilling to touch you because I knew once I did I would be lost," he mumbled, nuzzling Anne's neck, vulnerably exposed now that she had thrown back her head in passionate surrender.

"But then, I couldn't help myself," he continued, his mouth finding the peak of Anne's breast and his words vibrating along its sensitive surface, causing her to moan in uninhibited eagerness. "No matter what the consequences, I had to have you."

His hands were possessive as they explored every delicate area of Anne's yielding body, finally coming to rest near the moist, secret core of her being. Stroking surely and expertly, Ian ignored Anne's cries for release, seeking to magnify their pleasure by teasing them both just a bit longer.

"More," Anne begged, her voice broken by desire when she feared that he would stop this wondrous torment.

"Yes, more," Ian echoed in a ragged voice, increasing the steady rhythm of his hand. "That's what I wanted, too...more and more until nothing less than all of you would do."

"Then take me, Ian," Anne enjoined, finding strength in the power she had over him. "Take me now."

Hearing his name uttered with such yearning by the woman he loved, Ian was no longer able to control the urgings of his demanding masculine instincts. He discovered that he needed Anne every bit as much as she needed him.

He entered her almost reverently, encasing himself in the warmth she offered, luxuriating in the feel of her. Then primal impulses dominated all else, and he began to move, slowly and steadily at first, and then with increasing ardor. Anne's small cries and the tremors of her body beneath his spurred Ian on until he was half crazed with an urgency to please. The longing to have her had transformed itself into an ache to possess her, and their rocking movements gave way to throbbing frenzy. Deeply he drove into the sanctuary Anne tendered so sweetly until finally their pleasure balanced on the brink of pain, so fiercely did he need to make her totally his.

And then, from the depths of his soul came a potent surge that carried them both into a mystical dimension of immortality, linking them to all lovers who had ever lived as well as those yet to be born.

"Do you have any idea now as to how I love you?" Ian asked Anne, cradling her gently in his arms, both of them content in the radiant aftermath of spent passion.

"I'd say very well indeed," Anne murmured, nestling closer. "And will you be just as loving after we are married?"

"More so," he promised, holding her tighter though his mind was reluctantly being summoned back from the paradise they had shared to face the realities of the world. Knowing in his heart that Anne and he would never again experience such abandon until they caught the villain stalking Victoria, Ian silently wrestled with the problems facing them.

After a while, his eyes aglitter with inspiration, he eagerly sought Anne's attention with a proprietary kiss placed on her bare shoulder.

"I know it might sound a bit outlandish, but as concerns your concert, what would you say if we..."

Chapter Seventeen

The rest of the week passed in a blur of activity until suddenly it was late afternoon the day of Anne's concert, and Brewster's petulant complaints echoed through Ian's front parlor.

"Miss Hargraves, truly this whole scheme is positively absurd. Why you believe anyone in his right mind would ever—"

"Now then, Matthew, you heard Nigel tell you quite explicitly that you were to cooperate with us in everything we asked."

"And haven't I? I mean, did I say anything whatsoever about your staying here with Mr. Kendrick—in his bedroom? Did I voice my disapproval of the slipshod way this household is managed or the cramped quarters I was assigned in the scullery, a man of my reputation?"

"True, you have been exceedingly patient," placated Anne in soothing tones as she avoided meeting Ian's amused glance by raising her own eyes heavenward. "However, now is when we need you most. Think of Victoria. You and you alone could well be the key to saving her life. Indeed, the success of our entire plan rests on your broad shoulders."

"She's right, you know, old man. Without your help, the villain might well be free to go after the real queen next Tuesday. You don't want that to happen," coaxed Ian, fighting to control his mirth as he and Anne pandered to the half-naked butler suddenly beset by false modesty and second thoughts. "Matthew Brewster, the fate of England's monarchy could well depend on your performance this evening."

Not completely convinced, the portly little butler stood anxiously before them, desperately clutching at the waistband of his trousers as he pondered his choices. This smooth-talking pair had already relieved him of his waistcoat and shirt, but surely even the queen wouldn't demand that he sacrifice his pants for her.

"I still don't see why I can't keep my legs decently covered. You said no one will be that close to me," he argued.

"Because with your trousers on, I'll never get the corset to fit properly."

"Corset?" The butler nearly screeched in apoplexy. "If you don't wear one, I don't see any reason I should. I'll warrant Victoria doesn't."

"Brewster, Miss Hargraves has a far more womanly figure than you do, thank God. As for the queen, I don't know her habits, but your lumps and rolls are in nowhere near the right locations, so we have to do something to approximate nature's design," chided Ian, finally out of patience with the man's vanity. If they were to keep to the schedule they'd worked out, there wasn't much time left to placate the old fellow. "Look here, Brewster, stiffen your upper lip and do your duty for England. As an agent of the Crown, I venture you've suffered far greater indignities than this on other assignments."

"Perhaps I have sir, but not with an audience watching," muttered the rotund man who would shortly appear in public as Victoria's double. With her private secretary's cooperation, Conway had arranged to secretly delay the queen's return from Balmoral to Windsor while at the same time quickly spreading the word that the monarch would attend Anne's concert tonight. If he didn't cooperate, Brewster realized, it would indeed all be in vain.

Reluctantly he took a deep breath, dropped his trousers and revealed the lower half of a union suit and exceptionally bony legs. Grimacing as he accepted the corset from Anne, he turned away from her.

"I can manage myself, miss."

"I'm afraid not, Matthew. You must be laced into this from the back, and even you can't do that," disputed the pert blonde as she began to adjust the metal stays about the man's considerable girth. Only after that could she tie up the confining laces. Who said revenge wasn't sweet, she wondered, tightening the restricting garment with a pleasure beyond compare.

"Ugh," grunted the butler, red-faced but clearly resisting the urge to protest any further. If his sovereign needed him to do this, who was he to refuse, despite the discomfort involved? At least that bounder Kendrick had disappeared for a bit; that in itself was a blessing.

"Well, of course, I realized you knew the Prince of Wales when he sent round that message, but, Ian, the queen?" Jack's eyes fairly popped out of his head when his older brother announced their sovereign's presence downstairs. "Are you certain she wouldn't mind meeting me? I mean, I'd understand—"

Ian grinned and shook his head, reflecting how much Jack had matured in the past few weeks. Despite what must have been an overwhelming temptation for him, he hadn't flinched at Anne's sudden presence in the house, let alone the sleeping arrangements she and Ian were enjoying. Of course, to be completely truthful, acknowledged Ian, the younger Kendrick's reticence on that score might have been the result of the murderous looks he had given his younger brother the night he'd brought Anne home, looks that left no doubt as to the sort of behavior expected. Still, the lad had complied with surprising grace, even abandoning his woefully adoring glances and accepting the singer as an older sister rather than an object of love.

"You mustn't belabor Her Majesty with idle chatter now, but a few quick words of courtesy are only appropriate," Ian said aloud, tugging at his stubborn lock of hair, which had again fallen across his forehead. This would be the final test of Brewster's costume, he and Anne had decided. If the butler could withstand close scrutiny, however limited, by Jack and Mrs. Land, he would certainly fool the would-be assassin from a greater distance.

*   *   *

"Now, raise your arms, Matthew, and let me slip the dress over your head. Fortunately, it's her usual black gown," said Anne in the front parlor. To her amazement, the butler complied immediately, apparently accepting his fate and anxious to see the end of the whole affair. Moments later, however, when she persisted in adjusting the folds of billowing cloth, circling him to tuck black bombazine here and pull the fabric there, he revolted against her efforts.

"Isn't it sufficient, miss, that I have to suffer such indignities as this styleless garment without your petty enjoyment of my discomfort?" he demanded in irritation. "I'll never look like Victoria anyway, so let me be, for heaven's sake."

"Well, I suppose if that's the effect you want, it's the best I can do," she said with a wicked grin, recalling his similar comment to her. "Here, let me help you on with your widow's cap and veil."

"What's your point? No one will ever believe this outrageous scheme of yours. I can't believe Nigel agreed—"

Then the door to the parlor slid open and he quickly accepted the opaque black head covering, dropping it into place just in time.

"Anne, Nigel is out front with the closed carriage. He'll take Her Majesty to Paddington and make it appear she's just arrived from Windsor and then he'll join us at the People's Palace while she comes in the royal carriage," announced Ian. Satisfied that Brewster's disguise was complete, he stepped aside for Jack to enter the room. Mrs. Land and Molly were waiting near the front door.

"Your Majesty, may I present my younger brother, John Andrew Charles Kendrick?"

Brewster's back stiffened and he seemed to grow slightly taller with indignation, but his features were sufficiently obscured by his veil that Ian couldn't see the scowl he felt certain was angrily fixed in place.

"Your Majesty, this is truly an honor I never expected to enjoy during my visit to London," said Jack, bowing stiffly from the waist as he reached out to grasp the queen's hand, surprised to see it covered with hair.

"Oh, Lord," cried Anne, "the gloves!"

"Sod off, you young pup," growled Brewster, hiding his telltale hands in the folds of his skirt and sweeping regally forward to the door. "Let's get this over with."

"Anne? Ian?" questioned Jack in confusion. While the figure before him had certainly looked like Victoria, he couldn't imagine his sovereign ever being so ungraciously crude, but then any old lady with hands like that . . .

"I'll explain everything after the concert," promised Anne, grabbing her shawl and Victoria's gloves and following the others to the door.

In the hall, Mrs. Land and Molly had already dipped into deep obsequious curtsies as the regal matron passed, grousing all the way to the front door. Fortunately, his angry words weren't clearly discernible to the women, who clearly relished their fleeting glimpse of royalty.

"Oh, Mr. Ian, thank you. I never imagined in my lifetime that Beatrice Land would be so close to the queen," exclaimed his housekeeper as she struggled to rise from her awkward position.

"I think she smiled at me, Aunt," rejoiced Molly as Anne and Ian entered the smaller carriage for their journey to the People's Palace. There were still some final arrangements to be made, and of course Anne had to dress before the curtain rose, but for the moment they could be alone.

The man's palms were damp and his hands shook as he contemplated the evening ahead. This would be his night; Anne Hargraves might think she was to give a concert, but his would be the performance that changed history. Awkwardly taking a swig of whiskey from the bottle, he swallowed it without tasting it, pleased that his trembling seemed to lessen immediately. His wound was probably infected, he knew, but that didn't matter now. All that concerned him tonight was his ultimate success; this time he wouldn't fail.

He had no choice anymore but to use a handgun; his side was too sore to withstand the kickback of a rifle and there was no way he could smuggle one into the hall. Still, the small revolver had a solid, comfortable feel to it. Slowly, ever so methodically, he cleaned and oiled each piece of his instrument one last time, stroking the steel with sure, even touches as he reassembled it, relishing the coolness of the shiny metal beneath his fingers.

Finally, eyes glazed with anticipation, he opened the drawer in his desk and took out the box of ammunition. Removing one bullet at a time, he caressed each and slipped it lovingly into the obliging chamber of the waiting pistol. This night wouldn't disappoint him, he knew; now only Anne Hargraves stood between him and Victoria, between those who had waited so long for deliverance and their salvation.

The singer had escaped him on three different ocassions; each time the haughty blonde had probably sat back and laughed at how she'd fooled the Fates, and she didn't know how close he'd come to shooting her outside the tenement. In truth, then, there had been four occasions the unwelcome interloper had cheated Death when by all rights it should have been hers. But tonight, tonight she would not elude her destiny.

With Victoria visiting Anne Hargraves backstage, it couldn't be better; he would corner them both in her dressing room and maybe, he contemplated, he would even make the singer watch while he killed the queen. Of course, he might not have time for such a coup, but if the orchestra was playing and the noise sufficient, it would please him greatly for Anne to die knowing how she had failed to stop him. For that matter, if Kendrick happened to interfere again, he, too, would share the women's fate. There were plenty of bullets. The would-be assassin smiled as he began to dress with inordinate care for the concert. After all, if this might be his final performance, he had best be properly attired.

As their coach entered Mile End Road on the way to the People's Palace, Ian had to raise his voice to be heard over the tumult in the streets.

"Anne, are you certain you want to go through with this?" he asked, despite all her earlier assurances that she did.

"Don't start that again, Ian. Of course I'm going to do the concert. What's come over you?" she asked in sur-

prise. Nigel had been the one who objected most strongly to
the plan; she had thought she had Ian's full support. Looking at his firm, masculine profile, she took measure of his
mood; his usually clear eyes were cloudy and his manner
more somber than she'd ever seen. Could it be that he was
afraid for her? "Goodness, Ian, I've been in more perilous
situations than this dozens of times—"

"Yes, but look at the crowds already gathering. It's almost ninety minutes until your performance, and there are
mobs of people everywhere. There is no guarantee we can
stop him before he gets you, especially if he uses a rifle," the
once-confident male said, clearly distressed at the situation. Anne had come to mean more to him than his own life.
If anything went wrong tonight...

"Ian, between Nigel's people and those authorized by the
prince to help out, we'll have backstage and the hall itself
blanketed with sufficient protection. In fact, there will
probably be more men in the audience concerned with my
safety than will be there enjoying the concert."

"I doubt that's possible, but at least you convinced the
government to pay for their tickets; that will be a nice contribution for Brighton's charity." Ian grinned, still amazed
at the audacity Anne had displayed in dealing with the bu-
reaucratic hierarchy.

"Of course, why should they have free seats? The money
is going to a good cause, which reminds me, Mr. Kendrick," said the pert blonde, an impish smile brightening her
lovely face, "you haven't paid for your ticket yet."

"For heaven's sake, Anne—"

"Never mind, two quid won't put you in the poorhouse,
and it could feed a family of five for a week," admonished
the songstress, her palm extended to receive the price specified.

"Actually, my dear, to be quite honest, you are worth a
great deal more to me than that," Ian whispered huskily,
"though I did think our relationship gave me some privi-
leges."

"It does," she agreed sweetly. "At home, you're the only
one who can make me sing—and most of those notes aren't

on any scale I had ever encountered before you took me in your arms."

Chuckling at her casual reference to their lovemaking, Ian obligingly handed his lady the coins she demanded and stole one last kiss as the carriage came to a halt outside the People's Palace.

"Well, sir, I guess it's time," she murmured, taking a deep breath and accepting his assistance out of the coach. "Do you suppose he's here yet?"

Ian needed no explanation as to whom she referred.

"I gave strict instructions that no one was to be allowed backstage before we arrived, even our people," he reminded her, "but that doesn't really guarantee anything."

"I think he'll want to wait for Victoria now," Anne theorized. "I might have attracted him before, but she's his main interest. I might not even be in his sights any longer."

"I only pray you're right, my sweet," Ian answered, leading the way inside, where it appeared no one had violated his directive. Everyone, the members of the orchestra, the ushers and stagehands and all Nigel's operatives, had gathered in the orchestra rather than behind the curtain.

Looking about Queen's Hall, Anne felt a momentary twinge of apprehension as she remembered the attack on her the previous week, but then Ian squeezed her hand, drawing her back to the present and erasing her sudden qualms.

The huge room had been prepared exactly as she had specified, with its many chairs and divans, couches and ottomans set to face the stage. The only exception was one seating arrangement to the left of the orchestra, carefully blocked off from full public view by the decorative palms, designed for Victoria, the Prince of Wales and their respective entourages. Since the architects of the People's Palace hadn't seen fit to include either a royal box or a retiring room for the heads of state, Nigel decided this was the only feasible arrangement, though it would mean the queen would have to return backstage at intermission, if the concert ran that long.

"Anne, it's time you began to dress," suggested Ian, gesturing to the alcove prepared as her dressing room. "I'll help you."

"That's all right, thank you. Bess—"

"Isn't here. I wasn't about to take chances with her life, too. I'll be your lady's maid for the evening. After all, I've seen you in considerably less than you'll be wearing tonight," Ian reminded the singer.

"I'm certain you'll be better at it than Brewster," Anne agreed, "as long as you can keep your mind on business."

And he did. The songstress marveled as he assisted her in undressing and donning her costume. Even as his solid fingers gently unrolled her stockings and eased them up her shapely thighs, the man was nothing but pure efficiency, making no improper gestures, passing no suggestive comments. How so lusty a male managed to control his usually overwhelming tendency to lovingly caress each and every muscle of her body, she couldn't fathom. Indeed, for a moment, Anne felt rejected by his impersonal attention, but then she realized his apparently singular sense of purpose was costing Ian dearly. His tightly clenched jaw gave evidence to the self-control he was exerting, and when she leaned forward to reward him with a kiss, he grimaced in pain.

"Damn," he muttered in annoyance, sweeping her into his arms. "Here I've been gnawing the inside of my lips to keep my mind off your nearly irresistible charms and you go and ruin my sterling efforts."

"Oh, my," said the willing blonde, unable to hide her amusement, "the sacrifices you make for your country know no bounds."

Across town, Nigel Conway was finally enjoying a deep sigh of relief. He had successfully transported the disguised Brewster to Paddington without notice, and their ruse of having Her Majesty enter the back of one side of the train and exit the front of the other side had worked quite satisfactorily. Indeed, the only real difficulty was convincing Brewster not to walk so energetically and to use small steps, leaning on his cane instead. But even that hurdle was now behind him. He settled the bogus monarch into the royal carriage and prepared to leave.

"Where do you think you're off to?" snarled the queen, catching Nigel's hand and refusing to let it go.

"To the People's Palace, naturally. I'll meet you there," consoled Conway, attempting to release his hand. "I can't ride with you, Your Majesty; there's only room here for your ladies-in-waiting. Besides, my presence would only attract undue attention."

"And you think I won't do that in this silly getup?" demanded the butler, already out of patience with this masquerade. The corset had been bad enough when he was standing, but in the carriage ride, it had been torture. And now, he'd be beset by chattering females, as well. No, he'd not have it. "Nigel, see here—"

"Excuse me, Sir Nigel," interrupted one of the queen's attendants. "We really must join Her Majesty and be off. The prince's carriage has already left."

"Of course," agreed the nobleman, yanking his hand from Brewster's grip and turning to assist the women up into the coach before the butler could protest further. "We mustn't delay the procession."

"The procession?" echoed Brewster suspiciously.

"Just from here to the People's Palace," reassured Nigel, earning a grumble from his man. "Everyone is frightfully anxious to see you, Your Majesty. This is your first appearance since your return from Balmoral—and your jubilee parade next week won't include this part of London."

"Harrumph," snorted Brewster, knowing he was trapped.

"Just wave your hand once in a while," advised Nigel as the carriage pulled away. He hoped that was the only gesture the man would employ, he thought, hurrying to his own transportation and a shorter route to join Anne and Ian.

Floral tributes of all shapes and sizes, fragrant yet ominous, had been arriving at Anne's dressing room at such an alarming rate that they began to unnerve Ian. Despite Anne's reputation and recent visibility in London society, he hadn't expected such an overwhelming response to her public appearance that the place would resemble a Covent

Garden flower stall. In an attempt to monitor backstage activity, he had given clear instructions that no unknown persons were to be permitted behind the curtain, but it soon became clear that the delivery of the flowers made such orders imminently unworkable. The appearance of a huge arrangement of white lilies finally eroded the man's patience.

"Take that one outside. Put it on the stage if you like," he directed the stagehand. "For that matter, take half of the pieces from in here and all the rest that arrive and use them to decorate the hall. Just save the cards for Miss Hargraves."

"Ian, why?" asked a mystified Anne, quickly plucking the sender's note from the lilies as the arrangement disappeared from view but having no time to read it. "I thought it was rather nice."

"Call me superstitious if you want," the gray-eyed man muttered, running his hand through his already unruly hair, "but that one looked altogether too much like a funeral tribute. I've never cared for lilies."

"Well, that's fortunate," remarked the Duchess of Moreland as she entered with two magnums of champagne. "Otherwise Lillie Langtry might have snagged you before you even met Anne. Good evening, my dear, I just wanted to wish you luck on your performance this evening, not that I have any doubt you'll be splendid."

"Mother, it's bad form to say such a thing backstage," cautioned Audrey. "Performers consider it unlucky."

"Nonsense, Anne is too sensible to believe such nonsense," chided Aurora. "She knows I mean well. Anne, dear, I must say you look positively superb tonight. That extra sparkle in her eyes must be your doing, Mr. Kendrick. I applaud your persistence."

"Thank you, Your Ladyship, I've found it quite rewarding myself, but wouldn't you be more comfortable out front? Anne has reserved seats for you," said Ian, trying to herd the women toward the door. Though he'd included their names on the list of visitors permitted backstage at Anne's insistence, he didn't want them present when the assassin appeared.

"Oh, we've plenty of time. You know the queen will be late, she always is," replied Lady Moreland, sinking down onto one of the sofas, obviously prepared to remain until the monarch did appear. "I understand everyone who is anyone in society was scrambling frantically to find a ticket, you left them so little notice. But it was very clever of you, Anne, suggesting generous donations rather than a set price per seat. Everyone I spoke with was fearful of giving too little and being frowned upon. You must have done quite well for Andrew's cause."

"I don't know," the singer began, only to be interrupted by Brighton himself.

"The latest accounting is for almost five thousand pounds, my dear," he announced gleefully from the doorway of the dressing room. "Your efforts have even made Oliver Digby smile, quite a feat, I might add."

"And where is that gentleman? Surely he wouldn't miss Anne's performance?" inquired Ian, attempting to make it seem a casual remark as he monitored their suspects' arrivals.

"Oh, he'll be along shortly. He was going to entrust the money to our banker rather than leave it unprotected. Much as I hate to admit it, one can never be too safe, you know. Look at what happened to our building," said the reformer, settling himself on the divan next to the Duchess of Moreland. "I must thank you, Aurora, for introducing me to Miss Hargraves. She has helped our cause immeasurably. Indeed, after tonight, I daresay things in London will never be the same."

Ian's startled glance met Anne's over the heads of their visitors, but a few chance phrases couldn't serve as evidence. They needed more concrete proof, but where was their man? For that matter, where was Brewster?

"How much farther is it?" murmured the butler in tones as soft and feminine as he could muster. Uncertain as to whether or not the women with him were agents, he couldn't take the chance that one of them might suddenly cry out impostor, so he had sat stolidly enduring the ride as long as he could before finally speaking.

"Oh, it's only up the road," replied Lady Enright-Owens, a minor noblewoman amazed at her sudden good fortune in being asked to serve the queen this evening. In the past she had only stood around at interminable tea parties, not been part of the monarch's inner circle.

For, while Nigel's first impulse had been to use operatives, he had eventually decided society wouldn't believe in a queen accompanied by ladies-in-waiting whose faces were totally unfamiliar to them. Besides, he had reasoned, if the assassin wanted Anne, he would have to wait until Victoria had arrived at the People's Palace before he attacked; these women would be safe enough in the carriage with Brewster.

"Yes, I smell the breweries, and the People's Palace is just beyond them," agreed Lady Milton-Hughes, eager to be part of this royal conversation. It didn't seem the queen was as given to chatter as usual, but perhaps she was still weary from her train excursion.

"Hmmf, at least the audience can enjoy a lager," grumbled Brewster to himself as he once again raised a gloved hand to the cheering throngs along the route. It was just his luck Victoria couldn't drink in public.

Chapter Eighteen

Backstage, the formally garbed gentleman waited patiently as a stagehand checked his name against the list of approved guests. Showing no overt signs of his purpose here tonight, he would have blended well with those already seated in the audience, but he needed to see the arrangement behind the curtain to plan his strategy for later. As he had anticipated, Victoria had not yet appeared; she was forever tardy, feeling it her privilege to arrive when she wished, not when someone else had scheduled her to do so. That was the primary reason he hadn't intended killing her before the concert. No, there would be plenty of time at the interval, or if Anne Hargraves was in especially good voice, he might even delay his performance until after her last song.

Finally the stagehand approved his entry and the man in black crossed the large stage to Anne's small suite of rooms. Noticing his arrangement of lilies had been placed on the platform near her piano, he smiled with pleasure. It seemed an appropriate omen of his success. He had no doubts now; tonight would see the end of it.

Ten minutes later, Ian's nerves were ready to snap. The dressing room and the alcove behind it, prepared as a private retiring area for the queen, were mobbed with all their key players and numerous others who felt compelled to stop and wish Anne well. How he could be expected to protect her in this crush of nobles, reformers and socialites, he couldn't imagine. And, to add to his frustration, Victoria had yet to appear, though Nigel was signaling frantically from the doorway.

"What's wrong?" Ian demanded anxiously as Anne excused herself from her other guests and joined them outside her quarters. "Where is he?"

"The queen's carriage is at the front gates."

"Finally," approved Ian. "The curtain is supposed to go up in three minutes."

"The crowds along the route of the procession delayed Her Majesty," explained Nigel. "What about our killer? Is he here?"

"I don't know," admitted Anne, the strain beginning to show about her eyes. It was one thing to make herself the target, but risking Brewster's life, as well, when she was no closer to identifying the villain was becoming troublesome to her conscience. Still, he was an agent, knowing the danger the job entailed. "I hugged all the men as enthusiastically as I could without raising too many eyebrows, but no one seemed uncomfortable in my embrace, and I couldn't detect any bulky bandages. Maybe his wound was superficial."

"Or maybe you didn't actually hit him," countered her superior coldly. Never before had Anne failed him like this, and he still couldn't conceive of a case beyond her expertise. What would happen if she didn't find the killer? "Well, what do you want to do now?"

"We go ahead with the concert, of course," Ian stated quietly as he squeezed Anne's hand encouragingly.

"I think that's the only choice we have," the singer agreed. "I hope we'll draw him out yet."

"Are you certain it's safe?" questioned the government's authority.

"No one can ever be completely sure, Nigel, but your men have searched the hall for weapons and found nothing. If he's going to shoot, it will have to be from close range. I'll be backstage with Anne, and you'll be out front. We'll take him."

Before Conway could again voice his concerns, Brewster entered, leaning heavily on his cane and barely acknowledging the curtsies and bows from those he passed.

"Get me a drink, fast," he demanded in a hoarse whisper as he swept past the trio and into Anne's dressing room, leaving his ladies-in-waiting trailing in his wake. Inside the door, he stopped short at the sight of the assemblage gathered and adopted his most regal tones.

"We require a few private moments before the curtain, ladies and gentlemen, excuse us," he announced grandly, moving toward the small alcove bearing Victoria's crest.

"And I believe Miss Hargraves should have a few minutes alone to compose herself, as well," urged Ian. Fortunately the nobility were accustomed to what they perceived as Victoria's imperious manner and aided in moving the others along. In short order, the only ones left in the suite were Anne, Ian, Nigel and the Queen. Even the Prince of Wales had left.

"So?" Brewster challenged, doffing his cap and veil as he reached for the flask of brandy Nigel obligingly produced. "Who is trying to kill me?"

"I—ah, we don't quite know yet," admitted Ian. "But don't worry, we'll stop him."

"A damnably difficult job that will be if you can't even identify the bounder," grumbled their decoy, only slightly mollified by his intake of alcohol. At least it helped warm him; his legs were near frozen from this foolish costume. A dress, indeed! "How can you even be certain the fellow is here?"

"Oh, there's no doubt of that," said Anne in a steady voice as she noticed a new addition to the pile of calling cards. The one she picked up was heavily edged in funereal black, its message curtly hand printed. "So sorry for your upcoming loss." There was no signature.

"Bloody hell, the devil was here and you missed him," fumed Nigel. It seemed nothing was going right on this assignment, and of course, the final blame would be his. "How could you let him slip through your fingers like that?"

"He's still in the audience," Anne retorted, growing tired of the man's carping. "If you think you could do a better job—"

"The evening is only just beginning," interrupted Ian, seeking to soothe everyone's nerves. "We've plenty of time yet, though I do think you should see about starting, Nigel." Pulling Anne into his arms, Ian wanted her to feel his reassuring presence rather than be distracted by Conway's badgering. There was no reason for her to be more nervous than she undoubtedly already was.

Not resisting Ian's gesture, Anne stood quietly in his embrace for a moment as Nigel turned away in annoyance. Just briefly, the singer allowed herself to relish the gentle strength offered by her lover and sought to tell him so with her answering kiss. They had survived the angry recriminations, the painful doubts and the illogical fear; now, security in one another's love was theirs forever—or would be after tonight. All this and more she conveyed with her silent but evocative lips, promising the splendid glory that would soon belong to them alone.

"Well," suggested Brewster, Nigel's flask now empty, "let us get this concert started. The audience won't wait forever."

"Maybe not for you," muttered Ian, "but they would for Anne."

"Perhaps." The songstress smiled, gently stroking her lover's cheek. "But I'd rather not test that theory. Nigel, please see Her Majesty to her seat and instruct the orchestra to begin my introductory music."

In the audience one man sat particularly mesmerized by Anne's dulcet tones, all the more so because he hadn't expected to be. He was utterly amazed that the singer's physical allure could be so easily dwarfed by the magical sounds that escaped her sweet mouth. The way in which she had captured her audience would make this night more wondrous every time he recalled his triumph. He was glad then that he had waited to hear her sing, though in reality he had had little choice, being afforded no clear shot of the queen, who was sitting half-hidden behind a clump of palms.

As for Anne Hargraves, this was indeed her night. Performing in England for an audience of this size for the first time in years, she was in her element, an arena of willing listeners and a puzzle that required solving. For the time being, she had banished the specter of the unknown killer from her heart and concentrated on singing, her songs directed to Ian alone, an image of their future making her perform as never before. Whether accompanied by the orchestra or the simpler melody of the piano, the songstress managed to evoke for her audience passions undreamed of and hopes long forgotten as her voice called to the innocence of youth and the maturity of age, promising to each the opportunity for love and joy.

Shifting slightly to ease the throbbing in his side, the self-appointed savior of England was caught unawares, experiencing feelings he'd thought forever lost. For a brief moment, he sensed a hesitation in his determination, but then his goal prevailed.

"If she already sings like an angel, I'll be doing God a favor to make her one," he persuaded himself, applauding with the rest of the audience as they rose to their feet. An unheard-of standing ovation, and it was only the interval! What a fabulous tribute for her last performance, he decided. Now *was* the right time. "Besides, she could hardly sing any sweeter than she already has. If I let her perform again, it would only be a terrible disappointment," he reasoned, patting his revolver as he rose to go to her dressing room, led on by disillusioned dreams of personal glory.

Backstage, the scene in Anne's suite was absolutely chaotic, thirty people pressed into space for ten, each demanding proximity to their monarch and the empress of the evening, Anne Hargraves. What might have seemed extravagant words of praise were all too true this night as each visitor sought to impress Anne with how wonderfully she'd sung, each echoing the others yet believing his words unique.

Subtly as possible, the songstress circulated among her guests, trying to be available to all, serving champagne and cheer as she searched for a clue as to who represented death for Victoria and perhaps her, as well. The strain of the evening had begun to wear her down, and her smile was a bit more forced, her voice a touch more brittle, but Anne Hargraves was still a consummate performer, allowing only Ian to suspect her weariness. He willingly stayed at her side, encouraging her with a soft whisper or touch of the hand, reluctant to leave her unguarded even as he yearned to take some forceful action. Yet, what could he do until the villain revealed himself?

For his part, Victoria had pleaded exhaustion and retired to the rear chamber, accompanied by Nigel, Bertie and another flask of brandy. At least the assassin would have to deal with him first, reflected a thankful Ian, trying in vain to listen to the many different conversations in the dressing room as his eyes followed Anne's every movement.

Finally, as the orchestra began to play softly, signaling the end to the intermission, and as her guests moved toward their seats once again, Nigel caught Anne to one side.

"Well, you said this scheme of yours was going to produce results," her superior said accusingly. "All these folks have done is praise you, express some insincere interest in Brighton's efforts and preen over Bertie and Victoria. What's gone wrong? Why hasn't your killer tried something?"

"I don't know," the weary blonde admitted softly. The stress of playing an obliging target for the killer and the energy she had expended on her performance had totally exhausted her reserves. At the moment, she had neither the stamina nor the interest in satisfying Nigel's questions when she couldn't even answer her own doubts. "I was so sure—"

"Sure isn't enough, Anne," berated Conway, angry as much with his own impotence as with his agent. "We don't have time for mistakes. The jubilee is in four days."

"For Lord's sake, you act as though Anne can force this maniac into action. She's a singer, not a miracle worker, and how the hell do you expect this madman to think he can strike in such crowded surroundings?" snapped Ian, deciding it was time to set the man straight. For the past forty-eight hours, Nigel Conway had been pressuring his agent for answers though he himself had contributed no tangible suggestions or improvements to the plan. However unreasonable it was, the man seemed to consider everything her responsibility. Anne certainly didn't need that kind of bother at this point. "Come on, Conway, let's clear these rooms and give Anne and the queen a few minutes of peace before they return to their adoring public. Besides, I've got a few things to say that you need to hear."

Sending a grateful kiss to the man who owned her heart, Anne sank down on the divan and closed her eyes. She heard Nigel and Ian speaking to Bertie in the adjoining alcove, and then, as they left, there was only blessed silence. Practicing her breathing, she tried to soothe her tumultuous thoughts so she could go on again, an effort that appeared futile.

What had gone wrong? The black-edged card had indicated the killer had been in her dressing room earlier. What had stopped him then? Oh, she recalled, Victoria hadn't arrived yet...but where is he now? Mentally, even as she slowed her breathing and tried to relax, she called to mind her visitors during the interval. Had any of them not shown?

Bradford and Wallingcroft, even Chadwick and Bothwell had dropped by to congratulate her, and of course Brighton and his ever present shadows, Digby and Morrison... Suddenly the pieces seemed to rearrange themselves and she recalled Digby's late arrival before the performance. Had he been the one who left the black message? He had been on the other side of the door at the burning tenement, but Morrison had been oddly reticent during the interval, as though distracted. Could the two of them be working together?

Massaging her sore temples as she tried to ease the pounding in her head, Anne didn't open her eyes when she heard the door to the dressing room creak ajar.

"Ian, give me another five minutes, please? I can't face the audience yet," she confessed softly.

"Five minutes? Suppose you don't have that long?" asked a male voice that was not Ian's.

Anne's eyes flew open only to find Alex Morrison looking at her, his manner wild and distracted. He stood tall, possessed of an authority he had never demonstrated before, very unlike the smitten young man who had followed Brighton so meekly. Yet was it possible he could be here for any other reason than to kill her?

"If you wanted a private performance, Alex," she whispered throatily in an attempt to find out, "you only had to ask me. I very rarely say no."

"You said no when I asked you to stop snooping around the East End," he muttered, pulling the gun out of his coat pocket and turning it on Anne. He had no idea when Kendrick would return, so he knew he had better hurry. Grabbing the singer's upper arm, he yanked her to her feet and motioned her toward the curtained alcove where the queen waited.

"I never thought it might be you," Anne said sorrowfully.

"I was certain that you knew, but it doesn't matter anymore; you know my identity now—and that means you have to die."

"I only wanted to help your cause—"

"I didn't need your help. I had everything planned," complained the reformer as they moved toward the area set aside for Victoria. He was prepared to shoot at once if need be, but to his amusement and Anne's dismay, Victoria had nodded off, her chin resting on her chest, a tentative snore escaping the weary sovereign from under her veil.

Evidently the exertion of his disguise and two flasks of Nigel's brandy had been too much for Brewster. Anne frowned. A fat lot of help he would be.

"You see, Miss Hargraves? She's no good to anyone anymore; the old lady is past her usefulness and needs to be put away before she gets England into more trouble. I'm only trying to save the country," Morrison muttered, pushing Anne toward the seated figure, clearly pleased at this further evidence of Victoria's aging. "Only someone younger, a man of vision and virility, should rule a nation this great."

"But she helped to make it great," argued the blonde.

"Once upon a time, I'll grant you that," agreed the man with the gun. "But hundreds of innocent children die in the East End every month, starved or beaten to death—and she does nothing but appoint commissions to investigate. Oh, she's giving jubilee mugs to thirty thousand cleanly starched and pressed public school students, what good is that? The old orders have to be swept away and vital new ones put in their place."

"Miss Hargraves? Your Majesty?" A call from the corridor interrupted Morrison's rambling as the stagehand echoed the age-old traditional warning. "Five minutes, Miss Hargraves."

"Answer him," snarled her captor, holding the pistol to her head. Breathing heavily with eyes blazing, Morrison was clearly out of control, an idealist turned fanatic, the singer realized, and if she was to save Brewster and herself, she would need assistance. But how could she signal without alerting this deranged man to her cry for help?

"Go ahead, answer him."

For an instant, Anne hesitated, but she knew she had no other choice. She hoped Morrison was as unfamiliar with theater traditions as she prayed the waiting agent was knowledgeable. Quickly she whistled a few bars softly until the call came again.

"Miss Hargraves, did you hear me? Are you ready to go on?"

Once more she whistled just the opening notes clearly and she hoped accurately, trusting the stagehand would understand her message. No one, but no one whistled backstage in a theater. It was a superstition older than the Greek gods.

"That's it then, miss," came the ready reply. "I'll tell them."

Oh, I hope so, Anne thought, as the madman became all the more agitated. If only Brewster would stir, the distraction might give her a chance... But no, he was dead to the world, a phrase she hoped wouldn't become true any time soon.

"I want to know why me," the songstress said softly. "I see how you feel about the queen, but—"

"I thought at first that you were one of us, that you were going to make a difference—it was going to be you and me changing the East End, helping the poor," he told her, eyes wide and unfocused. "But then Digby opened my eyes. He told me you were working for the monarchists and were there only to spy on us... to put an end to our good works. I couldn't take a chance that he was right. I had to get rid of you, especially when it seemed like you knew what I intended. But, no matter what Brighton and Digby say, I have my own plans. Once the queen is dead I don't need anyone else."

"It was you who tried to kill me during the tenement fire?" Anne asked, stalling for time. Surely they had told Ian of her whistling by now, but would he know its significance? After all, this wasn't a theater, it was a concert hall, she worried.

"I dropped a match in the piles of rags when I was searching for my matchbox," he explained, a note of irrational pride in his voice, displaying the box in one hand as his other retrained the gun on his blond victim. "But I'd never lost it, see?"

"Yes," answered the songstress, trying to back away from Morrison as he began to advance closer, his jaw set with determination.

"And that was me at the Bothwells', too, and even here last week. You'd have been dead three times already, except that Kendrick interfered—"

"And he's going to do so a fourth time," said Ian, stepping into the curtained alcove, his own gun aimed steadily at the man who threatened his beloved.

"But I saw you going into the audience," protested the assassin.

"It was easy enough to retrace my steps," Anne's darkhaired savior answered simply. "Now give me your gun—"

"No! I have a job to do. I mustn't fail again," said Morrison, backing away from Ian, his expression confused and his chest heaving. "You don't understand, I must kill the queen."

"Maybe you're right," agreed Bertie's man, holding his gun on the reformer as he stepped between Anne and the would-be assassin. "But that is not Victoria. It's only Miss Hargraves's butler, and while he is rather irascible, I don't think he deserves to die for it."

"No, you're not telling the truth," denied the reformer, moving forward and pushing aside Brewster's veil. "It's all been for nothing," he screamed. "You tricked me, but worse than that, you've condemned England to an ignoble fate."

"Alex, let us help you," Anne urged, sympathy rather than fear foremost in her heart.

"No, no, get away. Don't you see? Someone has to die or I've failed," cried Morrison in despair, taking aim at the last victim available to him. Though he would never be able to rid his homeland of Victoria, this treacherous singer's death would call attention to his cause.

"Ian," called Anne as Ian's bullet struck home and Alex slumped to the floor. "Ian, he was only a boy."

"A boy who nearly killed you," muttered Ian, pulling the woman he loved into his arms and leading her away from the still twitching body. Shaken by how close he'd come to losing Anne, he was not about to leave her alone.

"Oh, did you get him then?" asked Brewster, aroused by the gunshots.

"With no help from you," retorted Anne as Ian captured her hand with his own and welcomed her into his fervent embrace.

"Nonsense, if I hadn't played Victoria, he would never have come here tonight," pronounced the butler. "Indeed, I shall go tell Nigel so."

"Fine," murmured the songstress, placing her finger over Ian's protesting lips, "and while you're at it, tell him I've retired. This man and my career will keep me much too busy to spy in the future."

Holding her tightly to his chest, Ian showed Anne just how true that was, raining kisses on her lips, which she drank in as eagerly as a parched garden does an early shower.

It was only Brighton's discreet cough a few moments later that drew the two of them apart.

"Excuse me, Miss Hargraves, but will you be finishing the concert?" he inquired, Nigel at his side. "Or shall I send the audience home now?"

"Never let it be said Anne Hargraves didn't complete a performance." The weary singer giggled, clinging once more to Ian's hand. "I'll sing one last song, but only if this man stays beside me. I love him and want the whole world to know it. I have finished with dangerous deceptions," she added, with a pointed look at Nigel.

"Fine, Anne, fine," agreed the government's man, "but, tell us, what was that you whistled to signal us? There were too few bars to be sure."

"My heavens, wasn't it obvious? 'God Save the Queen.'" Anne smiled contentedly. "And He did."

Epilogue

A triumphant Duchess of Moreland was one of the last guests to leave the wedding breakfast following the simple ceremony that had united Anne Hargraves and Ian Kendrick only one week after the long-touted but uneventful golden jubilee of Queen Victoria.

Of course, the marriage had not come as a surprise to society after that deliciously scandalous and romantic incident at Bothwell Manor, when Ian Kendrick had whisked Anne away in the middle of the house party and returned to London. Some had even whispered that the always roguish Ian had immediately installed the seductive blonde in his household without benefit of clergy. But Lady Aurora would never comment upon such speculations. She would say nothing more than that she had predicted this match between these two passionate souls long before it had ever occurred to either party involved.

Standing in the vestibule of the house off Russell Square after bidding Aurora and her family goodbye, Anne looked radiantly lovely in her gown of palest pink. As Ian slipped his arm possessively around her tiny waist, she found that she had never felt so loved and cherished, not even when bowing before a wildly applauding crowd following a successful performance.

As Ian bent his head to hers to plant a kiss on her cheek, a muffled cough reminded the newlyweds that they were not yet alone.

"Anne," said Sir Nigel, coming forward to finally kiss the bride, "I wish you happy, though I regret having lost you. I don't suppose I could persuade you and Ian, now that he is no longer working for the prince, to..."

"Sorry, Nigel," Anne replied, looking up into the face of the man she loved so dearly. "But the answer is a resounding no."

"Well then, are you going to continue your singing career?" Anne's former superior asked, at a loss for anything else to say.

"Yes, at least for now," the bride replied.

"And I promise, sir, that Anne will sing more sweetly than she has ever sung before," Ian commented dryly. "Besides, she's used to wandering the globe, and I've a yen to see the world with her."

"I see," the silver-haired spymaster said thoughtfully, nurturing a small hope that at some future time he could induce both Kendricks to change their minds.

"Chin up, Nigel. You still have Brewster," Anne said with a wicked smile when the butler entered the vestibule carrying Jack's satchel. "I think he might enjoy a few jaunts to exotic places at the moment."

"Yes, I hear that when he was dressed as Victoria, he all but won the hearts of several old codgers in the audience who found him incomparably lovely. I understand he's been hiding from them ever since," added the happy groom.

"I beg your pardon, sir!" Brewster began to protest.

"It's useless to scowl at me, old boy," Ian said with an amused grin. "I'm never frightened of men I've seen in skirts."

Unintimidated by the servant's continued grumbling, Ian turned to wish his brother a safe journey home.

"Well, Jack, I hope you found the education you came seeking in London."

"If not, at least he has found Audrey Palmer," Anne said, delighted to see, by her brother-in-law's reddening face, that she had guessed correctly.

"I say, Kendrick," Nigel interrupted, catching Ian's eye. "No one would ever suspect a boy of Jack's age to...I don't suppose your brother would..."

"Would what?" Jack asked immediately, interested in anything that would delay his return home. Northumberland was going to be so utterly boring after his adventures in London.

"No, he wouldn't," Ian proclaimed, hastily escorting his brother to the doorway, where he watched him enter the new coach that waited for him.

"Give my love to Mother and Father, Jack, and tell them Anne and I will soon be home for a visit," he instructed before he shut the door of his house.

To Ian's way of reckoning, that left only Nigel and Brewster to be gotten rid of before Anne and he could be alone, Mrs. Land and Molly being circumspect enough to have taken a half day.

The baronet's son used every polite device at his disposal to hint at their departure, and had resorted to looking pointedly at his watch, when a knock sounded at the door.

There wasn't a person standing in the vestibule, including the usually unruffled Brewster, who wasn't taken by surprise at this newest intrusion.

Victoria, late as always, and escorted by the Prince of Wales, had come to attend the wedding breakfast.

While the gentlemen bowed deeply, Anne sank into a graceful curtsy, wondering just what this visit portended.

"We have arrived," the august monarch announced, "to partake of the celebration."

"You do us a great honor. May I suggest we retire to the drawing room?" Ian said smoothly, indicating the direction with a sweep of his hand.

"I thought you called it the parlor," Anne whispered as they followed the royals into the front room.

"For today, dearest, it's the drawing room," Ian replied, a meaningful gleam in his eye.

Within moments, a bustling Brewster had produced trays of coffee, tea, fruits and dainties plentiful enough to satisfy even the sweetest tooth.

"We understand, Mrs. Kendrick," said the queen as she plucked a sweet from a pile with a pudgy hand, "that you and your spouse have done us a small service. Of course, due to the nature of your work, we cannot recognize you publicly, but we have come here this morning at the urging of our son, to render a token of our thanks. Albert, present the newlyweds with our gift."

With this, the smiling prince produced a small, flat rosewood box, and handed it to Ian.

With the queen's permission, the beaming groom gave it to Anne, who nervously opened it, expecting to find a set of butter knives or some such thing.

Neither bride nor groom had thought to see a deed lying on the velvet lining of the box. The paper made them the owners of a sizable estate in Dorset.

"Your Majesty," Anne began, "your generosity is..."

"Nothing, Mrs. Kendrick. You will find that a husband must feel he can adequately support his wife. And besides, having a little home of this sort will allow you both a pleasant escape from the rigors of society," the queen said, a faraway, romantic look settling upon her usually austere features, as though remembering her own Osbourne House as just such a place.

"We are more than grateful to you, Your Majesty, and to you, as well, Your Highness," Ian said, unconsciously slipping his arm around his bride once more.

"After a suitable time, there will be a title, as well," Victoria promised, suddenly distracted from what she was saying by Brewster's appearance with more hot water for the tea. "But tell me, Kendrick. Who is that sturdy little fellow? Though we know we have never seen him, we find him, nonetheless, hauntingly familiar."

Even Anne, who had grown used to his grumbling, was embarrassed by the indignant butler's fierce muttering as he scuttled from the room.

"If I may, Your Majesty, that is Matthew Brewster," the new Mrs. Kendrick explained. "He is an eccentric old fellow, to be sure, but my husband and I feel that it is our duty to be loyal to old retainers after all the loyalty they themselves have demonstrated."

"Then he has been with your family for years?" the queen inquired.

"At this point, as you can see, he has been with me much too long. But then, what can one do?" Anne asked with an innocent shrug of her shoulders.

"How refreshing to find such kindness and wisdom in a lady who is so beautiful, as well. Mr. Kendrick, you have done yourself proud," the sovereign pronounced as she rose to take her leave.

"Yes, Your Majesty, very proud indeed," Ian agreed, looking down at his Anne with such tenderness that the others wisely deemed it time to withdraw while the sophisticated and worldly Anne Hargraves Kendrick blushed as red as any new bride.

"I thought I'd never have you alone," Ian said, enfolding Anne in his arms when the door closed behind the last of their departing guests.

"But now you do," she said pertly, her eyes alive with promises.

"So I do. But tell me, Anne," Ian muttered, bending his head to place a kiss at the base of her throat, "do you think you will ever come to miss the excitement of your old life?"

"I'm quite sure my life has never been as exciting as it will be with you," the curvaceous blonde replied breathlessly, as the very essence of Ian's demanding cravings was transmitted by his touch, bringing every bit of her more alive than she had ever been before.

In response, Anne answered Ian's fire with her own. And when her husband swept her into his arms to carry her up the stairs, Anne knew that her dalliance with espionage was in truth ended, replaced forever by her newly acquired passion for the intrigues of the human heart.

* * * * *

HISTORY IN
THE MAKING!

Join Harlequin Historicals as we celebrate our 5th anniversary of exciting historical romance stories! Watch for our 5th anniversary promotion in July. And in addition, to mark this special occasion, we have another year full of great reading.

- A 1993 March Madness promotion with titles by promising newcomers Laurel Ames, Mary McBride, Susan Amarillas and Claire Delacroix.

- The July release of UNTAMED!—a Western Historical short story collection by award-winning authors Heather Graham Pozzessere, Joan Johnston and Patricia Potter.

- In-book series by Maura Seger, Julie Tetel, Margaret Moore and Suzanne Barclay.

- And in November, keep an eye out for next year's *Harlequin Historical Christmas Stories* collection, featuring Marianne Willman, Curtiss Ann Matlock and Victoria Pade.

Watch for details on our Anniversary events wherever Harlequin Historicals are sold.

HARLEQUIN HISTORICALS . . .
A touch of magic!

HH5TH

HARLEQUIN PRESENTS®

is

- ☑ exotic
- ☑ dramatic
- ☑ sensual
- ☑ exciting
- ☑ contemporary
- ☑ a fast, involving read
- ☑ terrific!!

*Harlequin Presents—
passionate romances
around the world!*

HARLEQUIN ROMANCE®

is

- ✓ contemporary and up-to-date
- ✓ heartwarming
- ✓ romantic
- ✓ exciting
- ✓ involving
- ✓ fresh and delightful
- ✓ a short, satisfying read
- ✓ wonderful!!

Today's Harlequin Romance—the traditional choice!